MW01102018

DANIEL

a novel of discovery

JOHN OSBORN

authorHOUSE®

AuthorHouse™
1663 Liberty Drive
Bloomington, IN 47403
www.authorhouse.com
Phone: 1-800-839-8640

First published by AuthorHouse 7/6/2009

ISBN: 978-1-4389-7826-0 (e)
ISBN: 978-1-4389-7825-3 (sc)

Library of Congress Control Number: 2009903666

Printed in the United States of America
Bloomington, Indiana

This book is printed on acid-free paper.

Other Books by John Osborn

MICHAEL

SAMANTHA

SET IN 1998 IN ENGLAND this is the third novel in the life of the Lord family after Michael and Samantha. Daniel Lord works hard to manage the family Fotheringham Manor Forest Estate, his golf game and his new girl friend Katya Howard. He does this while still helping his parents retire from their software company and his sister Samantha bring some order into her life with her son James. As Daniel works with Katya looking for green revenues from the forest estate the pair discover golden coins and the story of past murders. While helping Detective Inspector Terence Field, his sister's new man solve the murders, Daniel becomes personally embroiled with the Whelks family and perhaps finds the long-lost Lord family legacy. A final murder decides the fate of the Ferris cottage.

Why did Idwal come back?

Daniel Lord looked around the Estate office and decided there were enough chairs.

'Mum, there will only be the four of us won't there? I expect Betty will drive herself up from the village and not get her dad to drive her. I don't think Toby wants to see John at this point in time.'

'Right Daniel. You arranged the meeting for ten?'

'Yes Mum, but I wanted to sit and think a little about what we might say. I want to be fair to both of them and that may prove to be difficult.'

'Well let's review the facts as they stand. Correct me where I go wrong. Idwal Ferris returns to Fotheringham after what, eight years when we sacked him and John?'

'Yes, right after their father got killed.'

'Right, so eight years ago Idwal disappears and John stays around and we eventually hire him back again six months later. In fact I offered him his job back if I remember rightly. Do you know what happened to Idwal in those eight years?'

1

'I think he was in gaol Mum most of that time. There was a strong rumour floating about the village that he was found guilty of manslaughter; someone up in Bristol and he served time. As far as I can gather he had only just got released.'

'So he comes down here with some floozy who sounds as if she is completely spaced out most of the time and barges back into his dad's old cottage.'

'Which you and dad gave to John and Betty as a wedding present back six years ago now. So yes, I caught Idwal that Wednesday afternoon sitting in an old van with this Lola or whoever about to light up a cigarette. I put a flea in his ear about forest fires and told him to get lost but next thing I hear is that he and John are as thick as thieves in the pub that night drinking up a storm.'

'Now according to Betty Daniel, Idwal came crashing into the cottage before John got home from work and was rude and abusive to her, frightened the kids and generally tried to take over. She told John when he came home that night that his brother had to go. Betty was furious and John just said he would sort it. Even then Idwal was ranting on about having some revenge for the death of his dad. Betty didn't know all the details because she lived with her parents at that time but she said Idwal was absolutely crazy about sorting Enrico out.'

'Right so far.'

'And then they went on the Thursday morning, Idwal and John to find Enrico and when they couldn't find him Idwal vandalises Enrico's cottage. He attacks and tries to rape Samantha, and when he's finished there he goes back to John's cottage and beats up Lola, rapes Betty and ties them both up in that cellar-like place.'

'Yes Mum, that's about what I gather. However, because Samantha really pissed him off he stayed around complete with a gun if you remember and tried to kill the horses by burning down the stables.

2

Fortunately Samantha and Danielle saved the horses and I got the crew to contain the fire until the fire truck arrived.'

'But you went back to John's cottage?'

'Yes Mum. John and I didn't know exactly where Idwal might go but John reckoned that Idwal coming back to get Enrico was only part of the story. He said that Idwal was going on about some gardening he had to do. John only remembered this because it was so unlike Idwal to even dream of such a thing. John thought there was something else on Idwal's mind and so we went down to the cottage.'

'And all hell had broken loose. That must have been a bloody disaster zone Daniel.'

'It wasn't pretty Mum. By the time that John and I had got there, along with PC Meadows Idwal had shot Lola and was attacking Betty. Well John charged in and well you know the rest. John said he just lost it. Even now John can't really remember what happened there that night. After he charged into the cottage it all goes blank he says and he finally came to sitting in a police cell. He couldn't tell you who was in the cottage or what had happened.'

'So he kills Idwal and you arrive when everything had gone quiet.'

'Mum it's good that you never had to see it. Their kitchen looked a right mess. Betty was huddled in a corner wanting to disappear; John was in a trance still holding the knife; Lola was shot dead against the wall and Idwal was naked with his throat cut. Betty had tried to defend herself and she slashed at Idwal several times so there was blood everywhere.'

'And then my beloved daughter comes crashing into the scene on an errand of mercy; typical I suppose.'

'Yes, but in retrospect everyone thought what she did was good. Even Inspector Field thought what she did was good and it was his crime scene. He's usually really officious about proper procedures and although he wasn't happy professionally he thanked Samantha much later for what she did.'

'So John gets arrested for manslaughter; Betty gets raped and therefore traumatised; Lola gets killed by Idwal and Idwal himself ends up on a slab; bloody marvellous. Just when I thought the forest crew were really starting to work so well together this comes along and it will cause enormous friction between the various personnel.'

'It has already Mum. We now have people who are pro John and those who think he deserves to be arrested. You're right, it's not helping productivity. Fortunately the workload isn't too heavy at the moment but I really don't need the aggravation.'

'More importantly, much more importantly there's Betty and the children? Actually I was relieved and delighted that she came out of this nightmare as well as she has. She's a fighter Daniel. She put up one hell of a struggle in that cottage I hear. Apparently it was she who got loose in that little hidey-hole in the cottage and untied Lola. She was just about to go and get help when Idwal came bursting in that second time after setting fire to the stables. Betty said he was like a mad thing but she cut him several times with a knife before he completely knocked her out. She says she still has nightmares, not so much about the rape but about the attack. She thought he was going to kill her. That's why she doesn't want to go back to the cottage I think. She says she'll wake up in a cold sweat dreaming of the attack. There's just too much there to remind her.'

'John seems to have managed to live with it. He's been there now for four days. He started work yesterday and he seemed pretty normal. He's really pissed off at the terms of his bail, not being able to see Betty and the kids you know. He says he really misses the kids but he seems to have got some sleep in the cottage.'

'Yes Daniel, that's as maybe but he really doesn't have any memories of what happened there. You just said that he can't remember what he did. So it's not surprising that he can live there without bad dreams but Betty just can't take it. I'm not sure I could either and that rather poses a problem. You know that Samantha suggested Betty expand her pie-making passion into a business, possibly using the money from the sale of the cottage and she was quite interested. Anyway, after we left Toby's place this past Monday morning, leaving the family with that idea Betty came back to me and said that she, and her mum and dad thought it was a good suggestion and could we discuss it further? So she will want to sell the cottage.'

'And John will want to keep it as he needs somewhere to live. Jesus, what a bloody mess and all because that useless brother returned. Seems a shame they let him out from wherever he was. Perhaps I should find out from Terence Field exactly where Idwal was and why?'

'Daniel I'm going to go outside and make sure I catch Betty before John appears. I don't want any ill feeling being generated before we have this meeting. Don't forget it was a special compensation from the court to even have this get-together. Inspector Field wanted to be here, and so did Samantha of course. I managed to persuade them and the court authorities that it would be more productive if we keep the numbers to a minimum so there'll just be the four of us.'

I looked around the room; clean, tidy, and functional. It had been the Forester's office on the Estate for as long as I could remember. When I was still very young we had Ronald O'Rourke here, a very astute Irishman who really managed the Estate on a commercial footing, something dear to my mother's heart. My mother was the economist and accountant for both Brainware Pty Co., our family's software development company and for the Fotheringham Manor Estate, our home. Although petite in stature my mother is a force to be reckoned with as regards finances and the bottom line. O'Rourke really helped put the Estate on a firm financial footing and took most of the pressure off my parents so that they could concentrate on the Company and raising their four children.

Yes I thought, Ronald O'Rourke the Forestry Officer who had come here and worked so well with Edward Templeton, our Estate foreman. Edward's father had been Albert and he had fought alongside my great grandfather George in the First World War. In those days, well just before the Great War George Lord and Albert Templeton had run the Estate for shooting and hunting. We had pheasants, we had foxes, rabbits galore and the occasional deer but while the men were fighting in Italy George's wife, my great grandmother Virginia had changed all of that. After seeing some really productive forestry operations in India as a young lady Virginia had turned the Estate from a rural retreat for gentlemen into a commercial enterprise. When my great grandfather returned in 1919 the direction of the property had changed and it never looked back. We became a commercial forest, although it did take time to gradually convert the old somewhat rural woodlands into an economically viable managed forest. When O'Rourke arrived, fresh from Oxford and four years commercial forestry practice just down the road so to speak in Devon, Fotheringham really started to make money.

I had been born here at Fotheringham in 1974 and so I could remember the warm and friendly Irish Ronald O'Rourke. As I was growing up Edward Templeton, Albert's son died and Ernest Edwards took over as the foreman for the work crew. Against my dad's better judgement but on the insistence of his eccentric mother Rosamund, the Estate hired Norton Ferris in 1984 as a Forester. The Estate had become sufficiently complex and the forestry part had expanded. We now intensively managed many hectares of plantations and natural woodland. We had increased the size of the nursery and added drying kilns along with our sawmill. It's true we didn't directly market our finished products on site but in essence we had a completely vertically integrated company and dad felt we needed a Forest Officer O'Rourke and a Forester Ferris overseeing the foreman Edwards and the rather large forest crew. And as I grew up everything was going along wonderfully until that fateful natural disaster in October 1987 when a tremendous windstorm laid flat and broken a large part of southern England's woodlands, ours included. Unfortunately for us it also laid flat Ronald O'Rourke as he and his Landrover were crushed by a massive fallen oak tree.

My memories of 1987 were the storm, O'Rourke's death and the quiet passing away of Ernest Edwards and the beginning of the pseudo reign of Norton Ferris as head of the Estate. Although Bob Edwards, Ernest's son became the foreman that really didn't matter to Norton Ferris as he had his two sons Idwal and John to take over the forest crew and get the cushy jobs.

During the following year the Estate had been lucky and my oldest brother Geoffrey, who was ten years older than me, had married Christina DeLucci. I can still vividly recall that day because it is the first day I can ever remember my sister Samantha wearing a dress, well a pretty dress. Samantha was two years older than me and a tomboy. She and my mother would shout and scream at each other. Well they are alike in so many ways and both want to be first, and Samantha insisted she wasn't a lady and could beat her brothers at anything. She had always been a tomboy but that day, I never did know why, Samantha decked herself out with a really lovely off-white bridesmaid's dress. At that time I was a boarding pupil at Bristol House, a boys only school all the Lord family men had attended and I had special permission to be home for my brother's wedding. Geoffrey had been a pupil at Bristol House and my elder brother Michael was in his final year there. Sitting in the Estate office I smiled to myself as I could remember that I had recently become aware of girls. Now being in an all boys boarding school the opportunities to see let alone talk to girls is limited and my hormones had recently kicked into gear, so it was a startling revelation to realise my sister was a truly vivacious young lady. Samantha usually didn't notice me because I was both younger and not aggressively competitive. It was Michael, and sometimes Geoffrey she chased and wanted to beat but that particular day for whatever reason she spent some time with me. It might have been the drinks she had me go and collect that were the attraction because I could remember she ended up getting drunk and being sick behind the bushes but she did notice me that day.

To really understand part of the dilemma behind this morning's small meeting you have to know a little bit about Norton Ferris and his two sons. I suppose Norton Ferris must have been about fifty eight when dad hired him in 1984, perhaps not an auspicious year in many respects. Norton had been born in Liverpool in a broken home, scraped around doing odd jobs before finally getting into the army. While in the army Norton learnt to keep his head down, scrounge what he could and try and work as many scams as possible. Unfortunately he was not all that bright and one scam in particular, in Naples I think but certainly somewhere in Italy resulted in a knife scar right across his cheek which he tried to mask under a dense beard. As a consequence of this embarrassing incident Ferris developed a fierce hatred towards Italians. After the war Ferris had his superior officer, who unfortunately was an old beau of my grandmother's wangle his way into Forestry School. Right after the war there was a desperate shortage of skilled forestry people and he managed to graduate as a Forester. From 1948 to 1983 Norton Ferris worked at the Forest of Dean for the Forestry Commission and the rumour was he was about to get fired when this loony superior officer from the army days persuades my grandmother that 'he's a fine chap, just needs the odd break but a skilled worker, keen too you know'. Well it really was a crock of shit but grandmother was verging on senility at the time and bought the story and we ended up with the skilled, keen Norton Ferris and his two equally skilled and keen layabout sons, Idwal and John.

Now for some unknown reason dad never hired a replacement Forestry Officer when O'Rourke was killed and so Norton Ferris ran the show. Dad and mum were really busy with the software Company; Geoffrey had recently graduated from University and was helping with E.U. regulations and although he was officially in charge of the Estate he really didn't have the time and so Norton had a rather free hand. Now Norton's wife had died some years ago and when he got the job as Forester in 1984 he brought his two sons with him. I suppose Idwal was twenty three and John three years younger.

Fotheringham Manor Estate had two cottages in the forest as well as Home Farm. Two Italian brothers, Antonio and Enrico Branciaghlia rented one and both men worked on the Estate as forest workers. They had been with us since 1943 when great grandfather George hired them from a P.O.W. camp where they had been interred. As a boy I had spent many happy hours in their cottage as both brothers were exceptionally patient with children and both had wonderful skills in toy making. All of the Lord family children as well as many other children in the village had received carved or sculpted toys from Antonio or Enrico.

Dad installed Norton Ferris and his two sons in the other cottage. From 1984 to 1987 Norton was under the firm direction of Ronald O'Rourke, who he really resented. Ronald was strict and expected a job to get done when it was required and done properly. Norton Ferris didn't quite see it that way and neither did his two sons. In 1987 much of the immediate forestry work was logging, cutting up and clearing away the mass of fallen and broken timber. Lumber flooded the market but the forest activities were simple. Here Norton Ferris was relatively efficient, especially when he could work all sorts of side deals for items he sold himself and pocketed the money. After this salvage work ended and the

Estate got back into the broader activities of forest management many of these schemes weren't so easy to create and by 1990 dad had had enough. It had already been a bad year with my eldest brother Geoffrey getting killed in June. That left a gap in the Estate Management and my other brother Michael was more interested in his own schemes, some of which involved Norton Ferris himself. It must have been in December that dad and mum decided to fire the entire Ferris family.

However, one or two days before dad actually came out and told Ferris this something else happened that was really relevant to this morning's meeting. Even to this day no-one is really sure who caused the accident, if that is what it was or who was the real target. Michael had skived off somewhere for the day and Norton Ferris decided to "borrow" Michael's Landrover and collect and illegally sell some of the Estate's fence posts. Norton had already creatively miscounted the inventory and the surplus material he was going to sell to a shady character called Larry Whelks. Well Norton was driving the Landrover and quietly filling the back with the surplus posts when a stacked skidway of logs up above the forest ride came loose, thundered down the hillside knocking the Landrover with Norton Ferris inside it down into the stream below. As chance would have it the Landrover must have rolled, several times according to my dad and ended up upside down in the stream. It was Norton's two sons who found the Landrover when they were out looking for their dad but they didn't know that he was inside. As it was Michael's Landrover they thought that Michael was inside and came rushing back to the Big House to tell my dad. Well mum and dad charged out, collected some help and hot-tailed it to the scene of the accident. When they pulled the Landrover out and opened it they found it was Norton Ferris who was dead inside, drowned. Dad waited a few days until after the funeral before he gave Idwal and John Ferris their marching papers. Right pissed off they were dad said. Norton himself hadn't been exactly loved on the

Estate or in the village where he owed a lot of money, and to the bookies too I heard so there were several people who could have wished him ill. Anyway, the two brothers left but those events were overshadowed for me by other personal upheavals within our own family. We had Michael's twenty-first birthday party, his supposed announcement of engagement to Melanie Rogers, a shocking and public dis-engagement about a week later and then in early January of 1991 Michael was shot and killed on the Estate.

But to come back to the Ferris family and this morning's meeting. As my mother had recapped the two Ferris boys went separate ways. Idwal had some deal going that sounds like it went wrong somewhere, shades of his dad's scams not working out and John hung around and settled down. Now John Ferris, the younger brother was quieter, less aggressive than his older brother Idwal. After getting away from his father's and brother's influences John seemed to have changed. Dad had found him working in a factory in the local town and when he stopped to say hello John mentioned that working indoors wasn't really his thing. When she heard this my mother rehired John Ferris. I never did know whether this was because she wanted another person in the cottage paying some rent, because she had faith in John, or because she had a guilty conscience firing them right after their dad's death. At the time in 1991 this seemed a really good decision and John did settle down as a good forest worker paying rent for the cottage. Looked like a win-win situation.

Mum must have felt even better when John married Betty Travers. Now Betty's parents, Toby and Mary run the off-licence and the greengrocer's shops respectively in the village. Good hard-working honest people with three kids and Betty the eldest, and they were a little apprehensive when their daughter started walking out with John Ferris. The village hadn't forgotten the name of Ferris and it wasn't a good memory. Still, John worked hard, proved trustworthy and he married

Betty with perhaps reluctant best wishes from Toby and Mary. What was a better win-win deal for my mother was to give them the cottage in the forest as a wedding present. Now Betty was over the moon with this because for a young bride from her background to have her very own house, well cottage right after her wedding was a dream come true. The gift was conditional on them living in the cottage, which would be typical of my mother's forward thinking but John was delighted too. He saved on the rent and he proved himself worthy of the gift by making some improvements to the cottage. The two bedrooms in the cottage also came in useful as Betty had Katey a year later and then along came Paul after that. So we had a very happy family living and working on the Estate. Earlier on, probably in the 1980s dad had renovated all of the properties by putting in mains electricity and telephone lines so the properties were not so isolated and had modern light and power. Betty Ferris, who won John's heart partly through her prowess in pie-making took a while to get used to an electric stove because at home she had always cooked on gas but no-one could make pies the way she did. This rather blissful state of affairs had just been blown sky high nine days ago when Idwal Ferris returned.

'Come in Betty, it's good to see you. How are you? And Katey and Paul?'

'I'm fine Mr. Daniel, really I am. I was just telling your mother how grateful I am for you to go to all this trouble for us. I hope we can start to sort a few things out.'

'Betty you know there will just be the four of us?' Mum asked.

'Aye Mrs. Lord, the court clerk told me that when she phoned. I think that's for the best too. I could see no need to involve others although I wondered whether Miss Samantha would be here too thinking about all she had done for me. I was so grateful to her Mrs. Lord.'

'Yes Betty, well my precious Samantha wanted to be here, claiming that it was her and Inspector Field's idea but I persuaded her, none too gently I might add that it would be easier with just the four of us. In the end Inspector Field also told her that it would be better this way.'

'Ah, here's John,' I said and John Ferris knocked at the open door and stood there rather uncertain what to do next.

'Come in John, come in,' I said, 'and sit yourself down. John before we start would you and Betty like some time together, just the two of you? Betty do you want that or not? This get-together is really to help you two you know?'

'Mr. Daniel I would like a moment with John if that's all right. As you know we haven't had a chance to say anything to each other since that night. John love I'd like a word.'

'Aye Betty, fine with me.'

Mum and I silently stood up and walked outside into the soft weak sunshine of the yard. Friday October the second, just eight days after that bloody attack and mayhem. I walked some distance away from the office buildings and looked at my mother.

'Well Mum, how do you think they both reacted?'

'I think Betty knows what she wants to do but I think John is still in shock to be perfectly honest Daniel.'

'Personally Mum I'd like it to go back to the old situation but somehow I can't see Betty living with that unless she's a lot stronger than I give her credit. I think John will gradually recover but then he has to go through it all again in court and probably serve some gaol time. In some ways his future is mapped out. He's never been very imaginative and so I don't think the cottage and the forest will bring back those vivid images of last week, whereas Betty..'

'Yes Daniel, whereas Betty may be a lot tougher but she has a lot more to think on, including Katey and Paul. I will guess she wants to stay in the village with her parents and let John stay here until the court case. I will also guess she would like to sell the cottage, depending a lot on the outcome of the trial. But we'll see. Betty, you and John ready for us?'

Just down the way from the Estate office were the buildings and house of Home Farm. My eldest brother Geoffrey's widow Christina lived in Home Farm with her son Peter, my nephew. In the Lord family there is a strong, old-fashioned tradition that the entire Estate passes to the first-born male in each generation. So, when he turned twenty one my brother Geoffrey was officially made the heir to both Brainware Pty Co., the software company and the Fotheringham Manor Farm and Forestry Estate. This was twelve years ago. Geoffrey married Christina and they had a son Peter who is now nine years old. In June of 1990 my two brothers and I decided we three should go for a "boy's weekend out" somewhere, which at the time we all thought would be great. Dad and mum thought it was a really good idea as they were worried about the antics of Michael at that time. They hoped that Geoffrey's more serious nature might influence and curb a little of Michael's outlandish behaviour. I tagged along because I really loved my brothers and enjoyed being with both of them and I was desperately anxious to get out of a bullying event at school. Geoffrey had sort of rescued me from Bristol House one Friday evening and driven us up to Bangor in North Wales. Michael, who was at London University at that time, had just wrecked his car and lost his licence in the process and so he went up by train. The three of us met early on Saturday morning at Bangor station. It looked like being a splendid weekend and Geoffrey and Michael were both in good moods and joking about this and that. Now this was unusual for Geoffrey as he was usually quite serious and conservative. He was always one step at a time as opposed to Michael's incredible leaps of faith, usually into the unknown or someone else's unknown. Anyway, after we found breakfast at a local hotel the other two decided on a hike over the Carneddau mountains. Rather surprising for Geoffrey he took us up into the slate mining village of Bethesda and made us observe what was special about this village. In the end I realised that all the pubs, and there were several of them were all only on the one side of the street. Apparently one side of the street belonged to one estate and the other side of the street was owned by someone else. The teetotal side was owned by a family Geoffrey said that had had a drink-caused tragedy and so there was never any alcohol selling establishment on that estate.

I mention this because Geoffrey was in a really brotherly and friendly state of mind that weekend which was a little surprising as he had experienced a busy and exhausting week so he had told me. Perhaps he was just happy to escape like I was. I think his son Peter was teething at the time too. Unfortunately the friendly state of mind wasn't to last. Our hike turned into an easy rock climb, so Michael said and that in turn led to an accident where Geoffrey fell. I couldn't hold the fall as the friction of the sliding rope burnt my hands. Geoffrey was hurt and unconscious and I was in shock. Michael left us to go for help. Sad to say Geoffrey died, he actually choked on his own vomit in the end but I was in shock at the time and didn't realise. Michael ran away and I ended up on a real guilt trip thinking it was my fault that Geoffrey died. The other end result was Christina became a widow and her son Peter became heir to the Lord family futures.

Antonio and Enrico Branciaghlia both worked well in the forest, quiet, thorough, conscientious. My grandfather Desmond and my father both thought they were excellent workers. Unfortunately Norton Ferris had this long term resentment against Italians and he took every opportunity to belittle and harass the two brothers. In August of that fateful year of 1990 Antonio and Enrico were felling white pines late of a beautiful summer's afternoon. One of the large misshapen wolf trees got hung up in the neighbouring trees when it was cut by Antonio and in trying to free it the top broke off, fell and smashed Antonio's head. He didn't die immediately and after doing as much as he could Enrico set off for help. The rest of the forestry crew were working to bring in the farm harvest and so they were all out in the fields. Norton Ferris was drunk and incapable and my precious brother Michael told Enrico he had other priorities, namely a date with a lady. Antonio died in the forest and Enrico didn't forget who had or had not done anything. This partly gave rise to the thought in Idwal's mind that it was Enrico who had sent the pile of logs down on Michael's Landrover and killed his father.

When Idwal Ferris had gone looking for Enrico, to "sort him out" for supposedly causing his father's accident and death Christina had been rushing Enrico into hospital after he had collapsed in the kitchen of Home Farm. Now at this moment Enrico had just come out of hospital. Seeing that Idwal had vandalised Enrico's cottage Christina offered to have Enrico stay with her and Peter at Home Farm. For Christina, who is Italian, emotional and lonely this is another adult, someone who speaks Italian and a man in the house. Peter, who is nine now tells everyone he is the man in the house and Peter is very adult for his years. Actually Peter really helps his mother with her emotional condition by keeping everything low key and simple. He is a good lad and takes after his father, my brother in his serious and logical demeanour. Enrico had originally been a woodworker in Italy as a youth and now he sat in Christina's backyard in the sunshine and slowly carved wooden figures.

Just over a week ago now, the day after Idwal's rampage there had been another attack at Fotheringham. Michael had had a girlfriend, one amongst many who came originally from Mozambique. Danielle Made had a son, Tony and Michael had been the father. Originally Danielle had expected Michael to marry her after Tony arrived but my brother was looking for more affluent families for marriage. After Michael was killed my mother really wanted her grandson Tony to live at Fotheringham but Danielle wouldn't have any part of that and she moved back to London with her son. Later in the year that Michael was killed it was my dad who slowly re-established contact with Danielle, through a mutual business friend in London and as my dad is really good at team building, bringing people together, he persuaded Danielle that my mother wasn't that bad. Over time Danielle came to know all of us better and she visited a few times with Tony. Just last week the home of Danielle and Tony had been attacked by some people from Mozambique. Danielle had nowhere to go as all her family were dead and so she packed up a few things and rushed down to Fotheringham for sanctuary. Vindictively the two men followed her down and subsequently attacked us here. With a couple of friends who were staying at the house we managed to rescue Tony but Danielle ended up going to hospital with knife wounds. Unfortunately the serrated knife had churned up her insides and she subsequently died. Christina promptly "adopted" Tony and as Tony was about the same age as Peter this seems to have worked out quite well and so Christina suddenly had two new people at Home Farm. Enrico was carving a wooden football player for Tony.

Peter had several carved figures that had come from the skill of Enrico's hands and Tony thought they were "wicked", and so Enrico who loved children decided he would do something for the new resident in the house. Now Tony had lived in London virtually all of his short life and had played football at school. Although they had lived on the west side of London Tony supported Tottenham Hotspur, a north London football team. Danielle never knew much about Tony's passion and so she was surprised when someone explained to her that Tony was a

Spurs supporter. Most people living in west London support Chelsea. 'But it's obvious Mum,' Tony had apparently explained, 'Spurs play in black shorts and white shirts and that's just like me. I'm black and white because of you and my dad.' Danielle wasn't quite sure whether this was good or bad but she did accept her son's realisation of his background. So Enrico carved this football player in the act of kicking the ball and was all set to help Tony paint it black and white.

Although Christina had begged Peter and Tony to let Enrico get a little settled at Home Farm as he had just come out of hospital, already Peter was quietly asking Enrico to show him how he carved wood. The two boys were really fascinated with this. Tony had been excited all this past week because he had just started school down here with Peter and the new school was "smashing" as far as Tony was concerned. So Christina was having her hands full with two very active youngsters and an old man who was a charmer. All of a sudden her rather quiet and placid world had changed and that is a good thing I thought. 'Daniel, are you coming in or are you going to sit out here and look into space? I know the trees we have are fascinating and that being a forester you like to talk to the trees love but I think Betty and John are ready to talk with us now. You know Daniel, talking with people, you remember?'

'Sure Mum, sure. I was just thinking about other people here on the Estate. I was thinking about Christina and how the changes in her life are positive. Suddenly Home Farm is a little livelier.'

'A lot livelier I'll bet with Tony and Peter under her feet but Enrico will calm them down. He really is a wonderful person with children Daniel. You could learn a lot from him you know.'

'Mum I not married let alone have kids so stop pushing eh? You keep an eye on that sister of mine and little James. Actually James is fine so just keep an eye on Samantha because I think she has set her eyes on Detective Inspector Field.'

Here my mother sighed and looked a little quizzical.

'Yes Daniel, I just wonder what little Miss Muffit has in mind. We talked a lot you know just last Sunday when we went climbing. That was a really good day with your sister Daniel. We both enjoyed ourselves that day.'

'Well you certainly looked like you had enjoyed yourselves when you drove up. I had been telling the Howards all about you and they were quite fascinated with the family and our activities. James of course had embellished all the stories and I'm not really sure what Deidre expected but you bowled up and emerged from the car dirty and carefree and immediately looked like the lady of the house. I was impressed Mum really I was.'

'Well as we came up the driveway Samantha had remarked that there appeared to be a reception committee waiting for us and when she saw you there with a pretty young thing her antenna went on red alert. She really cares for you you know?'

'Who Katya?' I asked, sort of hopefully.

'No dummy your sister. Samantha thinks you need to find someone and settle down.'

'Coming from her that's rich Mum. She's never settled down anywhere: she doesn't know the meaning of the word. Still, it's nice to know she does notice me. That's taken a while.'

'Daniel Daniel Daniel, your sister has always been an aggressive competitive challenger in all things, life included.'

'And I'm not?'

'Daniel you are who you are. All my children have been individuals son and you weren't old enough or aggressive enough to be competition for your tomboy sister so she never saw you when you were young. Now,

now she's come home she's seeing you for perhaps the first time as a man in charge of his own life. She was really praising you for how you handled last weekend you know, and for how you manage the Estate. I think it is Samantha who has changed Daniel and she now can see the family in a different light.'

'So that's perhaps why she rushed down to see Betty right after Idwal's attack in the cottage.'

'Maybe, but I think she was probably still in shock herself after Idwal's attack on her earlier. Still, she did continue and ask continuously after Betty following that incident.'

I smiled and remembered the stories of my sister trying to see Betty in hospital and Inspector Field thwarting her efforts. Perhaps Terence Field does have what it takes to contend with my sister I thought. He'll need to be a strong-willed man.

'Well Betty, what have you and John got to tell us?'

After thirty minutes it appeared that we were repeating ourselves so I gently called the meeting to a halt. Betty and John were both very civil to each other but I could sense the vibrations and they weren't all positive, a sort of mutual truce. God how sad I thought. Just over a week ago these two people were happily living together with love, family, expectations and a future and now all of that was in a shambles. The outcome was as mum had predicted and given the terms of John's bail perhaps appropriate. Betty would live with her two children at her parent's house in the village and John would continue to live at the cottage and work on the Estate. He would have no further contact with them, although I did promise to ask the court whether there could be visiting conditions. There would be if he was in gaol I reasoned. John could go into the village pub on Saturday evenings and Betty and the kids would avoid that location. I arranged to collect groceries for John. It wasn't good but it could work for the benefit of all parties. The only uncertain point was Betty's possible future pie-making business. If that was to flourish the way that Samantha suggested Betty would need some capital. My mum agreed she would look into that and get back to Betty.

When mum and I stood up Betty was on her feet immediately and partway out of the door. Well I thought, that answers the question of whether the two of them want to say goodbye in a more loving fashion. Mum went back the Big House, Betty drove herself back into the village while I ran John over to the work crew in the forest.

'So you got things settled Mr. Daniel?' asked Bob Edwards when I brought John back to the crew. They were working on a fencing project around a compartment scheduled for planting next spring.

'No not really Bob, but then again perhaps yes as well as it could be.' I was a little uncertain whether it really would work. 'John stays in the cottage. He finds he can live there despite what happened.'

'That was a mess Mr. Daniel. I've never seen anything quite like it. I'm glad I didn't have to clean that up. I'm squeamish about blood at the best of times and it was all over down there.'

'Yes Bob, it wasn't pretty but it appears that John can't really remember being in the cottage or what he did there so it's not too bad for him living there. Still, we'll need to watch him because there may be some delayed reaction. Keep an eye on him will you?'

'I'll do that Mr. Daniel. In fact I've got to keep my eye on all of them now because there are some bad feelings about John being back from some of them. A few people here think he shouldn't be here at all, that you should have fired him.'

'It's about lunch time Bob that right?'

'Yes Mr. Daniel, it is, why?'

'Just call them in and I'll have a word right now. I'll try and nip any confrontation in the bud before it has a chance to fester so to speak.'

Bob went out along the fence line and called the lads off for lunch. He had them come back to where I was and they hung around a little bit sheepishly because they might have guessed what I was going to say. When they had all arrived I just held up my hands for a moment.

'Okay, just a quick word please. First, I want to thank each and every one of you for the job you did last week over Enrico's cottage. I know it was a mess but you all did a really excellent job and I know Enrico will be pleased. At the moment he is out of hospital as most of you know and staying with my sister at Home Farm. Needless to say Enrico is not letting things sit still and he is carving a wooden figure for my nephew Tony. I understand it will be a soccer player as young Tony is a fan. Perhaps you George can take him out on one of your training sessions and we'll have him playing for the village team before long.'

'I'll take anyone Mr. Daniel. The present team is a bunch of no-hopers and that includes young Ronnie here.'

'Hey, I ain't that bad George. I'm only a little slow.'

The rest of the crew laughed and several of them agreed with Ronnie that yes he was slow.

'Now I also want to thank you for work on the patrols and fighting the fire in the stables. Thanks to you, and my sister and Tony's mother we saved all the horses with no damage and we only lost part of the stables. It could have been a lot worse and it was your efforts that made sure it wasn't. Finally, you all know what happened after the fire and John here was the one who put an end to that. Now I realise that each and every one of you has some feelings about this. Understood, but it is likely that none of you know the whole story behind this so I would ask you to accept two things. First, John has been charged and will go to court but in the meantime he is here, out on bail and the family has agreed to have him work for us. We all think he is a good worker and has been a valuable employee for over seven years now. My dad stood bail for him so that gives you some idea how we feel. I've just come from a meeting we arranged with special permission from the court between John and his wife Betty to decide a few things. That done John works here and continues to live in his cottage and so that leads me into the second thing. If any of you feel you don't like this arrangement then say so, not now and not here but sometime later speak to Bob or come and see me. I'm quite sure we can find a way of keeping you employed and comfortable in your own thoughts. We realise life would have been a lot easier, a lot more peaceful if Idwal Ferris hadn't returned but he did and what happened has happened. So learn to live with it one way or another. We have. Finally, it's Friday so think on what I have said over the weekend.'

I turned to Bob, 'thanks Bob, enough said I think.'

'Fine Mr. Daniel. That was a good idea. Let's them all know that you're aware of the situation and tells them where you stand. Think they'll appreciate that. John Ferris will too I think.'

'I'll be off then Bob. I've got to sort some things out with my mother over the meeting we just had with John and Betty but I think things will work in the short term at least. See you later.'

I drove away and back to the Estate office but my mother wasn't there. I found her organising a quick bite to eat for lunch and so I joined her. Samantha was there with James.

'Uncle Daniel is my friend Katya coming back here tomorrow? She promised she would.'

'Yes James, your friend Katya will be coming tomorrow …'

'Oh good. She can see me ride Dainty again and I will show her how I can turn Dainty into a polo horse.'

Samantha leant across and whispered in James's ear, 'just remember whose friend Katya really is.'

'She's my friend,' retorted James loudly and he looked quite indignant.

My mother laughed. 'James,' she said, 'you may have to share your friend with some other people in this room. I think your uncle Daniel may want Katya to come out with him on Sunday, at least for his golf match.'

'Perhaps,' said James looking thoughtful, 'of course it might be easier if we can play with the railway Uncle Daniel, just the three of us. That way I could share Katya with you.'

'Don't I get a share young man?' my sister asked. 'Can't Katya be my friend too?'

James became even more thoughtful after this question from his mother and in the meantime my mum intervened. 'I thought you were going climbing on Sunday Samantha, with another of James's friends?'

'Who Mummy, who, who is it?'

'I arranged to go climbing with your Evelyn Nicols. You remember WPC Nicols your superheated steam engine driving teacher.'

'Can I come too?'

'No love I'm sorry but this is a girl's only expedition but your grandmother, bless her heart has decided she will take you for a serious riding lesson. You remember what I told you about my mother teaching me to ride?'

'Yes Mummy, you learnt not to fall off because the ground was frozen and you had to ride Nightmare.'

'She said what James?'

'Mother that's not quite what I said. My son seems to have only a semi-retentive memory. Like all men he tends to remember the parts that suit him and then occasionally he embroiders the rest. Anyway James, grandma will take you out on Dainty on Sunday morning and I will be home sometime in the afternoon so do we have a deal?'

'Sure Mummy and thanks Grandma; I just love riding Dainty you know. She likes it too. Uncle Daniel don't you think we should go and look at the railway now? You've finished lunch and you're not doing anything. You're just looking out of the window but you aren't seeing anything.'

'Shush James, your uncle Daniel is seeing Princess Katya riding up the driveway in her coach.'

'Where, where, show me.'

James jumped off his chair and rushed to the windows.

'I can't see her. Where is she Mummy?'

'In his head darling.'

James turned from the window and decided that he had heard enough of adult word games and he just grabbed my hand. 'Come on,' he said, 'let's go.'

I got off my chair and holding James's hand I looked over at my mother and my sister. 'If you'll excuse us ladies I think we lads have a date with God's Wonderful Railway upstairs.'

'Yes yes,' said James, 'can I drive?'

I walked upstairs with James and we went into the room clearly labelled "Railway". Inside I had developed over the years a rather comprehensive model railway. I suppose I had grown up like many young boys playing with toy trains but I had wanted more than a circular track and an engine chasing its tail. I had graduated from 'O' gauge cheap tinplate into 'OO' gauge quality precision locomotives and a comprehensive array of rolling stock. Over the years my "toy train" had evolved into a model of the Devon countryside complete with hills, a river, small villages with buildings, a farm with animals and served by a railway line. As with all model railways there is always something that is "work in progress" and I had several extensions and reworking in mind but at the moment it was operational and James had been fascinated when he first saw it a couple of weeks ago.

Although the Fotheringham Manor Estate is in Somerset I had modelled my location and railway on the Great Western Railway (GWR) or as it was sometimes called God's Wonderful Railway. Again, like many English railway modellers it was supposedly set in the 1930s when steam still ruled the rails. So, I had a good selection of engines of the Saint, Castle, Hall, and King classes plus several goods locomotives like Dean and Collett. My collection also included the inevitable GWR pannier tanks and a couple of Prairie tanks. For passenger rolling stock I had models of old clerestory coaches and more modern Collett corridor coaches. I had assembled over sixty goods wagons of different types and companies as Private Owners vans and wagons were very common in the 1930s.

'Can I drive, can I drive please?'

'Fine James,' I said, 'but let me get things all turned on first and make sure nothing is off the tracks or fallen over before we let you loose. Which engine would you like to drive? Can you remember what we said about the wheels?'

'Yes, you have a lot of 4-6-0s for the passenger trains but I would like to drive the King, the best and the fastest.'

'You're just like your mother James,' I said, 'you want to be out in front.'

'All the way Uncle Daniel. Is it ready yet? Is it this control? This way?'

'Hang on one moment you impatient little monster and let me get these couple of other locomotives out of the way so it will be easier for you. There, now try but slowly slowly.'

I spent thirty minutes with James before his interest waned and we arranged to put the engines to bed. I turned off all the controls and we went back downstairs.

'Now what are we going to do?' asked James.

'Well surprising as it might seem James my lad I have to do some work. I've got to go and talk with your grandmother about the Estate and then we might go and practice.'

'Can I practice whatever it is you're going to practice?'

'Well I'm not going to practice eating trifle so it won't be that exciting but give me half an hour James and you can come with me. Can you find your mother for that time and then when I've finished with grandmother I will come and find you for practice.'

'Goodee,' and a pair of little legs pumped into motion like engine pistons and James took off to find Samantha.

I found my mother in her office and we spent some time going over Estate finances plus a brief exchange on the outcome of this morning's meeting. I agreed I would check with the clerk of the court about further meetings for John and Betty and I would ask Terence Field about Idwal's previous conviction. I was about to go and find James when I had another rather vital thought: Katya. I went out to the telephone and called.

'Can I speak to Katya Howard please? Yes I'll hold. Who? Tell her the Lord at Fotheringham Manor is calling, she'll know who. She's not there? Can I leave a message? She's just returned. Hi Katya, it's good to hear your voice. Yes we're all fine here. And you? Look, I'll keep this short because I'm between obligations. With who? Well who do you think, with Master James of course. Yes, I'll say hi for you. Now, you are coming down this weekend? Brilliant. Bring some good shoes for walking. No not hiking but just for walking. I'll explain when you come down. Yes, outdoor clothes too. No, I persuaded James that although you are his friend we could share you. Yes there was bribery involved. That lad is his mother's son there is no doubt about that. Yes the hot woman, I remember. Samantha hasn't forgiven me yet for that expression. So, I'll pick you up at the train station around nine. Yes I'll be there. I've missed you. We'll talk later. Bye Katya, see you tomorrow at nine. Bye.'

Great I thought, absolutely bloody marvellous.

'You look happy Daniel.'

'Yes Mum, I've just confirmed I am picking Katya up at nine o'clock tomorrow morning for the weekend. Oh, she sends us her best wishes by the way and says she is looking forward to coming down and seeing us all again. I told her that James agreed to share his friend with all of us. Now, talking of James I promised I would take him to practice although he didn't bother to ask what we were practising.'

'He likes you Daniel, he really does.'

'Well Mum, despite the fact that my dearly beloved sister is his mother I also like him. What do they say, you can't choose your parents?'

'Daniel Lord you should wash your mouth out. You know you really love your sister and this is all a big act.'

'Actually Mum you're right. I do feel closer to Samantha since she's been home but then a lot has happened to promote that. Perhaps this is the first time we have really met and had to experience things together as adults. Before she went to Canada I was always just her baby brother. Well, after the last two weeks I think Samantha has realised otherwise.'

My mother looked at me and let her head tilt slightly to one side as she mused on my last comments.

'Yes Daniel I agree. I think Samantha has come home to a different household than the one she left and she has come home with a different attitude, a more mature and comprehensive attitude. I hope we can all continue this healthier state of affairs. Too much has happened recently and I think it has put a strain on your father. He won't say anything, you know your dad but I think he is feeling things a little more difficult these days. I'm hoping that Rosalind Cohen comes back to us with positive thoughts and ideas about the Company. That is worrying your dad a lot and when Samantha and you both said thank you but no thank you he was somewhat at a loss to know where to go next. That's not like him Daniel. Anthony is never at a loss about where to go next. Just watch him Daniel will you, please?'

'Sure Mum, I'll keep things away from him where I can and deal with them. Actually I did just that this morning with the work crew. I told them where we stood with John Ferris and that if any of them didn't like that they should come and see me and we'd sort it out.'

'Thanks Daniel, I appreciate that. Now, why don't you find James and go and practice? At least I know what you are going to practice.'

Enrico slowly twisted the knife in his gnarled hands and a sliver of wood fell to the ground. He grunted and gently rotated the figure around in his hands.

'It's marvellous Enrico,' exclaimed Tony coming out of Christina's car home from school. 'I'd never have believed you when you started with that ordinary block of wood, and now it's absolutely marvellous.'

'It's not finished yet Master Tony. There's still some work to do but you can get the general idea.'

'Look Peter, now ain't that awesome?'

'Isn't that awesome,' corrected Christina but she ruffled Tony's curly hair and smiled as she added, 'and yes Tony you are right, but then Enrico is a craftsman; a man with skilled hands.'

'And a vision Mum,' added Peter. 'You've also got to see the result when all you have to start with is a simple block of wood. You need the vision too.'

'Peter you are right lad. I've always been lucky as was my brother Antonio. Both of us could see what we wanted to create right from the beginning. It is a gift, and if you are double blessed to have hands that go with the vision then you become a craftsman.'

'An artist Enrico,' added Christina. 'It truly is a gift that both you and Antonio had. You have made many people happy the pair of you with your numerous creations. Most of the children around here Tony have one or more of Enrico's creations.'

'Unfortunately you lost some of them Enrico when your cottage was vandalised.'

'Hush Peter, don't mention that,' said Christina. 'That was a tragedy best forgotten.'

Enrico put down his knife and held out his hand to Christina. He gently held her hand with his rough and calloused fingers and looking up from the bench he was sitting on he smiled and said, 'it's not a problem Christina. It happened but let's try and learn from the incident not just dismiss it. All things, good and bad can give us insight into living a better life. We can try and do better next time, whatever we do. Actually, I was thinking of going down to the cottage in a few days time and see what there is I can do with the place.'

'Enrico give it another week please. We've only just brought you back from the hospital. If you're so insistent why don't you leave it until next week and then we'll see.'

Christina grasped Enrico's hand a little more firmly. 'Please take it slowly my friend.'

'Mum we could go down with Enrico, perhaps next weekend. Tony has never been there and we could both help if there was anything to be moved or brought back here. Could we do that Enrico with you? Tony I know you would be fascinated with Enrico's cottage.'

'It's not too far into the forest is it?' asked Tony. 'I'm still not comfortable with all these trees. They all look the same and I can hear them talking to me. Some nights I find it quite spooky here. It's so different from living in London with the street lights, the traffic and all the people. I'm still trying to get used to it Peter.'

'I'm sure you are Tony. I can understand. When I first came here from Italy I found the same thing. It was all so different and I too came from a town and not the country. I too found the forest a different place and quite spooky as you say but it is just a different place and over time you will learn to be comfortable with it.'

'I find it fabulous Tony. It can be so different between day-time and night-time. The birds are different, the animals are different and the light can make different patterns. At times it is enchanting and other times exciting too. We should persuade Uncle Daniel to take us out in the Landrover at night some time and see the eyes of the animals in the headlights. It's like those pictures on TV of being on safari.'

'Maybe,' said Tony rather hesitantly, 'but first time can we go to Enrico's cottage in the day-time?'

'Tony of course we will,' said Enrico. 'My eyesight won't let me go traipsing through the forest in the night-time any more, not like my eagle-eyed young friend here. Anyway you two, let me carry on and finish this for Tony before the football season is over. Christina, take these two scallywags away and let an old man continue with his labours.'

The two boys laughed and Christina bundled them off into the house.

'That's a smashing carving Enrico is doing for you Tony,' said Peter. 'It looks just like the man is kicking that ball.'

'Just wait until he's finished. Enrico said I could do the painting Peter, seeing as I know the colours. I'm going to keep it right by my bed so I can see it all the time.'

'Will you put a cover over the player's head when the team loses?' asked Christina jokingly.

'No auntie, never: they'll never lose, well not often anyway. Come on Peter, let's get changed out of these school clothes and see about your tree fort.'

'Yes, off you go the pair of you while I fix your and Enrico's teas. Be back around six Peter please.'

About a kilometre away, just tucked below the Big House I swung smoothly and the golf ball sailed in a gentle arc to land softly on the green and roll to within two feet of the cup. I pulled another ball into position and took a couple of easy practice swings. With my feet fairly close together I swung gently again trying to keep in balance with my weight evenly distributed and let the swing and club propel the ball up, down, release and roll to stop again within two feet of the hole.

James watched with his mouth half open.

'Can you do that every time?'

I laughed. 'I only wish James, I only wish but this does help do it more often with this practice.'

'I never knew this was here,' he said looking at the little area I had persuaded my parents to create. I had started to play golf soon after I went to Bristol House School. I must have been about eight I suppose. Dad and mum had made sure I could ride, could sail and could climb but none of these really fascinated me, in fact climbing rather frightened me. I certainly didn't have Michael's crazy stunt mentality or Samantha's incredible competitive drive. What I did have though was an inner peace to be competitive within myself and I found that golf provided that. True it was a wonderful outdoor sport usually set in some attractive and occasionally dramatic scenery but in addition to all that I found a real inner peace of mind striving to improve myself. I didn't need someone else to beat like my sister did. My challenge was with the course and with myself. No doubt when I started I never sat down and rationalised everything this way but I know I enjoyed golf. As part of the family I didn't give up on the other sports but I concentrated on golf. My parents were a little uncertain about this. Mum had never played and found it hard to understand why anyone would want to beat a little white ball around for three and a half hours and then complain about frustrations. She thought golfers were masochistic. I didn't even hint that climbing was sometimes like that too, especially on those cold and wet days when the cliff is streaming and you would sooner be indoors by the fire. Mum would come back from such expeditions vibrant with her attitude of success irrespective of the elements. I came back feeling there must be better ways of spending the day. Mark you, golf under those conditions can be rather depressing too but somehow I didn't feel that way on the course. Okay, so we're all different and golfers tend to be a breed apart.

After a couple of years I found that I was quite good. Mum accepted my playing, in fact she became very supportive but then I was her precious child. Dad played, primarily as a social and business activity and he enjoyed the camaraderie more than the game itself. My father has this fascinating ability to meld people together into a powerful unit irrespective of who they are and so dad became a good team player and many people liked playing with him. I on the other hand played for myself. I, me, myself became both the team and the competition and so when I was younger I often played alone. This was good in many ways because I didn't have to worry about finding a partner or even a competitor. As our course was never very crowded, except in the height of the tourist season I could play almost anytime.

My parents watched my game improve, and eventually after a lot of badgering on my part my father set aside an area out of sight of the House where I could practice. We had sat and discussed this and eventually dad created a putting green with seven holes and adjacent to this was a chipping area with three holes and a sand trap on one side. We kept the grass short, just like a fairway for about one hundred and fifty yards to an area that served as a tee-box. This meant I had a practice area for any shot up to that distance, the area where you can lose shots very easily if you are not concentrating. Just to add to the challenge we planted a hedge that eventually we kept trimmed at about ten feet high about one hundred yards from the green and partly in line with the tee-box. So, I could stand on the tee-box and hit an eight or a nine iron the one hundred and fifty yards with a clear view of the flag or I could move a little sideways so the hedge blocked my line of sight but still with the same shot hit with feel alone. I had another advantage as with the clear view to the green I could also practice using any club to hit anywhere up to the flags using all kinds of bump and run shots. Finally, and almost as an after-thought we put up a net for full-swing shots with woods although I spent virtually all my time in and around the green.

I had brought out some junior clubs for James but even these were too long for him at four years old. I watched him struggle trying to swing and frustratingly keep hitting the ground before the club head reached the ball. 'James, leave that club son and just try putting. I don't have any clubs short enough for you to swing fully. I'll try and find some at the Club if I can.'

'I can't hit it Uncle Daniel.'

'Come here then and try this one James. Here, stand in front. That's right. Feet a little wider apart. Good. Now hold the club gently in your hands and sweep the ball towards the hole. Whoa, gently now. Just like driving the train.'

'Engine Uncle Daniel.'

'Yes engine. Gently though as if you were stroking the ball. That's better. Softly softly with the hands.'

'That's what grandma says when I ride Dainty. I'm riding Dainty with grandma on Sunday Uncle Daniel.'

'Yes I know, and I'll be out on the golf course so I need to practice.'

'Is Katya going with you?'

'Yes James.'

'Does she play?'

'No I don't think so.'

'Why's she going then?'

'She's going to be my caddie.'

'What's a caddie?'

'Someone who carries your bag.'

'Why can't you carry it and then Katya could come with me and watch me ride Dainty?'

I laughed and picked James up off the surface of the putting green. I spun him round in my arms until he was facing me. 'All right little monster; I can see that practising with you tends to end up in a long dialogue and that's not helping my concentration.'

'You want me to go and find Mummy?'

I was about to find a way of saying yes in a diplomatic and avuncular fashion when Samantha suddenly appeared and solved my problem. 'Samantha this young golfer needs his mother to help improve his stroke. Why don't you take him over into the nets there and teach him to swing?'

'Daniel you know I can't play golf for toffee. I never could see the point. There's no adrenaline rush brother, no feeling of freedom.'

I didn't argue because if you're not a golfer there is no way you can ever understand the feeling of absolute marvel, absolute amazement that does happen at times. You've walked up to your ball and pictured the shot in your mind. You can see the stroke, the perfect flight and the correct landing of the ball so that it rolls across the green to end up in tap-in birdie range. Then you select the club, take your stance, one last quick glance at your target and swoosh. You hear the click, feel the clubhead bite through the earth creating a perfect divot and your little white ball soars through the air clear against the blue backdrop sky to land just where you visualised it and then roll truly to the flagstick. The feeling is marvellous but I could never explain all that to Samantha.

When Samantha dutifully wheeled her inquisitive son away to the safety of the nets I felt I could go back to the tee-box and practice some longer shots. I selected a couple of wedges and a nine iron. With a bag of thirty or so balls I started to practice chipping and lobbing shots onto the green. Gradually I moved further and further away still striving to have the ball finish close to the selected hole. When I was down to five balls I moved to be behind the hedge and tried to visualise the shot. I looked up at the trees that made a backdrop for the chipping green and tried to imagine the distance and the power needed in the shot. First I hit a full swing pitching wedge and the ball soared straight up into the sky to land just short of the green but straight I noted. I closed the face just a little and swung a little easier so there was less backspin and this time the ball pitched forwards onto the green to end up close to the flag. After looking around the end of the hedge I went back to my hidden line of sight. I hit three nine irons and managed to get two of them within five feet of the flag. Although not satisfied, I mean what golfer ever is, I did note that all the shots went straight. Walking back to the green to shag all the balls I saw that Samantha and James had stopped swinging golf clubs and Samantha had James climbing and swinging about in one of the neighbouring trees. Just like his mother I thought. For all his questions it's good to have them both back home.

Just ten days ago Samantha had come back to Fotheringham with James and my parents. A month before that, back in late August Samantha's husband Andrew had been killed with his co-worker in a rather horrific accident. They had both been trapped in a forest fire and burned to death. Andrew had been a forester too like me but Andrew had done postgraduate at Oxford specialising in modelling forest fires and developing strategies and tactics to fight them. He and Samantha had gone to Canada three years ago now and Andrew had worked at the Federal Forest Research Centre in Sault Ste. Marie, Ontario. My sister had ended up working at the same Lab but in the Forest Economics Section. She had just come home from some sensational new rock climbing route she and a friend of hers had done to find an empty house and a message from Andrew that he would be away for the weekend. Sad to say the next day Samantha heard that Andrew had been killed. Mum and dad went over straight away and after a while they all arrived back here where the past ten days have been a whirlwind and nightmare of activities.

First we have had the return of Idwal Ferris and his series of attacks, plus the burning of the stables and Idwal's eventual death at the hands of his brother John. The following night Danielle had been attacked and Samantha had taken Danielle, Tony and James into hospital only to have Danielle die there. With a couple of friends, Donald MacLeod and Stanley Rogers the three of us had dealt with the intruders in a rather final way. As a result of all this criminal activity Detective Inspector Field arrived on the scene and now it seems that my sister has taken a fancy to Terence Field so I'm not sure where that will take any of us. And to cap off a rather active weekend my mother and sister go climbing on Sunday and achieve reconciliation, well so they both say but we'll wait and see on that one. That same Sunday I took James to see the trains and we all meet up with the Howards from Jacksonville, Florida. Ah yes the Howards, Deidre, Delaney the IIIrd. and their lovely daughter Katya who is in her final year at Oxford University and will be coming here tomorrow. Roll on tomorrow.

Stay indoors when it rains

'Katya Katya Katya,' I cried as I hugged her and whirled her around on the platform.

'Daniel, Daniel!'

'What?' I said.

'It's not what I expected. Here I was thinking you were a proper English gentleman.'

Suddenly I realised what I had done and started to release my hug.

'Now I didn't say stop Daniel, it's just not what I was expecting, but it's nice though.'

I blushed. 'It's not really me,' I said. 'I'm not usually like this at all. You really do have a special effect on me Katya. That's it, you've bewitched me.'

'Have I Daniel? I rather like that.'

I unwound my arms and picked up Katya's overnight bag. Holding her by the hand I almost skipped down the platform and Katya giggled.

'It must be the trains,' she said, 'the atmosphere of railways obviously does something to you Daniel Lord.'

'Well there is that but I think there is more to it than that, much more,' and I turned and smiled at her.

'Everyone's going to be delighted to see you so soon. James was demanding all of yesterday that you would spend the entire weekend with him as you were his friend. He says this with such seriousness and authority you could almost believe him.'

'He's sweet Daniel. He's a fine young man. I am pleased to be his friend.'

'Well I bribed James by letting him drive engines yesterday and then we had golf practice so that I could have some time with James's friend. Come on, the Landrover's just down the way. Here, I'll put up the umbrella so you don't get wet.'

We drove back through the ever-increasing rain and a green but soggy countryside. Grey mists sunk lower and lower over the hills and there were dense patches of cloud in the bottom of all the swales. We chatted about University and Katya getting prepared for her final year. She didn't have much course work and would concentrate on getting her thesis organised. Apparently her supervisor was being very supportive with the objectives of Katya's research and it looked like being a very successful and productive year.

'Actually Daniel, when I saw the weather forecast I did pack some work with me. I thought we could go over it together if we run out of things to do.'

I smiled and then my smile broadened into a grin. 'Remember all the books in the library and my ability at explaining things in pictures in books?'

'Yes,' said Katya, a little unsure where this conversation was going to go.

'Well, I think there are enough books in the library to keep us occupied for a long time.'

'But Daniel I know how steam engines work and I've already explained why some engines are blue and some are green even without pictures in books.'

I laughed and we both remembered just last weekend when I had first met Katya and her parents while taking James out on a special train trip. As usual James had been an absolute volcano of questions and to try and keep him from exploding I had prevaricated and told him I would answer some of them back in the library of Fotheringham. I had explained that I had several railway books with pictures that would answer some of his demands for knowledge. Well Katya, who spent much of that day with James and I caught on to this answer of mine and anytime that James asked a particularly awkward question Katya would jump in and tell James that I would explain it later with pictures in a book in the library. Every time she would smile at me and dare me to contradict her. It had become a game between us to see whether I could answer James before Katya offered the library books as a default answer.

It didn't take us long to reach home and I cruised slowly up dad's beloved gravel driveway at a sedate pace to park around by the blackened shell of our stables. Again, only two weeks ago these had contained six horses all happily munching their feed and looking over stall doors at each other. Idwal Ferris's arson attempt had ruined all but one of the stalls and destroyed the feed barn. Happily the horses were fine although they wouldn't be so happy today I thought in this grey cold rain. I expect that they are all huddled up under the shelter of the oaks at the foot of the paddock where we had temporarily placed them.

'Is James going to ride Dainty today Daniel?'

'No Katya, my mother has arranged to do that tomorrow morning, which is just as well too given the weather.'

'Do the horses mind the rain?'

'No not really but the riders don't usually like it, especially if you are racing. The hooves tend to cut up the ground and there is mud flying everywhere, usually in your eyes. Helps the horses if they wear blinkers under those conditions. Even the jockeys wear goggles but you do get dirty.'

'Have you raced then?'

'Not seriously, partly because I am not the right size or shape but I have raced a little in steeplechases.'

'That's over jumps?'

'Yes, usually hurdles but it is also uphill and downhill in this part of the world so you have to judge your horse's condition and stamina.'

'And you've fallen off like James the other day?'

'You bet and that's when you want it to be soft and wet like today, and be the last horse in the race.'

'Why the last horse? That doesn't sound like a Lord ambition, certainly not your sister's?'

I laughed and turned to Katya. 'You're right, and you're learning a lot about this family but so true. Samantha wouldn't want to be last but then she probably wouldn't fall off either. The danger when you fall off, especially in a jumping race is being underneath another jockey or worse under a falling horse, or its hooves of course. Not a friendly place to be. Still, I never did it seriously so the risk wasn't high. Anyway, let's go inside before this rain gets any harder.'

'Hello Samantha, it's good to see you again. How are you and how's your sister/mother or is it mother/sister?'

I looked up just at that moment. I had put Katya's bag down in the hall as Katya greeted my sister. I watched Samantha's face go through a whole series of expressions before she laughed, stepped forward and gave Katya a big hug. Once again Katya looked a little surprised. When I saw Samantha look puzzled at Katya's expression I explained. 'Katya has, or perhaps had until recently this misconception that all English people are reserved, aloof, and not given to showing emotions. I hugged her at the station and you sister dear have just hugged her again, and that is why she is wearing that rather puzzled look on her face. By the way I am interested too whether it is sister/mother or mother/sister?'

Samantha looked daggers at me as she stepped back from hugging Katya. 'I'll let you guess,' she said, 'but woe betide you if you guess wrong.'

'Katya, this is a wonderful vision this early in the morning,' and just to add to Katya's continuing confusion my father swept into the hall and gave Katya a big hug.

'It's a big Lord conspiracy Katya,' I said trying not to laugh too hard. 'We all planned it this morning over breakfast, that we would show our American cousins how human we stiff upper-lip Brits can be. I'll bet James gives you a hug too when he finds you. Mum you're just in time.'

'In time for what dear? Oh hello Katya,' and my mother held Katya by her upper arms and kissed her on one cheek and then the other.

Katya looked mischievously at the other three of us and said, 'obviously your mother didn't have breakfast with you this morning?'

When we all stood there laughing my mother slowly peered at each of us in turn. 'What have I missed? Is my slip showing or something? Have I put my head on backwards this morning? You're all standing there grinning like apes. Anyway, come along Anthony, we've things to do in the village.'

As my mother moved at speed out of the doorway and dad followed he called back over his shoulder, 'I'll explain it to her as we drive off,' and away they both went.

The three of us stood there in the hall grinning at each other for a brief moment before the peace and quiet was violently interrupted by a small pair of legs supporting a torso that had a pair of arms flailing like

42

there were three pairs. As usual the mouth was open and words issuing forth.

'Katya, Katya my friend,' and without any change in pace the bundle of humanity that was called James by his mother and other names by me charged straight into Katya. As predicted there was a flurry of arms into a hug and Katya crouched down to be at eye level. 'Hello friend,' she said, 'how is my favourite engine driver this morning? You look like you are all fired up for a long journey.'

James went into overdrive and there was a long explanation without too many breaths of all the hundred and one things James had done since he got up this morning. This ranged from 'jumping on mummy before she was awake, going for a pee without dribbling, trying to open the door while mummy was dressing, having a porridge-eating race with Uncle Daniel' and so on. Katya crouched and listened attentively to this entire extremely detailed monologue. Eventually Samantha decided that other people could only take so much of monster James and so she hauled him off and told him there were some serious mother to son discussions needed and that he could see Katya later in the day.

'Samantha, before you haul monster mouth away is there something special you have to do with James? I ask because I was thinking of taking Katya down to Christina's and meeting her plus Peter and Tony. If you wanted we could take James down to see whether Peter and Tony wanted to play. If they didn't we could bring him back but that way he would get out of the house a little bit in this poor weather. It's just if you didn't have other plans.'

My sister stood with James in her arms and thought about that. 'Why don't I give Christina a call Daniel? First I can tell her you are dropping by and can ask about your other suggestion. Keep in mind that Peter and Tony are nine.'

'Fine, Katya why don't you come upstairs to your room while Samantha is doing that and then you're all settled in.'

'I'll come. I'll show Katya Uncle Daniel. Come on Katya let's go upstairs. You're in the special guest room.'

'Yes James,' I said, 'the one with a secret panel and behind that there is a hidden passage and it leads to....'

'I know I know it leads to my room so I can go and visit my friend without anyone knowing.'

'He's incorrigible Katya he really is. Come on then Guest Guide lead our guest to her room. Would you like to carry her bag?'

'It's a bit big Uncle Daniel. You can do that though.'

'Well, gee thanks James,' I said as the three of us traipsed upstairs leaving Samantha on the telephone.

Samantha said she had other things to do and so the three of us climbed back into the Landrover with James firmly ensconced between Katya and I. The rain continued to fall fairly seriously and the dry ground soaked it up readily. Dead and dying tree leaves twirled to the ground and the forest floor became a mosaic of different colours. Tendrils of mist still clung around the low-lying areas.

'I can see Dainty's head,' cried James. 'She's like the cat which kept appearing and disappearing in that book on Alice mummy reads to me. See, there's Dainty's legs now.'

We pulled in around the back yard of Home Farm and Christina stood in the doorway to greet us.

'Good morning Daniel, although perhaps it is not such a good morning but do come in please.'

'Christina I would like you to meet Katya Howard. Katya is doing her final year at Oxford and I met her and her family last weekend.'

44

'Katya welcome my love, welcome to Home Farm. James, there you are, well Peter and Tony are upstairs love. Just pop up and see them. Sorry Katya but James demands to be first.'

'Christina it's really nice to meet you and I fully understand young Master James. I had a lovely day with him last Sunday and learnt quite quickly that he takes after his mother in many ways.'

'Does he ever,' agreed Christina. 'Don't you think so Daniel?'

I laughed and agreed. 'Christina you are so right although James probably asks more questions than my sister. Samantha used to jump in and ask afterwards. Perhaps in Canada she became older and wiser and has passed the questioning thing on to James.'

'Anyway come in Katya and meet another good friend who is here. Enrico we have a visitor, as well as Daniel of course.'

I watched Enrico slowly rise from a chair and walk towards us with both arms outstretched. He has got old I thought and I hadn't noticed. The hands shook a little but the smile was still the same.

'Katya is it? I'm very pleased to meet you. I am also delighted that you have found this young man to bring you here to see us. It is about time that young Master Daniel brought pretty ladies to see me. Usually he brings me frogs and dead mice, and occasionally an interesting tree stump for carving, but you my dear are a brilliant change.' Enrico turned to me and just said 'thank you.' He turned back to Katya and held her two hands. He looked at them in his own brown well-worn wrinkled hands. 'Precious these are my dear and yours are lovely. One's body is a wonderful god-given machine but these can do some really beautiful things. They say the eyes are the path to your soul but I am a great believer in the capabilities of the hands.'

'Enrico carves Katya,' I explained and his hands have created some truly wonderful things ranging from art, to toys and to tools and other useful things. I heard you were working on something for Tony Enrico? Do you have it to hand?'

Enrico turned and walked over to a table. He pulled a cloth off his latest endeavour and brought it across for us to see.

'Young Tony here is a football fan and he was a little disappointed to leave London and his beloved favourite team who I think are called Spurs.'

'That's right Enrico, Tottenham Hotspurs.'

'So, to help him settle here, and because Peter has several things I have carved for him and Tony thought they were truly "awesome" I think he said, I decided to make something just for Tony. He wanted a football player and when he is finished I will help Tony paint him in the team's colours which I think are black and white.'

'Tony is my husband's brother's son Katya,' explained Christina, 'Michael's son but his mother was Danielle and she came from Mozambique so Tony says he is a mix of black and white, and so he supports Spurs, who are also black and white. He is sometimes a very serious boy.'

'And quite like Peter too Christina,' I added. 'Peter is very thoughtful and mature for his age, in fact very like Geoffrey was.'

'Yes Geoffrey,' said Christina wistfully.

The tension in the room was suddenly lessened when three young men burst into the room and came to an abrupt stop when they saw who was there.

'Caw, who's the smashing bird Uncle Daniel?' asked Tony.

'Tony!' said Christina emphatically, suddenly going from sorrowful emotion to embarrassed shock.

'Oh, sorry,' said Tony and he embarrassed himself further by blushing which Peter noticed and promptly added to the situation by saying, 'Tony, you're blushing.'

'No I'm not.'

'You are.'

Katya stepped forwards and defused the situation beautifully. 'James,' she said, 'who's this smart young man you have brought to me who so gallantly thinks I am smashing?'

James, never one to notice adult nuances stepped forward and in his serious little voice said, 'this is my cousin Tony Katya and this is my other cousin Peter. They both live here with Auntie Christina and Enrico. This is Home Farm you know and my great auntie Stephanie looks after the sheep that are very special. They win all sorts of prizes don't they Uncle Daniel?'

Katya decided to step in before James ran through the names of all the sheep.

'Tony I'm pleased to meet you. I am Katya Howard, a friend of your Uncle Daniel and he has brought me here to Home Farm to meet you all.' She turned to Peter and took his hand. 'Hi Peter, it's good to meet you. I can see your mother in your eyes.'

Katya had no sooner stopped when James took over again, 'and Katya is my friend too, not just Uncle Daniel's. Aren't you Katya?' and he came over to Katya and took her hand as if to take possession.

'So are you three getting along successfully?' I asked. 'No tree fort today Peter, too wet for outside? How is it coming along? I must have a look one day, if I'm invited of course.'

'Of course Uncle Daniel, you could be a special guest. Yes, it is a little slippery when the bark is wet and Mum thinks we'll fall off the ladder.'

'It's dangerous Peter. You never know when you might fall.'

'Mum, it's fine really. It's not very far up to the fort and we've piled some straw around the bottom of the ladder. James gets up and down easily enough.'

'James goes up there?'

'Sure Mum. He loves it. Don't you James?'

'It's smashing Auntie. You can peer out and no one can see you. It's like being on the roofs back at the Big House and hiding behind the chimneys.'

I watched Christina hold her hands up to her face in horror. 'Your mother knows you are climbing this tree James, and up on the roofs too. Mama mia, I would have a fit if Peter had done that at your age.'

'But I'm nearly five Auntie, aren't I Uncle Daniel?'

'James is fine Christina,' I said. 'Samantha has had him out in all her usual risky places already. You know what Samantha is like?'

'Yes,' said Christina, 'I know what Samantha is like and that is what worries me. Still, if you say it is okay Daniel I will have to accept it but it will still worry me this tree fort.'

'Christina, have no worries. Boys are boys and they are very good at bouncing when they are young,' said Enrico. Antonio and I used to scramble all over the cliffs back home when we were little, just like young goats and the chamois we were chasing. They are fine.'

Christina wasn't convinced and dusted her hands on her apron.

'We just popped in to say hi Christina and let James play with Peter and Tony if that is okay,' I said. 'Samantha did telephone didn't she?'

'Yes Daniel, and Peter and Tony said that would be good. There was something special going on and they wanted James here anyway so that's fine. I'll bring him back later in the day. Katya it is really nice to meet you. I heard that you had a good day last Sunday with Daniel and James and that your family stayed an extra day. Please visit us again if you come back.'

'She'll be back next weekend, won't she Uncle Daniel?' quickly interjected James.

'Yes Christina,' I said, 'well I hope so' and I turned to Katya. 'I hope so' I repeated and held her hand. Katya smiled. 'It's been lovely to meet

48

you all and I promise I will come back.' Here she turned to me and added 'I promise.'

'We're just going to tour around part of the forest Christina and make the most of a wet day. I know it doesn't do much for people but the rains really help the trees so part of me welcomes this weather. It's always a weird situation you know being a forester. Much of the time you are praying for weather that isn't what people want for themselves. Anyway, thanks for taking James. We'll see you all later. Look after them all Enrico?'

'Goodbye then Daniel, and you too smashing lady,' said Enrico with a chuckle and he turned to watch Tony turn red again.

Katya and I ran across the yard in the rain and jumped into the Landrover. We sat inside and shook ourselves. 'Here,' I said, 'I think I've got a towel or something somewhere.' I rummaged about behind the seat and produced what had been a white towel at some time in its life. 'Use this.'

'No way Daniel, that's dirty. I'm just a little damp and that will soon dry. Men!'

I dropped the towel back again and switched on the ignition. I didn't have a suitable retort so I kept quiet.

'Can we go and see Enrico's cottage?' asked Katya. 'He's a very interesting man. You obviously know him very well and I can see that he likes you too.'

'That's true Katya on all three parts. He and his older brother Antonio came here during the war. My great grandfather George wanted workers and he had lived with and fought beside Italians in the First World War. He thought they were good workers and dedicated people and so when he heard about Antonio and Enrico he pulled a few strings from his army days and brought them here. It worked out well for all concerned. Enrico loves to carve.'

'He is really talented Daniel. That soccer player is magnificent. I think Tony will be delighted. He certainly should be. He's sweet too Daniel, even if he does think I'm a smashing bird.' Katya laughed. 'I think that's the first time I've been called a bird.'

'That's one of the more polite London expressions Tony brought down with him. I'm glad he didn't use some of the other descriptions Londoners have for women. But to come back to what you were saying earlier I suppose I have known Enrico all my life. In many ways I grew up with him and his brother. I was the youngest in the family as you know, the baby so to speak. Anyway, somehow or other I spent a lot of time at Antonio and Enrico's cottage. I still have several of the toys that they made me. And yes, I suppose I did develop a special rapport with Enrico. We get on really well but I was just noticing there in the house that he is getting on in years. It could be he has just come from hospital and still feeling a little weak but I noticed that his hands shake a little more now and he moves slower.'

'We all get older Daniel,' Katya said quite quietly and she put her hand on mine very gently. 'I noticed with my parents before they went back to the States that my mother has slowed down a little in the mornings and my father, well he really does move slower.'

'I thought that was because he came from Louisiana: wasn't that what your mother said? He was a proper southern gentleman and not one of the speedy products of Florida like your mother.'

'Daniel,' said Katya laughing as she spoke, 'the only really speedy thing about my mother is her mouth. She does a mile a minute with her mouth but otherwise she too is a typical Florida resident, slow baby slow. The whole world goes slowly in Florida Daniel.'

'But not the trees though,' I said. 'My dad was really impressed talking with your father about forestry operations and your rates of growth. He was talking of rotations that were twenty years or even less. That's pretty fast in anybody's book.'

'Yes Daniel, that's true but you have some American trees that grow quickly here don't you?'

'Sure, when you can see them,' I said as I peered through the murk. The rain had eased off a little but the mist had rolled in and you could hardly see the trees on either side of the forest ride. 'We're here. We're at Enrico's cottage.'

'Where Daniel? I can't see anything in this mist. I certainly can't see any cottage.'

'Come, I'll show you.'

I turned off the engine and got out of the Landrover. Walking round to the other side I helped Katya down and continued holding her hand. It seemed a good excuse at the time, so that she didn't feel I was going to lose her. Sure. We walked through the mist and Enrico's cottage gradually emerged like a phantom.

'I see you've been here before.'

'Only a few hundred times I think.'

I unlatched the back door and we walked into a rather bare but now tidier kitchen. 'Just two weeks ago this was a really comfortable and homely room. I've spent many a happy hour here. Then, what nine days ago now this kitchen was a scene of utter vandalism. Everything that could be was smashed, food scattered all over the floor, broken plates and bottles. It was gross. I had the forest crew come in here and clear up as best they could. Mostly they just took stuff out to the lorry and we burnt it. They did do a good job on cleaning up the floor though. It actually looks liveable again, just empty and impersonal. Did you want to see the other rooms?'

'No Daniel, not really. I'm sorry. I didn't mean to intrude on something that is both personal and rather unhappy. No, I don't think I want to see you so upset. Let's go back to the car.'

Rather slowly I walked out and relatched the door. Idwal Ferris I thought you have a lot to answer for. Your return seems to have caused one disaster after another. Why did you ever really return?

Back in the Landrover the mist hadn't moved and there seemed to be no real point in driving round in the mist other than I was alone with Katya but it was cooler than we both thought and even with the heater on I saw that Katya shivered a little. 'Look, it's almost lunchtime. Let's go and get a bite and discuss a warmer and more constructive plan of action for the afternoon. I can see you shiver Katya and that's no good. What do you say to some lunch?'

'Actually Daniel I say yes please. I didn't really have breakfast and so I'm quite hungry. So yes, let's go and have lunch, and what did you say, discuss a more constructive plan of action? I can go for that.'

I drove back through the mist and Katya wondered how I knew where I was going.

I turned towards her with a grin on my face. 'Guess what I'm going to say?' I asked. Katya looked at my grinning face and thought for a moment.

'You're going to show me a picture in one of those large books in the library so I can understand how you know where you are going out here?'

'Right on,' and we both laughed as we remembered pictures in the books in the library.

My parents had returned from whatever they were doing in the village and Samantha also joined us for lunch. Because they were still talking about whatever they had had to do in the village dad and mum didn't pay much attention to the three of us and so they were rather surprised when I told them Katya and I were going to spend some time in the library.

'Doesn't seem a very exciting thing to be doing Daniel, especially when Katya has come all this way.'

'Mum, Katya very smartly looked at the weather forecast, rather unknowingly being American she believed it and brought some of her thesis work with her. I was going to help with it and we thought the library had a more academic atmosphere than the drawing room. If you look outside you can see that you can't see anything and that rather detracts from taking extended tours of the forest, the countryside and probably most of southwest England.'

'Yes Daniel, you've made your point. Anyway your father and I have some business to discuss so we'll be in the office if you need us.'

'Mum I don't think they'll need you at all, no disrespect of course but I think that Daniel and Katya will be just fine alone together in the library.' Samantha turned and smiled like a Cheshire cat as she spoke.

'Isn't that right brother?'

'Katya it's time we left,' I said and stood up, 'before my beloved sister here makes any more innuendos.'

'I'll just go and get my things then Daniel and meet you in the library. Don't go looking at any of those pictures in the mean time; you know the ones I mean.'

'Why does everyone think I should be the fall guy?' I asked the room but everyone had their faces elsewhere.

Up in the library I browsed around waiting for Katya. This was a rather splendid room in our house. The view was down the driveway and that in itself was impressive but the interior had a charm of its own. Great grandfather George had a passion for the light pale colouring of oak and the entire lower parts of the walls were panelled in this lovely timber and above that the walls were subdivided into sections for books with oak dividers and shelving. At about six feet in height the panelling was pulled forward to line up with the front end of the book shelves and continued to the ceiling. The ceiling itself was painted white and the whole room had a very light appearance even though the walls themselves were covered by dark looking books. On the inside wall, the one directly opposite the large driveway-facing windows was a space from books and there stood the family shield. The room had grace in both its dimensions and its appearance. I had never measured it and I wondered whether my great grandfather had had it built to any classical size and shape. As architectural design had not been a compulsory or even an optional subject for a Forestry degree I had never learnt very much about such things but I did have an eye for beauty and this room had it. Had it twice over I thought as Katya came in through the door.

'You look like you've seen something delightful Daniel standing there with that sort of bemused look on your face. It is a lovely room isn't it? When you first brought me in here to show James pictures of steam engines I thought it was a lovely room. That's what you were looking at isn't it?'

'Yes and no Katya. I was looking at the room and I do agree with you that it is delightful and then you walked in and I thought the room looked even better.'

'In your dreams Daniel Lord.'

'Usually,' I muttered.

'I think there is some Irish connection somewhere in the House of Lord Daniel: you all seem to have this silver tongue thing. Now let's get some work done can we, or shall I just pull a book at random and you can explain the pictures to me?'

Katya dumped her thesis material on the table and stood in the centre of the room.

'I'll close my eyes, spin round three times and walk to the shelves and then pick at random. Warn me if I end up walking towards the windows. Ready?'

Not knowing quite what mood Katya was in and after our verbal sparring not sure where this was all going I just said 'right, spin away.'

Katya closed her eyes and turned. Finally she walked rather slowly and carefully towards the shelves. 'You're safe,' I said, 'just go slowly with your arms outstretched.'

'You'd better not be in front of me Daniel. It doesn't sound like it. Am I okay?'

'Close, nearly there. There, can you feel the shelves?'

'Yes, now let me see, or rather let me feel. Can I feel some vibrations from any of these books? Is there a fascinating story, with pictures of course somewhere here? Here we are. What have I got here Daniel?'

I walked over and looked at the book in Katya's hands.

'It's entitled "Needlepoint for ladies" and it must have been written in Victorian times. Yes, dated 1881. However, it does contain pictures, well diagrams at least.'

'I'm not really a lady Daniel so I'll pick again.'

'Just a minute Katya, just hold it a mo'. I've just seen something I was looking for a week ago, something Samantha was asking about and that is interesting. Here in this box file.'

I moved along the shelves a little and lifted down a rather modern dark grey box file and took it over to the table. 'Come and look. You may find this more interesting than petit point.'

'Needlepoint Daniel but that file looks modern. Why would that be more exciting than genuine Victoriana?'

'Well come and look and I'll show you. What's inside this modern box as you so rightly point out is something much older than Victoriana.

I put these papers in this box some eight years ago now I suppose and the papers are old, very old. Come and see.'

I started to take the papers out of the box and spread them on the table.

'I'm surprised at you Daniel, getting so excited when there are no pictures. Are there pictures?'

'Look at these and tell me what they are?'

I handed Katya two rather faded and tattered sheets of paper. She took them carefully and looked at one and then at the other. 'This is a map,' she said and she handed me one of the pieces.

'Right, so not really a picture but a sort of picture representation of something, or somewhere. And the other?'

'This, I'm not sure about this Daniel. What is it?'

'Just put it down for a moment and let's look at the first one, the map.'

'Tell me where you found them first Daniel so I can understand why you are so excited about some mouldy and rather torn pieces of old paper.'

'It's a long story.'

'Daniel, I've learnt that most things associated with your family tend to be long stories but it is raining, it is misty and I don't really want to work on my thesis so why don't you tell me why you are so excited? Deal?'

'Deal, but as it really is a long story why don't we go and sit in those two more comfortable chairs by the window and I'll explain. We'll take the two pieces of picture paper with us.'

'You're not happy without pictures are you?'

'Hush, sit back comfortably and I'll begin.'

I relaxed back in my chair and thought over how best to explain my excitement. Where to start? I suppose right at the beginning, even if that was painful. I looked at Katya.

'This is a family story with a sad start, an exciting middle part and a sad ending.'

'Must it have a sad ending Daniel? I don't want to cause any grief but you seemed so happy and excited just then when you found the papers so it can not be all that sad.'

'Well you can judge for yourself when you've heard it. Maybe the story will have a happy ending some time.'

'I hope so.'

'You may remember I told you that some eight years ago, in June of 1990, Geoffrey, Michael and I went climbing up in North Wales and Geoffrey died.'

'Yes, I remember Daniel,' and Katya looked at my hands as I too looked at the scars on my palms from the rope burns.

'Well Christina was devastated. Peter must have been just over one and there was a great row in the house because Christina thought Michael was to blame for the accident and she accused him of killing Geoffrey. This got serious and Christina went back to Italy to see her parents. By this time my mother was really upset. She was looking after me because I was still in shock and on my guilt trip and now Geoffrey's son, the heir to the Lord Estate was in Italy and not at Fotheringham. However, Enrico came to the rescue.'

'He did, but how?'

'He quietly suggested to my mother that she should take me and herself to Italy and see Christina at her parent's home. I would be a tutor to little Peter so he didn't forget his English. My mother would see Peter and talk with Christina's parents and Christina and hopefully this might defuse the situation. Enrico thought it would be good for me, sort of take my mind off myself and think about someone else.'

'And did it, did it work?'

'Well, several very positive things came out of that trip. My mother bonded well with Christina and learnt more about Christina's Italian volatility as described by Christina's father. My mother is not a people person the way my father is but she did learn to understand Christina's emotions. But perhaps better, for me at least was I really got on well with Peter. He was learning to speak and we developed a kind of special language between the two of us, sort of babyspeak Anglo-Italian mix. Anyway we bonded. When we came back to Fotheringham later that summer Peter wanted to be with me most of the time and gradually I left my sorrow behind.'

'So Enrico's suggestion really helped?'

'It turned out to be better than that Katya. Let me continue and I'll tell you how. It relates directly with these two pieces of paper. When we came home Christina was still a little emotional over Geoffrey and so I volunteered to help clean up all Geoffrey's belongings with Christina. In that process we included Peter and it was a sort of therapy for all of us and that's where the papers came in.'

'Where Daniel?'

'Quite by chance in the attic. Peter and I were supposed to be tidying up but playing really in the attic of Home Farm and he accidentally knocked over a stack of boxes and this pile of papers tumbled out all over him. Peter shouted more in alarm or shock as he wasn't hurt at all but he suddenly found this piece of paper and for some reason he was entranced. He wouldn't let go of it. It was this piece of paper,' and I showed Katya the piece of paper she hadn't deciphered.

'What was so special about it Daniel? It doesn't look like much to me. In fact I'm not really sure what I am looking at.'

'Well this is the exciting part, but let's get back to all the papers and the story. After I bundled everything up back into the box and with Peter still clutching his special piece of paper we went down into the kitchen to see what we had found. There's only one light in the attic and we couldn't really see anything. So down in the kitchen I quickly made a copy of Peter's special treasure map and by sleight of hand I substituted the original. He was happy colouring the copy and I managed to salvage this piece.'

'Did you think it was important then?'

'At that time I didn't know but thought it might be. It might turn out to be old rubbish and then it might not but at that time I was just an excited teenager and had all sorts of fanciful ideas and imagination.'

'And now you're an excited twenty something and just as full of ideas and imagination?'

We looked at each other. A warm vibration bounced to and fro across the table and I put out my hand and placed it softly on top of hers.

'That feels like yes.'

'Well Christina and I slowly went through all the papers and most of them contained writing including some lists with numbers but only two were pictures of some sort. In the end Christina and I thought it looked like a series of lists, with what appeared to be numbers associated with each item on the list and then some form of commentary. We sort of guessed without any evidence that it might be an inventory of cargoes. Now the family of Lord a long time ago was involved in shipping out of Bristol. In fact some of the old family money came that way according to hearsay. Many of the old families here were involved in shipping and for a period of time that meant slavery. Bristol was really into the slave trade for a while and we wondered whether the lists and prices were shipping manifests.'

'But what about these two pieces of paper?'

'This one, the one you thought looked like a map is a map. It's a map of parts of Fotheringham. Maybe this was a map of the entire estate in those days but it certainly does portray part of our land as of today.'

'How did you find that out? This is rather like a detective story or a kind of treasure hunt with clues?'

'You're closer to the truth than you think. But let's get back to the map. I brought it back here and showed my father and told him about the other papers. He thought the family had had land in Jamaica at one time and he agreed the lists may be shipping manifests. But the interesting thing was dad thought he recognised the map. He had seen something like it in this room and that his grandfather had shown him once. Dad thought it was in one of these books.'

'But there are hundreds of books here Daniel. How did you ever find which book?'

'I bypassed the library. It's not what you know Katya it's who you know that helps in life and that's what I did.'

'But your great grandfather was long dead, even your grandfather was dead you told me.'

'Yes Katya but great grandfather had a gamekeeper named Albert Templeton and he had a son called Edward Templeton and Albert Templeton knew all about the so-called Lord treasure and the existence of a map.'

'Treasure Daniel, you did say treasure?'

'The rumour was that some of the money the family made a long time ago came from some illegal activities, as did most of the old old families here. We were all involved in smuggling and probably other undercover and unsavoury activities. Anyway the rumour was that some monies were buried somewhere on the estate. Great grandfather knew quite a lot about it but he never needed the money so he let the story die but his gamekeeper knew about it and the map. He told his son Edward and Edward was the foreman when Antonio and Enrico came here. The three men got on really well and talked a lot together. Now Edward died when I was just four but Enrico was still here and so I took my map to Enrico, who I knew.'

'And he knew about the map?'

'He did better than that Katya. He took me to the northern part of the estate and I could see exactly what the map showed me. But better than that, much better than that was the second piece of paper. Look here, look at it again and change the map scale in your mind.'

Katya took the two pieces of paper and scrutinised them. 'This one is a smaller scale of part of the estate you say. This is the one Enrico saw and took you somewhere special?'

'Yes.'

'What was special about the northern boundary that I don't know? What did you see there?'

'The estate ends at a cliff which is perhaps fifty, sixty feet high. The cliff is really part of a limestone escarpment that rises and falls along our northern boundary. There are some really old trees growing along the foot of the cliff, separate from our much smaller plantation trees.'

'This other piece of paper could be a larger scale version of part of the other map and this sort of matches here on the first piece but there are too many just wriggly lines Daniel. Tell me please?'

'We found this one first, the one that is confusing you. When I saw it I suppose I saw two pictures on one sheet of paper. See here, we have a possible map view, a top down view. The one wriggly line has a really sharp indent in it and there are a couple of circles inside the indent and a sort of square in between. There is a circle just beside the indent and if it's a top down view then the circle represents some round building or round object anyway.'

'But what is the other part of the paper supposed to mean?'

'Think side view of a cliff; the two lines represent the top and the bottom of the escarpment. See the bottom one is relatively straight and the upper one bounces up and down just like the top of the cliff does. On the bottom one there is a sort of semicircle and beside the semicircle is what looks like a forked tree. Now when Enrico brought me to the cliff and we walked along the foot of the escarpment I suddenly saw it.'

'Saw what Daniel?'

'The tree, the forked tree although now it doesn't have a fork. One of the limbs has broken off but it is a very old tree and that is natural. Anyway, I went down to the tree and then I found out what the semicircle was, and the big indent in the map picture. It was a cave. It has a very small entrance which is partly hidden by the big old tree.'

'So you went inside and found the treasure Daniel?'

'No, I didn't go inside at that time. Enrico had to go back to work and I didn't have a torch. In fact I never did go inside the cave before my brother found it.'

'And Michael discovered the treasure and that is why he was killed?' asked Katya looking anxiously at me. 'Don't go on Daniel if this is too hard, too painful.'

'Well you have the right idea but it didn't work out that well, not for any of us really. Sure Michael must have found my maps where I had hidden them and gone out sometime in early January. I know he went into the cave from the reports after the accident. I have been inside the cave but long after Michael's death.'

'So what happened to the treasure? No, let me back up a moment. Was there ever any treasure?'

'We don't know, and perhaps we'll never know. There certainly wasn't any treasure in the cave when Michael went there the last time. Apparently he had gone to the cave to dig in this spot, this square inside the indentation and he found nothing. But someone else must have found out about all of this because on that fateful night someone else set a trap for Michael. According to hearsay Michael was lured out to the cave on some pretext, perhaps someone offered to give him the treasure for something, maybe some secrets of my father's Company. We may never know. Michael went out there and was shot, just outside the cave. It was a funny event, funny peculiar that is as there was one shot through his head but no search ever turned up any shell casing or any evidence of what killed him. Still, as I said at the start it had a sad ending as Michael died and no treasure was ever found.'

'But you've been into the cave since Daniel? What was it like?'

'It's small, really just an enlarged fissure in the limestone and doesn't go in very far but it is typical with a dry floor, a couple of incipient stalagmites and a hole between them. I suppose the two circles in the indentation are the stalagmites and the square is where the treasure may have been many years ago. It wasn't there when they found Michael and we haven't heard anything about it since. So that is the end of the story but the two pieces of paper were exciting when we first found them. Peter is still excited about the story. Enrico made him a model of the cave for his birthday. I think he still has it.'

'Daniel I would like to go there.'

'That's a bit morbid Katya.'

'No I don't mean as a ghoulish tourist, I mean as an interesting facet to eco-tourism. Your mother was rightfully pointing out I should be looking for revenues. Well a cave is a natural phenomenon but a cave with an added human interest story is an attraction. It is part of Fotheringham heritage, treasure or no treasure. I really would like to see it. Consider it part of the research for my thesis Daniel. Could we go?'

'How about tomorrow afternoon Katya? I need to get my head around this first. Michael was my brother and I loved him dearly and going back there is a bit of a challenge. I don't think Samantha has ever been back there. She was really close to Michael, perhaps more than any of us. He was always her primary challenger. If we do go don't mention it, please: certainly not to mum and dad. For them it's almost a shrine. No that's too melodramatic but I know dad only goes there close to the anniversary of Michael's death.'

'Daniel, let's forget it. I'm sorry I asked. I didn't realise the personal significance. Forgive me?'

'Katya there's nothing to forgive and I did tell you the story, and yes I do still find it exciting. We'll go tomorrow afternoon after my match. I'll have a clearer head by that time and we'll take a closer look at the cave. I have never looked thoroughly all around the area. We'll do it together and I'll feel better. So, what about your other thesis work?'

'Look Daniel, the mist has lifted and you can see down the driveway. Didn't you say you needed to practice some time this afternoon? After a story of a musty dusty cave let's go outside and I can watch you swing. Come on, too many pictures in books gives you ideas. Come and show me how good you are on the golf course. Perhaps you could come and play in Florida on one of our tours. That would be neat Daniel.'

But neater I thought were some other ideas I was having and that didn't involve going as far as Florida. We left the library to its secrets and I went and found my clubs.

'I didn't know you could play golf.'

'Well you never asked, and how could anyone from Florida not play golf Daniel?'

'I'm almost embarrassed to ask whether you have a handicap watching you chip the ball like that.'

'As it happens I do Daniel. I play off six. Have you never seen anyone chip this way off the fringes of the green? I suppose we have quite tough Bermuda grass around our greens and this use of a fairway metal sort of pops the ball up. That way it clears the fringe and the tough grass doesn't grab the club as it might if I used an iron. You need to practice it a lot as it is a feel shot.'

'So I wouldn't embarrass you if I asked you to caddie for me tomorrow? I was just going to ask you to come round with me as a spectator but watching you I think I'd sooner have you as a caddie. Any preferences?'

'There wouldn't be any difficulties with my not being a member or anything, or an employee of the Club?'

'No certainly not. Tomorrow is just a normal club event for the monthly medal so there are no strict protocols or anything. Hey, I think it would be neat. Still, just let me get my head around some more conventional shots but try any club in the bag you like Katya. The more I think about it the more I like the idea that you play, and play well too off six.'

'I suppose you're a scratch golfer Daniel?'

'Yes, around there but as you know it just depends on the day.'

'Can I practice too Uncle Daniel?'

'Hello tiger, where did you spring from? Were you a big tiger lurking in the bushes just waiting to spring on poor unsuspecting Katya here?'

'Certainly not Uncle Daniel. Katya is my friend and tigers don't eat friends. Do you have that little putter? Come Katya I'll show you how well I can putt. Uncle Daniel was teaching me to putt with my eyes closed. What did you say uncle, just hear it fall into the cup before you open your eyes?'

'Something like that James but will you let me concentrate for a moment old chap? I'm playing in a match tomorrow and I need to be at my best so can we hush a little?'

'Of course, I know when to be quiet too. I'll be a very quiet tiger and only growl occasionally. Come on Katya, let's leave this grumpy bear to his practice while I show you how to putt with your eyes closed. Completely closed Katya, no peeping.'

After thirty minutes I decided that things were as good as they were going to get with James being a quiet tiger. I came and watched James with Katya on the putting side of the green. James had learnt well and could do what I had shown him but as a teacher he is a walking talking disaster, but then he is only four I thought. Samantha came walking through the surrounding trees and found the three of us in a putting competition. By this time I had realised that if I can't beat them I may as well join them.

'James I hope that you are winning my boy?'

'Of course Mummy. I'm not sure why Uncle Daniel thinks he can play golf because he can't putt for toffee.'

'That's because I am playing from twice as far away from the hole as you are little scamp.'

'But Katya is quite good Mummy.'

'She shows promise does she James?'

'Yes Mummy, she beats Uncle Daniel nearly every time.'

'Daniel, I think your course umpire, referee or whatever is not being very fair with you. Do you need him quietly removed from the course? I hadn't realised that he was home. Christina must have dropped him off.'

'She said she would Samantha, but no I was finished and thought James might like a little competition. Katya has just finished her lesson from the young pro here and he was demonstrating how to be first, just like his mother. Anyway, did you come down for something special?'

'Well to find you and Katya and tell you I would be out this evening so you will have to suffer mum and dad's interrogation at dinner tonight. I happened to overhear mum telling dad she thought it would be a good time this evening to find out more about Katya so be warned kid.'

Here Samantha put her arm around Katya and smiled at her. 'My mother is a very sharp lady but underneath the initial hard shell she is a softie. Dad has always been a softie so no problem there.'

'I don't seem to remember you ever describing mum as a hard-shelled softie. I know you and mum were always throwing things at each other; mostly verbal barbs thank heavens but a softie, never Samantha. Mum's like you, tough through and through.'

'Well thanks Daniel. I love you too little brother.'

'Just to change the subject are you going anywhere special this evening that I should or should not know about? Related question, do mum and dad know where you are going, or should they?'

'My, when have you developed this sort of custodial brotherly or maybe parental attitude? Just to help mum and dad do know where I'm going and to fill you in I'm going for a drink and then dinner with Terence Field. Satisfied?'

Here I paused and thought about the many implications of this answer. Detective Inspector Field had been the officer who arrested John Ferris, who had investigated the whole series of events with Idwal Ferris, and, perhaps more importantly been making inquiries into the attack on Danielle. The attack had resulted in Danielle's subsequent death in hospital so it had ended up as murder. At the time three of us, Donald MacLeod, Stanley Rogers and I had disarmed the two attackers as they were trying to kidnap Tony. The slight complication here was that Stanley Rogers disarmed the knife-wielding attacker by shooting him in the knife hand with his rifle. Stanley Rogers, who was actually a business acquaintance of dads had been a sniper in Viet Nam and was still a crack shot. Trouble was that shooting people was not really legal: there is no open season on kidnappers in England and so Terence Field was rather disturbed by this aspect. Following the dis-arming we had told Detective Inspector Field we had made sure the two attackers left the property. They had been claiming diplomatic immunity and we wanted no part of messing around with the authorities. We had got Tony back and didn't know at the time that Danielle would die. All we wanted to do was seriously warn them off and make sure they never came back again. Unfortunately Inspector Field now had two murderers to find and wasn't very happy when we weren't very interested in helping finding them. What Inspector Field didn't know and the three of us plus Samantha vowed we would never tell was that the two murderers didn't both leave. Sure we saw one of them off the property but only after he had seen us bury the knife-wielding Portuguese mulatto alive! While Samantha had taken Danielle to the hospital the three of us had decided we would take the law into our own hands and we all agreed that this was an appropriate fate after we had heard Danielle's description of what these two men had done in Mozambique. Samantha had insisted on knowing and I had told her with the agreed-upon promise not to tell anyone else, my parents included. Now Samantha was going out for a drink and dinner with Detective Inspector Terence Field. Sure he liked my sister and I understood that she liked him but I hoped this wouldn't complicate an already nefarious activity.

'Fine Samantha, enjoy yourselves. He seems a nice bloke despite the job he has to do. However, are you going to take this monster away and tidy him up? He has acquired a rather green shade to various parts of his body and clothes. I never realised that golf could be a full contact sport. Away you go James. We'll see you later. Maybe your good friend here will read you a bedtime railway story. Would you like that?'

'Awesome, thanks Katya,' and two little legs took off with his mother, holding her hand and his mouth going non-stop with a minute by minute account of today's eventful activities. James you are really a great nephew. It's so good to have Samantha home.

'You look very happy and yet pensive Daniel. Is all well? You seemed to hesitate when Samantha explained what she was doing this evening. Isn't Detective Inspector Field the officer who was with you at John Ferris's cottage?'

'Yes Katya, in some ways we saw rather a lot of Detective Inspector Field last weekend, well before that really I suppose, from Thursday night onwards almost daily. For a policeman with a rather nasty job to do he's okay, in fact quite sensitive and compassionate but he is a policeman and one with a reputation for being very good and very thorough. Unfortunately the events here were somewhat complicated and I think we may be seeing Inspector Field here again as a policeman, as well as a friend of Samantha's. I just hope that my sister doesn't further complicate the entire can of worms.'

'Can of worms?'

'There I go again, telling you what's for dinner.'

'Daniel, Daniel!'

'Take it easy lady, that's not an official Rules of Golf use of a seven iron. For your education a "can of worms" is an expression describing a mess, a mix-up, a disturbing set of events. Now, with James having left us perhaps I can spend maybe ten minutes with some eight and nine irons to the green from back here. These are a good test of depth perception with the hedge we put in. Can you stand on this side Katya and tell me how close I am if I keep this side of the hedge? Thanks.'

We spent another short time going through this routine before I felt fairly comfortable that my swing was smooth and easy. We went and shagged the fifty or so balls from around the green and walked back to the house chatting about whether dinner would or would not include worms.

Samantha took her mother's car down into the village and parked beside the Saint George and Dragon public house. She sat in the car and looked at herself in the rear-view mirror. Hair's fine, lipstick's on evenly, eyes look clear and bright so why the hesitation kid? First date for a long time isn't it? Hell, I feel more certain of myself on a hard climb. Still, it's just like climbing: look, think, see it, and do it, well then let's do it and she opened the car door and strode purposefully across the parking lot and pushed open the pub door. Terence was sitting by the bar and chatting quietly with George the landlord. Samantha walked up softly and lightly laid her hands upon his shoulders. 'Hello Terence,' she whispered in his ear.

Unfortunately this rather startled Detective Inspector Field and he swung round quickly letting the beer from the glass in his hand describe a mathematically precise arc of golden liquid and softly wetting a considerable area around the bar. Being behind him Samantha was spared a wetting but two other customers weren't so lucky.

'Christ mate, you're supposed to drink it not fling it all over the rest of us. That'll cost you a fucking pint for the bloody aggro.' The speaker suddenly noticed Samantha and put his hand over his mouth. 'Oh sorry Miss Samantha, I didn't see you there. Pardon my language but this 'erbert 'ere has just pissed all over my best coat if you see what I mean,' and he held up his arm to show the soaked sleeve.

'Freddie I accept the apology and I'll buy you a pint. I startled my friend here and caused your wetting. George, another pint here for Freddie and his friend next to him. Terence you okay with that?'

Terence stood and looked at Freddie rather seriously. Before he could open his mouth and be the policeman with some reprimand Samantha stepped between them and just said, 'thanks George,' and she paid and passed the two pints further down the bar. Slipping her arm into

Terence's she pulled him away from the bar and over to a table by the window.

'Better view here Terence,' she said, 'but let sleeping dogs lie. Freddie there looks like he's had too many already and I didn't want to start the evening with any confrontation, official or otherwise. He's our gardener if you're wondering how I know him.'

Terence looked out of the window and Samantha could hear the wheels going round in his head. She reached across the table and put her hand on his.

'Stop detecting for a moment Terence, please. Just be with me. This is my first date for a long time and I'm already all a flutter. I don't need any upset this early in the evening.'

Terence shifted his gaze and looked at Samantha and smiled. He turned his hand over and held hers and brought his second hand to cup hers between the two of his. He squeezed gently. 'Sorry,' he said, 'it's sometimes hard not to be a policeman. I know who that is and you're right he's already had enough to be belligerent so thanks for your swift intervention. Now, let's forget Freddie and have a quiet drink before we go to dinner. I've a confession too. I haven't been out with a beautiful woman for a long time either so this will be a first date for both of us.'

'Then let's toast two virgins,' Samantha joked, 'and don't you dare say hardly!'

Freddie sipped his pint while leaning on the bar but as he looked over his shoulder at his mate he noticed who had come in. 'Well look here,' he exclaimed to the room, 'see who the cat's dragged in, our own local knife-wielder, the brother-lover himself. Evening Ferris.'

'Can it Freddie, leave him be. Just drink your pint.'

John Ferris came into the room and looked around. He went over to the bar and ordered a pint and told George he'd take it over by the dart board corner.

'Going to practice throwing darts at people eh Ferris? Not content with just being fast with the knife? Going to learn to throw it at folks next?'

'Freddie leave him alone. Christ man he's had enough trouble without you stirring things around. Drink up mate.'

John was joined by another lad from the village and the pair of them started to play a game of darts. Freddie watched and continued to down his pint. He slammed the empty glass down on the counter. 'Another pint George. It's Saturday night and I feel fine.' He turned and grinned at his mate. 'Well Danny boy do you think we could beat those two at darts? Have to be careful though that Ferris doesn't get angry and slash you across the throat with a dart. Ain't that right Ferris, dab hand you are I hear with the throat shot.' Freddie giggled into his beer.

'Samantha have you finished your drink? We should be getting on. The conversation and the atmosphere here's not conducive to sweet talk and soft lights. Can we go?'

'Sure Terence. I don't need this either and before much more I would be in there banging heads. Christ, can't they leave John alone? He only gets to come down here once a week as you know and then he gets Freddie or someone else on his case. He'll end up being virtually imprisoned in his cottage and go cabin crazy or whatever people get in northern Canada.'

'Cabin fever.'

'Yes that's right. No, let's go before either of us do something we'll regret. Night George.'

Terence and Samantha left the pub and walked over to Terence's car.

'I'll leave mine here if that's okay with you and then you can drive and I can relax.'

72

'I heard that would be somewhat out of character......no correct that, forget that. Good, I'll like that: you sitting next to me and relaxing. Let's have a good evening Samantha.'

Back inside the pub Freddie continued his baiting of John Ferris and it wasn't long before George decided he'd heard enough. He warned Freddie and eventually Danny managed to get Freddie to leave but not before Freddie had needled John sufficiently for John to turn aggressive. George had all four of them leave but he was wise enough to let Freddie go a good half an hour before he ejected Ferris. More people came in and George settled in to a steady regular Saturday night.

Much as Samantha had warned me my mother was in one of her inquisitive frames of mind over dinner. We all managed to find time to eat but mum interspersed bites with questions. She wanted to know more about Katya and the questions covered birth to up-to-date with who, when, where and sometimes even why. I tried to ease this pseudo inquisition by asking mum and occasionally dad some questions of my own about our family. In the end, by the time we reached dessert Katya and I were leading the questioning trying to find out more about the condition of the estate at the turn of the century. It was dad who had most of the answers to this but even he wasn't certain of many of the details.

'It's all a long time ago Daniel. Heavens, it's almost a century ago now. Unfortunately everyone who knew anything at all about the estate then has long gone. My Aunt Veronica and Uncle Matthew are both in their eighties now but neither of them was very interested in the outdoors as children. Sure Veronica skied but that was in Switzerland and Matthew spent all his time taking things to pieces. The Templeton family who knew everything about the estate has all died out. No, that's not quite true as young Gary Templeton is working for us now. That family was traditionally our old gamekeepers but that stopped with the death of Edward over twenty years ago now. There is no-one on the work crew who has any really long term connection to the estate. Although, come to think of it, Bob Edwards's family have worked here for generations if I remember right. Still, your best bets are buried away in the books in the library. Weren't you in there this afternoon?'

'Yes Dad and we were looking through some old documents.'

'Not that set of papers you found at Home Farm Daniel?' my mother asked.

'Yes Mum, actually it was. Samantha had asked to see them a week ago and I couldn't find them but today I did. I was showing Katya and telling her the story of the possible list of goods shipped to Jamaica.'

'What did Samantha want with them?'

'I'm not sure Dad but I think Samantha developed an interest in the Lord family when Janet was telling her about Heritage Adventures and finding people's pasts. Samantha told me she didn't know anything about her own past and she thought it would be instructive to see how she could find out a bit about her own heritage.'

Mum looked at my dad and that questioning glance went between them.

'I'm sure Samantha's fairly serious about this Mum,' I said. 'Actually it would be good for her to have a tough assignment the first time she works for or with Janet. If she had to concentrate really hard on something it would focus her attention. She does well when she's focussed. She doesn't let anything stand in her path when the goal's clear cut and that's much more like the sister I knew.'

'You're right Daniel,' my mother said, 'which was why last Sunday was such a success. That last climb we did was really tough and I had to use the runner for aid on the top pitch but Samantha came out of that climb really happy, really vibrant. It had been truly positive and I just hope that this deal with Janet does help Samantha focus her emotions.'

'Not too single-mindedly I hope,' said dad. 'Well not for Terence's sake,' he added. 'I would imagine he would prefer her emotions concentrated more on him that Janet Donaldson at this point in time.'

'Yes,' said my mother rather thoughtfully, 'I hope this evening doesn't develop into one of Samantha's old encounters with the opposite sex.'

'Darling give her a chance. She's a widow with a young son and not a teenager any more. She's come home a changed woman. I had a really good heart to heart talk with her last Saturday. She was much more thoughtful, much more interested in the people around her, even a little uncertain where to go next and that is a very different Samantha from the girl who went to Canada.'

'Katya, I'm sorry, we're sorry we've been discussing the family and completely forgetting our manners.'

'Mrs. Lord, Sylvia please. I'm interested in this family and I really like and feel for Samantha. From what little I have heard she has had an extremely rough ride in life over the past few weeks and I'm not surprised she is somewhat uncertain. I too hope she can find something to, what do you say here, get her teeth into. James is an absolute treasure, isn't he Daniel?'

I started. I suppose I had gone inside my head and was thinking about my sister for a moment and Katya's question caught me by surprise. 'Absolute treasure are not the words I would use to describe James Katya but he is a rather entertaining young man. You are never quite sure what he will do or say next. Actually, talking of James where is he this evening? Samantha went out and so where is James?'

'Samantha asked cook to have him for dinner Daniel.'

'I wonder whether he tasted good Mum? Or was it worms we had for dinner?'

Katya chuckled and my mother looked at me as if I had lost my mind. 'Never mind Mum, it was a joke in poor taste,' and I laughed again.

'Daniel son, quit before your mother thinks you've lost it. Don't you have a tournament tomorrow or something? What's poor Katya going to do with you swanning around the golf course?'

'Actually Dad Katya here plays off six and she has agreed to be my caddie tomorrow and very glad I am about that too. So, poor Katya will not be swanning anywhere but helping me win. How about those apples?'

'You obviously play pretty seriously Katya?' my mother said.

'I enjoy it Sylvia. I find it helps me concentrate. Listening to Daniel describe rock climbing perhaps it's a little similar in that when you get ready to take a shot you do better if you really concentrate. Just for those ten, fifteen maybe twenty seconds you need to focus your entire mind on that particular action. Daniel was telling me about Anthony's instructions when he first learnt to climb. How did it go Daniel? Look, think, see it and do it? Was that right? Well golf in some aspects is the same. As you walk up to the shot you need to look. How far away is the target, what is the lie like, what is the wind doing, all those sorts of things and then you have to think about how you're going to move that little grinning white ball from where it lies to the target. After that, when I have decided what kind of shot and therefore what club I visualise the shot. I literally see it in my mind. I can play golf surprisingly well seeing my way round the golf course but the last action is where most of us struggle, the doing it. The body doesn't always do what you want it to do and the result isn't quite what was wanted. I can presume that much of that process is the same in climbing, certainly for a very short period you have to concentrate. Maybe the major difference is that in golf we have relatively long periods of just walking in a very pleasant environment whereas I presume climbing has fewer or shorter periods of easy going.'

'Interesting Katya, I suppose I have never really thought of golf in quite that light.'

'No Dad, that's because your routine is a little different. If I remember correctly you walk up to the ball and aggressively swing without a lot of forethought. Yes you might look but if you do the thinking and seeing bit you do it very very quickly before you're into the do it part of the process.'

'You might be right Daniel but I sure enjoy it. For me the score is not really the issue. I just like the camaraderie. You know me, I like people and getting out on the course with a bunch of blokes and relaxing is fun. We have a few laughs, take a few swings, ...'

'Take a few more, and a few more.'

'Okay, okay, so we don't shoot in the seventies.'

'Or the eighties, or even the nineties Dad.'

'I told you, sometimes we don't even bother to keep score. It's a fun game.'

'Trouble is Anthony you come home with a few really pitiful jokes and a handful of crazy ideas. Many of your golf chums must be really cuckoo dear with some of the ideas you bring home. Perhaps it is the stress of having to drag all those useless clubs around with you? What is it you take, thirteen, fourteen and when you come home only three or maybe four have mud on them? Why do you take all the others Anthony? It's not very efficient.'

'Sylvia my love, if I come down to your level I will explain that there are some very effective clubs in my bag and then there are some reserve, sort of insurance style clubs for those unexpected situations. The unexpected doesn't happen very often, just like in business but when it does you need to be prepared. You need a fall-back position. You want to be flexible enough to cope with any emergency and so many of the other, often unused clubs are my security blanket.'

'Dad, you are silver-tongued tonight. I've never heard such a load of old codswallop. Even Mum won't buy that lot.'

'Katya, how many clubs do you take with you dear?'

'I take all fourteen Sylvia and I do use all fourteen pretty regularly. In fact I will change which fourteen I take depending on which course I am going to play. Sometimes when the fairways are narrow I need to make sure I am really accurate and can get out of the rough for long distances. So there I might take a wider selection of utility clubs, tight lies and so forth. Why, on some courses I may not even take my driver at all. It's a little like Anthony was saying, you need to be prepared.'

I watched my mother sit back in her chair and think on all this.

'It's three to one,' she said finally. 'I'm not so keen on the odds and so I think I will bow out gracefully. Keep him honest tomorrow Katya will you?'

'Mum,' I protested, 'a gentleman doesn't cheat in golf. It's an honourable game.'

'From some of the jokes your father brings home I'm not so sure Daniel. I hear some tall stories.'

'Stories, yes Grandma, that's just what Uncle Daniel promised me, stories, didn't you Uncle Daniel?'

'Yes James I did, and I also promised your mother I would make sure you got to bed on time, and looking at the clock it is past time already so how about we go upstairs and get started?'

'Will Katya read to me? Will you Katya?'

James turned his relatively clean face, which did show a little evidence of his recent dinner towards Katya and walked over to hold her hand. He looked up into her face and pleaded, 'please.'

Katya stood up from her chair and then crouched down to be level with James. 'Yes, I will James but only after you're in your pyjamas and comfortably tucked up under your covers. Is that a deal?'

'Deal,' said James and he slapped Katya's outstretched hand.

'We'll go and deal with Katya's *absolute treasure* and then go and look at some of those old books in the library when we've silenced this little monster. Night Mum, night Dad.'

'Sure Daniel, we'll see you both in the morning. Now Sylvia dear, what time do we expect to see Samantha?'

'Anthony I got very firm instructions from our dearly beloved Samantha that I was to stay out of her love life. There's to be no boyfriend vetting, no getting home by whenever times, no controls whatever and surprise surprise I agreed. We came to a mutual pact. Live and let live.'

'Well, that's a switch. The two women in my life have suddenly changed. Perhaps there may be some peace and quiet in the House of Lord for a while.'

I heard my mother laugh as I walked up the stairs with Katya. We each held one of James's hands and he was still talking non-stop. Katya glanced across at me and smiled and I felt weak in the knees. Yes mum I thought perhaps there may be some peace and quiet in the House of Lord for a while.

IF ONLY I COULD PUTT

I WOKE ON THE SUNDAY morning to find that yesterday's damp and dreary weather had cleared away and the sun shone through the windows. Looking at the clock I realised that I had better stir my stumps as my tee-off time was eight thirty and Katya and I had to reach the course long before then. Already Katya was prowling about downstairs nursing a piece of toast in one hand and a cup of coffee in the other.

'You've got some warm clothes as well as what you're wearing?'

'Sure Daniel, I came prepared. Remember what I said last night about choosing which clubs to take out on the course, well I do the same with clothing and other accessories too. So yes I do have some additional clothing. It's here in a duffel. Hadn't you better eat something or do you play better on a growling stomach?'

'Right, a quick bowl of muesli and we're away. My parents not up yet?'

'I haven't seen anyone Daniel, except for cook. Did you hear Samantha come in last night?'

'No, did she?'

'I don't know but seeing as how I didn't get an invasion from James I think she must have. Do you want me to put coffee in a flask for you?'

'No thanks, I'll be fine. I'll probably grab a juice or something just before tee-off. Set?'

'Let's get at 'em tiger. Isn't that what you say?'

'No not really, this is much more laid back than that. It really is just a Club medal competition, a monthly deal between members so it is rather low key. Sure there's competition amongst the members but it's all rather friendly and not too serious. Now the Annual Competition for both the men and the women is a little tighter but that's not for another month yet in November. The Club has its Open competition in July and we get many people competing in that and so sometimes we have to have a knock-out round or use a low score cut like on a Tour event. It's a genuine Open, all-comers and includes men and women. Comes up with some interesting results over the years.'

'Who won this past year Daniel? Anyone I should be aware of this morning? Are you playing with this year's winner or anything?'

'Actually I am Katya, and no it wasn't me. I was runner-up this year, primarily because I couldn't putt. I'm still struggling with that part of my game. Anyway, let's go before the house wakes up and wants to talk.'

'Daniel you off?'

'Hi Samantha, yes we're just off. I've an eight-thirty tee-time and it's gone seven already. How come you're up so early?'

'I'm going climbing with Evelyn Nicols and I'm supposed to meet her at eight down in the village.'

'Well you've lots of time then.'

'Sure, you're right. Good luck then Daniel. Have a good day Katya.'

'By the way Samantha how did last night go?'

'Fine, why?'

'No reason, just curious.'

'Curiosity killed the cat, now scoot.'

I chuckled as I walked Katya out to the car. Opening the boot I checked that my clubs and shoes were safely there. Back in the car Katya turned to me and asked, 'why the interest in Samantha's night out?'

I sat and thought about the question. 'I suppose for two reasons. First I love my sister and now that she's home here in Fotheringham I want to make sure nothing or nobody upsets her any further and two, I'm still a little cautious where Inspector Terence Field is concerned. After you left on the Monday of last week Inspector Field telephoned Samantha and amongst other things he told her that Moboto, he was one of the two attackers and being a huge man he is not easy to miss, anyway he had been seen leaving the coast of England with two other men. So in some ways we all hope that the two attackers have left England and Detective Inspector Field can desist from further inquiries but I suppose I'm always a little curious about him still being around. If you like I'm not quite sure which hat he is wearing when he comes to call.'

Katya looked at me. 'You're quite a sensitive and thoughtful man Daniel Lord. Still, let's go and see whether you can turn that into some advantage on the course shall we?'

I had Katya hold my golf bag while I went and changed in the men's locker room. After that we walked over to the putting green and I took out three balls and my putter. 'Well caddie, do I have more than fourteen clubs in my bag? It has happened before you know and just when you think you are having a good game you suddenly realise you have accumulated a whole slew of penalty strokes, well up to four anyway.'

Katya put my bag down and stood behind a practice hole. She held the little flag and crouched down behind the hole. I started from two feet out and slowly putted each ball into the middle of the cup. Katya picked them out and rolled them back to me. I stepped back another foot and rolled the three in again from three feet out. Slowly I gradually increased the distance. At six feet I missed with two of the balls.

'Suggestions?'

'I don't know your stroke well enough Daniel to be constructive. This round is a learning session for me too remember. I can't really help today until I've seen you play seriously.'

I grunted and moved back to five feet. Three balls I rolled into the cup in quick succession and so back to six feet. This time I only missed one of them. 'Shit,' I muttered under my breath. 'Let's try a few long ones just to get a feel of the green. I hope that Billy Anderson the greenskeeper had them cut this green the same as all the others on the course.'

I took six balls and trundled them thirty to thirty five feet across the putting green towards Katya. Three were short and I quietly cursed but two were close and one went a good five feet past. Two distinct parts I thought: this game has two very distinct parts and I might be able to do well on one of them but on the greens I struggle. Learn to relax Daniel I told myself, let the club do the work like the full swing.

'You do a lot of muttering Daniel. Are you a quiet Lee Trevino on the course?'

Now Lee Trevino was never quiet on the golf course. Perhaps James has been watching golf I thought because he was a little motor-mouth too but I had never noticed that I kept muttering: never seemed to affect my swing or anything. Still, now wasn't the time to make any changes; keep that for practice sessions.

'Hi Larry. Larry meet Katya Howard. Katya this is Larry Sykes, and this is Peter Ruttledge and here comes Alan Grey. Chaps, this is Katya Howard from Florida who I have persuaded to come and caddie for me and distract the three of you. I checked with the Secretary and old Humphrey Davies says it's quite within the rules so you'll have to play against the two of us today.'

Larry, Peter and Alan exchanged glances and wondered who was going to say anything. After a pause it was Alan who gallantly held out his hand and said, 'welcome fair American cousin. This will be our pleasure for the morning, along with beating your playing partner who has to rely on subterfuge and distraction to win these days.' The other two shook hands with Katya and also added pleasantries. After this I noticed that Katya looked at me as if to say well that wasn't so bad Daniel, three nice fellows to spend some time with: what else would any girl want?

The first hole at our club is a fairly difficult par four. In fact it is the hardest hole on the front nine and just the way to sort out the men from the boys right from the start. At two hundred and fifty yards out the fairway doglegs to the left with the inside corner thoughtfully protected with a long narrow sand trap. Over most of the right side of the fairway are a dis-organized jumble of bushes ever-ready to catch the errant slice or pushed hurried first drive. These bushes get a lot of visitors over the length of the season. From the corner it is still just under two hundred yards to a long narrow green flanked with sand traps on both sides. Just to keep everyone really awake on the first hole the designer made the green with two tiers and a false front so the approach shot had to be precise or else you found trouble. As I said it was a difficult hole.

Larry dutifully spun a tee and we worked out the honours on the first tee-box. Our course starter was a dour Scotsman named Campbell and he was never happy unless it was pouring with rain and blowing hard. This morning, with just a zephyr of a breeze and the sun weakly shining made him a taciturn old codger and it was a very abbreviated 'play away gentlemen' that let us start the round.

'Alan, you're a Scot, did old Campbell here say we could go? I couldn't understand a word out of that last comment of his.'

'Aye Larry, we're away. Just let me get settled and you'll see why the Scots invented this game.' Having tee-ed up his ball Alan made a couple of serious practice swings and took up his stance. With a very simple but effective swing Alan launched his drive straight down the fairway and we watched the ball bounce over two hundred yards down the middle. He bent over to pick up his tee and turned and grinned at all four of us. 'Start as you mean to go on I always say.' He walked over to his bag and carefully put the head cover back on his driver and into his bag. I heard Larry mutter to himself as he took his place on the tee-box. Now Larry stands over six feet tall and has long arms and legs and when he swings it appears that most of his body is in motion. It may be unorthodox but Larry manages to achieve the desired result and he too found the fairway but on the right hand side a good two hundred and forty yards off the tee-box but still some two hundred and thirty yards from the green.

We all made the usual inane comments that golfers make and I pulled my driver out of the bag. Katya sort of started as if she was not quite with me but then smiled as I tossed her the head cover. I have always enjoyed the challenge of this first hole and I felt really good as I tee-ed up my ball and swung my driver. As usual I aligned myself with the centre of the fairway intending to draw the ball towards and around the left-hand trap. As it was the first tee I remembered to swing easily and not force anything. There are eighteen holes out there in front of me and things will come if I am patient. It was a good balanced rhythmic swing and I cleared my hips at the right time, pivoted over my feet and let my head stay behind the ball as the inertia of uncoiling swung my arms through and around. I heard the neat click of the ball leaping off the club face and after that initial second I let my eyes turn to follow the flight of the ball. It sailed up on a good launch angle straight down the middle as planned and slowly but surely drew gently left to bounce on the fairway some four yards right of the trap and leap forwards another five yards so that it ended up only one hundred and sixty yards from the flagstick. It really was a good shot.

'Great shot Daniel,' I heard Katya whisper.

'She's right there Daniel. You're caddie's right on the money with that comment. It was a great shot.'

Peter was the last to play and he too was a good golfer with a single digit handicap. His drive unfortunately was over powered and he pulled it severely into the nearest end of the left hand sand trap. As the trees on this left hand corner were quite high he was effectively blocked out from easily turning the corner of the dogleg. Such is the design of our first hole I thought: hit is straight and hit it far or else.

When we reached Peter's ball he had a good lie in the sand trap and he played an excellent shot hooking the ball very successfully around part of the corner and ending up one hundred and seventy yards out. Both Larry and Alan went for the green on their second shots but Larry was well short and Alan pushed his second shot into the right-hand greenside trap. Katya and I reached my ball and I stood and looked at my next shot. 'Just like your practice area Daniel. About the same distance isn't it? This is the shot you were practising at the end of yesterday remember?'

I sort of grunted and looked at the distance, the flagstick, and watched the breeze very very gently moving the tops of the trees. That's hardly a factor I thought. So, where have they put the flag today? The green's committee had been kind on this hard opening hole and placed the cup up on the back upper shelf which was quite wide and beyond the sand traps on each side of the green. I knew there was no real trouble over the back of the green so going long was a better bail-out than being short I thought. One hundred and sixty yards to the stick: a smooth seven or a hard eight? This early in the round I prefer to swing easy and so I turned to Katya. I was about to ask for my seven when she handed it to me.

'Just like yesterday,' she said, 'nice and smoothly. You'll be hole high with this, yes?'

'Yes.'

I took one last look and in my mind I saw the shot land up on the top shelf just right of the flag and draw gently towards the hole. Smoothly I thought, nice and smoothly. I took a couple of practice swings and aligned for the right hand side of the green. My swing naturally produces a draw and this is just what I wanted to do here as the flagstick was more over to the left side of the green. See it, do it and the ball soared away to land just on the shoulder of the right-hand side of the green where the backspin made the ball jump left and trundle happily towards the flagstick. The ball came to rest some six feet from the hole on the back shelf.

I turned to look at Katya and saw her smile with admiration. 'Great team work partner,' I said.

'Just like last night Daniel. I saw you hit that shot five or six times really well. Looked good.'

When we were all on the green Peter was lying four and Larry and Alan were lying three. They were all away before my putt and I prowled around the green keeping out of their line of sight but trying to see what my putt would do. Katya tended the flag for all four of us. The other three putted out and I had my birdie to make. It looked straight and the green looked flat so just hit it I thought. Be a kid again. Remember when you just walked up to a putt and holed it without any real thought every time? No pressure just hole it. Trouble was I was older now and thought too much. What do they say about paralysis by analysis?

I hit it and we all groaned. I thought about all the many many golfing clichés like never up never in and several others. I walked up and tapped in for par. Good four.

'Good opening par partner,' my caddie spoke supportively. 'Tough hole your opening hole here Daniel.'

Katya was really good. She dutifully raked sand traps for all four of us. She tended the flagstick on the greens. She kept quiet when she was supposed to. She quickly amazed me with knowing my club selection. All in all she was an excellent caddie and as the morning progressed my game improved. After the front nine I was two under par, primarily from making birdies on both the par fives. Alan was two over, Larry three over and Peter was having an off day but then don't we all in this crazy game?

'Is that twenty six or twenty five putts so far Katya?' We were standing on the sixteenth tee-box with three holes to play and I was feeling good, apart from my putting that is. I was five under par and my swing this morning was looking smooth. 'It's twenty six Daniel but don't worry about that now just think on this next shot. What do you usually take here?'

'Well it's just two hundred yards to the middle of the green but there's a long carry over the water as you can see.'

'Daniel the water's not in play for you but what's over the back of the green? That flagstick is up at the back but you don't want to go over if there's trouble.'

'Actually there is. There's a great big sand trap that is quite deep over the back. So, what do you think?'

'Tell me what you usually take here first?'

'Either a five iron or a four iron depending on the wind. This tee-box is rather high up on the course and it is often windy into our faces.'

'Fine, but that's not an issue this morning and it's a downhill shot so take the five and play for the middle of the green, or take the four and fade it slightly to land softly.'

'No, I can't do that to order. I'm just as likely to come over the top and pull hook it. I'll take the five.'

I had the honour on this hole and stood for a moment on the tee-box as the foursome in front of us cleared the green. Standing there I had noticed that the green was slow and quite uphill from the front to the back. One of the foursome in front had taken three putts and was still short of the hole. My swing was still good but a gust of wind came up out of nowhere and knocked my ball down in mid flight. It cleared the water but not by much and I was just on the front of the green, a good sixty feet from the flagstick.

Katya didn't say anything as I handed her back the club. She quietly put it in the bag and moved off the tee-box. The three others had seen what had happened to my shot and all three promptly changed clubs. The thought of a knock-down wind made Peter try and hit too hard and he half-skulled his ball into the water. Larry and Alan went the other way and both found the back bunker.

'Good job this isn't one of the KP holes,' Larry said.

'Well at least I'm on the green,' I joshed.

'Maybe true Daniel but Alan and I are closer,' added Larry.

Peter played from the drop zone and landed his third shot within two inches of the cup; a tap-in bogey. I was next to play and remembered the foursome in front. I couldn't see the hole easily from the bottom of the green and so Katya tended the flag. Unfortunately I had this sudden burst of adrenaline or something because my putt scampered up the hill eager to reach the flag and then charged another ten feet past the hole. I ground my teeth and thought for a moment about seeing whether my putter could swim in the pond behind me. Wisdom prevailed. I knew my putter couldn't swim.

Alan blasted out of the back bunker on his second attempt. The first swing had generated an incredible volume of sand, some Scottish swear words and a golf ball moving three feet closer to the flag but still in the trap. His second blast however did get the ball onto the green. I watched it miss the flagstick by inches, and Katya's quick-moving feet and gradually pick up speed as it found its way down the slope towards the pond. It stopped before the pond and before Alan had emerged from the deep bunker so he never did see how close he had been. All he saw was the result, which engendered a few more but quieter Scottish oaths.

Larry took his time. The foursome behind us appeared on the sixteenth tee-box and started taking practice swings as some kind of message. Larry's shot flew neatly up over the lip of the trap and trickled ever so slowly down the green and tried to stop just before it reached the hole and the flagstick. It failed and quite smoothly tapped the stick and dropped into the cup. 'Birdie!' cried Larry somewhat obviously but still correctly. Alan walked down to his ball and eyed his putt. Again Katya had to hold the flagstick to show Alan where the cup was. Ever so smoothly Alan released his putter and his ball hopped and skipped initially but settled down into a roll that was on line right from the start and dropped into the cup well after Katya had correctly pulled the stick. Sixty foot putt; impressive. Peter tapped in to be out of the way and that left me and my ten-footer.

The foursome on the tee-box was now joined by the foursome behind them. We looked around for a marshall but fortunately none were in sight. However, the pressure was there. I had seen putts down the green and up the green. I lined up with the toe of my putter to try and take some of the weight out of the shot and swung ever so gently. The ball went six feet and stopped. Katya looked up at the sky. The other three looked back at the tee-box up on the hill above the pond. I tried again and ended up four inches past the cup. The ball had found that golfer's mythical cellophane bridge that occasionally is unseen but there across the top of the hole. Four putts. I picked up the ball and wondered whether it could swim any better than the putter. In the end I gave it to Katya who promptly cleaned it on the wet end of the towel. After drying it she put it in her pocket. 'It will go further if it's warm Daniel,' she said.

'I'd have thought it was steaming hot by now,' I growled.

We walked off the sixteenth green listening to a light clapping from the eight men on the tee-box behind us.

So I was last to hit on the seventeenth tee-box. Katya handed me my driver but she didn't let go of it immediately. I looked at her face. She smiled and all she said was, 'smoothly.' With that single swing thought I moved the unrepentant golf ball two hundred and eighty yards down the fairway. I picked up my tee and handed my driver back to Katya. 'Smoothly,' was all I said and we both turned and followed the other three off the tee-box and down the fairway but I was back to three under par.

From an excellent position in the middle of the fairway on that five hundred and twenty yard par five I hit my fairway three metal like never before and it soared over the line of traps blocking the fairway for most second shots to bounce in front of the green and run right through just off the back some two hundred and fifty yards. 'Two fantastic shots Daniel, really good,' said my positive caddie as she cleaned some imaginary grass off the face of my club. When we reached my ball over the back of the green we found it nestled down a little in the grass that lay towards us as we looked back at the flagstick. 'It will try and grab your club Daniel. Any thoughts of popping your fairway metal like I did yesterday?'

'But you said I needed to practice that before I tried it Katya. Think it'll work?'

'It's what I would do Daniel, especially the way that grass is lying but then we have Bermuda and that is tougher and grainier. This is bent isn't it?'

I didn't answer because I hadn't really heard the question. I was looking looking looking and thinking how I could hole this. After those two previous shots I was feeling charged up and this was a great opportunity to get back the shots I had just lost. Slow down Daniel. One shot at a time but this shot, how to play this shot? Could I use a fairway metal here or would I make a balls-up? Cut out the negative, think positive. I thought back to what I saw Katya do yesterday: just pop it.

'Take the stick out Katya please. I can see the hole fine.' I picked the five metal out of my bag lying beside the green. I took a couple of practice swings noting how the grass tried to grab the hosel. It really didn't as the large metal head just brushed through the grass and kept on line. Standing over the ball I saw the line and without hesitating I chopped down on the back of the ball and made it pop out of the fringe onto the green and into the hole without a second glance. Bingo, eagle!

Katya silently clapped her hands together as she held the flagstick. 'Way to go partner,' she whispered. The three others had been closer to the flag than me and they in turn putted out. Looking back down the fairway the following foursome was well out of range and so we had made up our time as the foursome in front had only just left the eighteenth tee-box. Great I thought, five under.

'Where did you learn to do that?' Alan asked. 'That's a very useful idea with a rather unconventional club. I used to have a chipper that had a very large and heavy head for doing something similar but to use a fairway metal is clever.'

I turned to Katya. 'My caddie showed me. She's a lot more than a pretty face gentlemen. She's my secret weapon.'

'Well you can teach me anytime Katya,' said Alan. 'Here, I'll give you my business card and we can discuss fees.'

'Hands off Alan. Katya is my nephew James's special friend and even I must ask permission. Isn't that so Katya?'

'He's right Alan I'm afraid. Young James would not take kindly to people trying to hustle his special friend. He can get right uppity if he found out but as you're someone special I won't tell, for now anyway.'

Katya walked quietly off the green carrying my golf bag, including my unconventional fairway five metal.

The eighteenth offered a variety of options as to how best to play this hole. It was only three hundred and ten yards long and steeply downhill to a bowl-shaped green. On a good dry day when the ground was hard you could easily drive the green. The ball would run for miles. Trouble was there was a hungry pond behind the green that bounded the Club House on the far side. Through the green meant a penalty shot. About one hundred and fifty yards from the tee-box there was a flat plateau conveniently perched on the downslope. This was about fifty yards long and it was an easy wedge shot to the green from this plateau. Each side of the fairway the ground rose a little and so it was like hitting down a chute. The trick was to decide how far down the chute was the best for the kind of game you played.

I looked at Katya but this time she didn't offer any club but looked at me with her eyebrows raised. She didn't know how I wanted to play this hole. Sure I was pumped up after the last hole but could I control my length? I had just hit a fairway three metal through the last green. This was not the place to repeat that kind of shot. 'Two shots like your practice area Daniel?'

Good idea Katya I thought. Swing easily to land on the plateau and then flick a wedge in close. The flag today was back right and very close to the water. There were no sand traps on this hole at all and both sides of the green short of the pond had long lush grass which was much more challenging than any sand trap. Think Daniel dam it. Go with Katya's advice. 'Give me a seven iron please Katya.'

Katya pulled my seven iron and ran her towel down the grip. Gripping the head of the club she handed it to me. I settled the grip gently into my two hands and swung half-heartedly. Looking at Katya again she said just one word, 'firmly.'

The shot clicked off the club face and I took a respectable divot pinching the ball in the process. The backspin let the ball land softly on the plateau one hundred and seventy yards out and jump back a foot before settling happily. Position "A" I thought.

Larry had had a very uneven round with some exciting birdies like the one on sixteen and another on twelve but also a couple of double bogeys. He'd just come off a bogey on the par five seventeenth and was ready to charge in frustration. Pulling out an old wooden three wood he swung hard and true. He only just caught the upper half of the ball but the amount of topspin drove the ball like a projectile and it shot off down the fairway staying about fifteen feet above the ground. The first bounce about halfway to the hole caught something hard on the ground and the ball suddenly arced upwards still carrying its topspin. A second bounce was more conventional and the ball leapt forward to just reach the green before coming to rest about ten feet from the hole. He turned to the group of us and bowed in a very Elizabethan way with his hand flowing under his body as if doffing his hat. Unfortunately he caught the club in the ground as he did this and nearly speared himself. Stumbling off the tee-box he reached his golf bag and reverently kissed the club before gently easing it in with the others.

'Impressive Larry.'

'Old club but lots of talent.'

'That wasn't what you said when you used that club on the last hole. You came close to trying to hide it as far into the bush as you could throw it.'

'Well that was then and this is now Alan so you're up.'

Alan decided to follow my lead and he too placed a good shot on the plateau some one hundred and forty five yards from the hole.

Peter had watched the different strategies and he decided that he couldn't drive the green normally but as it was downhill and fairly dry he would at least use his driver. With the contours of the hole he reasoned that the ball would roll towards the green and if anything be well short. He might be left with a nasty downhill short chip shot but he might be able to putt it down the slope. His drive again hooked left but caught the sidehill and true to his intentions the ball rolled past the plateau and fetched up some fifty yards short of the green.

'Good decision Daniel?'

'I think so Katya. After that last hole I didn't want to go through the green and the length to the plateau is like the area back home. You've got a good eye. What do you think of the course?'

'The obvious thought Daniel is that it's so hilly. Everything in Florida is flat. All of the State is flat except for some minor bump in Tallahassee I think. The joke in Florida is the definition of a hill.'

'Which is?'

'Any land above water. Still, this course has some real variety from hole to hole. It makes you think and that is good. Like this hole where the course architect gave you some choices on what is really quite a short straightforward hole.'

We reached Alan's ball on a flat lie. His simple swing propelled the ball a little to the left and he ended up thirty feet from the hole but on the green. He looked at me and grinned. 'Gives you lots of room to get inside me Daniel. Actually I don't see why you don't get inside Larry. He's what, ten feet from the hole?'

I was one hundred and forty yards from the middle of the green and the flag was another seven yards further on and to the right with the green sloping to the right. One possibility was a high fade. Throw the ball just past the flag and to its left and let the spin stop it and trickle down to the flag very gently. Sure, but could I stop it doing that? As it was downhill I could really put spin on it with a pitching wedge and still get the distance. Once again Katya kept quiet and still. There were too many options and she didn't know how I wanted to play this. I made up my mind and pulled the pitching wedge out of the bag. Katya lifted the bag and stepped away from my line of sight.

I saw it, I saw it clearly and I did get the ball up in the air with a ton of backspin but it was off line. The ball hit the right side of the green just in front of the flag and spun violently right and off the green into the long grass well past the fringe. Silently I handed the club back and just as silently Katya slipped it into the bag.

Before we reached the green we all stopped around Peter's ball. The grass was cut to fairway height all the way to the hole and Peter didn't hesitate. He pulled out his putter and very effectively rolled his ball down to the green and slid it sideways to the right to come within two feet of the hole. 'Texas wedge,' muttered Katya.

'That takes some nerve Peter with that pond behind,' I said. He looked at me and smiled.

'I'm like Larry Daniel, old club and lots of talent.'

Down on the green Alan was further from the hole than I was and he had Katya tend the flag. With very little time spent assessing the situation Alan lined up his putt and softly stroked the ball. Very efficiently it followed a good line and dropped into the cup for a round of applause from all of us. Good stuff.

I found my ball sitting well on the lush grass and a couple of feet below the level of the green which sloped towards me and off further right to the pond. Again the options I thought. High flop, chip and run, lob shot? Then I saw the shot I could make.

'Katya can you pull the flag please?' The three men looked more keenly at my intentions. Katya stood back from the hole with the flagstick in her hands. She looked really pretty standing there in a plain pastel skirt and a light-coloured sweater. She shook her hair and the sunlight glittered. Pretty, really pretty Daniel, but back to reality for a moment.

The lie was soft, too soft for a flop shot and I might go right under the ball without moving it so make sure you do hit the ball cleanly. Fine, little wedge sharp to the back of the ball and just lift it onto the green to track to the hole. Hold the club lightly but firmly and tap. The ball jumped cleanly off the face and landed over the long grass on the edge of the green. Once on the short grass I watched it roll very true in a lovely curving arc straight into the hole. Thank God I don't need to putt was all I thought. Birdie and six under par.

Larry had watched all of these shots and needed to hole his putt to win the hole and achieve last hole bragging rights. The tension built up around the green as Larry took his putter and prowled around his ball and the hole. The putt rolled and rolled and looked really good until it found a slight bump on the green and then caught the lip of the hole to describe a one hundred and eighty degree semicircle and stop six inches away. We all looked at one another. 'Good hole Larry whatever the score. Talented drive as you said.'

Larry had the good grace to grin at us all.

'Perhaps the golf gods decided the drive didn't really warrant an eagle.' We all nodded wisely.

Alan putted out for his birdie too and we all felt really chuffed as we walked off the green. Four birdies on the last hole is a great way to finish we all agreed. Katya shook hands with the three other players and we walked to the Club House feeling it had been a grand morning.

'Thirty putts Katya, thirty. Just think what I could have scored if I could putt?'

'Daniel that little word comes into golf quite a lot. It bedevils us all.'

'What word?'

'If.'

I chuckled and held her hand. 'That was a great morning and we made a fabulous team. Thanks for all the support and advice. Your chipping technique saved my bacon back there on seventeen.'

'Talent, wasn't that what Larry said? You've got it Daniel. You're good. Have you ever considered playing professionally?'

I thought about Katya's question as we walked back into the Club House. 'Let me just change my shoes Katya and I'll answer your question. Is it okay to have lunch here and then we'll go back and explore as I promised?'

'I'll be here. Just don't take too long telling tall stories in the locker room about the birdie that got away.'

I changed my shoes and Katya and I put my gear back in the car. We walked back into the dining room of the Club House and joined Larry, Alan and Peter who were already downing pints. Alan stood up and asked Katya what she would like to drink.

'I'll have a white wine please Alan.'

'You know my poison Alan.'

'Sure Daniel. Are we all having lunch? Can I order something for anyone while I'm at the bar?'

'The Sunday Special Alan please.'

'Me too.'

'You Daniel, and Katya?'

'Sure Alan, make it easier and we'll both have the Sunday Special.'

I looked at Katya and she gave me that questioning expression on her face. 'Trust me you'll love it.'

Alan brought back Katya's white wine and my pint and we toasted one and all and congratulated ourselves on a good morning's work.

'That was a dramatic recovery Daniel after the sixteenth.'

'True, but I don't need to be reminded any more about that sixteenth. How good is our Pro Toby with giving putting lessons? After today's escapade I could do with some improvement. I can't expect to chip in on all eighteen holes now can I?'

We all commiserated around the table as golfers are apt to do: never satisfied because there is always room for improvement, sometimes more than one room. Katya listened to the usual banter around the table. She turned as one of the dining room servers came over with our five plates of the Sunday Special. Each plate had a splendid steaming Cornish pasty. There was a large central bowl with a ladle with gravy for those that wanted and another large plate of raw vegetables including carrots, broccoli, cauliflower and onions. To complete the meal the waiter brought bowls of small cold boiled potatoes and beetroot. It was an unusual mix for an English dining table but the members had really approved and it was a very successful lunch item.

'Daniel, should I ask what is inside this pastry item?'

'Certainly you should. It contains chopped up pieces of skrag end beef which I suppose you might think of as hamburger and potatoes, onions, and maybe yellow turnips and some other secret ingredient known only to our chef. It is a product of Cornwall where my mother comes from. Prepared properly it is a delightful dish and as our chef comes from Redruth in Cornwall we think it is pretty authentic. Please don't tell me you are vegetarian or something Katya?'

'No, not at all, I just wondered. It certainly smells appetising.'

'You'll notice that Larry and Peter put gravy on theirs, as do I whereas Alan here thinks the only liquid worth consuming has to be alcoholic but we draw the line at letting him pour his beer on his pasty. Anyway try it and see whether you like it. We can always find something else if not.'

'No Daniel I was just curious, and I do trust you, although you still haven't answered my question of ten minutes ago now have you?'

I purposely sat still and made out as if I was trying to remember what it was Katya had asked. She looked puzzled at first but as I started to grin she punched me on the shoulder. 'Joker,' she said, 'what's the answer?'

'The answer is yes,' I said. 'I've thought about it but never done anything seriously about it. I suppose I've never really had the time to do anything about it as I moved into managing Fotheringham straight from University. My father took it for granted that with a Forestry degree and no desire whatsoever to continue and do research that I would come and work for him. I don't think we ever even discussed it. It was as if it was a foregone conclusion.'

'But that's awful Daniel and you didn't say anything?'

'Let me think on that a minute. I turned twenty one nearly three years ago now and at that time dad asked me whether I wanted to take over the estate as Samantha wasn't interested. That summer, Andrew her husband had been over to Canada lining up a job which he subsequently took the following year. Samantha was just starting her final year and wanted to graduate and be with Andrew. She was much too interested in being with Andrew and furthering her own career and so she didn't really give it any thought. In some ways my dad offered it to me as a last resort but he knew I would be well qualified even if I had this leaning towards "green" forestry rather than commercial.'

'Your mother didn't ask you either?'

'No, I think my mother took it for granted that when I elected to study Forestry rather than Geology, which was my other specialised subject at High School I was going to manage the estate. Without being too cynical she was probably looking at the bottom line and having someone who already knew the history of the place meant I could walk in without any necessary learning period. Recently though I did voice my desires. Look I'll tell you more about it later.'

We all finished lunch and I made arrangements for a game next Wednesday afternoon, another regular club event. Katya and I said cheerio to the other three and we walked back to the car. Katya was still very pensive and I offered her a penny for her thoughts.

'I was thinking on your parent's assumptions Daniel. Perhaps I have been very lucky because from a very early age my parents have been asking me what I really wanted to do. Mark you that hasn't stopped my mother from a whole array of suggestions that aren't me but my dad has always listened carefully. Yes, I have been lucky.'

Somewhat surprisingly the day stayed sunny. When you live in a country where you can get all four seasons in a single day you grow up with an expectation for change but this particular Sunday the morning passed into the afternoon with a sunny sky, fluffy cumulous clouds and a light breeze; most unusual.

Back in the house mum was going over some figures in her office and obviously didn't want to be disturbed. Dad was taking a welcome siesta and snoozing very contentedly in a comfortable drawing room armchair. We tiptoed out again and climbed into the Landrover.

'My mother's lesson with James on Dainty must have been pretty gruelling this morning as the house is quiet and so little James is probably having an afternoon nap as well. Actually mum makes a good teacher for riding but she is strict. It's definitely her way or the highway.'

'Did she teach climbing and sailing too?'

'No, our family is quite diversified with regards to Instructors. Dad taught all of us climbing, well the basics. He was the one we all started with. After we improved then we switched around within the family and I climbed with both Geoffrey and Michael. I also climbed with my cousin Henri. Henri's father was Charles who was dad's younger brother. Charles and his wife Helene were fantastic climbers, alpinists really and did some very hard first ascents in the Alps. Helene was French. Samantha has done a couple of their routes around Chamonix. Anyway, Charles and Helene both got killed climbing when their children were all quite young and my Aunt Stephanie adopted all three of them. She's the aunt who does the research with sheep at Home Farm. When I was younger I climbed with Henri who was a good climber too.'

'And sailing?'

Here I stopped and chuckled. 'Do you remember your father asking me last Sunday whether I sailed and who taught me?'

'No, not really.'

'What about James's story of his mother leaping out of the boat with a rocket up her knickers?'

'Oh yes Daniel, now I remember the frightening Aunt Veronica, or your great aunt I suppose? She was the Instructor for sailing?'

'That's right and each of the Instructors taught us more than just the fundamentals of the sport. We learnt life skills associated with the environment of the sport. You learn when a climb is too hard it is sensible to retreat and that applies in business. Learn when to push and when to back off. You learn when your horse feels one with you you can really leap anywhere and that can be a team thing. For instance back there on the golf course this morning on the seventeenth, when I had my ball on the back fringe and you just looked at me and reminded me of what you had shown me yesterday. I felt really good. I felt we were playing well together, as a team and that your contribution was to show me how and my contribution was to just do it, so I did. Now that's small team feeling that I have learnt in climbing, in sailing and in riding.'

'Professional golf?'

'I'm still just thinking about that Katya but it did come up a week or so ago when we had a serious family meeting about the future of both my parent's Company and about the Estate. They are trying to find someone to take over the Company and let them ease back a little, maybe even retire so to speak. Of course they offered the Company to Samantha and to me when Samantha said no thank you but they already knew what we would say. Neither of us had changed our minds and we both said no thank you again. Dad is seeking someone else that we know fairly well who would be really well qualified.'

'But what about you Daniel?'

'Well after we had discussed the Company I said that they should think about a successor for the Estate Manager position too as I might have other things I wanted to do as a career. Dad sort of knew about this but mum and Samantha were quite amazed that I was not one happy camper. It's not often I can shock my sister. It was quite funny really to watch her reaction.'

'Yes but what did they say Daniel?'

'It's under review. We'll take it into consideration.'

'That's not an answer. That's a cop out.'

'We'll see but today that's not an issue. Today we're going exploring. Today the team is on the hunt for the elusive treasure.'

'Are we?'

'It's just around the next couple of corners and up the hill.'

I drove the Landrover round to the left and up a compartment boundary that led to the northern edge of the property. The escarpment stood up clearly at the end of the lane. We parked and I looked about me as I always do when in the forest. It's an automatic reaction to look at the trees and do a quick estimate of what is there and how is it looking: a quick scan up at the crowns to see whether they need thinning and is there any damage: is the fence still intact? I suppose it is all part of being a forester that you just do these things without thinking. Katya had watched me spend the minute or two doing this.

'You care don't you? They're like your babies?'

I laughed and turned towards her and held her hands in mine. 'Yes I care. Like any forester I care about the state and dynamics of my forest environment but they're not my babies. They belong to all of us and I'm just the temporary caretaker and at the moment all is looking quite good so let's go and explore.'

'You said this cave is not very large?'

'You're not frightened of small spaces are you Katya, claustrophobic or anything?'

'No Daniel, we have a lot of caves in Florida because much of the area is limestone so I have been out with friends in small caves and large caverns. No I was just curious.'

We followed the northern boundary by walking along the foot of the escarpment with a young plantation on our right. On our left the cliff rose and fell and then we came to a part where all of the ground sloped downhill and I could see the tree. It was a very old oak and you could see where there had been a fork about ten feet from the ground but sometime in the past one of the limbs had split away leaving a considerable scar in the trunk. The remaining limb rose another sixty feet skywards and still held its leaves. Given its age and damaged trunk the oak looked amazingly healthy.

'Is that the tree you talked about?'

'Yes, that's right.'

'Come on then.'

'Carefully Katya, the ground's really rough underfoot here. There are a lot of loose rocks that have fallen off the cliff over time and the vegetation hides them. Just don't twist any ankles out here. It's a long way to carry you back to the Rover.'

'Daniel you're an old woman at times. Don't worry so.'

I was about to make a retort but bit my tongue instead. This proved to be a mistake as I trod down heavily at the same time and a rock under my foot caused a jolt up my spine and I bit too hard. I swore under my breath and could taste blood in my mouth. We scrambled down to the tree and Katya stopped and turned to look at me.

'You're bleeding,' she said. 'How did that happen? Come here Daniel and I'll wipe it away. You won't be able to see it.'

She walked up to me and took a tissue from her pocket and gently dabbed at my lips. 'There, that's a little better.' Still standing close she whispered, 'perhaps I should kiss it better?'

I didn't answer in words but wrapped my arms around her and replied with my lips. Gently, softly and trembling a little I kissed her. As we both increased the pressure slightly I parted her lips with my tongue and I felt her giggle. She pulled away for a moment and looked into my eyes. 'I can taste your blood Daniel. Will I turn into a vampire?'

I shook my head and pulled her closer again and we kissed harder this time and I felt her body pressed up against mine and both our tongues slowly embraced in a sensuous dance.

'Did you bring a flashlight?'

It took a moment to understand what Katya had said but then I replied quietly, 'yes.'

'Let's look in the cave and explore afterwards. Did you bring a copy of that large scale map, diagram thing? You know the one that shows the details of inside the cave?'

'Yes.'

'Good,' and she turned to look behind the tree. 'Isn't the entrance right behind this tree?'

I turned on my torch and slid past Katya into the very narrow slit of an entrance. Once just inside I splayed the light over the interior walls. I held out my hand behind me for Katya to hold.

'Come on in then but mind the bumpy floor.'

We stood inside what was really a very narrow fissure in the cliff. It slanted and narrowed to nothing as it went deeper into the mountainside. Just here inside the entrance it was larger and looking at the walls I noticed that might have been done by hand and not nature.

'Are these the round circles on that diagram?'

'I think so. It would make sense but they may have been bigger when the map was made and people have smashed them down, almost like making places to sit.'

'And between them is this hole, well hollow really. It's not very deep.'

'Again, I'm not sure what it looked like even eight years ago when Michael was here Katya. Remember I never came into the cave originally and I don't know what it was like.'

'But it could have been bigger, or deeper Daniel? Shall we dig?'

'There's nothing there Katya. Michael dug and he found nothing and if I remember correctly he was pretty desperate. He must have been for Michael to actually dig. No, there's nothing there. Perhaps there never was.'

'Interesting though Daniel, a piece of history even if it is unknown or unsolved. Thanks for showing me.'

Katya turned and put her arms around my neck and this time she initiated the kissing. It felt really good standing there holding her. She hugged me tighter and knocked against my arm holding the torch and I inadvertently dropped it with a crash on the floor. The light went out and we were there in the complete darkness.

'Don't say it,' she said. 'I know what you are going to say but there's no need.'

'What am I going to say?'

'The car's run out of gas and we're stuck here for the night. You know the standard male ploy for trying to get his wicked way with a woman.' She giggled in the darkness.

'Hold still a minute while I crouch down and see whether I can feel it.'

'That's another standard line Daniel.'

'Katya, listen up a moment. I didn't plan this, believe me.' She must have crouched down beside me because I felt her arms around my neck again and our lips brushed each others cheeks before finding each others lips.

'Katya,' I whispered, 'this would be much more comfortable and much more delightful for me if I could see you so let's get ourselves out into the sunshine before this goes any farther?'

She kissed me harder and then slowly let go and stood up. 'Yes yes kind sir.'

I found the torch and flicked at the switch but nothing happened.

'I must have bust it when I dropped it. Right, let me think for a minute. All that kissing is most delightfully distracting Katya but getting out might be a higher priority. We were standing here and so the entrance would have to be.. shit.'

'What?'

'I just banged my head on the roof and it's not smooth.'

'Hold my hand Daniel while you go charging about. I don't want you to knock yourself out and have to find you in the dark.'

'Ah here, yes here we are. I can see a faint light and yes this is it.'

Although the cave wasn't deep it had a very narrow entrance and it angled twice to reach the expanded cavern area. We threaded our way through the tight entrance slit and out beside the tree again. Katya stumbled as she made the final step and pitched forwards partway down the slope.

'Ouch, I caught my foot in some root or something.'

'Is it still caught? You're lying awkwardly so hang on a moment while I look at your foot. Yes you did catch the edge of a root, probably after that rock slid away and hello, what's this?'

I lifted Katya's foot out from the area of roots and dug away at something that caught my eye.

'Katya, are you okay?'

'I think so Daniel. Let me try and stand up. Ouch, my foot is a little painful but no I can walk on it. It's probably just a slight sprain. No I'm fine really Daniel. No you don't have to kiss it better. Come here and help me recover properly.' We held each other and kissed again. 'Now I feel much better Daniel but what did you cry out about?'

'Look what I found by your foot.'

'Well it looks like a dirty pebble or flat disc from here. What is it?'

'See this edge it glitters, well it flashed in the sunshine when I first saw it.'

'Looks pretty dull to me and it's covered with dirt.'

'We'll take it back to the Landrover. I've got a water bottle there so we can clean it up a little. I think it might be an old coin.'

'Go on Daniel, you said there was no treasure in the cave. Michael didn't find anything and if people had found it before they have never come forwards. You've never heard anything else have you?'

'No, but never mind that let's get this cleaned. We'll never know whether it's something or nothing until we've looked closer.'

For some reason I felt excited. Perhaps I was overly optimistic after kissing but I felt really good. I couldn't wait to get back to the Landrover but I had to be patient as Katya's ankle slowed her down. Back at the Landrover I dug around in my pack and found the water bottle.

'All right then Mr. Treasure Hunter. Let's see what you've found?'

I sluiced a little water over the dirty object and rubbed with my fingers. Fragments of limestone and earth slithered off the surface and gradually the object became slimmer and rounder. I ended up with a disc, perhaps a coin which was somewhat circular but twice as big as an old English penny. It was heavy and a dull golden colour.

'Well, what is it Daniel?'

'I haven't any idea Katya. It could be a Saxon medallion, a Spanish gold piece, or a token for the tram on the seaside at Weston Super Mare. I really have no idea but you found it and so it is yours. Here, my first gift to you,' and I put it in her hand and kissed her at the same time.

'Daniel the kiss I liked but how can you give me something that is already mine. Think about it. If I found it and therefore it is mine how can you give it to me as your first gift?'

'Katya that's much too intellectual a question. Just kiss me again and say thank you.'

'"Thank you Daniel, very very much,' and she kissed me with the whole length of her beautiful body pressed up hard against me and her arms tightly around my neck. I held her close and shared the kiss.

'Let's go home Daniel?'

I unfolded my arms from around her waist and opened the door for her to climb into the Landrover. I slid into the driver's seat and turned on the ignition.

'Heavens, is that the time Daniel? I'm supposed to catch the train at five.'

'There'll be a later train Katya.'

'No Daniel, I checked, not on Sundays.'

'Look, let's not rush about. I'll drive you home and we'll pick up your things and I'll drive you back to Oxford. It's not very far and that way there's no panic and you'll get home safely probably before you might by train. Is that a deal?'

Katya leaned over and kissed me again. 'Deal.'

It was a quiet afternoon down in the village. Betty Ferris had taken Katey and Paul down to the little stream by the mill where Paul's friend lived. With some old bread they had fed the assortment of mallard ducks, coots and moorhens.

'What's that Mummy, down the river standing by the edge of the bank? You have to look carefully because it is standing very still.'

'I can see it Paul. It's a heron isn't it Mum? Can you see it?'

'Yes Katey I can see it and your sister's right Paul. It is a heron, looking for his supper I expect.'

'We never saw them heron-things at the cottage did we Mummy?'

'No Paul, the birds are different in the forest from down here by the stream. Do you remember what we saw in the forest?'

'There were big black and white birds that walked funny, and there were lots of singing greenish birds, and of course those brilliant flashy birds. What did you call those Mummy?'

'Those were jays Paul, and your funny black and white birds were magpies.'

Betty thought back to the time in the forest. It had been different, peaceful but not quiet. There was always the swishing of the tree branches and the morning and evening bird song, not like living in the village at her parents with the traffic, the human chatter and the bell ringing in the shop. Different. She wondered what John was doing. I miss him she thought. John I miss you.

John was missing too. He'd set up a row of empty beer bottles and was throwing stones at them but he was missing, which was not very surprising as he had emptied all the beer bottles personally. Work all bloody week he thought and then Saturday with a chance to escape this open prison. Christ what a bloody mess. And Saturday all I seem to get is abuse and aggro. I'll brain that stupid Freddie. Just because dad kicked his arse doesn't mean he has to take it out on me. I never did him any harm.

He threw angrily at one of the bottles and by chance he hit it. Bingo he shouted to the surrounding forest and the forest just swallowed up his cry. It was good here John thought. Normally I'd be out with little Paul and Katey and we'd be walking through part of the forest looking at the trees and counting the birds we saw. Little Paul was starting to recognise the different birds. The scream of a jay startled John. Shit I could do with my family around me.

'Mummy, grandma says I'm getting better at riding and Dainty thinks so too.'

'Darling that's wonderful. Did you get to trotting today?'

'No Mummy, grandma says I must learn to walk first. Is it school tomorrow?'

'Yes love. I've seen the teacher and she is really looking forward to seeing you.'

'Will Peter and Tony be there too?'

'No James, this is a different school from them but you will see them after school. Would you like to go down to Auntie Christina's for tea? You could see Enrico too.'

'Did you have a good day Samantha? How did Evelyn make out?'

'Mum we had a terrific day. Evelyn did very well. We only did four climbs but the last one was harder than anything else she had ever done. She's a great woman to climb with and we've arranged to go next weekend if nothing changes her schedule.'

'Yes, being a police constable is not exactly a nine to five job I would imagine. Still, James and I had a good day and he is improving even though he needs to sit up a little straighter and not look like a sack of potatoes sometimes. Let's go and have dinner.'

'Hello Dad, did you get a chance to have some rest or did my little scallywag come bothering you?'

'No Samantha James was fine. He was out riding with your mother in the morning and we went for a drive in the forest this afternoon. He is getting to recognise his trees Samantha. Daniel, where were you this afternoon? Did Katya get home safely?'

'Yes Dad in answer to your second question and we were touring the forest too like you earlier.'

I felt Samantha looking at me and wondering whether this is what I was actually doing but I just smiled at her and she was none the wiser.

'We saw John Ferris in the pub last night Daniel. He didn't look a very happy camper although he did end up drinking with some friendly faces. That Freddie was giving him a lot of aggro though Daniel. I thought you should be aware.'

'Thanks Samantha. Freddie normally works around the gardens and the stables and so he and John shouldn't cross paths too much in the normal course of a day but I'll keep that in mind. How was your evening?'

'Just fine thanks brother. Terence Field is a gentleman and we had a very enjoyable dinner at Westland House.'

'And?'

'And nothing. He was on call but fortunately the villains were all quiet last night.'

'Did you get to ask him why Idwal Ferris spent time in gaol? If he was put away for all the past eight years it must have been something fairly serious. Did you ask him?'

'Yes in a way Daniel. We agreed early on we wouldn't talk about his work. Terence said he had had that all week and could really do with a break but we did touch on John Ferris because we had seen him in the pub earlier. I asked about Idwal and Terence thought he had done time for manslaughter. He had killed someone in Bristol, a Larry Whelks I think he said, and yes he had got eight years. Terence thinks he had only been out a couple of weeks when he arrived here.'

'Larry Whelks. Wasn't there a Larry Whelks in the village Dad? Isn't he, or perhaps I should say wasn't he old Ma Whelk's boy? There were two of them surely, brothers and the younger one went to Australia or something? I was still at school but I seem to remember hearing old Ma Whelks having two sons. Do you remember Mum?'

'Well old Florence Whelks still lives in her dilapidated cottage just on the edge of the village. Nobody ever sees her very much, she more of a recluse but yes Daniel she did have two sons and they both disappeared. The younger one, I think he was called Phillip ran away when he was a teenager. Larry disappeared about eight or nine years ago now. So many other things were going on then with this family that I can't really remember them. Anyway, both boys disappeared and that's perhaps why I had forgotten about them. Did Terence say why Idwal Ferris killed Larry Whelks Samantha, presuming we've got this story straight?'

'No Mum, we didn't pursue it as I said. It just came up as a single question when we were talking about John. Does it matter? Daniel, does it matter?'

'Not really Samantha. It's just something John Ferris said about why his brother came back here. It's niggling but perhaps I'd better go back and ask John to make sure I heard it right. It was just something unusual and that's why John remembered it. Anyway, thanks Samantha. No other questions from Terence to you?'

'None that were significant as far as you are concerned thank you very much.'

'Dad, talking of concerned questions have you or mum heard anything back from Rosalind Cohen? Wasn't she supposed to call back within a week?'

'Daniel I telephoned this past Monday so it hasn't even been a week yet. Let's allow Rosalind her week at least before I start to sound desperate. I hear you had a rather successful game of golf this morning. What was it, six under?'

'Daniel you didn't, did you?'

I turned and smiled at Samantha. 'Actually dad's right. It was very successful thanks to Katya actually and yes I did finally end up at six under par.'

'But that's terrific, and how did Katya help you? Did she caddie in the end?'

'She's a good player in her own right and yes she did carry my bag around the course. Actually she makes a good caddie.'

'And good other things too?'

'Yes sister dear but this morning she was a good caddie thank you very much. She quickly sensed what shot I would make and therefore what club I would need. When she was uncertain she was quiet and let me decide, but a couple of times she suggested I play a shot I hadn't really thought of and it worked out really well, especially on the last two holes.'

I turned to my mother. 'Mum, I've asked Katya down again next weekend. I hope that's okay? On Saturday I was planning to take Katya for a cliff walk somewhere. Samantha, where are you going climbing next weekend?'

'We hadn't decided where Daniel, why?'

'Why don't you go down to Bosigran and we'll come too in the car and walk along the cliff there. That way we can all have a day out together.'

'What, you with three ladies? Bit cheeky Daniel.'

'Where do I go?'

'True enough Daniel, who takes James?'

I sat and thought about this for a moment. I knew Katya hadn't done a lot of hill walking. Sure up and down the golf course wasn't flat but it wasn't quite like the Cornish cliffs either. I looked at my sister but she decided to let me speak first.

'Mummy, where do I go if you're going climbing?'

'James how would you like to come with Katya and me?' I said turning and holding James's rather sticky hand.

'Can I, can I? Can we go on the train again, like last time with Katya and King Delaney and Queen Deidre?'

Everyone around the table laughed. I suddenly realized that was only a week ago and yet it seemed an age.

'No James, not on the train this time young fella but on shank's pony.'

'We don't have a pony Uncle Daniel. Even Dainty is a horse although she is small. Where will we find a pony?'

Dad decided I shouldn't tease and so he leaned across the table and caught James's other hand. 'Your uncle is teasing James but he wants you to walk. You know your grandma is teaching you to ride. Well your Uncle

Daniel wants to teach you to walk. His words "shank's pony" is another funny English way of saying walk.'

'But I know how to walk. What's so special?'

'Well, how about you come out next Saturday with Katya and me and we'll see how well you can walk shall we? We can walk while your mother is climbing with Evelyn, your WPC Nicols. Perhaps after we've had lunch we can watch your mother climb if we can find a route to overlook. Think we can do that Samantha? How's that for a deal, although I think you owe me one?'

'Thanks Daniel, that'll be a big help and James gets on well with Katya.'

'She's my friend,' piped up James in his assertive voice.

'Mum, I nearly forgot. I invited Terence Field for dinner on Saturday, for seven o'clock. I hope that fits in with everyone's plans.'

I watched my mum smile and glance across at dad. 'It's good just to sit here and listen to you two get on with your lives, it really is, and yes Samantha I'm sure cook will do just fine as long as she has some advance warning. What do you think Anthony?'

'You're right my dear. It's good to have a little more activity going on in this big old house. What's the plan for Sunday?'

'Dad I'll go and play golf as usual with my trusty caddie.'

'And you Samantha?'

'Dad I was hoping Terence could stay, in a spare bedroom of course and we could go round the forest on Sunday with James. I'd like them to get to know each other a little better.'

'Will he have my other special friend with him Mummy, you know the lady who knows all about steam engines?'

'No darling, we'll see your other special friend WPC Nicols on Saturday but she won't be with Terence on Sunday. We'll have him all to ourselves and we'll go and have a special visit in the forest somewhere.

Perhaps we'll go and find your uncle's badger gate, if I can find it that is? What do you say?'

'Is there any more pudding?'

In the bathroom just down the corridor from her room in Oxford Katya sluiced warm water over the dirty pebble-like object she found by the cave. It was really encrusted with dirt and even bits of limestone grit. She used an old small brush to scrub quite hard at the brown and black surface and slowly bits of other colours shone through. After some thirty minutes of arm-tiring activity she had a round object in the palm of her hand that was heavy, more or less circular and a dull bronze to golden colour. It looked like a medallion or even a coin but the inscriptions and raised relief on the faces were too worn to be able to decipher. After drying it Katya slipped it in her pocket and walked thoughtfully back to her room. She wondered who she knew that might unravel its secrets.

ALL THAT GLITTERS MIGHT BE

GOLD

John Ferris rolled out of his restless bed and shook his head. He looked around his bedroom and thought back to just twelve days ago. Christ, just twelve days ago Betty would be calling me for breakfast and little Paul would be in here wanting to wrestle. All changed thanks to my fucking useless brother. Cursing forlornly John climbed into his rather dirty and smelly clothes and wandered out into the kitchen to find the kettle and the tap. While the water boiled for tea John looked around in the various cupboards for some sort of breakfast, and maybe even a lunch if he got his head together. He was still nursing a headache from yesterday's attack on the twelve or more beer bottles. After thirty minutes of eating, drinking, sluicing cold water over his face and head, and finding a lunch bag he walked out of the back door and set off across the forest to the office. Another day in paradise he mumbled and a jay screamed back at him.

Up at the Big House breakfast was just as disorganised but a lot more vocal. James, who started nursery school today was asking questions like

118

there was no tomorrow. I watched my sister trying to cope with feeding James, answering questions, and getting his shoes on all at the same time. Did I really want children I asked myself? Wonder what Katya was doing right now? Enough Daniel, you're off to work and Katya will be here soon enough at the end of the week but right now let's go and sort out the work crew. Just keep Freddie out of John Ferris's face.

The first two days of this first week in October passed quickly and before I knew it I found it was Wednesday already. As well as getting James off to nursery school Samantha was also rushing around getting organised to go up to London to see Janet Donaldson. After more talks with mum and dad, plus getting in touch with a real estate agent in Canada to sell the house in Sault Ste. Marie, my sister had decided to offer to become a partner in Janet's Heritage Adventures Company. I wished her luck and said that I would pick up James at lunch time.

Having deposited a very voluble James back with my mother I reversed direction and arrived at the golf course a little late for my afternoon regular Club's Men's Day event. Although I hadn't had much chance to practice the last two evenings I did manage to do the front nine in level par.

'Not quite as good as last Sunday Daniel, but then you had a helper?'

'Right Larry and she really was a helper. I could have done with some advice or perhaps just encouragement back on the seventh hole. There was a birdie for the having.'

'If Daniel, if only, the magic golf phrase. Is Katya coming out this Sunday? She sure brightened up the foursome. Actually Daniel I think we all played better under her critical gaze. You say she plays off a six? If she's staying around why don't you propose her as a non-resident temporary member, then she could play in some of the Club tournaments and we could see how good she really is?'

'It's an idea Larry. Perhaps I'll ask her this weekend. Trouble is she is rather busy as it is her final year and the thesis takes top priority. I know I didn't find much free time in my final year.'

'You here this Saturday 'cos we're looking for a fourth? Old Phil had to drop out with gout or something equally painful. Says he can hardly walk which is not in itself a problem but he can't swing a club either and that is more serious.'

'No Larry, sorry. Katya and I are out walking on Saturday down in Cornwall on the coast. We're babysitting young James while his mother dices with death on the cliffs there.'

'She's still doing that crazy climbing thing? I thought going to eastern Canada which is pretty flat would put an end to the cookie passion.'

'Don't laugh Larry. She and my mother were out a couple of weekends ago and they had a positively wonderful day according to them. I know they both came home looking really together and happy.'

'I thought you told me they used to fight like cat and dog. Couldn't stand to both be in the same house at the same time?'

I turned to Larry and laughed. 'You're right. Before Samantha went to Canada that's just like it was but last Sunday week they had a sort of reconciliation day and it worked. Quite amazing really. I'm still waiting for the roof to fall in but so far the house is quite peaceful. But yes, Samantha climbed quite a lot in Canada, some really hard things apparently, new routes and new areas and so she has come home gung ho to continue. It's interesting really because she has found a new partner, one of the local WPCs.'

'What, she's climbing with a copper?'

'Yes, nice girl actually and apparently she can climb well enough to keep up with Samantha so she must be pretty good. So, Saturday we will go and see this mighty duo in action. Just hope the weather stays clear.

Anyway, isn't your shot? We've been here chitty-chatting long enough and the foursome behind us is starting to look agitated.'

I didn't tell Larry that not only was Samantha climbing with a copper but she was also going out with another copper to boot. Larry wasn't a strong fan of the police with several of his deals probably close to the edge of legality. There were a few rumours going round about some of his cars but then in a country area you learnt when to ask and when not to ask questions. After the round I ended up at one under par but didn't feel the elation that I had felt last Sunday; perhaps it was just the company.

Back home however my dad did appear elated and he rushed me into the office almost as soon as I walked in the door.

'Hold up a sec Dad and let me get my coat off at least. There's no bloody fire, well I hope not. Can I at least wash my hands or is this an on-line crisis?'

'Yes, sure Daniel, sure just don't take too long will you? It really is good news. I'll get your mother.'

Realising it wasn't quite as earth-shattering as dad would have me think I took about ten minutes to change and clean up a little before going back into the office. Dad was already there with my mother.

'Will Samantha be here or is she still in London?'

'She phoned earlier in the day Daniel and she is planning to stay up in town with Janet and come back down tomorrow. Actually she had something to do with today's news.'

'Knowing Samantha she probably precipitated a decision from Rosalind,' said my mother. 'She never could stand any long term delays in decisions.'

'So Rosalind called I assume? What did she say?'

My father looked at my mother as if to say who would speak.

'Yes Daniel, Rosalind called and with good news, well we think so. Samantha did go round there with Janet and they spent a little time explaining what they were thinking of doing and a little more about our situation. Anyway, after their visit Rosalind called and said that she had talked with her people. She'd also talked with some financial people she knows up in the city and was prepared to enter into some form of gradual buyout. Overall she was both positive about the idea of combining the two companies and she was personally delighted we had thought to make her the offer. It was a very positive message. As a result your mother and I have arranged to go up to London next Monday for a couple of days and start the process. It looks really promising Daniel. That suggestion of Samantha's was a good one.'

'But that's excellent news. I can see now why you were so excited when I came in. That would really be a good news story if we can push it through to the obvious conclusion. As Samantha said you would have passed a successful venture into a new environment and walk away with no worries and a sizeable investment opportunity. That should please Christina and Peter too Dad. That's what they both wanted. Sounds like a win-win situation. What do you think Mum? You're awfully quiet.'

'Daniel I'm as delighted as your father is. Given Rosalind can find the right sort of financing then it would be a win-win situation as you say. Still, I'm keeping my fingers crossed as I know some of the possible financial hurdles and there are a lot of places this can fall apart but overall I'm feeling good about it. Anthony I think a drink is in order dear. Perhaps not a toast for "reaching the summit" but definitely "camp one".'

We were sitting there in the office sipping dad's scotch when the telephone startled all of us.

'It's for you Daniel, sounds like Katya. Your mother and I will leave you in peace. Come on Sylvia and don't forget to bring that bottle.'

'Hi Katya, I was going to call you later this evening but you beat me to it. All set for Friday evening?'

'Daniel, Daniel hush up a minute. I've found out something exciting, really exciting.'

'Okay, I'm listening.'

'You know that grubby old thing I kicked up coming out of the cave? You remember?'

'Uh huh.'

'Well, guess what it is?'

I could hear the excitement strumming down the telephone wires and wondered what it was that Katya had found. I decided for once not to be corny. 'A gold piece, maybe a Spanish doubloon, a piece of eight, an American golden dollar.'

'No, no, no and no again, although the first guess was probably closest to the truth. When I got back on Sunday I let it soak for a while to get some of the grime and dirt off it. It was really encrusted you know. Well, I checked back on Tuesday night to look in the pot where I had soaked it and it turns out to be a coin of some kind. So, today I went over to a friend of mine who is a bit of a fanatic about old coins and she jumped up and down. Mark you Daniel she's English and a little weird at the best of times. I think she comes from one of those titled families from the year one although you'd never know it by the way she dresses. Her room is a real shambles with books and clothes sort of scattered all over and you should see where she cooks. It's positively gross. It beats me how she doesn't get food poisoning or something, she's....'

'Katya, can we come back to the coin or whatever and forget lady whoever and her dangerous living environment?'

'Sorry Daniel but I don't know how some of you English ever survive. I had to hold my nose part of the time and appear not to be doing so but really.'

'Katya!'

'Oh yes, the coin, well it seems it might date from somewhere in the seventeen hundreds. Apparently it's English, or so Penelope thinks. She went looking for some books to check but of course she couldn't find them in the chaos of her room and then she stumbled across something else she had been looking for and kind of lost interest in what I had and went off on some sort of tangent. Whatever it was she found proved to be exceptionally interesting and she ignored me after that and so I left.'

'Did she think it was something special or just a regular coin?'

'She didn't say Daniel. Initially she was really excited and I was expecting some fantastic revelation but it sort of fizzled out. I will try again. I got the impression it was a regular coin although if it was gold it would still be worth something, even as a regular coin. Wouldn't it?'

'I don't know Katya, I really don't, but it sounds interesting even if not valuable. I'm glad you found it and hope that it is valuable for you. Anyway, what about Friday?'

'Yes Daniel, I will come down. Were you going to play golf again on Sunday? I enjoyed that day and I think you did too?'

Thinking back on all that happened that day I agreed. 'I sure did, all of the day, afternoon as well as the morning.'

I heard Katya laugh down the telephone.

'And did you talk to Samantha about Saturday?'

'Yes, she is going climbing with Evelyn Nicols again and I persuaded them to go to Cornwall and said we would go too and walk along the tops. As a compromise I said we would take James. He can walk part of the way and I can carry him if he gets tired. I told Samantha to pick a climb in the afternoon where we could sit and watch her climb. I think James would like to see that.'

'I would too Daniel. I've never actually seen anybody rock climb, in real life that is. Sure I've seen it in the movies but I would like to see Samantha actually climbing. It must be quite exciting.'

'Yes it is and I would like James to see it before he goes any further. So, bring warm clothes for hiking and some sturdy shoes or even boots if you have any. They'll be better for your ankles on the cliff top.'

'Anything else?'

'Samantha's up in town for two days talking over business partnerships with Janet Donaldson.'

'So she's made up her mind to go for Heritage Adventure?'

'I think so. We'll see. Oh, by the way, that friend of dad's rung up from London, I think after some talking with Samantha and Janet actually, and said she was interested in merging Companies and/or buying Brainware.'

'That's great Daniel. Isn't that what your parents wanted? Wasn't she the lady you had talked about, who had worked with your father before?'

'Yes, looks like a positive step forward although as my mum says there's a long way to go yet. Still, it is a good news story. So, here at the moment everyone's kind of positive but I'll be happy when Friday comes and I see you again.'

'Me too Daniel, but I've got to work in the meantime so I'll let you go for the moment. See you Friday. Bye.'

I heard the phone click and wistfully replaced the receiver on the cradle. Friday, roll on Friday.

I picked Katya up from the train station on Friday evening and we drove back to Fotheringham. Once Katya had dumped her gear in her bedroom we reassembled in the drawing room with Samantha who was telling mum and dad about her discussions with Janet. They in turn were briefly describing the call from Rosalind. When there was an unexpected gap in the conversation I decided it was time to move onto tomorrow's agenda.

'So now all of you are fairly happy with your achievements this past week can we move into thoughts for the weekend? Samantha we need to understand what you have discussed or arranged with Evelyn. Is she still on for tomorrow or has the omnipresent Terence decided she is needed elsewhere?'

'Daniel stop portraying Terence as some kind of ogre. Anyway, as far as I know Evelyn is on for tomorrow and we'll pick her up around six thirty in the village. As you know it is a good three hundred kilometres down to Zennor and it will take a while. So we should plan on leaving here soon after six. Think you can manage that?'

Samantha smiled sweetly at Katya and me as if to say defy me. I grinned back and held Katya's hand.

'Sounds fine but what about mighty mouse, the non-stop questioning four-year old wonder of the world?'

'I'll worry about James Daniel. You just be ready. You planning to walk in the morning and then come and ogle in the afternoon? Is that right?'

'Yes, we were planning to walk along part of the coast path until lunch time and then come and watch you and Evelyn climb. That will be enough walking for James and I thought it would be good for him to see you climb.'

'With one of his special friends?'

'Yes, although it amazes me how all his special friends are female.'

Samantha just gave me one of her smug looks as if to say it was part of the education of her son but she said nothing. Katya also developed one of those feminine "cat has found the cream and is licking its whiskers" looks and she too smiled at my remark.

'Sounds like you three should all be off to bed if you've got to get up that early,' mum said. 'Anyway, have a good day all of you. The weather forecast is fine but windy, which is rather typical for this time of year.

126

Climb carefully Samantha, especially in front of your son. Daniel you make sure that grandson of mine doesn't try and climb off the coast path. If it's windy that can be quite treacherous in places.'

I turned to Katya and quietly said, 'you should have heard my mother when we were teenagers after listening to those pieces of advice. Perhaps she doesn't realise that we're in our twenties now.'

'Daniel, being in your twenties doesn't make you immune from mishaps. Your dad and I just want to make sure you enjoy yourselves and take care of James.'

'Sure Mum I know what you mean and I'll make sure your rebellious daughter behaves.'

'Out, out, out the lot of you. Katya take these two disrespectful children of mine away, but do look after them for me?'

'Sure Sylvia, I'll look after them.'

The three of us left my parents and laughed our way upstairs. Soon the house slept.

At six o'clock the next morning four of us were quietly munching away on various bits of breakfast. For once James was quiet, a mixture of half asleep and half hungry. We quickly sorted out the various things we would need for the day and left the house quietly still sleeping around six fifteen. Evelyn was waiting in the village by the pub and we let her sit in the front seat with Samantha while Katya, James and I snuggled up in the back. For the first hour we all peacefully dozed as the drive wasn't all that exciting but after we left the motorway at Exeter and drove west over the top end of Dartmoor Katya started to take a greater interest in the countryside. Tendrils of mist hung in the low spots on the road but there was very little traffic and Samantha maintained a good pace. We passed from Devon into Cornwall near Launceston and then through the bleak open spaces of Bodmin Moor. Although Katya had been in England for over two years now she was still amazed at the variety and changes in the countryside in such short distances. We talked almost in whispers as James stayed delightfully asleep. Samantha and Evelyn chatted quietly in the front about various climbs and suggestions for today's agenda. The sun slowly climbed up in the sky behind us and the mists dissipated.

On the bypass around the town of Bodmin itself Samantha stopped for petrol and we all had a chance to stretch our legs and use the facilities. James had woken up by this time and was asking for breakfast as I took him into the men's toilets. We managed to take care of him having a pee without too many questions as men have difficulty doing two things at the same time. Back in the car Samantha had wisely packed a second breakfast for James as she knew he would be hungry again as soon as he woke up and this kept him relatively quiet even though there was a certain amount of bread and peanut butter scattered over Katya and myself. James would insist on trying to speak and eat at the same time and of course he waved his hands while he spoke. Obviously he has spent too much time down at Home Farm with my Italian sister-in-law with all the hand action.

By the time we reached Hayle and navigated around the weird set of roundabouts at the western end towards St. Ives the sun looked like it would stay visible for most of the morning and it was a cheerful crowd of people in the car driving the wooded part of the road through Lelant and Carbis Bay to overlook the artist's village of St. Ives. It now being October all was relatively quiet and I explained to Katya that in the height of summer this place was really crowded with holiday-makers.

'Back by the ocean again James, like in the train ride a fortnight ago. In fact, down below us is another railway that runs from St. Erth to St. Ives. The railway runs right by the edge of a challenging links golf course.'

'Will we see blue engines Uncle Daniel, or are they all green here like on your GWR?'

'Unfortunately James there are no steam engines here and all the trains are diesel electric, which is efficient but not very romantic or picturesque. Still the scenery is dramatic. Just look at the sunshine glittering off the water down there. Much of Cornwall is rather austere and forbidding, especially where there are old mine workings but here in the sheltered St. Ives bay with the sand dunes of the Towans stretching away in the distance this corner is quite pretty. They say the light here is rather special which is partly why it became quite a haven for artists from 1880 onwards I suppose. In the very olden days the town had two other activities. One was mining and living by the sea what do you think the other might be James?'

'Hunting for seals?'

'Interesting answer James as we might see seals here but there are no ice floes like you get in Eastern Canada. What else could it be?'

'I know I know,' said James leaping up off the seat. 'Fish, they went fishing, salmon fishing.'

'Yes and no James. Yes they went fishing but no not for salmon but for a smaller fish like a sardine.'

'Ugh, that's cat food. Nobody eats sardines Uncle Daniel.'

I heard Samantha laugh as she carefully navigated the narrow lanes around the top end of St. Ives.

'James you obviously haven't been around English climbers very much my love. There are many people here who will eat sardines and love them but your Uncle Daniel is talking about another little fish, even smaller than our pickerel.'

'What are they Daniel?' asked Katya. 'I'm not sure that I know which fish you are talking about.'

'Well I suppose it was back in the last century that the fishing was in its hey day but they used to catch pilchards here in the bay with seine nets. Apparently they'd pile them up in big mounds on the pier and let the blood and the oil run out so they were partly dry and then they'd salt them and pack them up in hogsheads for export to Catholic countries like Italy.'

'The smell must have been pretty awful?'

'Yes I can imagine. Samantha we should buy some and let James try them?'

'Leave that until we get home Daniel. I don't want him being sick in the car thank you very much, even if he wants to try but I'll bet he thinks they are even more like cat food than sardines.'

'But I might like them Mummy. I might love them.'

'Yes darling you might but can we leave the experiment until later. We're nearly there.'

'What I was leading up to with my trivia about St. Ives was the town really had these two groups of working people, the fishermen and the miners. The fishermen lived in a set of houses in an area of the town just above the harbour called 'Downalong' and the miners lived in a set of houses called 'Upalong' and of course the youngsters used to fight each other in gangs.'

'Daniel I'm not sure James needs that kind of history lesson thank you very much. Tell him something more constructive, something about the lifeboat for instance.'

'Sure Samantha.' I turned back to James. 'All along this coastline James it is very rocky with rough seas piling waves and swells in from the open Atlantic ocean. There have always been lots of boats in the sea here and so in bad weather some ships get into trouble and might get wrecked on the rocky coast. So, along much of Cornwall many of the villages have a lifeboat which they send out to sea when someone is in distress.'

'This is like an ambulance on the road Uncle Daniel?'

'Sort of yes, but the lifeboat may go and just help rescue the people. The crew might not be hurt but they will probably be wet, cold, frightened and in danger so the lifeboat goes out and saves them. Anyway, what I was getting to is that the lifeboat down in St. Ives and in many of the other villages too around here sits in a shed on top of a slipway into the water. With the tides here and the nature of the coast it is easier and safer to build the lifeboat house higher up on the shore and then let the boat slide down into the ocean to launch it. It is exciting to see it go rushing down the slip into the rough ocean.'

'This is Zennor and we're all but there. Daniel are you going to walk from where we park the car or do you want to drive on to somewhere else after Evelyn and I get our gear?'

'No Samantha we'll walk from where you park. That'll be easier and we'll all know where the car is.'

There were a couple of other cars in the parking lot when we arrived. The wind was blowing but not too hard and the air was cool but not cold. Samantha organised the various layers for James and I received the usual mother's admonitions of do this don't do that and I looked at James and winked. He giggled and wriggled. 'James stand still a minute love while I get this zipper closed. Daniel, can you and James play after I've done with him? Now look after him for me. James, you listen and do what your Uncle Daniel tells you. I know you're both really a couple of youngsters but listen to Daniel. Perhaps I should have Katya look after both of you.'

'Samantha, sister dear, why don't you and Evelyn sort out your gear and go and climb? It might surprise you but I can look after your precious son. We managed very well two weeks ago. Didn't we James?'

'Yes Uncle Daniel, and we found Katya too Mummy.'

131

'Well don't go finding any other young ladies this morning please James. Just enjoy the walk with Katya and Daniel.'

'Come on Katya, let's go before Samantha gives us written instructions. I've got the rucksack with your spare clothes, map, binoculars, camera, enough gear for James for a week, spare food, drink, and the tents and stoves for camp one.'

Evelyn laughed. 'I can see why you get on so well with your brother Samantha. He's a laugh a minute.'

'Let's go Katya before Samantha can think of a funny answer to that comment. Have a good morning you two and we'll see you both after lunch. You've got your red anorak Samantha and yours is yellow Evelyn? We should be able to find you although this wind makes communications difficult. Don't worry, we'll find you. Come on James. Would you like to carry the rucksack to start with?'

I watched James look seriously at the full rucksack sitting on the ground and then turn and look at me. 'Do I have to? It's almost as big as I am but I'll try.'

Katya walked over to James and gave him a big hug. 'Your Uncle Daniel is pulling your leg James. Just hold my hand and you'll be fine. We'll let Daniel carry all our gear. He can be our porter while we have the easy life. Come on, let's go and find what we can see from the top of the cliff.'

I had decided to walk westwards to start with as that would be into the prevailing wind. Then, if James got tired we would at least have the wind at our backs. Leaving Samantha and Evelyn sorting out their climbing gear we walked towards the coastal path. As in any climbing area there were lots of paths to start with but eventually we found our way nearer the sea and the familiar Coast Path signposts came into view.

'This is one of England's longest long walks Katya,' I said. 'I suppose it is nearly one thousand kilometres long from one end to the other, all around the coastline of south west England.'

'And people walk that far Daniel?'

'Dedicated fanatics do the whole thing but most people walk sections of it and they might do a few sections each year, or they might just do the parts that are in Cornwall. Today we're just going to do part of one section, well one section according to the guidebook. Here, I'll show you. We're walking a part of Section 29 in the Southwest Way guide, from St. Ives to Pendeen Watch. Pendeen's the next main village further down the road we were on.'

'Uncle Daniel I'm hungry.'

'Of course you are James. I'd be surprised if you weren't hungry. I was always hungry at your age and if we look in my rucksack we can probably find something for you. Here, let's look. Does this interest you James?'

'Oh, that's awesome Uncle Daniel. How did you know I liked these?'

'Your mother loves you James and she gave them to me to give to you.'

'Are there any pictures in your book Uncle Daniel? Can I see?'

'No James, just words and I am going to show Katya where we are going.'

'It says "Grade: Severe" Daniel. Is that a warning?'

'No, not really a warning but in comparison with other parts of the path this section is more demanding than most. It explains below that this section is very long between places to stay, refreshments are non-existent, and the trail is often muddy but all that is in comparison with other parts of the walk. We'll take our time and try and keep James out of the mud.'

The three of us walked down the path towards the ocean and within ten minutes we came to the coastal path and a little stone bridge. Here I turned west and pointed up the hillside in front of us.

'We've got to climb up there Daniel?'

'Yes Katya,' I said as I laughed. 'We'll walk slowly but steadily and try and develop a rhythm. You go first, then James and I'll bring up the rear. In a way you have to learn to walk all over again as it is quite a trick to walk steadily on this kind of terrain.'

Katya set off up the hillside that leads to the top of Rosemergy cliffs and Trevean Point. It was a steady climb and a couple of times I urged Katya gently to take it slowly. It was hard to teach James how to walk slowly as he wanted to rush up everything. As we came over the brow of the hill we met the breeze from the west and the air was really full of salt. You could almost taste it.

'So this path runs all the way along the top of the cliffs, beside the ocean the whole way?'

'More or less Katya. James keep out of that muddy hole please. Watch that wind, it will blow in gusts up here and I don't want to chase a rolling ball of James across the cliff tops. How about a picture James? How about a photograph and a little rest after climbing up that hill?'

We stopped near the crest of the hillside and I slipped the rucksack off my shoulders and dug around for the camera. The sun was still shining but it was a rather weak and pale effort at warming this part of England. The usual westerly wind blew in gusts and we were all glad we had sweaters on.

'There Katya, yes just there please and you James come alongside Katya. Look at me James and try to think of something funny, like mummy with a rocket in her knickers.'

Katya smiled and James laughed as I quickly took three or four shots. With James wriggling about I hoped one of them would look reasonable.

It was a great backdrop with the ocean in motion and a good view of the rugged coastline down towards Pendeen Watch and its lighthouse.

I gave James a drink from my water bottle and we set off again towards Pendeen. Across the top of Rosemergy cliffs the path was quite flat and the walking fairly easy. After another twenty minutes I decided we would find a sheltered spot and just look at the ocean. We were approximately an hour from the car and about time to reverse our walk.

'Daniel, we've seen some pretty serious-looking walkers along here, complete with enormous rucksacks, boots and looking like they should be up in the mountains somewhere.'

'We'll see all sorts Katya. I'm surprised we haven't seen more OAPs, especially as it is such a nice day but perhaps they only come out during the week and leave the path for the masses on the weekend.'

'What are OAPs?'

'Old Age Pensioners, old folks, old crusties, retirees, whatever you call them in Florida. Snowbirds isn't it?'

'No Daniel, snowbirds just come down for the four or five months of winter and then go north again but we do have several people who have retired to Florida.'

'What else do we have to eat Uncle Daniel? My toe hurts. Where did mummy say she was going? Can we see her? This ground's awfully lumpy Uncle Daniel.'

Katya laughed and put her arm across James's shoulders and gave him a hug. 'Here James, sit on my coat and I'll look at your toe. Just let me slip your shoe off for a minute. Is it this one?'

'Yes, and the sock too. Oo, that tickles.'

'Hold still a moment and let me look. Wriggle your toes. That's good. Daniel do you have a bandaid? James's toes look like they are rubbing a little and a bandaid will keep them apart. Thanks.'

We fixed James's feet: gave him a sweet: told him where Samantha was and that we would see her soon after lunch. Katya put his sock and shoe back on and I stood up.

'Okay troops, it's back to base. Think we can manage that troops? It's mostly downhill, well at the end it is.'

Katya stood up straight and saluted. 'Yes my captain,' she said. 'Stand up tall private James. Pull those shoulders back, bottom in, tummy in, stand tall, eyes front.' James giggled and tried to do what Katya was doing.

'Right troops, slow march, slow, slow, slow.'

Katya set off back across the cliff tops and with the wind behind us it made for easier walking. I looked back to check we hadn't left anything behind and then followed on after James. Pretty soon we were back on the top looking down into Porthmeor Cove. I must have turned to look behind me for a moment when I heard a cry and looking back I saw that James had slid on the muddy path and cannoned into Katya who in turn had tumbled over the edge of a piece of heathers' roots. I shot down the path at speed and grabbed James by his sweater to keep him from falling further. I held him upright and reached down for Katya who had tumbled over a steeper section. All in the blink of an eye I shouted at James to stand very still while I reached down for Katya but couldn't reach so I let go of James and stretched my hands down to Katya. Unfortunately I had too much momentum and rolled forwards. To avoid landing on top of Katya I half leapt and half dived downhill to miss her. There was quite a drop as the hillside was fairly steep down into Porthmeor and I twisted in the air to land on my shoulder and roll. I was doing fine until my body weight rolled over onto my wrist which didn't take kindly to the immense stress. I felt a jab of pain as my body eventually came to rest some five feet beyond Katya. Rolling over my eyes scanned across the blue sky and

136

I must have looked pretty silly as my feet were uphill and the rest of me was spread-eagled down the hillside.

Katya's face suddenly blocked out the light. 'Daniel, Daniel are you all right?' I must have grunted and then feeling the pain in my wrist twisted my face a little.

'What hurts? Lie still, you might have concussion. Let me look into your eyes?'

'Willingly,' I said and grinned.

'You sham, you're not hurt at all. James your uncle is fibbing.'

James was standing still quite shocked and when I managed to sit up and look around me I noticed his expression. It was a mixture of fright and pain. I got up quickly and climbed back up to him and folded my arms around him. 'We're fine little fella. You're not hurt and it's all a bit of a shock.'

I knelt down in front of him and looked into his eyes. 'James, you in there? Everything is okay. You slipped a little in the mud and fell against Katya. Look, she's smiling. Nothing hurts does it? You only stumbled and didn't actually fall so we're all fine. Nobody's hurt and everything's okay. We're all safe.'

'I knocked Katya over Uncle Daniel. I didn't mean to. I just slipped.'

'I know James but no problem. See, Katya's not hurt. Let's all just sit down for a moment and have a breather? This slope is steep and the path is quite slippery with that mud.'

I looked up at Katya. 'Are you okay?' I mouthed. She nodded yes. I turned back to James.

'Shall we see what else I can find in my rucksack?' I rummaged around in my sack and found a couple of jube-jubes and a rather battered small chocolate Easter egg. 'Do you know what these are James?' I asked as I made an offer of my two finds.

'Can I have them please?'

'Would you like all of them? Do you know what this really is?'

'It's an Easter egg silly. Mummy always hides them all over the garden for me and we often come across one or two later in the summer. So this is a very late Easter egg Uncle Daniel, but I'll try it just the same. I bet it still tastes yummy.'

'Do you have any bumps or bruises James from your stumble or did I catch you before you hit the ground?'

'No just my arm where you held me before you dived over Katya. It looked very dramatic Uncle Daniel.'

I looked at James's face and quickly ran my hands up and down his body. There was no wincing or avoiding my touch and so I hoped that all was well. By now James's face was looking less frightened with chocolate spread around his mouth and he seemed happier. I stood up slowly, aching a little on my side and looked at Katya. 'Are you really okay? It all happened so quickly and I couldn't hold up James and catch you before you rolled over. Then I couldn't stop you falling and had to leap over you so as not to do any more damage. Fortunately the ground is pretty soft and the clumps of heather cushioned my fall but are you unhurt Katya?'

'Daniel I'm fine, I really am. Sure I've probably got a couple of bruises and some dirt over my clothes but otherwise I'm not hurt Daniel. What about you? You seem to be holding that wrist?'

'I suppose I fell on it at a funny angle when I rolled in mid flight to land on my shoulder rather than my face. I think it's in one piece, perhaps just a sprain. James appears less frightened now I have distracted his mind. Let's walk and that will minimise any memory.'

I turned to James with his happy chocolate-smeared face. 'How about we have a little drink and then I'll wipe most of the excess chocolate off your cheeks James? Can we manage that?'

'Sure. This egg tastes good. Can I have the jube-jubes next?'

We cleaned ourselves up a little and set off slowly down the rest of the hill into Porthmeor Cove. It was getting on for lunchtime and I thought the best place to try and see Samantha and Evelyn would be from the headland across the cove rather than the less safe top of the main cliff. With Katya leading again we slowly walked up the hillside until we found a good spot to view the cliff.

'How about lunch here James? Perhaps I can find some real food other than just sweets.'

'As long as it's not that cat food Uncle Daniel. What did you say they were called, pulkins, like those serrydenos? In a can but really only for cats. Ugh, tastes horrid. Katya won't like them either. Will you Katya?'

'Hold up there James. First I think you mean pilchards rather than pulkins or whatever and they are rather like sardines being small fish in a can. But no they are not cat food, and, most importantly, we don't have any and so we'll never know whether Katya likes them or not shall we?'

'Good. I'll have peanut butter and jelly please.'

'Let's look and see what your mother hid in these boxes shall we? She did this last night James and I'm not sure what your mother eventually gave us but we'll open them and see.'

I winced a little as I twisted the top off the plastic sandwich boxes Samantha had prepared and Katya noticed what happened. 'That hurts,' she said.

'Just a little. Perhaps I'll bind it up after lunch. Can you open the box for me though and I'll see what else we've got buried away in this rucksack. Here James, here's a coat to sit on so you're not on the damp cold ground. Are you warm enough or do you want another sweater?'

'Where's mummy?'

While Katya was looking in the lunch boxes I did a quick scan of the cliff opposite. There were a couple of ropes on the cliff and I looked for the colours of Samantha and Evelyn. I couldn't see them and so I turned back to James. 'Not obviously in sight James but let's have lunch and relax a little. You had a good walk this morning. You did really well.'

'Do you miss it Daniel? Do you miss climbing, or perhaps I should ask do you still do it?'

'On and off Katya but I haven't had much time over the last couple of years what with the Estate. I suppose I've been out maybe two or three times a year but come to think of it I haven't climbed at all this year. In some ways I do miss it because it can give you a real high, a real adrenaline rush but then I can get a similar and perhaps safer kind of rush on the golf course. Climbing is mentally good, leastways it was for me. I never had a super strong physique and so I learnt to climb like most people with my head. Dad was really good about that. He taught me to climb within myself, and, more importantly to think about the moves and the climb in total. Mum's always been fairly fit and she's neat, flexible and her power-weight ratio is excellent. She also has rather long arms which really helps her as she's short overall. In contrast my dad was a typical middle of the road kind of guy and he found he had to climb with his head or he wouldn't be able to keep up with mum. You should watch Samantha climb though because she thinks dad was an excellent teacher. She still climbs with exactly the same routine and approach she learned as a beginner. Sure she does it automatically now and she's really good but when you see her you can almost hear her thinking before a move or a sequence of moves. Actually she's a delight to watch but she does make it appear so easy. I did enjoy it in a way but never like Samantha did, or Michael for that matter.'

'But didn't Michael push too hard, climb a little dangerously?'

'Usually. I can remember climbing with my cousin Henri, a long time ago now when I was still a young teenager. Henri was much older than me and already a really good climber, although not as good as his

140

parents had been. They had been super climbers but Henri was still good. Anyway Henri took me climbing a couple of times and warned me about Michael and his rather aggressive attitude. Henri also taught me a little more about safety and climbing with people you trust.'

'But you did trust Michael, and your eldest brother Geoffrey? I thought you had told me that Geoffrey was quite conservative, rather a plodder I think you said. Peter isn't like that though Daniel. Peter is quite a livewire and a leader when he has to be. He certainly steers his mother when she gets a little emotional.'

Checking that James was now deeply engrossed in his peanut-butter and jelly sandwich I looked up at Katya and nodded. 'Peter is fine. He's growing up really well given what has happened and yes I did trust Geoffrey. I even trusted Michael that day in Wales when we had the accident but unfortunately it all went pear-shaped. That did put me off climbing for a long time, over a year in fact before I went back on the cliffs again. Even then I started back on some small easy climbs that I could have got up in my sleep.'

'But as you just said Daniel, a lot of it is mental and that was what was important, the mental challenge to go back on the cliffs again. Oh look at James!'

We had both been rather engrossed in our conversation and not noticed that James had succeeded in smearing his peanut-butter from one ear to the other and over a large area of his sweater.

'It sort of slipped Uncle Daniel. I was watching the sea-gull swooping and my sandwich sort of slipped. I think the sea-gull would like peanut butter though. Can I feed him? He looks really hungry. He has those beady eyes. Why are the other ones brown and white? Are they gulls too? They look like gulls with that sharp beak. They've got beady eyes as well.'

'First things first James. Let's try and move some of the food back towards your mouth area from the other parts of your body. That's better. Now, gulls? The brown and white ones are young herring gulls. As they grow older they gradually become grey and white and look like their parents. And finally, yes I'm sure they will like peanut butter because they will eat virtually anything.'

'No pelicans Daniel?'

'No Katya, not round here anyway. I don't think we have pelicans in England at all but we do have another funny-looking bird. Look, there's one now with that large multi-coloured beak. The small bird, well smaller than the gulls here but with the rainbow beak. Do you know what they are James?'

'I've never seen a bird like that Uncle Daniel. Do they carry things in that beak?'

'Well they eat fish James and they are called puffins.'

'Neat. Is there pudding?'

I delved deeper into my rucksack and found one of James's favourites: a sort of pudding cup thing that was a mixture of custard-like semi-liquid mixed with fruit. Inside one of the rucksack pockets I found a spoon that I licked clean as I wasn't sure exactly what else had been in the pocket with the spoon. While James shovelled contentedly from cup to mouth I looked for some bandage. I usually carry a small waterproof zippered bag of first-aid items and inside this I pulled out an elastic bandage. I was about to hand it over to Katya to strap around my wrist when she suddenly stood up and cried out, 'there they are Daniel, just coming over the top of the cliff now. Look, they've stopped and seem to be sorting out their ropes. What are they going to do?'

I put the bandage down and looked back in the sack for my binoculars. James continued very seriously scraping the last remnants of his pudding from the plastic cup onto the edge of the spoon and carefully transferring the slight smears into his mouth. I focussed on Samantha and Evelyn.

'Looks like they're arranging an abseil. They'll throw the two ropes down and then slide down them to the bottom of the cliff to start the climb.'

'And then climb back up the ropes?'

'No, when they are safely down at the bottom of the climb, probably just above the reach of the waves they will pull the ropes down and then climb back up again.'

'Well why pull the ropes down then if you're going to climb back up again? Isn't it easier to climb up the ropes?'

'Katya imagine if they came to the foot of the cliff by boat, across the water and landed at the bottom. Then, in order to get to the top they have to climb up the cliff. Think of doing it that way which is the more normal way you see people rock climb. It all looks a little weird here because you start at the top of the cliff but that is what is different about sea cliff climbing. Normally we walk up the mountain side to reach the bottom of the cliff.'

'So how do they use the ropes?'

'Watch. James, can you see mummy over there in her red anorak with Evelyn in yellow? See, no more to the right. Follow my finger, now see them?'

'I see them. Mummy!!! Mummy!!!'

'James they can't hear you from this distance, not with the wind and the noise of the waves. We can just watch and I'll tell you what they are doing. See they are now both at the bottom of the cliff just above the water and your mother is looking back up the cliff to see where she will climb.'

'Will she fall off?'

'No James, your mother will not fall off. Watch what she does with the rope. See she has tied it to herself and Evelyn is holding it.'

The three of us sat and watched Samantha climb neatly and steadily up the cliff across the water placing her protection and continuously looking up the line of the climb. I explained to Katya and James that Evelyn was making sure that the rope ran out carefully with no jerks or knots. I didn't explain how Evelyn could safeguard Samantha if she fell off because James didn't need to know about his mother even thinking of falling off. After running out a long first pitch Samantha belayed in what looked like a very dramatic position on the cliff face and she took in the small amount of slack down to Evelyn.

'See how your mother takes in the rope and safeguards Evelyn James. The two climbers are joined together by the rope and protect each other. Only one climbs at a time and the other climber is safely tied to the cliff. If you do it properly it can be very safe as well as very exciting. Just look where they are on that very steep cliff face.' Seen face on across the water the cliff looked steeper than it actually was.

'So if Evelyn slips Daniel the rope protects her from falling very far?'

'Right, and that is why the leader is usually the stronger of the two climbers. But watch when Evelyn joins Samantha. If they both think they can do the climb Evelyn may pass Samantha and take over as the leader. That is called leading through and can speed up the process. If Evelyn finds it is too difficult then she will stop where Samantha is and tie herself to the cliff and Samantha will go on again in front. You and your partner sort all this out as you climb.'

'But how does Samantha know she can climb this cliff at all Daniel? How does she know either of them can climb it? What happens if neither of them can climb it?'

'My mummy can climb anything. She's good, isn't she Uncle Daniel?'

I put my arm over James's shoulders and hugged him closely. Leaning over to his head I whispered in his ear, 'yes James, your mummy's very good but let me answer Katya's question.'

'Okay, but she is good.'

'Coming back to your questions Katya you remember my guidebook for the coast path and you read out the words "Grade: Severe"? Well, Samantha has a guidebook for all of the climbing routes here at Bosigran. After a route is climbed for the first time the leader will give the climb a name and suggest a grade of difficulty for the climb. He or she will also write up a brief description of where the route goes and how to find the start. They may also add anything that is special about the climb, like the start is likely to be wet at very high tides or the top is very loose, something like that.'

'So Samantha reads this book and decides which climbs she can do?'

'Yes, in a way but she reads it with Evelyn and they both decide which routes they would both like to do. Routes that they both will enjoy. As I said before it is a team thing. But yes Samantha will know she can climb routes up to a certain level as can Evelyn and they will pick routes that they both can do or expect they can do. You never really know until you rub your nose on the rock. The climbing grades are a suggestion not an absolute like a golf handicap.'

'So before they started to slide down the ropes they both knew that one or both of them could climb back up again?'

'Yes.'

'But what about the first person? The person who did it the first time ever. How did they know they would get up? How did they know where to go if they had no picture or photo or anything? It would be a bit like playing golf and standing on the tee box not knowing where the green was and whether there was any fairway or any hazards.'

I laughed. 'It's not a fair analogy but it is similar. The first time someone does a climb they literally go looking for somewhere no one has been before. The first person ever to climb on this cliff would sit down where we are now and look across at the cliff and see where he thought he could go from the bottom to the top. Then they would walk over to the place they thought they could start and try climbing upwards. After you've been climbing for a while you learn how to look at the cliff face and see ways up. Some ways are easy and some are hard. After a while there would be several routes already on this cliff and so to find a new climb, a new route you have to look between the existing climbs where it is harder to get from the bottom to the top. I imagine the route that Samantha and Evelyn are on right now is hard and was only climbed recently, say in the last five years whereas some of the easiest climbs here go back to the sixties or maybe even the fifties.'

'But you still haven't told me how the first person can get up. What if they can't?'

'On a normal cliff, not a sea cliff, if you can't get up you climb back down and walk away. It's just too difficult for you. Or, when you get stuck you look and see whether you can go sideways and find an easier line. For example, look where Samantha is now.'

At this stage Samantha had climbed up above Evelyn but the overhanging face had made her traverse sideways some thirty feet and she had paused looking upwards. 'See, Samantha couldn't continue straight up and so the route goes left and now she is seeing whether she can continue upwards. If she can't she will continue to look further left.'

'Is there any more pudding Uncle Daniel?'

James brought me back to our immediate surroundings. 'James, shall we have a big search inside this magic sack and see what else I have here?'

'Yes let's.'

'Fine. Then you reach inside and carefully pull things out one by one. We'll lay them here above this rock so they can't roll down the hill. Can you do that for me?'

'She's moving up again Daniel, but she's left something hanging below the rope. It's sort of pulling on the rope but she's climbing on.'

'Yes, she's fine Katya. Carefully now James or we'll have everything everywhere. Just one at a time please.'

In the next thirty minutes Samantha and Evelyn successfully finished their climb, Katya was amazed at where they had been and James and I thoroughly emptied and investigated the entire contents of my rucksack. The latter exercise convinced James that there was no more pudding and he was about to protest when Samantha came jogging up the hillside. She grabbed James up off the grass and swung him around in a violent circle while he shrieked with delight.

'Careful Samantha, he's full of peanut-butter, jam, sweets and fruit cup.'

'My little vacuum cleaner,' laughed Samantha.

Evelyn plonked herself down on the grass beside us and dropped her climbing gear. 'Daniel your sister is a fabulous climber. She really did some great leads today. The cliff was wonderful. What did we do Samantha, "Doorpost", "Little Brown Jug", "Anvil Chorus" and whatever that last climb was called?'

'How hard Evelyn? I was telling Katya here about each climb having a name and being graded.'

'Severe, VS, HVS I think.'

'Katya, that mean hard, very hard in fact, nearly at the top of the scale. Like a scratch golfer.'

'But you make it all look so easy from here,' Katya said.

'You should come out on the rope Katya and you'll see I didn't find it easy at all. In fact on the last climb I wasn't sure I could make a couple of the moves but your sister Daniel can be very persuasive. She doesn't take any hanging about from her seconds.'

'Evelyn you did fabulously, you really did. It was a great day and we both had a blast.'

'Uncle Daniel had a blast Mummy. He dived over Katya. He looked really fine but he hurt his wrist. I didn't get hurt at all, neither did Katya. Perhaps Uncle Daniel got a blast too?'

'Daniel?'

'It's nothing Samantha. James tripped and slid a little coming down the hill. It was a mite muddy and slippery so I grabbed James but he had slid into Katya. I got James upright and leapt to catch Katya but she caught herself and I had to dive over her to stop crashing into her. I just rolled a little and turned my wrist the wrong way. James is fine, although a little muddy. The brown around his face is chocolate not mud by the way. But you obviously had a great day and the weather has been brilliant. We had a good walk and James did exceptionally well. We were right up on the top of Rosemergy cliff and could see a long way south towards Pendeen. Katya was all set to walk to Lands End but we didn't think we would get back in time and so we left it for another day.'

'Sure Daniel, Lands End indeed, still I'm glad James had a good walk.'

'We managed to feed him most of that time too Samantha,' added Katya. 'I think he has finished all of Daniel's emergency food supplies as well as the regular lunch.'

'And the gulls really like peanut butter Mummy. I fed them, even though they have beady eyes.'

We lingered a little longer just sitting on the hillside watching another pair of climbers on the cliff and the endless motion of the waves. Katya wrapped the elastic bandage around my wrist which had swollen a little and was still painful if I tried to twist it. We'll have to see what it's like tomorrow I thought.

We dropped Evelyn off in the village on the way home and it was four tired, dirty, dishevelled bodies that slowly clambered out of the car soon after six o'clock that evening. I had driven most of the way home and my wrist had seized up a little with the more or less fixed position for driving. We traipsed into the hall and suddenly Samantha gave a muffled shriek. 'Terence, that's Terence's car in the driveway. Oh God I forgot. What time is it? Shit, he must be here already.'

My mother appeared in the hall and looked quickly at each of us before turning her eyes back to Samantha. 'Yes Samantha dear, Terence is here as you invited him for six o'clock. A quiet drink and a chat before dinner I think you said. Looking at you…'

'Hello Samantha,' butted in Terence, 'I think I'm a little early but your parents have been most gracious and delighted me with their company and a quiet drink. Your mother told me to expect you when I see you and I must say you do look, well quite how shall I say, alive perhaps, exuberant?'

My mother laughed and threading her arm through Terence's she wheeled him back into the drawing room. 'We'll see you when we see you,' she chuckled.

'James, up those stairs young man and let's get cleaned up toute suite. Forgive me Katya but in all the excitement of today I quite forgot.'

'Who'd you'd invited to dinner,' I added. 'I think all of us might benefit from soap and water actually Samantha. Even dad might wrinkle his nose after today's exertions.'

The dart's match was in full swing when John pushed open the door to the pub. A waft of hot air full of beer fumes, smoke, and supporters' comments rolled across his face as he walked in. He looked around and nodded at a few faces.

'Pint please George. How's the game going?'

'Think we're beating them but it's more noise than talent from what I can see lad. Perhaps they should 'ave kept you on the team like. You always were a dab hand with an arrow.'

'Pretty fast with the knife too eh Ferris?'

'Shut yer mouth Freddie afore I shut it for yer.'

George leaned over his bar. 'Freddie, any more comments like that son and I'll bar you. Just go back to your mates in the corner there and keep your mouth buttoned up. John here's done you no harm.'

'We'll have four more pints George and then perhaps I'll button it. Just surprised you serve his type in here George, bloody scousers.'

'Here Freddie, take these over to your mates but it'll cost you twelve quid first son.' George handed over a tray with the four pints to Freddie who glared at John Ferris and then walked his order back to his mates in the corner. Several laughs and comments wafted back towards the bar.

'Don't mind that lot John. Freddie has always had it in for you but that was because your dad never let up on him when he was a kid. Your dad didn't make many friends you know and you're unfortunately reaping the scorn and abuse.'

'Don't I know it George, but your right, my dad was an idle bugger and never could get on the right side of people. He always had this chip on his shoulder as if life had treated him badly from the get-go. Christ, enough other people have had to struggle in their lives but dad never saw it that way. It was always someone else's fault.'

'Keep your head up John. You'll come out of this okay. Most of us here in the village think you've done some good things over the past eight years, what with marrying Betty and settling down with the kids like. You've all pulled your weight. Done things to help in the village. Most of us think what you did was right. It's just a bloody shame it had to end up the way it did. Do you know why Idwal decided to come back here? We all know Enrico had nothing to do with your dad's death so why did he come back?'

'George I really don't know. When he first arrived it really puzzled me. We were in here that first night and he kept going on about getting revenge, how he'd been thinking about it all the time inside but I got the feeling that was just an excuse. Even when we went to the cottage the next day he didn't make any big effort to find Enrico just vandalise the cottage. Then he went kind of crazy.'

'There was a rumour that he met Miss Samantha up there in Enrico's cottage.'

'Don't know about that George but he was muttering that night down here in the pub about gardening. Now Idwal has never done any gardening or anything in the garden in his whole life. All he ever did in our garden was piss in it.'

'I agree with you. I can't see your brother doing any gardening either. What else did he say?'

'Can't remember really. He was rambling on about life inside and how long he had been nursing this grudge and wanting revenge. He did ask about Florence Whelks though. Asked whether she still lived here.'

'Old Flo' Whelks. Whatever would Idwal be doing with Florrie Whelks? She's as crazy as all get-out. Nobody ever sees her. Whatever things she ever wants people get for her. I don't think she has left that cottage of hers for years. And her garden looks like a jungle so that couldn't have been where Idwal was thinking.'

'Has she always been like that George? I don't seem to remember her when I first got work here.'

'No you wouldn't would you? She went a little crazy when her younger son Phil ran away to sea. I heard he ended up in Australia. You must have come after that. Then of course she became even weirder when Larry got killed.'

'How do you know that Freddie?'

We hadn't noticed that Freddie had come back to the bar with his empty tray looking for refills.

'My old gran' used to know Florence Whelks back twenty or more years ago. She was quite lively then but wham bam she loses Phil and her other son Larry starts a life of petty crime. Shut up shop she did. Closed the door and wouldn't see anyone, even my gran'. She turned even worse when Larry got killed. Actually Ferris I think your brother had something to do with all that too. He was a friend of Larry's if I remember right. Well they did some business together at least.'

'You leave my brother out of this Freddie. Just shut your mouth about my family.'

'Freddie, I thought I told you to button it. Do you want any more pints or did you just come over here to cause trouble?'

Before Freddie could answer the room erupted with loud shouts and cheers as the dart's match ended and a swarm of players and lookers-on swarmed over to the bar. John took his pint away to a window seat and sat and thought about what had been said. Fuck you Idwal, why did you really come back?

The dining room conversation bounced around the room sometimes between couples and sometimes embracing the whole table. James intervened with unexpected comments when there was any break in the voices. Waving his custard-laden spoon he startled us all with a loud exclamation of 'my Uncle Daniel went diving today but I didn't give him very high marks. Mummy was much better.'

This inevitably led to an explanation of my bandaged wrist, the slide down the hillside and my efforts at keeping the party safe. Terence was interested in what we had all done today and was quite surprised to hear that his WPC Nicols had been out climbing with Samantha.

'Seems I might know something about your staff that you don't,' she teased.

James reasserted himself to make sure everyone understood that WPC Nicols was his friend, although he let mummy climb with her today while he went walking with his other special friend.

I suppose I still felt a little uneasy sitting at the dinner table with Terence Field. I couldn't get away from the fact that he was Detective Inspector Field and had been the investigating officer in all of the events that had taken place here in the last two weeks. Seeing as how Inspector Field didn't know the whole story and I did I felt a little uncomfortable about how to act. I tried not to keep glancing at Samantha every time she spoke but I was never certain what my sister might say. She had a dangerous habit of speaking first and thinking afterwards and she too knew more things than were good for her. It didn't help when Katya suddenly asked 'why was Idwal Ferris gone so long from the village if his brother was here all that time? Where had Idwal gone?'

The table went a little quiet and we all sort of looked at Terence. I could see he was thinking how best to answer Katya when Samantha jumped in with, 'he was in gaol Katya, in gaol for all that time.'

This could have been the end of it but Katya muttered under her breath, 'must have been something serious to be in gaol for seven or eight years,' and Samantha who was sitting next to her heard this and she said, 'yes,' and looked at Terence.

Terence had obviously decided to explain some of this story as he saw that both mum and dad were also looking at him with expressions that said answer please, it affects us all.

'Okay, a brief answer seeing as how it affects all of this family. As far as I can learn Idwal Ferris killed a man in Bristol. At the trial it appeared that there was some business deal going on between Ferris and his partner with a well-known family of villains in Bristol. The partner knew this family in Bristol and Ferris and the partner had something to sell to the group. Somehow Ferris got double-crossed, or thought he had been double-crossed and the family told him and Ferris ended up killing his so-called partner. It was fairly obvious who had killed this partner and the jury found Ferris guilty of manslaughter so he got eight years. End of story.'

There were too many unanswered questions but I thought this was not the time or place to pursue them and so I turned to Katya and said, 'so that's why he was away from the village for so long and now all we have to worry about is what happens to John Ferris.'

'And his family,' added my mother.

'Well you can all help his family,' said cook as she came in with two pies. 'I've taken the liberty Mrs. Lord of buying two of Betty Ferris's pies for dinner this evening. She's a lovely lass is Betty and I know she makes a wonderful pie so I thought I'd help out with her family. One's blackberry and the other's rhubarb. I'm sure you'll like them both. I might make pies Mrs. Lord as you well know but Betty Ferris has the touch so she does. Enjoy them.'

154

SUNDAY HURT

I STOOD ON THE FIRST tee-box and took a couple of practice swings. My wrist still hurt and I had kept the elastic bandage on.

'Every Sunday Daniel you come with a new gimmick to help you win. Last week you brought your lovely caddie here and distracted all of us. This Sunday I see you have some imagined injury and we're all supposed to feel sorry for you. Well tough luck my friend. You battle like the rest of us poor mortals.'

'Sure Larry. Hi Peter, hi Alan. You remember Katya?'

'How could we forget last Sunday Daniel, especially with all that good advice your caddie gave you? Good morning Katya, it's good to see you again.'

'Morning Peter, morning Alan.'

'Good morning to you too Katya. How can I persuade you to carry my bag today instead of Daniel's?'

After nine holes the mood had changed a little. My wrist seemed to be affecting my swing and I was not getting much length off the tee. More importantly I had little feel for any short wedge shots and my score reflected my quality of play. I was five over par. Katya kept quiet and just handed me clubs. On one of the chip shots she had handed me a putter as a possible alternative but I elected to chip and afterwards wished I hadn't.

I finished the eighteenth hole with a par but the overall score was a disappointing four over. Larry had played really well and was one under par. 'Looks like the wrist really is a bit of a bummer there Daniel.'

'Maybe Larry, or maybe this is just not my day. You know what golf's like? Anyway chaps, I'm going to love you and leave you as Katya and I have some urgent things to do this afternoon and she has to get back to Oxford so we'll see you all next Wednesday. Bye for now.'

'Bye,' said Katya, and she carried my clubs back to the car.

Once we were inside and ready to go Katya turned and asked, 'you feeling okay Daniel? Was it your wrist today or do I get in the way? I tried to be quiet.'

I leaned over and gently held her chin in my hand. I lifted up her lips and softly kissed her. 'You were perfect Katya and I love being with you. You are a wonderful caddie and I missed two opportunities because I wouldn't take the club you suggested so it was my mistake, but no I'm feeling fine. I am a little bruised from my swan dive yesterday and the wrist does ache, especially on wedge shots as you saw but overall I'm really happy to be with you.' I kissed her again and a loud banging on the window made me look up. Larry was grinning down at us. I rolled down the window.

'I thought you had some urgent things to do this afternoon Daniel, or perhaps this was the urgent thing? Well good luck to the pair of you. Bye.'

We laughed and I started the engine and drove home.

Terence had stayed overnight and somewhat surprisingly he had not been summoned anywhere with an urgent telephone call. He and Samantha had been driving round the forest this morning and over much of the lunch time Samantha was explaining what they had seen. Terence Field was obviously more a city person than someone from the country and he was quite interested in all the things Samantha was explaining.

'It's a whole different world out there,' he said, 'and I could get lost quite easily as nearly all those trees look the same. What amazed me was Samantha telling me the history of all the different blocks of trees.'

'She can spin a good story can my sister,' I said, 'especially when her audience wouldn't know whether she's got it right or not.'

'I had a good teacher the same as you did Daniel, two good teachers actually, Antonio and Enrico. They were always really good to us kids and we all spent a lot of time down at their cottage.'

'It used to be one of my sister's favourite hiding places when there had been a battle royal with my mother.'

'Really Daniel,' Sylvia said, 'you make it sound as if there were continual fights here.'

'Fortunately Mum your dearly beloved daughter was in Europe for much of the time so the battles were mostly during the holidays.'

'What about when I was at University brother dear, at jolly old Cambridge?'

'Samantha when you were at University the discussions here were not battles but simple differences of opinion between two ladies and as a gentleman I will not even mention those. Let's just say we all knew when you were here at Fotheringham. But yes Terence, Samantha and I did get a really good grounding on the history of the woodlands from Antonio and Enrico.'

'And when they had their heads full of silviculture and the delights of forest operations I would bring them down to earth with the bottom line. Isn't that true Anthony?'

'Yes Sylvia dear, you were never very romantic about the forest but you sure knew where the costs went.'

'And the revenues Anthony, remember the revenues? Talking of revenues Katya have you had any more ideas how we can charge for experiencing the delights of Fotheringham?'

'Er no Sylvia, not really. I've been too busy with trying to make some good arguments based upon data from my father's company in Florida. I'm starting to wonder whether the financial figures my dad's boss gave me are really the truth. I'm a little suspicious about some of his costs.'

Terence was looking a little perplexed and I suddenly realised that Samantha hadn't told him much about Katya's background or her fathers. I turned to Katya and asked her to tell Terence why she was here at Oxford and what her father did.

After a brief explanation Katya continued with the previous question from my mother.

'So Sylvia's quite inquisitive to see whether I can find some commercial but green sources of revenue from the forest here. I'm trying to have the forest become more natural, less man-made so to speak and yet still pay its way.'

'It looked pretty wild to me,' said Terence, 'apart from the forest rides of course. Most of them are so straight.'

'See there's an example of how to change things. Gradually we could let the rides become more twisty and less artificial-looking.'

'Now that would take the forest back over one hundred years or even more,' my dad said. 'The straight lines came from the days of hunting, for deer down here. Sitting on your horse you could watch from a junction and see whether the deer crossed from one compartment to the next as your beaters flushed them out. If the rides had not been straight you wouldn't be able to see very far.'

'And the deer would have had a fairer chance.'

'Now who said life was supposed to be fair? It's dog eat dog out there in the wild. But I suppose it is the same on the streets too isn't it Terence?

Mankind is just another animal and the rules don't change just because we've turned the trees into wooden walls?'

'True enough Anthony, and life on the streets is anything but fair. Still, I must say that being out in your woodlands is a much better breath of fresh air than some of the streets I have to visit.'

'This is great Enrico. It's really awesome being out here in the forest. It's so different from where I grew up in London.'

'Well Tony you are right. Here in the forest the trees breathe in some of the pollution and city gases and breathe out oxygen. It's healthy being out here in the forest.'

'That's right Tony,' Peter added, 'the trees sort of suck up carbon dioxide I think and change it into something else inside the leaves. What comes out as Enrico says is oxygen for you and I to breathe. It's like a great big oxygen producing factory so breathe deeply. Come on Tony let's run and breathe even deeper.'

The two boys ran ahead as they walked through the forest to Enrico's cottage.

'Do you really live out here Enrico? This is neat. It's so quiet. Can we come in?'

'Let me go in first please Tony. I haven't been in here since I came to your mother's Peter, over a week ago now. Sir Anthony and young Master Daniel said they had cleaned up after the disturbance here but I would like to go in first.'

'Of course Enrico. It is your cottage.'

Enrico pushed open the back door and walked into his kitchen. As I had promised it was clean and tidy but virtually empty. Most of the furniture had been smashed to pieces along with much of the crockery.

The foodstuffs that had been strewn and smeared all over the floor and walls had been washed away and it was clean.

'Come in, come in you two. I'm just going to look further into the other rooms but come in.'

Enrico continued on into the bathroom and the two bedrooms. Here there was a little more furniture and the floors were swept and everything looked tidy but empty.

'All of your carvings are gone Enrico,' said Peter. 'You used to have several of them on the kitchen dresser but that has gone too.'

'Your Uncle Daniel said there were some bits and pieces up in the shed by the forest office,' said Enrico. 'They saved some items for me to look at in case I thought I could repair them or even restore them. Perhaps some of the carvings are up there too Peter. We might look later in the week. Still it's home, it's clean and tidy but it is a little empty right now, like I feel. Perhaps I might sit down for a minute. Peter can you find me a stool or something please?'

'Sure Enrico. Come on Tony let's find something for Enrico.'

The two boys rushed around and managed to find the serviceable remains of an old stool which Peter triumphantly carried back into the kitchen. 'Here Enrico, sit on this. We think it's safe.'

Enrico carefully lowered himself onto the stool and clasped his carved walking stick in his gnarled hands in front of him. 'Made a mess I heard, quite a mess. Now who's that I hear?'

I had driven up in the Landrover with Katya and we climbed out just as Tony and Peter came running out of the back door. 'Hello you two. Are you with Enrico? He said he might come down here this afternoon. Is he okay?'

'Yes Uncle Daniel, he's just sitting down and looking around his rather empty kitchen. There's hardly anything left in there, although the bedroom still has a bed in it. It must have been a dreadful mess.'

'Yes Peter it was. We cleared up as best we could but there were a lot of things broken and smashed beyond repair.'

'Did some of the carvings survive? I've been telling Tony about some of the carvings.'

'Yes, there are some we found and we took them up to the office. Talking of carvings has Enrico finished your footballer yet Tony?'

'Yes Uncle Daniel and it's smashing. It looks really lifelike and I've started to paint it, with some help from Enrico of course.'

Katya and I accompanied the boys back into the kitchen and we greeted Enrico. 'Just come to see what's left Master Daniel. I thank you for cleaning up and clearing away what must have looked pretty horrible.'

'Enrico the chaps on the crew were only too happy to try and make your cottage look liveable again. They all worked really hard but unfortunately most things were past fixing. I did have Bob Edwards pick out some of the items that might be special to you or might be important and put them by up in the office Enrico. As Peter was asking I know there are some of the carvings still there.'

'I will come and look tomorrow Master Daniel. You will be in the office?'

'Yes, sure Enrico. I'll be there. Anything you want moved we'll put it in the lorry and bring it down again.'

'It would be good to have some carvings back. Good so I can show young Tony here. Eh Tony?'

'Yes Enrico that would be awesome.'

'Are you all going back to Home Farm now Peter?'

'Actually Master Daniel I was thinking of walking with Tony and Peter to the Ferris cottage and make my peace with John. I have always liked John and I would like to make sure he knows how I feel. Would that be acceptable Master Daniel? Is John settled now?'

I stood and thought about Enrico's question. Sunday afternoon, I wondered what state of mind John Ferris might be in. 'Yes Enrico, I think that would be fine but just look at John first before you get too involved. He is lonely and feeling a lot hard done by so watch how he is. Just be a little careful with Peter and Tony although I think having the two youngsters with you will be a good idea. You are all going?'

'Yes Uncle Daniel, we were all going to go. I was sort of a showing Tony around more of the forest and when Enrico said he wanted to see his cottage I thought it was a good idea to come out too. Mr. Ferris must be really lonely out here on his own, especially after he was used to having his family with him.'

'You're right Peter. Go slowly and be rather quiet around John Ferris. Don't remind him too much that he hasn't got Katey and little Paul out here with him. Can you do that for me?'

'Sure Uncle Daniel. We'll be what do you say, sensitive about it. Is that right?'

I smiled as I said, 'right on Peter, good lad. Fine, take care the three of you and Katya and I will continue our own exploration of Fotheringham forest. See you later Enrico?'

'Yes tomorrow. Bye Master Daniel.'

We got back in the Landrover and I continued deeper into the forest.

'Can we revisit the "you know where" Daniel?' asked Katya. 'I want to see whether I can find any more of those grubby coins.'

We bounced off from Enrico's cottage and I grunted as an unexpected tree root made the front wheels jerk and my wrist told me all was not well.

'You should check that wrist out with the doctor Daniel. Have an x-ray at least. You might have broken something and not just be a sprain.'

162

I glanced over at Katya and saw the serious and concerned look on her face and so I refrained from some facetious comment I was about to make. 'Sure,' was all I said and drove on looking a little more carefully at the surface of the forest ride.

It didn't take long to reach the top of the compartment and the northern edge of the forest. As usual we walked along the foot of the escarpment and then scrambled down the last little steep bit to the old tree and entrance slot of the cave.

'I didn't bring a torch Katya. Did you want to go in the cave again?'

'No Daniel. We found that coin when I caught my foot in a root of this old tree so I wanted to look around outside.'

'Given this was a crime scene some eight years ago I would have imagined it was searched pretty thoroughly, especially as they were looking for a bullet.'

'That's true Daniel. I wonder how they missed the coin I dug up. Do you have something we can scrape around the roots? See whether there's anything else under the dirt?'

'No not really. Look, let's think for a moment rather than just dig about. If this area was thoroughly searched back then how come we managed to find the coin last week? Where might that coin have come from? What are the alternatives?'

'The first and most obvious Daniel is that someone dropped it here in the meantime and so there won't necessarily be any others. Sort of end of story.'

'True, that's one possibility but the other extreme is that it was buried before the tree was this big and quite by chance you kicked it loose. Wind, storms whatever caused the roots to move about and lift your coin towards the surface and your foot did the rest.'

'So we could dig around in the roots then?'

'Yes but what if the coin fell down from the tree, or even fell down from somewhere on this cliff? We've never looked up you know. I suppose everyone's always thought any treasure there might be was buried in the ground or even in the cave with that "X" on my old map. It's possible that "X" was just a marker and not the actual final site.'

'Now that's sort of stretching the mindset of people back over a hundred years ago Daniel. Do you think they were that devious? I always thought that "X" marked the spot.'

'I suppose it depends who did what and under what circumstances. If the treasure was that hot I might be tempted to be a little crafty. Trouble is they may have been more crafty than we think and there is nothing here at all. Whatever there might have been is somewhere else or been found long ago.'

'Well I found that one coin last week Daniel and I'm going to look for more. If we've nothing to dig with how about your other suggestion that it fell off the cliff or out of this old tree? Wasn't it a forked tree in your old map? A hole in the fork would be a simple place to hide something and would be easy to remember for the person who hid it. The "X" in the cave could then be a misleading marker as you suggest. What do they say about trying to hide something? It's easier to hide something right in front of your eyes, out in the open so it's obvious but not obvious at the same time? Well in the fork of that tree in front of the cave is a possibility but before we look there can you see any other possibilities in the cliff above the cave's entrance?'

We stepped back a little from the foot of the cliff but the young trees of the plantation didn't let us go too far back and not lose a clear view of the cliff. I thrashed about in the trees trying to get a good look at the various faces of the cliff above us. The ground sloped downhill quite a lot and it was hard to be able to see very high but there was no obvious hole or cleft in the cliff face where you could easily hide something.

'I think your idea of the tree is the best one Katya. Some two hundred years ago it would have been much smaller and that fork is only some twelve or so feet off the ground so it wouldn't have been very hard to lift something heavy up that far with a couple of men. They may even have had a ladder or a rope ladder.'

'So, how are we going to reach up there? We don't have a ladder as you suggest.'

'Look, if I make a hold with my hands and you step from my hands to my shoulders you should be able to reach high enough up to find something to pull on around the scar where the fork was. You may even be able to pull yourself up to stand above the scar leaning against the stem that's still growing. The rest of the tree still looks healthy enough. Want to try?'

'How about your wrist?'

'Let's give it a try and I'll worry about my wrist if it hurts too much. You're pretty light and so we might be able to do this. Come on, I'll stand next to the trunk on the uphill side. That will give us another foot or so and the broken off piece is the uphill side anyway. Here, I'll make a stirrup with my two hands clasped together. Put your foot in there and your hands on my shoulders.'

I braced myself with my two feet placed apart and bent down with my hands locked together so that Katya could step up into my hands.

'Good, I can hold you there. Don't wriggle too much with your foot. Try and reach up with your hands smoothly up the bark and step your other foot on my shoulder. Yes, the uphill shoulder is safest. I still feel braced. Can you move more of your weight onto my shoulders? Ouch!'

Katya moved her right foot up onto my left shoulder but she half jumped and the sudden thrust down on my locked hands really strained the wrist again but now most of her weight was on my shoulder.

'Can you find anything to hold on with?' I grunted, hoping I wouldn't have to stand here much longer. Katya's left foot swung about in front of my face and I hoped she wouldn't get too excited. I reached up and put her left foot on my other shoulder.

'There, you more or less level now? Any better?'

'There's a hole in the tree Daniel. A hole where the fork used to be I suppose. There's nothing I can pull up on, it's all too smooth and slippery. Hold on a moment though I think I've found something.'

I could hear most of Katya's comments and some scrambling scuffling noises followed by 'shit, I've dropped it,' and a soft bump as something fell off the tree and landed near my feet. I couldn't look down to see it with Katya standing on my shoulders so I continued listening to her muttering above me.

'Daniel, there's nothing I can see and I can't get up any higher so I'm going to come down, slowly. Just watch my foot will you? I'll reverse how I got up.'

I managed to catch most of this and heard Katya's hands slide down the tree's trunk and felt her left foot slide off my shoulder and swing about in front of my face. I gently held her ankle and guided her foot into a cradle of my hands. Her hands reached down for my shoulders and her pelvis pressed itself against my face as she slowly lowered her weight onto the foot in my hands. She wriggled the right foot off my shoulder and reached her leg down towards the ground with her arms grasping my shoulders. When she was finally down I slid both arms around her waist and pulled her gently against me.

'That's taking advantage,' she whispered.

Very gently I rubbed my lips against hers and slid the tip of my tongue between her lips. She slowly opened her lips and I felt her teeth and then the soft tip of her tongue. Our lips continued to move very slowly over each others as our tongues slithered softly to and fro. I tightened my arms and moved my hands over her back and down over her buttocks. Katya moved the bottom half of her body against me and we both could feel the excitement building between us.

'Daniel, I dropped something. Something I found caught in the edge of the hole in the tree. I think it was another coin but I'm not sure. Can we find it before this goes any further?'

'Do you want it to go any further?'

'Yes Daniel, yes I do but I want to find that coin first and then find somewhere less rocky.'

I laughed gently and softly kissed her lips. 'Sure, let's find whatever you dropped and then find somewhere more comfortable.'

We separated and started looking on the ground. 'I heard it fall but couldn't see where Katya. Somewhere to my left I think. There was just one kind of light thump.'

'Yes Daniel, I only found one and I dropped it as I was getting it out of the edge of the bark. It was about the same size as the last coin I found but again it was all filthy and blackened so I'm not sure what it was.'

We searched about amongst the roots, the rocks, the moss and the dirt.

'Bingo,' cried Katya, 'I've found it. Look here Daniel, it's like the other coin I found. Well it will be when I've got it cleaned up.'

Katya slipped it quickly into the pocket of her trousers and almost leapt into my arms. I felt her warmth pressed up hard against me as she folded her arms around my neck and kissed me hard and passionately.

'Further Daniel, back by the car, further.'

An hour later I rolled over from lying on my back and looking up at the sky to gaze intently into Katya's eyes about six inches from mine. 'I should remember to put another blanket in the Landrover.'

Katya giggled. 'And an air mattress or something Daniel. These benchseat pads are cold vinyl.'

'I did offer to lie underneath.'

'I wanted to feel your weight on top of me love. The first time I wanted to feel you pressing hard on top of me Daniel. I wanted you to be in charge.' Katya shivered and I leaned forward and kissed her. 'We'd better get ourselves homewards before we freeze our buns off. I love you Katya Howard.' I kissed her again and put my clothes back on and helped Katya get organised.

The pale sunshine continued to sift through the leaves of the trees and reached the trio as they slowly walked along from Enrico's cottage to that of John Ferris. Golden tassels fluttered slightly on the slender branches of the larch trees. Bare stood the ash trees on the slight rise where the limestone rose up under the ground and came close to the soil's surface. Their grey green boles stood out stark against the washed out blue sky.

'It will be a while before they show you any new leaves,' said Enrico. 'They are the last tree to flush out in the spring. You'll see their flowers before you see their leaves but they're a grand tree for our limestone soils. They make nice and springy wood. Good for cricket bat handles Master Peter. You play cricket don't you?'

'Yes Enrico I do. I can bowl and bat of course. I can bowl googlies,' Peter added proudly.

'Googlies eh? Tell this old Italian who has never played cricket what a googlie is?'

'Well it's like this. When you bowl you can try and make the ball move sideways in the air and also try and make the ball bounce sideways off the ground. That way you fool the batsman, the hitter. Okay so far?'

'Yes, a little like bowling where you make the ball curve rather than go straight.'

'Right, well the ball has a seam and depending how you place your fingers over the seam you can make the ball move. I suppose it's like the bias on a wooden bowling ball, like they have on the green in the village. Anyway, the batsman can see how you hold the ball and work out whether it is an off break or a leg break and he can change how he is going to hit it.'

'And the googlie?'

'Let me describe the off-break and the leg-break first and we'll get to the googlie. For a right-handed batsman an off-break bounces from in front of you in towards the wicket, the stumps and you. It bounces from the batsman's right to left as he looks down the pitch. It bounces from the off-stump inwards. Now the leg break goes the other way. It is bowled almost behind you and tries to move sideways around your legs and catch the leg stump, so it bounces from your left to the right. I don't like leg breaks as I seem to get the timing wrong.'

'And the googlie?'

'Oh yes, well the googlie looks like a leg break the way the bowler holds the ball but in fact it bounces like an off break so it fools the batsman, but it's hard to hold the ball just right and flick the wrist to make it work. I can only do it some of the time but it's really neat when I get it right.'

'I'm sure it is Peter, and you Tony, do you play cricket?'

'Naw, I play football Enrico, always football.'

'Even in the summer?'

'In the summer I swim. We've got a pool in the local park and I swim in the summer time but mostly I play football. I've been teaching Peter here. We've been watching footie on the tele on Sundays as you know. Auntie Christina's been telling us what the players are saying. It's in Italian of course because it's Serie A on Sunday mornings.'

169

The three of them chatted amongst themselves as they quietly moved out of the ash compartment and through a darker avenue of beech trees.

'See how the trees here have kept their leaves for a while Tony? These are a different tree. Apart from the leaves can you notice any other differences?'

'It's a lot darker in there,' said Tony looking into the depths of the woodland, 'and there are no bushes or anything underneath. Is that because it's so dark and there's no light for anything else?'

'Well Peter, is he right?' asked Enrico.

'Good stuff Tony. You're right. These are beech trees and they keep their leaves longer and when they have all their leaves they shade out the light and so nothing gets to grow under a beech forest. What do you call them Enrico, are they shade-tolerant?'

'Very good Peter and the ash trees are light-demanders and they grow more openly and so other plants can grow beneath them.'

'So you know all these trees Peter?'

'Some Tony, or rather most of them but there are still some I'm not sure of. When I'm stumped I come and ask Enrico.'

'Or your Uncle Daniel Peter, Daniel knows all the trees. Ah here we are at John Ferris's cottage. Now keep rather quiet you two until we see what sort of a mood young John is in. There's smoke coming out of the chimney so he's at home. Wait here a moment while I check he's awake.'

Enrico left Peter and Tony on the edge of the clearing while he walked up to the back door. All sounded quiet within. 'John, John are you there? It's Enrico with the two boys from Mrs. Christina. Can we come in?'

Enrico heard a chair scrape over the floor, the sound of a glass plonked onto a table and dragging footsteps across the kitchen flagstones. John opened the door and peered out.

'Enrico, it's you. Sure sure you can all come in, not that there's much to come in for. Sure, bring the boys in. It'll be good to see some youngsters for a change. Can't see my own can I?'

Enrico stepped back so he could see Peter and Tony and waved them over.

'Come on in you two.'

The three of them trooped into John's kitchen and John clumsily staggered around to find chairs. The two boys sat on wooden chairs at the table and as Enrico had asked they kept quiet.

'Thought you might like to have some company John, and see some friendly faces. We've just been over to my cottage and tidied up a few things. I'm planning to move back in again some time soon so you'll have the chance of someone else close by if you ever need a chat or anything. It'll be good to be back in the woods don't you think?'

'I don't know I'm sure Enrico. I'm sitting out here in the woods when I'd sooner be in the village with Betty and the kids but that can't be can it?'

'That'll all get sorted out pretty soon John though. Have you had a chance to see Betty again after Mrs. Lord arranged that first meeting?'

'No Enrico and I do miss her, and the two kids of course. Would you two like a drink of something? I'm forgetting my manners but I might still have some lemonade somewhere. Would you two like a drink if I can find it?'

'Yes please Mr. Ferris, if it's not too much trouble.'

'How about you Enrico? Would you like a beer? I've a crate here somewhere around my feet.' John stood up and kicked against the crate on the kitchen floor. He looked at Enrico inquiringly.

'No John thank you, I'm fine but the two boys would probably like some of your lemonade.'

John walked unsteadily across the kitchen and looked in one of the cupboards. He rummaged around and finally found the bottle of lemonade. Turning round he triumphantly flourished the bottle and dropped it in the process. Tony who had been watching intently darted forwards and caught the bottle before it hit the stone floor.

'Good catch, good lad,' said John, 'should make a good cricketer. Play cricket do you? Grand game, lots of fun with the lads, bat on ball and sharp hands in the field. Lovely game, lovely. Don't play you say. Well never mind you've quick hands. I'll just find a couple of glasses.'

Tony handed back the bottle and John wandered over to the cupboard again to look for glasses. He poured a little lemonade into the glasses and managed to splash the right amount of water onto the concentrate. Having placed the two glasses on the table by the two boys John slumped himself back into his armchair and picked up his glass of beer. He lifted the glass.

'Well here's to a better tomorrow eh? Monday Enrico, tomorrow's Monday and the start of another busy but empty week. Cheers. Drink up lads, drink up. Here, have a toast with me. What will it be? How about "Marvellous Monday" eh? I'll bet Monday is a marvellous day for you two what with having to go back to school and all that? Go to school tomorrow do you?'

'Yes Mr. Ferris, we both go back to school tomorrow.' Peter looked at Enrico and shut his mouth after this reply.

'John, with you working you won't have had much time to get yourself organised over the past two weeks and I realise that like myself it must be a bit of a tough deal being alone in your cottage. How about I come over here tomorrow evening and give you a hand to get things sorted and you could come over to my cottage on Tuesday and help me. That way we'll both get our lives back together again and be a little less lonely. Can we do that?'

John stirred a little in the armchair and looked at the beer still in his glass. He gently swirled the amber liquid around and took a sip. Very carefully he put the glass back down on a little table and looked at Enrico. 'Think we can do that Enrico, after all that's gone on?'

'Yes John I think we can. The past is past. As you said tomorrow is marvellous Monday. Lets you and I make a new start tomorrow as neighbours in the forest? I know I would like that.'

'Why not Enrico why not? Sure, come over after work around six and we'll see whether we can tidy up here a little and I'll help you later in the week. Actually it's a good idea and might make my life a little more bearable.'

While John was speaking to his glass of beer Enrico glanced over at Peter and Tony and silently tilted his head to hint that they should drink up their lemonades. Both boys finished and quietly rested their glasses on the table.

'John that's settled then and I'll be over tomorrow evening. Now we've got to get on and I've got to get these two lads back home for their tea. It was good to see you.' Enrico stood up and hinted at the boys to do the same. 'Thanks for your hospitality John, until tomorrow.'

'Thanks Mr. Ferris, thanks for the lemonade,' Peter and Tony said in unison.

'Sure sure, thanks for coming. Makes a nice change from drinking alone. Yes, so we'll see you tomorrow Enrico about six. Might make tomorrow's work a little easier to take. Bye Enrico, bye Peter bye Tony. Thanks for coming by.'

Enrico and the two boys walked slowly away from the cottage and back towards Home Farm.

'Looks a mess doesn't it Enrico, his kitchen still looks a mess although you can't see the blood.'

'Yes Peter. I don't think John Ferris has really recovered from what happened in that room. Going to help him tidy up and probably the rest of the cottage too might help him a little. He could do with a break.'

'But he killed his brother Enrico and that can't be right?'

'No Tony, that's not right but you have to know all the circumstances and that will all come out in a court case so it's premature for us to decide how to treat John. Right now he's not going to do anyone else any harm and he's a hurt human being so we need to be respectful and friendly. Living out here after the life he had two weeks ago he is really lonely and that is not good for anyone.'

'But you lived alone Enrico,' Peter said very quietly, unsure whether he should say this.

'That's true Peter. After Antonio died I did live out here alone and I found that was hard and looking back I wish I hadn't done that. But, in many ways I had nowhere else to go so I really didn't have a lot of choice. But, your Uncle Daniel was out here a lot, as he always was and that summer he came out here especially. He was a great help to me then was your Uncle Daniel. Actually that summer your Uncle Daniel was a great help to you and your mother too. That's when you went exploring in the attic of Home Farm.'

'And when I found my treasure,' exclaimed Peter excitedly. 'Tony did I ever tell you about that, what I found with Uncle Daniel at Home Farm? Enrico knows the story.'

'Yes yes Peter,' laughed Enrico, 'I know the story only too well. It was a good story but it led to a very sad result.'

'Well tell me then Peter,' said Tony. 'This sounds interesting. What did you find with Uncle Daniel?'

Dinner that evening was a more subdued affair with Katya and Terence having left. James was his usual talkative self and he spent much of the meal describing how he showed Terence around the forest and Mummy kept interrupting when he was explaining about the trees. This monologue was occasionally halted when spoon and fork ladled food into his motor mouth.

'James love, please don't try and speak and eat at the same time. I'm sure your Nursery School teacher will not be very impressed with Canadian manners if you splutter crumbs all over her when you talk to her tomorrow.'

'But I won't be having dinner when I talk to her tomorrow Mummy, so there won't be any crumbs to splutter.' I watched Samantha wrestle with the logic of this profound statement and the three other adults round the table all smiled. Suddenly, with a wave of his spoon, which fortunately was empty at the time James asked, 'where did you go Uncle Daniel today? What did you see? We talked to Dainty but Dancer kept trying to push his nose in the way. You should teach your horse better manners Uncle Daniel?'

'Yes, where did you go today Daniel?' my mother asked quickly before James could take another breath.

'Well we were out this morning as you know hacking around the golf course.'

'But not very successfully I hear.'

'I suppose my wrist and shoulder are still a little bruised from Saturday, from master-minding Samantha's delightful engine driver.'

'Now don't you go blaming James Daniel if you dropped the odd stroke or two. That's what competition is all about, overcoming the obstacles. Anyway, James told me you swan-dived just as an excuse to hug Katya. He tells me you are always hugging Katya, every minute he says.'

'Samantha,' and I stopped in mid talk as there was nothing clever I could think of saying.

'So Daniel, your golf game was a little off this morning but what about this afternoon? Was that off too?'

'No Mum, we went down and saw Enrico. He was down at his cottage with Peter and Tony. He asked whether it was all right to take Tony and Peter on to see John Ferris.'

'And what did you tell him?' asked my dad.

'I said yes Dad, but I advised him to be careful around John and tell the boys to be rather quiet. I think Enrico wanted to hold out a helping hand to John Ferris, wanted to let him know that he was there to talk or perhaps just be there for him. You know Enrico, he is always so thoughtful around people.'

'And Peter and Tony seemed okay Daniel?'

'Yes Mum. I think Peter was explaining the different trees to Tony and letting him feel more at home in this rather different world. I imagine it's all very strange after coming from London.'

'Talking of London Daniel you remember your mother and I are going up there tomorrow to see Rosalind Cohen. We'll be away both Monday and Tuesday and probably coming back on the Wednesday.'

'Did she sound very positive Dad, about Brainware I mean? Did she say which way she was thinking or is this still a very uncertain situation?'

'She sounded quite enthusiastic on the telephone Daniel. Apparently she had talked with some of her staff and she had talked with some of her family, the Townsends. You may remember that most of that family were in the locksmith and now security business so it appears that some of them think the idea of merging companies is a good one. Rosalind was telling me that there is money in the "family at large" and they have

176

all stayed very much together. So at the moment it all sounds rather positive.'

'Well I hope so for both your sakes,' I said. 'It was a good idea of Samantha's and perhaps is the best solution if it comes about. What do you say Mum?'

'You're right Daniel. It could be a win-win answer.'

'Then you could spend more time on the Estate and my dear brother could hack around the golf course morning and afternoons,' added Samantha.

'Or we could go on the train more often,' added James, not wanting to be left out of the celebrations. 'Maybe we'd meet some more interesting people.'

'Hold up there James darling. I think your Uncle Daniel is still trying to get to first base with his present interesting people, despite all the hugging.'

'Well you can talk Samantha. What did you do going around the forest this morning?'

'We had James as a chaperone Daniel, well a tour guide really if you believe half he says.'

'And did Mummy hug Detective Inspector Field James or didn't you notice?'

'No Uncle Daniel.'

'No they didn't hug or no you didn't notice?' I asked.

'No I didn't notice, but we did go and see your badger gate, and we also went to Enrico's cottage but he wasn't there when we went.'

'So what about Terence Samantha? Will we see him again as a policeman or as a friend? Actually, talking about him as a policeman can you find out some more about what Idwal Ferris had done? I know Terence explained that he was in gaol for manslaughter but it may help in building up some sort of character defence for John Ferris if we can establish that it was Idwal who caused all the mayhem. We all heard what Terence told us last night but if we know more of the story we might be able to establish John's innocence or ignorance of the whole earlier situation.'

'Good point Daniel. What do you think Samantha? Think Terence can tell us a little more about the past background of Idwal? What happened after he left here eight years ago, in addition to what he has already said?'

'I can only ask Dad,' Samantha said. 'Changing the subject a little how has John Ferris been at work? Do you think Mum should try and orchestrate another meeting between John and Betty or isn't that an issue?'

I mused over my sister's question. John Ferris had come back to work last Wednesday and seemed normal, quiet but normal. The work gang were kind of split over how they should react but there had not been any trouble and Bob Edwards the foreman had made sure the work got done. It appeared that John had managed to settle back in his old cottage. If Enrico had gone to talk with him today then maybe things will slowly settle down a little. For the moment we should let sleeping dogs lie I thought.

'Samantha, Mum, I would let it alone just now. John seems to be working out just fine and I would sooner he gets resigned to a routine of forestry work, his cottage and the pub on Saturday night. Let's see whether he can slide into that routine, boring and unhappy as it might be. Betty hasn't requested any further meeting has she?'

'No Daniel, neither Betty nor Toby and Mary have got back to me since we last spoke. I agree with you though son, I would let things settle a little before we try and pressure things any further.'

'Dad, should we have a family dinner on Wednesday after you have come back from London? I'm sure Christina would be interested in hearing what you had to say and we could all get together and discuss the subject again. She could bring Peter and Tony and we could all plan what the next steps might be.'

'Well Sylvia, what do you say to that?'

'Makes sense to me Anthony. Let me call Christina now before she gets all in a fluster over getting the boys ready for school tomorrow. You know what she's like when she has to plan something. Wednesday evening then?'

I lay in bed that night thinking over the past events: Katya, gold coins, golf, Katya again, John Ferris, and the future of the Company. What did I really want to do? Was I good enough to play golf seriously, professionally? Did I want to? And what will happen with Katya? Do I really love her and will she want to go back home to Florida, and then what? Look what happened with Samantha, happy one moment and then devastated the next. Still, she has James at least, but maybe she will end up with Detective Inspector Terence Field. Not a bad chap really, obviously good at his job but what a job? Always into the rotten side of life. Can you ever turn that off, walk away from it for a minute? At least in the forest or out on the golf course it's relatively clean. You can breathe fresh air. So Daniel Lord, twenty three coming on twenty four, what do you really want to do with your life? I fell asleep thinking about more practical and answerable questions like where would I find better cushions or perhaps a sleeping bag to put in the Landrover for when Katya came next weekend.

BONES

MONDAY MORNING BROKE WITH A flurry of activity around the Estate. I had been out early at the Estate Office to see the work gang go out with Bob Edwards. Back at the Big House dad and mum were having a leisurely and civilised breakfast while my sister was running late as usual getting James fed, dressed and ready for Nursery School. I could picture Christina down at Home Farm going through the same conniptions while Peter would be trying to restrain his mother's emotional outburst. I smiled to myself as I could remember Geoffrey, my brother and Peter's dad who was always so calm and serious. Peter is a good mixture of his father's ultra caution and his mother's Italian emotions. You'll do well Peter I thought.

Down at Home Farm Enrico sat quietly on a chair in the kitchen watching the world of Peter and his mother gradually come together while Tony also sat and watched. Enrico caught Tony's eye and he winked. 'Think they'll get it organised Tony?'

'Sure Enrico, Peter will sort it.'

'How is your footballer coming on? Have you finished painting him yet?'

180

'No, not yet Enrico. I was busy working on the tree fort last night with Peter after we came back with you from John Ferris's cottage. I haven't had time to finish him yet but I will. He's really smashing.'

'Tony you all ready love? I think Peter has got everything.'

'Mum I'm fine. I've got all my stuff. Come on Tony. Let's go before my mum can find something else to worry over. Come on Mum. Bye Enrico.'

The two boys ran out of the door and jumped into the car. Christina looked around the room as if something else would jump up and remind her of things to be done. The car horn sounded outside.

'See you later Enrico. I must get these boys to school.'

'Drive carefully Christina. I'm fine here with my coffee. You go now before they wear that car horn out.'

Quiet gradually descended on the Home Farm kitchen and Enrico relaxed. Wonder what else I can carve for the boys he thought. Tony seems to be settling in here and making something else for him would be good. And then young James wants some kind of stick or bat for playing polo was it? Think I'll have to talk with Master Daniel about that: not quite sure what that should look like. Sitting in the chair and slowly sipping on his coffee Enrico thought about his cottage. Might have to make some furniture for that too I suppose he said to himself, but no rush. I quite like it here at Home Farm and the company is good for Christina, and me too I suppose. Good to have the two boys about as well. Good that Peter has someone to play with. It was lonely for the little lad. Perhaps we should stay here a while.

'Do you think it is safe Anthony for us to go away together, at the same time? The week before last when we did that all hell broke loose here. Can we trust Daniel and Samantha to look after the place? Right now we have Daniel thinking all the time about Katya and Samantha has her emotions split between Janet's wild adventure company and Detective Inspector Field. Will anyone be looking after Fotheringham?'

'Sylvia my love sit back and relax. We have a pleasant short drive to the railway station, a comfortable and stress-free ride on a train and a possible good news meeting up in London with Rosalind. I've booked us to stay at a fashionable hotel, see a show in the West End and take Rosalind out to dinner at a chic little restaurant in Soho. One of my golfing companions recommended the restaurant as a place with good food and a memorable ambiance.'

'Memorable ambiance, in Soho, recommended by a golfing friend?'

'Yes Sylvia, why the questioning expression?'

'How well do you know this golfing friend Anthony? Soho has quite a reputation you know. Did your friend explain how or why the ambiance was memorable, or whether this was based upon some "boys night out" experience?'

'Sylvia just lean back, close your eyes and ......'

'Think of England?'

Anthony chuckled and looking over at his wife he just said, 'peace woman, I'm trying to ease us into the golden age of rest and relaxation.'

'Yes Anthony but what about Betty and John Ferris? I still have to think what to do for them?'

'Just for the next couple of days my love keep your thoughts focussed on Brainware and its future. Think what you're going to do for the Company. Betty Ferris is fine for the moment with her family and John Ferris should be keeping his mind focussed on the job at hand somewhere in the forest under Bob Edward's careful supervision.'

The young Douglas fir trees had been planted back some twenty years ago now in neat rows and the survival had been good. Many of the trees had shot up to fifteen metres or more and the lower branches had shed their needles and died. Bob Edwards had the crew doing a first thinning in this dense plantation to let in more light and release some of the better future crop trees. Bob had walked through the plantation a week or so ago with Daniel and they had marked the trees to be cut.

Along with the other eight men in the crew John Ferris worked in his row of trees and cut those marked with silver paint. Once he had cut the tree he carefully used a hand-axe to trim off the branches from the lower part of the stem which he bucked into two and a half metre lengths. The trimmed branches and needles would decay on the forest floor and slowly release their nutrients back into the soil and the cut lengths would be hauled out to the forest ride as potential material for the sawmill or as farm fencing material. It was a slow but steady job and the air was filled with the smell of fresh-cut timber and the shrill shriek of chain saws.

'Keep that stump cut down low young Ferris,' said Bob Edwards. 'This site is level enough to get the skidders right into the plantation on any subsequent cut if we keep the stumps low.'

'Yes Bob,' and John cleared away the loose material from around the base of the next marked tree to ensure the cut was nearly at ground level.

'You be careful with that saw now Ferris. Don't you go pointing it at me. Heard what you can do with sharp objects. Bloody lethal you were I was told.'

John concentrated on the job at hand. Ignore the silly bugger he thought. What would he know, half-pissed in the pub with Freddie most of the time? Slow and steady; watch where to make it fall; clear up the slash and buck up the logs. Slow and steady, that's the way. One step at a time. One day at a time. Christ, I wonder what Betty and the kids are doing now?

'Oy, watch where you're dropping that wolf tree you silly bugger. You'll have the top down on Don here. Christ, if you ain't cutting people up Ferris you're trying to crush 'em. Bloody one-man wrecking crew you are Ferris. Bloody danger to all of us.'

'Freddie, any more lip out of you lad and you'll be on the bus out of here. You heard what Mr. Daniel said last week. John works here and if you don't like it we'll move you elsewhere. You hear me Freddie? Now less bloody yap and more bloody work.'

'Yes, bloody is the right word,' muttered Freddie under his breath but Bob didn't hear him.

'You hear me?'

'Sure Bob, just making sure I'm safe like.'

'Son if it's safe you want I'll put you back in the nursery hand-weeding and bending over all day tidying up the transplants.'

'No Bob, I'm fine.'

'Good, so stay fine.'

John Ferris moved to the next marked tree. All very well this one day at a time he thought but what the fuck happens down the road? Go to court and then what – gaol, shit but for how long, and what happens after that? Would Sir Anthony keep me on and who looks after Betty? Sure Mrs. Lord fixed that meeting for Betty and me but nothing much came out of that now did it? God I miss my kids, little Katey and Paul. How am I ever going to get together with them again? Betty told me she had explained that I had to go away for a special job and they wouldn't see me for a while but what will I say if they ask me where I've been? Mr. Daniel's been good about deliveries from the village but what a life, like a bloody prisoner stuck out here in the forest on my own. Still Enrico said he would come out and see me tonight. It's company I suppose, someone to talk with but when I think what Idwal did to Enrico's cottage I feel all choked up inside. I can hardly look at Enrico when I think about that. Perhaps I'll have a few beers so I won't really see him too clearly. John stumbled and fell over the edge of his chain saw. Fortunately he didn't have his fingers on the trigger and the saw was still.

'Trying to cut your own throat now are you Ferris? Just pull a little harder on the trigger next time and put us all out of our misery.'

John just looked at Freddie but he didn't say a word. Fuck him he thought, he's a nobody. Dad used to kick the shit out of him when he was just a lad and now he's all mouth. Ignore the silly bugger. What do they say about sticks and stones? He pulled the trigger on the saw and lifted it up to clear away some bigger material. The roar caught Freddie by surprise and he stumbled backwards falling over a bucked log.

'Freddie you're becoming a friggin' liability lad. Go over to the last row, the one Ken's working on and start carrying those logs out onto the ride. Stack 'em in a open square crib. Now go and do something useful before I lose my patience with you.'

'Yes Mr. Edwards,' and Freddie walked back down the rows to the plantation boundary but not before throwing a black glare over at Ferris.

'Just you carry on Ferris. I'll keep Freddie from being an arsehole.'

John went back to his steady routine: clear it, cut it, trim it, buck it.

After lunch and a welcome nap Enrico decided he should go and see his cottage. As he was well away from the crew thinning the Douglas fir his walk was peaceful and serene. There was still the secret project for Master Daniel's birthday but the boys were at school and he could continue that with them when they came home. After the peace and quiet of living alone Enrico found it a little strange with Christina bustling around at Home Farm, always somewhat on edge. Sure it was good to talk but everyone needed their own space sometimes. Here in the forest one could feel the quiet. Yes Tony still found it alien but so would I thought Enrico if I had lived on a bustling city street. We are all creatures of habit and a little bit scared of change.

Pushing open the kitchen door on his cottage Enrico stood and looked inside. Change he mused, well that has certainly taken place in this kitchen. It was clean, tidy and somewhat bare. Yes changed Enrico thought. Now what do I really want to do here? Would it make more sense to stay at Home Farm? Christina would be happy. Peter and Tony would be happy, but what about me: what do I really want now at this time of life? Enrico walked slowly through the various rooms of the cottage and thought about his last question. We're back to basics he thought: back to when Antonio and I were children with our parents in Italy. We had a roof over our heads, food on the table, clothes on our backs and some talents to make things for people to bring them a little happiness. Anything else? What else does anyone need? Well I suppose we had each other, we had family and friends. There were always people in the house: our mother's smiling face and welcoming greeting; our father's offer of a drink and tobacco for the pipe; and the talk. Always the talk. Perhaps it is time to go back to the beginning and a family? Perhaps I will just stay at Home Farm and enjoy the family. I will talk it over with Daniel, he'll understand. He always was a thoughtful lad, a little like his father being a people person. So, what if anything do we want out of here Enrico asked the cottage? Will I be able to take Antonio back with me to Home Farm? I miss you my brother. Enrico sat in his bare kitchen and reflected on his years spent within these four walls.

Not far away John Ferris also sat in one of the Estate cottages and reflected on his life within his four walls. He tilted the bottle up and let the beer slide down his throat. Just forget stupid Freddie he said to the

186

walls and think on Katey and Paul. Think how they used to run out to greet him as he came home from work through the forest. Laughing and chattering away, clinging to his legs and Betty with the kettle on the boil ready to make tea the moment he walked in through the door.

He carefully stood the empty bottle on the scrubbed kitchen table and looked around for the crate of full ones. He tried not to look too intently at the walls, at the floor, at the table even. Just keep it slightly foggy John lad and try not to remember. Tilt up the bottle and try not to remember. A knock on the door disturbed the quiet and Enrico pushed it open.

'John, I've come to see you as I promised. I was getting a little lonely at my place and thought I'd come over for a quiet drink and ask how the work is coming on. I heard that you were thinning in that young plantation, Douglas fir isn't it?'

'Sure Enrico. Like a beer? Want a glass? There's some in the cupboard over there by the stove.'

'No John, the bottle's fine lad. Thanks. Anything good coming out of that plantation or is it all small stuff being a first thinning?'

'Mixture really. Trees have grown real good so there's a few small logs but it's mostly farm stuff. Sticky bloody trees though with all those gum blisters. Can make quite a mess of the saw.'

'Bob Edwards making sure you keep the stumps low is he? Always was a stickler for really low stumps was Bob.'

'Yes, he thinks we can get the skidders in there for a later thinning, seeing as the site is fairly flat like.'

'If you can do that it makes it much easier to get the logs out, quicker too. How's Bob making out with the crew? I heard Mr. Daniel spoke quite clearly to all of you last week. Made sure everyone knew how he and his dad felt. They both feel for you you know lad, Mrs. Lord too.'

'Yes Enrico I know. Mrs. Lord and Miss Samantha arranged for a meeting for Betty and me, trying to help us sort things out but it's all a bit of a bloody mess Enrico. I know they are doing all they can given what's happened but it's still a bloody mess and I don't know what's going to happen next.'

Enrico quietly supped at his beer and thought on John's words. 'Given what's happened has happened John what would you like to do? Have you given it any thought, something to work towards?'

'What's there to think about? Christ Enrico, I killed him, right here my own brother.'

'No John, beyond that son. So court, yes, gaol maybe, but then what? You want to stay on here, continue working at Fotheringham?'

'I haven't really thought that far Enrico. I mean, what's the point? It's all gone tits up.'

'Have a goal John. Find something to work towards. Find something you really can do for yourself. Doesn't matter what it is but aim at something, something for tomorrow.'

'That's just another bloody day cutting down Douglas fir and coming back to an empty cottage.'

'Go beyond that. You're a good worker. You've made a solid contribution to the Estate. You have grown up a capable young man. Find a future you can work towards, things you can do to make that happen. There are people here to help lad but you have to pick the target. Look at Miss Samantha as an example. She came here somewhat at a loss like you, with a big tragedy behind her, haunting her but she's made an effort to pick a new future and work towards it. People here helped her. They'll help you too John.'

John sat in his wooden kitchen chair and looked at his beer bottle trying to see Enrico's vision.

'I want to go back to two weeks ago Enrico.'

'No lad, that's not an option. Done's done. We don't go backwards John, none of us can. We might live in today but we have to work for tomorrow. Yesterday is gone, over. I've just been going through the same questions. I was sitting in my own cottage kitchen and trying to answer my own questions. What do I want to do tomorrow? Where do I want to be next week? We all have the same questions lad and each and every one of us has to make up their own mind.'

'Enrico this is all too heavy man. Have another beer.'

'One more John and then I must away. One of the things I have to do for tomorrow is work with Peter and Tony. We all help each other John. Let people help you. You're not alone. Give it a try.'

After Enrico had left John continued to sit on his hard uncomfortable chair and tilt his beer bottle. He slowly looked around the quiet and tidy kitchen. Four or five more empty bottles joined the first three or four standing forlornly on the kitchen table. Carefully John tried to stand up. 'I'll clean up that bloody hidey-hole,' he shouted. 'Clean out any sight and sound of my poor Betty being stuck down there. Almost like a bloody grave that is you bastard Idwal. I won't have it. I won't have it you hear me you bastard brother of mine! Try to bury my Betty would you? Well I'll make sure that will never happen again.'

The kitchen reverberated with the shouts of John as he staggered around the room still clutching a half-full beer bottle. He moved into the little hall-way and peered rather myopically towards the long narrow closet. Very carefully and deliberately he reached down and placed the half-empty beer bottle on the floor, and then he hiccupped. 'Slowly mate, there's no rush, you've got all night to tidy up this mess,' he muttered as he focussed in and out on the array of mops, brushes, pails, pans and other cleaning utensils neatly stacked in the closet. One by one John moved the various implements out of the closet and dumped them haphazardly in the kitchen. Twice he went looking for another beer but seemed to forget what he was looking for and returned empty-handed to the narrow closet.

When John had emptied the closet he stood in the little hall-way and screwed up his eyes. He was trying to remember. Where was the loose board? Along the floor of the closet was a series of tongued and grooved floorboards but one of them was flat-sided. Which one? Carefully, so as not to fall over John crouched down and let his eyes move from board to board. Which board? He tapped with his fingers on a couple of boards but all that did was give him a headache. He tried his fingernails and after the third fumbling effort the board slid up a little. 'Bingo!'

Board by board John unslotted the fitted boards and painstakingly placed them behind him in the hall-way. The long narrow trench of his dad's "hidey-hole" slowly came into view. About three feet deep and three feet wide the trench extended the length of the closet. John screwed up his eyes and pictured poor Betty trussed up in here under the boards like a stuffed chicken. His stomach lurched and bile rose up in his throat. 'Bastard,' he shouted and he kicked out at the pile of boards. His foot missed the pile and the momentum swung his sideways. As he fell his head glanced off the cornerpost of the hall-way and he was drunkenly unconscious and very limp as he bounced off the walls of the hidey-hole and ended up an untidy mess of humanity on the floor of the trench. Soon his snores and exhalations of beer fumes filled the hidey-hole.

Christina brought Peter and Tony home from school and soon Home Farm kitchen was abuzz with the chatter of voices. Peter persuaded his mother that he could work with Tony and Enrico on Daniel's surprise before tea and so 'could we use the kitchen table please Mum?'

'Yes love but you'll have to have everything tidied away by six please.'

'Sure Mum. Enrico do you have the two jigs, one for each of us? We had two jigs when James was here.'

'To be sure Peter. Just let me go and get the various bits and pieces and we'll set up a production line.'

Very soon the kitchen table was carefully covered with newspaper, as was the floor around the table. On the table itself Enrico erected the two little jigs for holding the model figures. Each boy carefully placed one of the model people in the jig and thought about what colours. There was an array of little jars of paint between Tony and Peter and each boy had a selection of fine paint brushes. Enrico sat and watched as Peter and Tony carefully turned each little lump of match-sticks and glue into a model person with hat, coat, trousers or skirt, shoes, face and hands. It was slow fine work and each boy had a different expression on their face as they concentrated on the task. Christina had provided a couple of rags to re-arrange any mistakes where the paint for the face inadvertently dripped down the front of the coat. Tony peered intently at his figure with his tongue firmly slotted between his teeth. Enrico smiled as he watched Peter turn the jig this way and that way trying to get the colour into some little spaces.

Christina came back into the kitchen quietly and gently placed her hand on Enrico's shoulder. 'This is a lovely idea Enrico. I think Daniel will be quite surprised at the sudden increase in the population for his toy train.'

'Model railway Mum please. Uncle Daniel would be horrified if you referred to his layout as a toy train.'

'It's really neat Auntie and he lets us drive the engines, when he's there of course.'

'Yes Christina, it is not a toy as far as Daniel is concerned. We all have our own little passions. Can you guess what yours is Christina?' asked Enrico.

'Enrico I don't have time for passions or any such nonsense. There is always too much to do for the family.'

Here Enrico smiled and he winked at Peter who was watching his mother and Enrico have this conversation. Peter wondered what it was that Enrico was going to say and so he raised his eyebrows in his questioning face.

'You trying to guess Peter? You don't know what your mother's special passion is?'

Christina blushed when her son looked at her and Peter turned back to Enrico and shook his head.

'Should I know Enrico or will it embarrass my mother? Listen up Tony, we're about to hear another secret.'

Now Enrico had all three people in the room looking at him with interest on their faces and ears finely tuned. 'It's very special and very beautiful,' said Enrico, letting the tension in the room build a little. 'I think your mother's passion Peter is family. Not just the people here in this room, although you three are certainly the inner heart of the passion but also the bigger Lord family passion. Christina you do a lot and you certainly enjoy the family, the getting together and the talk. I was sitting in my old cottage this afternoon thinking about my life and I was realising that I have come full circle.'

'Full circle like Uncle Daniel's railway Enrico?' asked Peter.

'Perhaps,' said Enrico, 'but I was thinking of my life and particularly of my youth. We would sit in a kitchen like this my brother Antonio and I. There would be our mother and father and in would come the aunts and uncles, the cousins, nephews and nieces and all would be lively and non-stop conversation. My mother would be spinning or knitting and my father would be whittling away on a piece of wood with his pipe clamped in his mouth and the kitchen would be full of family. I think that is your passion Christina. When you are all together.'

Christina looked across at Enrico and she smiled. She walked slowly across the kitchen floor and held Enrico's hands. 'You decided to stay,' she simply said. 'You have decided to stay here at Home Farm.'

'Whoopee,' cried Peter, 'fantastic, smashing. Tony isn't that smashing?'

'Sure is. Awesome. Auntie that's great. Suddenly the family has doubled, just like the people on Uncle Daniel's railway.'

The Dean Goods tender locomotive number 2516 slowly moved forwards pulling three cattle cars away from the loading dock. 'Nice and gently James. That's good.'

The train gathered speed and left the station yard on its way to the next destination.

'Now slowly turn the dial and let it come to a stop back there behind the mountain. Shall we take the King out again? That's your favourite isn't it?'

'Yes Uncle Daniel. I shall call it King Delaney the IIIrd. although the nameplate says King Henry the something. What's VIII Uncle Daniel? It's number 6013 and it's a 4-6-0. Did I get that right?'

'You're a smart lad James. You got it all right and I don't think the engine will mind being renamed King Delaney IIIrd. Perhaps I should try and get a special nameplate made up for this engine if you're going to rename it.'

'Can it pull the new coaches? What did you call them – Couttet, Cooper? What were they called Uncle Daniel?'

'They were called Collett James because that was the name of the engineer for the GWR at that time and he designed them. Same as I have a Collett Goods locomotive over there. See number 2244 by the engine shed. What is the wheel arrangement for my Collett Goods?'

'There are no wheels in the front and I don't see any under the place where we climbed up on the real engine. The engine cab did you call it? And in the middle I can see three large wheels so it must be 0-6-0, yes? Am I right, am I am I?'

'Splendid James and now we have to find the Collett coaches. Just let me set a few points and you make King Delaney move forwards. Forwards James or you will cause a wreck in the engine sheds. Yes that's good and slowly out onto the main line. Hold it there can you? Now, I need to set this point to let you back it up slowly onto the carriages you wanted. Nice and gently and there you have them connected. Shall we wait for the passengers to get into the carriages? Can you see Daniel and James running down the platform and opening the door and...'

'falling all over Katya's legs Uncle Daniel and sitting down next to Queen Deidre.'

'But it was a good meeting James don't you think?'

'Smashing Uncle Daniel, the blue engine ice cream, the Sunday blue engine ice cream was smashing and we went up into the cab and Sammy blew the whistle and I jumped. It was a great day Uncle Daniel. Thanks for taking me to see the real engines.'

'So have we got everyone on board? What happened next? Do you remember?'

'Someone, the guard was it waved his green flag and blew his whistle and Sammy had to whistle in return and then we had to rush to get on board and the engine started moving.'

'Shall I wave a green flag and blow a whistle and let you take King Delaney into the countryside?'

'Yes, let's go.'

John Ferris let go and the beer bottle rolled off his chest and slowly chugged chugged its contents over his trouser leg. He tried to sit up but his head really hurt and there was wet on his fingers when he tenderly felt his cranium. He scrabbled a little bit with his boots and tried to get a firm footing but he was still too drunk and fell over again. Taking a deep breath John dug his foot in really hard and pushed with his arms and tried to turn over from his back to his knees. Again the feet dug around in the dirt and John managed to coordinate enough to end up kneeling. His foot kicked against something hard as he tried to stand and as he turned to see what it was his legs collapsed again and he fell full length back in the hole. The kitchen light was on but there wasn't any light in the closet.

Very slowly John turned round to see what his foot was kicking. It was hard, dirty white and looked like a long spoon. Still drunk and peering like a blind man John tried to prise the white thing out of the ground. It came free and John screamed. He scrabbled frantically about on the floor of the hole and managed to kick more of the ground about. Clutching the white object in his hand John tried to stand and scramble out of the hole. His feet churned up more of the ground and disturbed some more white objects. John didn't look back into the dark hole and he finally clambered, rolled and wriggled his body into the hall-way. Exertion, imagination and horror overcame him and he collapsed in a heap passed out. A little later the only sound in the cottage was John's irregular snoring.

I came out of the Forest Estate office next morning to see Bob Edwards and the forest crew. 'You're still thinning in that Douglas fir plantation in Compartment eight Bob? How far through are you?'

'We only started yesterday Mr. Daniel and I reckon it will take all week to completely finish the job. We will haul all of the farm materials out and then I'll organise a tractor to skid out any sawlogs we have. They're quite a few sawlogs as some of those trees grew really well. The part that we did yesterday looks good now it is thinned. I think our marking was spot on.'

'Any other concerns Bob? I won't be around much today as I've arranged a meeting with the manager of Penrose for him to consider some of our hardwood lumber for his factory. As you know we already supply him with pine logs for the framing materials but I think we could supply him with hardwoods too. It's a good potential market.'

'Sounds like a possibility Mr. Daniel but to come back to your question Freddie has been his usual annoying self. He won't leave John Ferris alone, keeps sniping at him. I threatened to send him to hand weed the nursery and that kept him quiet for a while.'

'How did John react?'

'Ignored the silly sod. Just refused to listen to him and kept on with his work. He's a good worker Mr. Daniel, given the chance that is.'

I looked over the crew milling about in the yard. Freddie caught my eye and looked away quickly.

'Don't see John Ferris out there this morning Bob. Did he show up?'

Bob too walked into the yard and looked about. 'Seen John Ferris anyone? Late is he?'

'He ain't showed up Bob. We ain't seen him this morning.'

'Thanks Tom. Seems he's not around this morning Mr. Daniel.'

'Don't worry Bob. You carry on and I'll check at his cottage on my way to see Penrose. I'll let you know what I find, probably around lunchtime.'

196

'Fine Mr. Daniel, I'll carry on then. Okay lads into the lorry and we're off to open out those Douglas firs again today. Everyone got their lunches, safety gear, saws? Jesus Tom, you'd forget your 'ead if it wasn't screwed on right. Go and get it mate and hurry up. See you at lunch time then Mr. Daniel?'

'Aye Bob.'

Having collected the few papers I needed for the meeting with Penrose I locked up the Forest Estate office. Putting the papers on the seat beside me I started the Landrover and set off. John Ferris, what has happened today I wondered? Slowly I coasted the Landrover to a stop beside the Ferris cottage. All was quiet. I tried to ignore the events that took place here just over two weeks ago and walked firmly towards the kitchen door. It was ajar. Cautious now I pushed it open and peered inside. Still all was quiet.

'John, you there? John Ferris, you in here?'

One step at a time I walked into the kitchen but there was still no sound. Then I could hear it, a low rhythmic snore followed by a whistling noise. I quietly walked through the kitchen towards the noise. John was sprawled in a mess of arms and legs contorted in the narrow hall-way with his legs half hanging inside the closet which was an open gaping hole. Clutched in John's hand was a bone.

'John lad, John wake up can you?'

John stirred. The snoring and whistling stopped as John opened his eyes. The first thing he saw was the bone in his hand and he opened his mouth and let out an ear-piercing scream and threw the bone away. He sat up like a jack-in-a-box and put his hands to his head. He groaned and his whole body shuddered.

'John you awake now?' I put my hand under John's arm and tried to lift him up to his feet. Almost in a trance John staggered to his feet and let me lead him back into the kitchen where I managed to help him into a chair. He collapsed into it.

'What happened man? You were all right yesterday. Bob Edwards said you were working really well yesterday. Looks like you tied one on last night. Am I right?'

I had spoken quietly and clearly but John just sat there looking befuddled. Slowly he raised his head and peered in my direction. 'I just wanted to tidy up Mr. Daniel. Enrico said I should set myself a target. Find something to work towards and so I tried to clear up where Idwal imprisoned my Betty. I wanted to make it tidy for her, sort of put that part to rest.' John shuddered again and a series of tremors convulsively ran up and down his body. He almost fell off the chair and I had to put my hand out again to steady him.

'Enrico was here?'

'Yes Mr. Daniel, Enrico came over yesterday. Had a beer, had a chat. He told me to put the past behind me. Done is done I think he said. Look to the future. He told me to sort out what I wanted to do and people would help me. So I decided to clean up that grave where my fucking brother tried to bury my Betty.' John broke down and sobbed. He leant forward in the chair and the sobs wracked his body.

'So Enrico tried to help John? He said that he and other people would help you?'

'Yes, but he said I had to decide on the object, the objective or whatever. No one else could do that he said but after that people would help me get there. We had a beer together, two beers, three beers I don't know. After he left I decided to clean out dad's hidey-hole but I must have fallen in. I think I banged my head.' John felt his head gingerly and winced as he found the bump and the scab of dried blood. 'I must have scrabbled about in that hole and gradually come to you know. Something sharp was digging into me and my feet kicked something hard. When I picked it up I panicked. I suppose I tried to get out of the grave and then collapsed half in and half out. Wasn't that where you found me?'

'Yes John it was. You had something in your hand and when you saw it on opening your eyes you screamed and then collapsed again. I helped you here into the kitchen. Sounds like a cup of tea might be an idea. Think you can manage that?'

'Sure Mr. Daniel.'

Samantha had collected James from Nursery School and as usual little motor mouth was explaining the minute by minute activities to his mother. It was only when Samantha had sat him down at the lunch table that there was any break in the verbal barrage. Fortunately James likes to eat although even that activity is often interspersed with vocal outbursts coupled with the hand actions, spoon-waving and occasional parts of the lunch menu scattered across the table.

'James love, just for a moment can we concentrate on eating without the hand waving action? I will sit and listen to your morning's adventures after we have eaten. Uncle Daniel really doesn't want to be wearing your lunch.'

'Sure Mummy but I have lots and lots to tell you.'

'Yes darling I don't doubt you.'

'Samantha can I manage to get a word in edgeways?'

'Daniel I'm sorry about James's hand actions.'

'I think he has been watching Christina and Enrico talking together and learning the Italian hand language but that's not what I wanted to tell you.'

'What's so important? Didn't you go and see Penrose this morning about some lumber order? Did something unexpected happen there?'

'No Samantha, it was before I went to see Penrose. Bob Edwards told me that Freddie had been giving John Ferris a hard time out on the work crew but John had been ignoring any snide remarks.'

'Yes Daniel, it was Freddie and some of his friends last Saturday night in the pub that were trying to rile John there too. I thought he was a gardener?'

'He is but Bob was looking for a full crew and there is nothing much happening in the garden at the moment so I agreed to Freddie working in the plantations. I may have to change my mind, but that wasn't my concern.'

'Can I have trifle Mummy?'

'No James love. You ate it all the other day but cook has made a special train treat for you. It is called engine driver's delight. It is an upside-down cake.'

'Awesome. With custard too I hope?'

'Here, I'll give you a special serving but can you let Uncle Daniel speak to me please without any further interruption?'

'Of course Mummy, you just have to say so.'

'Daniel, you were saying about John Ferris?'

'Well John wasn't at work this morning when Bob assembled the crew but he had been telling me about Freddie's mouth yesterday. So, I went round to John's cottage before I went to see Penrose. He was a real mess. I think Enrico had gone round yesterday evening for a social call and a supportive pep talk if I understood John properly. John was burbling about the help Enrico was offering and the need to set himself some achievable objective. Anyway John convinced himself that he needed to clean up that hidey-hole where Idwal had hidden Betty and Lola. He thought he could purge the memory of that frightening part of the incident.'

Samantha glanced across at James to see whether he was listening. She had come to realise that her son had an embarrassing ability to hear and repeat unexpected comments from conversations. James appeared to be fully engrossed in upside-down cake.

'So what happened?'

'John must have been drinking. A lot if I had bothered to count the number of empty bottles. He was seriously hung over and in a mixture of drunken stupor and sleep when I arrived. I woke him up, and then managed to move him to sit in a chair in the kitchen.'

'Where was he originally? You talked about him clearing up this hidey-hole or whatever?'

'He must have opened up the floor-boards covering this hole and it looked like he had fallen in. He complained of a bloody bump on his head so it is likely he knocked himself out and fell into the hole. When I found him he was half lying on the edge of the hole but that isn't what frightened him.'

'Frightened him, you didn't say anything about him being frightened, just drunk and asleep.'

'Well when I woke him up he was holding something in his hand and this was the first thing he saw when he opened his eyes. He just screamed and dropped it as if it was red hot.'

'But what was it Daniel? What did he have in his hand?'

I glanced across at James but he was still making progress on his cake.

'It was an old bone Samantha and it looked like a leg bone.'

'Perhaps his dog buried it Uncle Daniel, although I don't remember whether Mr. Ferris has a dog. Does Mr. Ferris have a dog Mummy? Why did Mr. Ferris scream Uncle Daniel? It was only an old bone.'

'James darling can we both let Daniel tell us the story?'

The spoon came up laden with custard and successfully found its way into the little mouth. James slowly and thoughtfully nodded his head. Samantha looked back at me as if to say continue.

'As I said I got John to sit down in the kitchen, gave him a cup of tea and slowly pieced together some of the events from yesterday evening. John couldn't remember much past opening up the hole but he presumes he did fall in and spent most of the night either in the hole or half out in the hall-way. He had a vague recollection of kicking up some bones while he was in the hole and that frightened him enough to scramble out and then he had another blackout. I slowly got him sorted, waited until he had dowsed his head with water, grabbed something to eat and then I drove him over to join the rest of the gang. I explained some of the details to Bob Edwards and told him just to watch he was safe to work. He seemed to be walking normally and so I advised Bob to have John just lift out the cut logs rather than use a chain saw today. It might be safer.'

'But what about these bones Daniel? What are they?'

'I don't know and that's why I'm mentioning this to you. I'm in two minds really and I wanted to touch base with you about a sensible course of action. Normally I might just ignore them but after all that has happened in that cottage I am more cautious. There is always a possibility that Terence Field may want to revisit for some more forensic evidence you know. So, I could go back to the cottage and investigate further. See whether I can find any other bones but then I might be disturbing one of Detective Inspector Field's "scenes of the crime" and we've already had one member of this family doing that.'

'Beast,' said Samantha.

'Who is Mummy? Are there seconds? That was smashing. What beast Uncle Daniel?'

We both turned back to look at James who sat there with an empty bowl, a clean well sucked spoon and an inquisitive look on his face. I looked at Samantha as if to say he is your son sister, you sort him.

Samantha looked at me and said, 'just a moment Daniel. I'll get back to you.' She turned back to James and gently wiped some of the adventurous custard off his nose and cheek.

'Let's leave some room for tea this afternoon James can we? I talked with cook this morning and I know she has baked some more special gingersnap cookies for tea and you need to leave room for them. Shall we go for a ride this afternoon? Dainty won't want to carry you if you have had two helpings of upside-down cake. Can you go and get changed into some other clothes, just in case you fall off.'

'I won't fall off Mummy,' James said indignantly. 'Dainty and I work really well together now. I didn't fall off when I was riding with grandma and I learnt to turn Dainty like a polo pony, real quick.'

'You're wonderful sweetheart. You're a champion rider but I would like to keep those clothes you have on just for school. So go and change for me please. I'll be right with you.'

Little feet scampered out of the dining room and we both heard the rapid rush up the staircase. Samantha turned back to look at me.

'Yes Daniel, it is a bit of a dilemma. Sort of dammed if you do and dammed if you don't. What does your gut tell you?'

'To tell Terence and let him sort it out. Two reasons really. One, if there is anything of concern with these bones we've done the right thing and two, it might focus Detective Inspector Field's attention on something other than what really happened the night of Danielle's attack. I'd like to find something to distract him from pursuing that any further.'

I watched my sister roll this answer around in her mind. It didn't take long but then Samantha tended to act first and think second. 'I agree, phone him. Now I'd better go and find what new adventures my little treasure has initiated. I found him yesterday going through my clothes and looking at them.'

'What was so special about that?'

'He was looking at each garment Daniel and muttering "hot woman?" under his breath. After looking at each garment he just said "yes or no".'

'Perhaps you need to rename Janet's Company to "Hot women's Heritage Adventures". That would attract female clients who thought they were hot women and wondered who in their ancestors was also hot.'

'What about male clients? No, perhaps don't answer that. Go and call Terence and let's get this bones thing taken care of.'

Samantha walked upstairs to find her son and I sat in the hall and looked at the telephone. Just keep it simple Daniel I said to myself. Let the professionals sort it all out, whatever it is. I lifted the receiver and tapped out the number.

'Detective Inspector Field please. Yes, I'll hold. Hello, Inspector Field, this is Daniel Lord here calling from Fotheringham. Yes good afternoon to you too. Something unexpected has happened and Samantha and I decided that you should be informed. Yes, I have discussed it with my sister. Let me explain what has happened where. It's because of the where I suppose is why I am calling. This morning I went down to the Ferris cottage to see why John Ferris was not at work. I found him there sleeping off a rather drunken night but I also found another disturbing sight. John had opened up his father's old hidey-hole where Idwal Ferris had hidden Betty and Lola. He told me he wanted to clean it up and purge the memory of Betty being buried there. What was disturbing? Yes, I'm coming to that. John Ferris was clutching a bone in his hand when I found him this morning and it looked like there were some other bones in the hole. He had found the bones in the hole and this had terrified him so that he had scrambled out of the hole but must have collapsed on the edge. When I woke him up this morning he was still holding a bone in his hand and when he saw it he screamed himself awake, violently so. What sort of bone? Well that's why I am phoning. I wasn't sure and I wasn't sure why there were any bones in that hole at all. Samantha and I decided to call you before we disturbed the scene any further. It might be nothing and we decided to let you decide, professionally that is.'

I listened for several minutes as Terence Field described what he intended to do and what I should do.

'No, John Ferris is out working in the forest and so there is no one at the cottage right now. I can go down there to meet you if that is what you intend to do. Yes, I can do that. About three o'clock then.'

I sat in the chair by the phone and thought about possibilities. Could be nothing, perhaps Norton buried a dog like James suggested although I couldn't remember any dog. Bone was too big for a dog I thought and I didn't really look in the hole to see what any of the others looked like. Forget it I told myself. Let Terence do his job. You've made your decision so let the chips fall where they may. Three o'clock. I glanced at my watch. Time to go and see Bob Edwards and the forest gang and check Ferris is still out there. See whether he is still standing too.

Samantha came down the staircase with James.

'We're going to ride Uncle Daniel but we won't be able to take Dancer. I hope your horse behaves and doesn't bother Dainty. He gets very jealous you know. You should teach him better manners Uncle Daniel.'

'Yes James. I'll go and talk to Dancer later but right now I have work to do.'

'Everything under control Daniel?' asked Samantha.

'Yes Samantha. I've phoned Terence and we're going to meet at the cottage around three o'clock. First though I'm going out to check with Bob Edwards. See you later.'

I drove out to the forest crew and talked quietly with Bob. Apparently everything was going peacefully and productively and I briefly told Bob what I was going to do and why. Just keep it to yourself Bob for the moment as it might be nothing of any consequence I told him.

Down at the Ferris cottage I found Detective Inspector Field along with a couple of white-coated specialists. I walked into the cottage and we decided that the police tape need only cover the hidey-hole area and so John could use the rest of his cottage as he had nowhere else to go. It was a grudging compromise from Detective Inspector Field but he understood the practicality of the arrangement. I briefly explained what had happened this morning, much as I had described on the telephone. Terence Field didn't think the process would take very long but he did commend me for the decision I had made. He smiled when I explained that I had discussed the situation with my sister. Still with a grin on his face he told me he was surprised not to come down here and find my sister industriously digging in the hole. We both laughed, shook hands and I drove off to tell John Ferris what we had done.

Back at the Big House dad and mum were sitting comfortably relaxing in the drawing room looking very pleased with themselves.

'Treat yourself to a drink Daniel. We think we all deserve it. Where's your sister by the way?'

'Last seen Dad taking her son out to ride Dainty and Gypsy. Samantha thought the ride might reduce the number of words issuing from young James's mouth.'

'Daniel he's a very imaginative and talkative young boy. He enjoys life and lives it to the full.'

'Sure Mum but it is sometimes difficult to get a word in edgeways and now he has developed the Italian form of speech so the arms and hands are going just as fast as the mouth.'

My dad laughed and as he leant back in his chair he was just in time to catch a fast-moving mass of arms and legs. 'Grandpa, grandpa we actually galloped. Dainty was going real fast and I didn't fall off, even when we turned the corner. Gypsy couldn't keep up with us and so we beat mummy. It was fabulous.'

James wriggled around on my dad's lap so he could face my mother. 'I did everything you taught me Grandma. I had soft hands and sat forwards. I talked to Dainty and she answered me. We ran like the wind Grandma. And I didn't have seconds for lunch so I wasn't too heavy for Dainty. Now I'm really hungry. When's dinner?'

'James love can we go and clean up a little before we entertain. I'm sure grandpa would prefer a clean and less smelly version of Master James. You can tell everyone all about your ride much better in some clean clothes.'

'But Mummy it's important to tell everyone right away, while I can still remember. I might forget after I am clean. The water will wash away the memory or something.'

'Maybe, but we do need to wash away the something and you will feel so much better.'

'Uncle Daniel hasn't changed. He was wearing that shirt for lunch.'

Samantha decided that action was better than talking and she picked James off my father's lap and spun him upside down. 'Just like upside-down cake,' she said.

'Yes Mummy, that's a good idea. I'd like some upside-down cake please.'

'Only after you have clean hands and a clean face you young scamp. Let's go and look in the mirror to see who has the cleanest face.'

'So it was a successful trip up to town?' I asked.

'Yes Daniel. We'll tell you all the details after dinner when Samantha has put James to bed and she can relax a little, but yes son it was successful.'

'That's good Mum, that's really good. Oh, by the way, we had another slight situation crop up today. Like you I will fill in the details after dinner but we made another discovery out at John Ferris's cottage. Actually John made the discovery. I've already told Samantha and we think we have done the right thing.'

Samantha came back into the drawing room with a scrubbed up James. She let go of his hand and James walked slowly over to my mother and sat down at her feet. He looked up at her face and said very quietly, 'it was really good Grandma, just like you showed me. Thank you so much for teaching me. Dainty thanks you too. She thinks I am a good rider and we make a good team.'

My mother leant forwards in her chair and quietly whispered in James's ear. 'It runs in the family James and we're so happy that you had a good time. I'm sure Dainty told you herself. She is a very sensible horse and will just love having you on her team.' My mum put her arms around James's shoulders and gave him a kiss.

'Samantha we just offered Daniel a drink and we think you should have one too. We have some good news.'

'Can I have a drink Grandpa please?'

'Yes of course James. We'll all have a drink and I want to propose a toast.'

When we all had glasses in our hands and stood in a circle in the centre of the room dad clinked his glass with all of us and said, 'here's to a less stressful future and a new beginning for Brainware. Cheers.'

'Cheers' rang around the room.

Soon after eight James was happily tucked up in his bed dreaming of galloping across the meadows on Dainty with all the other horses trailing behind. Out in front he muttered in his sleep. First. He rolled over and now he imagined swinging his polo mallet while Dainty charged up and down the field. Goal he muttered. His horse quietened down and the images gradually faded as deep sleep took charge.

'Rosalind has talked with some people and she had two financial specialists at our meetings plus Tina Morland who is a partner now. We all went over Brainware's financial statements, assets, personnel, and had some discussions about our likely futures. Given that Brainware has been doing very well, has some excellent staff plus some good future contracts this all looked a very positive asset and investment. The two financial people were suitably impressed with the numbers and the possible future. That's right isn't it Sylvia?'

'Yes Anthony. The future does look good and the ever-cautious financial bods were impressed.'

'So Rosalind thinks the idea of merger and/or buyout is a good investment?' I asked.

'Yes Daniel, we think we established that part of the situation.'

'So what about money, timing, and responsibilities?' asked Samantha.

'As you suggested Samantha we told Rosalind we wanted to have no future responsibilities. Once the deal went through we would walk away. It would be all hers and it would be up to her which way she went. That way your father and I would be "free". As you said earlier Samantha our baby has grown up and it was the responsibility of the new partner/owner to shape its future.'

'That's great Mum. No more Government hassles, no more shareholders concerns, no more personnel interventions.'

'So money and timing Mum?' I asked.

'We've had some estimates done Daniel. In fact we've been having valuations done for the past couple of years so we have a relatively good idea of the money and Rosalind agreed that was acceptable. We'll have to end up with some lawyers sometime soon to make this all legal but right now we were discussing management options and valuations. As regards timing we will end up with an agreed-upon schedule with an up-front settlement and then a series of payments over maybe five years. The financial folk got into some convoluted terms and conditions Daniel that your mother understood and I let them sort that out.'

'But overall it looks like a win-win?'

My mum looked at both Samantha and me. 'Yes, I think so. I'm more positive now than I was before your father and I went up to town but I think we have a deal.'

'And the show was good?' asked Samantha, 'and the dinner, and the hotel, and the shopping?'

'Samantha love we don't have your energy anymore so we had a very relaxed dinner with Rosalind and Tina and yes the show was good. The hotel was fine and we didn't have time for shopping but overall it was a very successful trip.'

Just when I thought mum had leant back in her chair and relaxed she quietly asked, 'Daniel, you mentioned another situation had arisen in John's cottage. You said you would explain after James had gone to bed. I'm assuming there is a good reason for the timing?'

'Yes Mum, it may be nothing but then again we're not sure.'

I looked at Samantha but she merely nodded as if to say carry on.

'John Ferris wasn't at work this morning and no one knew where he was. I told Bob Edwards I would go down to John's cottage before I went to see Penrose's about that lumber order Dad.'

'And?'

'When I got there I found John hung-over, asleep and half in and half out of that hidey-hole Norton had made in the closet. I woke John up and he screamed.'

'A nightmare?'

'No Mum, well maybe but what made him scream was the bone he was holding in his hand. As he opened his eyes the first thing he saw was this bone and so he screamed. When I eventually got him sitting in a kitchen chair I managed to get a rather slurry and disjointed story about Enrico, beer, personal objectives, cleaning out the hole, banging his head, kicking up bones and passing out. Slowly I pieced together the sequence of events. Enrico had gone over to offer some conversation, friendship, supportive advice and they had had a couple of beers together. After Enrico left John decided to clean up the hidey-hole, something about cleansing away the memory of Betty being buried in the hole. John must have been quite drunk by this time given the number of empty beer bottles scattered around the kitchen. After he got all the floor-boards up he must have slipped, banged his head and fallen unconscious into the hole. When he next came to he must have thrashed around a bit and kicked up the floor of the hole. He felt something hard underneath him and came up with a bone. Well this freaked him out so he tried to scramble up out of the hole and managed to half get out before he collapsed again and that's how I found him.'

'So, what was special about this bone? John getting drunk and falling in the hole I can understand but you are hinting about something else.'

'Yes Mum. When I briefly looked there appeared to be more bones kicked up on the floor of the hole. To digress for a moment I got John organised and ran him over to the forest crew and left him working under the careful supervision of Bob Edwards. I briefly told Edwards about the state he was in and to keep him doing non-dangerous jobs. When I came back here for lunch I told Samantha what I had found and asked her what we should do about the discovery in the hole.'

'Samantha?' my mother asked.

'Yes Mum, Daniel was being sensibly cautious and he wanted to discuss with me the pros and cons of telling Terence.'

'Detective Inspector Terence that is,' my mum added.

'Right Mum.'

'In some ways Mum I would have just dismissed the bones as something insignificant but given where they were found and all that has happened I told Samantha I would sooner advise Inspector Field and let him professionally sort it out. If it turned out to be nothing then no harm done. I don't think he would consider it wasted police time given everything else that has gone on in that cottage of late. If it is something of concern then we can't be accused of unprofessionally messing up any "crime scene" or whatever.'

'Like last time,' my mum said.

'Okay Mum, I get the message,' Samantha agreed.

'So Daniel, what has happened since?'

'Well Dad, after Samantha and I had agreed I telephoned Inspector Field and explained what I have just told you. We arranged to meet at the cottage and before that I went and told John what I had done and that the police would likely be at the cottage when he went home that evening. From there I went and met Inspector Field at the cottage and he had cordoned off that closet area and had a couple of specialists carefully working away in the hole. I told him, Terence that is that I had told Ferris and was it possible to just keep the closet off limits so that John could still live in the cottage. He really has nowhere else to go. After that I went back to see Bob Edwards and the forest crew and I suppose the police carried on with whatever it takes.'

'What do you think the bones are Daniel?' my mother asked.

'Mum I've no idea. Once I decided to tell Inspector Field the professionals can tell us. The Inspector explained that they would likely remove whatever bones they found and take them back to a lab for examination. I suppose they will determine whether they are animal or human and maybe they can tell how long they have been down there. He said he would telephone as soon as they learnt anything significant, probably tomorrow. In the meantime he would tell Ferris to stay out of that area and I think John understands all of that. Given John's out on bail and doesn't want any trouble I don't think that is a problem. He's as confused as anyone and he has no idea what the bones are or where they came from. Until the incident with Betty and Lola he'd never even known about his dad's hidey-hole.'

'I'll tell you one more thing Mum,' Samantha said. 'With this new development I'm pretty sure Betty won't want to come back to that cottage.'

'Especially if there is more to this than just some old animal bones,' my mother added.

'I think you did the right thing son. Given all the past events I think you made the right decision. I may not like the police traipsing all over our property but I think you got it right. Let the professionals make the decision. It's what we pay them for anyway.'

'Dad I talked this over with Samantha because I thought she might have a better insight into how Terence might react.' I turned to my sister. 'I'm still a little uncertain Samantha whether I'm talking with a policeman or an acquaintance, friend, whatever, you know?'

'Daniel we decided and I think you were right too.'

AND MORE BONES

I HAD NO SOONER COME in to the hall to get ready for lunch when the telephone rang.

'Daniel Lord speaking. How may I help you?'

Detective Inspector Field had been busy. I stood with the telephone against my ear and listened to a rather unexpected explanation concerning the bones.

'You say they are animal bones. You think a dog, no two large dogs? And your people think they are approximately eight years old, so that puts it around 1990. That's about the time that Norton Ferris got killed and my dad fired Idwal and John. There was no one in the cottage from January until around May I suppose when John moved back in. So the bones appear to have been put there around the time of Norton's death, Christmas time 1990.'

I listened to another series of comments and a rather relevant question.

'Just a minute Inspector, Samantha has come in and she might know. Personally I don't remember any dogs.' I turned to my sister as she crossed the hall. 'Samantha, I've got your Inspector Field on the phone, bringing us up to date about the bones in Ferris's cottage.'

'And?'

'Well they are not human but they are dog bones, large dog bones it seems and they have been there around eight years. Do you remember whether Norton Ferris or either of his two sons had any dogs?'

Samantha stood and thought for a moment. 'Eight years ago Daniel, I had just started at Cambridge and was home for Michael's twenty-first and then that rather uneasy Christmas. Norton Ferris was killed in early January wasn't he?'

'Dogs Samantha, large dogs?'

'I'm thinking Daniel. Give me the phone for a moment.'

Samantha took over the phone and went into a lengthy blow by blow account of where she was. This evidently didn't do anything for Inspector Field and just as fast the telephone was back in my hands.

'You want to have a more careful look? Unexplained dog bones are a little suspicious. Yes, I can understand that. I can meet you around six thirty at the cottage. You think your people will have had time to investigate further by then? Look Inspector, Ferris knows you are looking into this matter and that you have cordoned off that closet. He will just assume you are checking on some details so I will not tell him what you have already found. That way you can question him without any prior knowledge, but I will meet up with you around six thirty because I too would like to know exactly what is down in that hole.'

Because I had a one thirty tee-time I had my lunch before the rest of the family. In fact I had it in the kitchen and briefly chatted with cook. She couldn't remember any dogs either but as she said she never had much time for that Ferris family. Your grandmother was never quite herself in her later years cook told me. The hiring of Ferris and his two sons was a real mix-up what with that loony Colonel Travis and your grandmother misguidedly persuading your dad when he had too many things going on. Still, all done and dusted as they say.

'But no dogs?'

'Doubt whether your father would have allowed it Master Daniel. Any large dogs running around the forest could have done too much damage, disturbed the wildlife or even spooked the horses. No, they're weren't any dogs love. Do you need a snack for halfway around the course? That's where you're off to isn't it this afternoon?'

I laughed as I pocketed two cookies and left to find my golf clubs.

My golf game that afternoon varied from brilliant to lacklustre which I suppose is typical for most amateurs. Consistency, the ability to grind it out is usually lacking when it's not your sole livelihood. On a few of the holes I had some really good memory flashes of being there with Katya and the good vibes and positive thoughts resulted in a couple of first class shots. Two or three birdies came that way and Larry joshed me about my secret weapon. Unfortunately there were periods when the inspiration was lacking and a loss of concentration on the fourteenth resulted in a triple bogey which doesn't help anyone's score.

Bones kept trying to surface in my mind and I couldn't find a way to correlate bones with some positive golf thoughts. Old dog bones, old large dog bones but why? Snap out of it Daniel and live in the present. Find the line and then concentrate on the weight. Swing smoothly and let the putter head follow through and end up pointing at the cup. 'Clunk, brilliant, birdie. Easy game Larry.' I smiled and then the bones reappeared. I played the eighteenth my usual careful way with two iron shots and ended up with a conservative par and a total score of one over. We all dutifully entered the scores in the computer to keep our handicaps honest and I went to change my shoes.

'Set for Sunday again Daniel? Alan and Peter have reserved for our usual tee-time.'

'Yes Larry and I plan to bring Katya again. She seems to be a very supportive caddie and brings out the best in my game.'

'Thought you were muttering her name back on number eleven, when you trundled in that long birdie putt.'

'Yes, when I could recall some of her comments I had some good holes but then another of my problems kept resurfacing and the concentration went pear shaped.'

'Anything serious?'

'Trouble is Larry I'm not sure. In fact I had better get my skates on looking at the time. I've a meeting at six thirty which might help solve my problem, or make it more complicated. Still, I won't know until I get there. See you Sunday then, usual time. Thanks for the game, bye.'

I pulled the purloined cookies out of my pocket and contentedly munched as I drove back to Fotheringham. 'Bones, them dry bones,' I muttered to the countryside. Well, we'll just have to wait and see.

'So you see Daniel, when we dug a little further we found a layer of sacking and under that some more bones.'

'More dogs?'

'We don't think so but we'll have to wait for the pathologist's comments to be certain. We have already found a skull and that certainly didn't belong to a dog.'

'What has John Ferris said about all this?'

'I think he's as puzzled as we are. I really don't think he knew of the existence of this hole until a couple of weeks ago so any bones over eight years old will be a complete mystery to him. He doesn't come across as the sharpest tool in the box and I believe him when he says he knows nothing about any of this. Have you got any thoughts?'

'I was a teenager eight years ago, at school most of the time, boarding school that is. Sure I was home for my brother Michael's twenty-first birthday just before Christmas on the twenty-first of December and then for the Christmas holidays. Norton Ferris died in an accident early in the New Year and right after that my dad fired the two brothers. Norton Ferris was caught in my brother's Landrover supposedly collecting fence posts for some private sale, some scam he had going. He was always involved in minor theft, getting into debt with the bookies and doing very little work but I'm not sure any of this helps.'

'You never know Daniel. Sometimes a most insignificant detail, maybe insignificant to you turns out to be the key to something else. Funny business detecting. Never quite sure what will turn up next.'

Inspector Field turned back to look at the hole and his white-coated technician carefully brushing and scraping away at the bottom of the hole.

'Looks like a second skull sir but I'll be a while trying to get it free without damage. Some of this soil is quite tenacious.'

Back in the kitchen we found John slumped in a chair and looking into space.

'Mr. Daniel, this is all too bizarre. I just wanted to clean up the hole, Betty's grave like and erase that terrible memory. Enrico told me I should find a positive thing to do. Something to help me move forwards but this seems to be dragging me back further and further into the past. I never knew about this hole, honest. Thinking about it though it's just the sort of thing my dad would do. He was always one for some scheme, some light-handed work here and there, but this was huge. I don't know how I never knew about it but then dad was often in the cottage when Idwal and I were out, working or at the pub. Could keep quiet when he had to my dad.'

'What about your brother? Idwal must have known about this hole John. He tucked your wife and that other woman in here pretty quickly and tidied up too. When you and I came looking that afternoon we didn't see anything out of the ordinary.'

218

'Did you both search the cottage?' Inspector Field asked.

'We both looked in the kitchen Inspector but I suppose I didn't go any further. We called and there was no answer. John you went looking in the other rooms didn't you?'

'Yes Mr. Daniel but I didn't move anything or hide anything. There was nothing to see and it was all quiet like you said.'

'But you didn't actually look Daniel, other than in the kitchen?'

'No, that's right, but I suppose I could see up the hall-way. Not into the closet of course but there was no sign of any disturbance. No floor boards or anything.'

'So it appears that Idwal not only knew about the hole but he knew how to make it disappear?'

'Seems so Inspector.'

'Who else visited Ferris? Who came to the cottage, back eight years ago?'

'Don't rightly remember Inspector. We kept to ourselves out here. If we saw anyone it was usually in the pub in the village. Can't remember anyone ever coming out here. Of course Mr. Daniel came here sometimes, and Mr. Michael was here a few times talking with my dad. Don't think your other brother ever came to the cottage Mr. Daniel.'

'What about Enrico?'

'Never, dad wouldn't have had it. Hated Italians our dad.'

'There weren't any girl friends, any card games, any drinking parties? Think man, who else could have come here?'

'Shit I don't know Inspector. It's eight years ago now. We kept to ourselves as I said. I never had anyone out here. As I said I don't know about dad.'

'And your brother? Did he have a girl friend, any mates for the odd game of cards or just a booze up?'

'No, we did that in the village. Idwal never had no girl friend. He was more like dad, always looking for the easy chance but he was rough with it too. He was a lot bigger than dad and Idwal used to throw his weight around, especially when he got drunk.'

'What about any of the forest gang? Was there anyone special who was Idwal's mate?'

'Not bloody likely. Dad gave all the cushy jobs to Idwal, and to me I suppose Mr. Daniel, and so most of the rest of the work crew didn't like either of us. As I said Inspector we kept to ourselves.'

'Well someone Ferris, about eight years ago put the dog bones in that hole and I'll bet someone put the other bones in first, possibly about the same time.'

Inspector Field suddenly changed tack and looking at me he asked, 'anyone disappear about eight years ago around here? I'll look in the Missing Persons file back in the office but can you think of anyone disappearing Daniel?'

Christina had brought Peter and Tony up to the Big House for dinner because my father wanted to have another family get-together about Brainware and the money. James always delighted in these meals and he was torn between watching what Peter and Tony did and telling all of us what he had been up to that particular day. This dinner time James watched Peter try and cut his meat and vegetables with just his fork. Obviously Peter had been watching Enrico back at Home Farm but Peter was not quite so dextrous and two or three times the contents of Peter's plate escaped, sometimes violently across the originally white table cloth. I watched my mother to see whether there would be a reaction. If we had done that as kids there would have been sharp words but now mum was a grandmother she had changed her reactions. There were no words, well not from my mum although Christina did launch into an emotional plea for better behaviour. Samantha who was next to me just looked at James with a face that said "don't even think about it". I winked at James and he giggled. Samantha gave me her eye-piercing glare and just muttered 'behave.'

Tony was quite talkative that meal time and he sounded really enthusiastic about his new school, new teachers, his new wooden carving and being with Peter. I'm sure all of the adults around the table were both relieved and delighted that Tony had settled given the recent series of traumas in his life. It was only three weeks ago that Tony had seen his mother knifed and the attackers try to kidnap him. With a couple of friends I had thwarted the kidnap attempt but Danielle had died from the knife wounds. Tony had suddenly found himself alone in the world except for this new family he had just discovered. Having lived all of his ten years in London with his mother Tony had never really known about the Lord family. Tony was the son of my older brother Michael but after Michael was shot some eight years ago now Danielle had fled back to London and kept Tony there. Dad had re-established contact and Danielle had come down to Fotheringham a couple of times but Tony never really knew any of us. It came as a complete surprise when his mother rushed both of them down to Fotheringham to seek sanctuary from her attackers.

Right after the attack it was my sister Samantha who helped Tony and the pair of them went into the hospital to say goodbye to Danielle. Samantha surprised me because she is normally as tough as nails but she told me it was she who wept and Tony was really wonderful. He had kissed his mother goodbye and wished her well on her journey. Coming back in the car from the hospital Samantha had very thoughtfully talked with Tony about his future and how we were all his family and loved him. Tony had seen enough of our family in the brief time he was here to pick the relative stability of my sister-in-law Christina and her son Peter as a safe haven rather than the wild eccentricities of my sister Samantha. It was Christina who took Tony to live with her and Peter at Home Farm. My sister Samantha was still struggling with her own demons as she had just come back from Canada where her husband had been killed in a forest fire. She and her four year-old son James were trying to get their own life into some sort of stability and adding Tony to that mix probably wouldn't have been the best solution. So we were all very happy to see Tony adjusting to his new life.

Tony had one other advantage, although he didn't know it at the time. On the evening of the attack on Danielle and Tony another resident of Fotheringham Manor estate was recovering in hospital from a fainting spell and slight stroke. Enrico Branciaghlia had worked in our forest since 1943 when my great grandfather arranged for Enrico and his elder brother Antonio to be transferred from a P.O.W. camp to our estate. The two Italians had been trained by my great grandfather and by Albert Templeton and they had become excellent workers for us. Our family had put them in one of the estate cottages and Enrico had continued to live there quietly after his brother was killed back in 1990. Both Italians were very skilled with their hands and both men had made many many toys for our family as well as several of the children in the village. As a youngster I had spent hours in their cottage and Enrico was really a part of our family. He'd been working with Peter and young James at Home Farm a couple of weeks ago when he collapsed on the kitchen table. Apparently Peter had taken charge and although he is only nine he had organised his mother to drive all of them to the hospital where they kept Enrico in for observation for a few days. This was rather fortunate as Enrico had been the target for a proposed revenge attack from Idwal Ferris, the elder brother of John Ferris. When Idwal couldn't find Enrico at the cottage Idwal went on a rampage and vandalised the cottage, assaulted my sister, and later ended up raping John's wife. To vent his frustration over my sister Idwal tried to burn our horses and failing to do that successfully he then ended up killing his girlfriend and assaulting John's wife again. It was during this assault that John Ferris ended up killing his brother. All this time Enrico was slowly recovering in hospital. When Christina learnt of the wreck of Enrico's cottage she immediately offered Enrico a new place to stay, namely Home Farm. Peter was delighted and Christina was really happy as now there was another adult in the house and someone who spoke Italian too.

When Christina offered to take Tony and make a new home for him it was an even happier Christina and Tony also gained a new friend in Enrico who really loved kids. Peter had enthusiastically told Tony all about Enrico's ability to carve and Peter had several examples to prove the point. When Enrico learnt that Tony was a soccer fan, and an ardent supporter of Tottenham Hotspur in North London Enrico set about carving a football player especially for Tony. I had heard how grateful and excited Tony was when Enrico finished this and gave it to him. It had been a further bonding of the four people at Home Farm.

At the end of dinner, when James had finally had his necessary two helpings of pudding and custard, my father asked us all to get together in the drawing room as he wanted another family discussion. Samantha managed to persuade James that Dainty didn't care much for overweight riders. I watched James listen to his mother's comment and put on his serious thinking face. He really is quite a charmer when he has this face and he solemnly agreed with his mother that Dainty also needed not to overeat as her rider didn't like overweight horses. She had to stay fit for polo. Samantha crouched down to James's level and with just as serious a face she agreed with her son. It really was quite funny to watch my mother during this very solemn verbal exchange. All she said was, 'I see Samantha is learning,' and dad laughed.

We all trooped into the drawing room and sat down in a variety of comfortable positions.

'Dad,' I said, 'can you take charge of this meeting, not like Chairman Samantha Mao of last time?'

'Fine Daniel but this meeting may be a lot shorter than the last one.'

Here dad paused and looked slowly around the room. My mother nodded her head.

'Well, as you all know we met just under three weeks ago to talk about Brainware and what do we do. Christina and Peter really wanted it to stay in England and Samantha had the idea of asking Rosalind Cohen up in London. I talked to Rosalind soon after that meeting and she discussed it with several people up in the city. After a very positive phone call from Rosalind last Wednesday Sylvia and I went up to London on Monday. We spent two days with Rosalind and her partner Tina Morland and several other people Rosalind had involved in her deliberations.'

'And?' said Samantha.

'Hush Chairman Mao. We had two good days and Rosalind proposes to buy out Brainware and either merge it with her own company or run it as a separate entity. She will probably sort all that out after discussions with her accountant and lawyers but the bottom line as far as we are concerned is that she will buy the entire package. Sylvia and I will walk away with no responsibilities, which is what several of you suggested. So all that is very positive news.'

'Mum do you want to explain the timing?' I was about to add that dad said he had found all the financial details confusing but realised that I didn't need to make that comment so I shut my mouth.

'Fine Daniel. Rosalind is proposing, and we think we will accept the idea of a front end cash settlement of part of the value and an agreed-upon schedule spread over five years probably for the balance. We'll sort out the final numbers later as we will have to consider value changes over time, the effects of interest and other details but it all looks good. As Anthony said it all looks positive. Now, we know that we will have to get lawyers involved which means costs and time but overall we need to discuss what do we, the Lord family do next?'

'Mama, that is fantastic. I am so pleased for you.' Christina got up from her chair and came across and gave my mother a big hug. 'And you too Poppa. I am happy for both of you. Now perhaps you can take it easy. Put the feet up.

'So Grandma, what will happen next?'

'That's the question Peter. That's really why we are all here, to see whether any of us have any special thoughts or ideas what we might do with the money.'

'Dad this is Peter's and the Lord family long term heritage and I wonder whether we should step back just for a moment and ask whether there is anything on the entire estate that needs I'll say improvement? Thinking long term is there anything obvious in the infrastructure that would benefit the continued value of the estate? I know you have made several major renovations on this house but I am thinking, or asking if there is anything along those lines?'

'Daniel it is a good question and you're right. Some time ago, maybe eight years now we had a major overall and repair work done on the roof and modernised the kitchen here. We've got to repair the stables but the insurance will cover most of that and it is relatively minor. Is there anything to do at Home Farm Christina?'

'Nothing major Poppa. There is probably some regular maintenance like painting the boys' bedrooms and now we have Enrico staying with us we should ask him what he might like done with his room. Did I tell you that he told us yesterday he intends to stay with us?'

'Christina that is really good news.'

'It's good for Tony and me too Grandma,' added Peter. 'Now we can all learn to carve like Enrico and we'll be able to make suggestions what he should carve next.'

'Mummy can I go and live with Enrico too?' asked James, who never wanted to be left out of any situation.

'But darling I would be lonely,' said Samantha sorrowfully.

'You can have Terence, or his friend WPC Nicols, or perhaps that other hot woman Janet.'

'Samantha your son seems to have your life all mapped out for you, as well as looking after his own interests.'

'James, just for the moment darling can we both stay in this house until everyone else gets settled? Dainty would be very confused if you came visiting from a different direction and your other friend Katya might not be able to find you at all.'

We all watched James consider the ramifications of his mother's comment. After a moment he got up and walked over to his mother and seriously looked up into her face and said, 'I will stay and look after you Mummy. I won't let you be lonely.'

'Good lad James,' said my dad, 'and can we return to the basic question. I don't hear any major suggestions although there are some maintenance issues we can deal with later. It was a good suggestion though Daniel and worthy of consideration as we go forwards. Staying with your thought though Daniel is there anything else to do with the estate that perhaps we don't have that maybe we should have or would like to have that is a potential investment?'

'Dad, can I come back to some of the ideas we batted around when the Howards were here.'

'More badger gates Daniel?'

'No Samantha but I do have a couple of other ideas. One is educational and the other sport oriented and both could involve some infrastructure investment that might bring in some "green" revenues.'

Mum pricked up her ears and sat forward in her chair. She looked at me with that questioning face. 'What have you and Miss Katya been up to in the forest Daniel?'

'Mum I'm not sure you want to go there, well not with those words.'

'Okay Samantha but we did discuss and look at the possibilities of these two ideas. The first is an Educational Centre. Now this is just an idea and we haven't discussed what that might really envision. It could range all the way from a substantial building with class-rooms, hands-on laboratory-type rooms, little lecture room for presentations, exhibits, you name it all the way to just a series of featured walks with names on plants and trees along a self-guided tour. Depending on the time of year and certainly being aware of any forest operations we could offer the Estate as an Educational Resource for a fee. We would need to be very safety oriented and there may be some additional insurance premiums to cover liability. As I have said we haven't thought through any of the operational details but Katya and I thought this estate offered something special. Katya did mention this idea when she was first here.'

'It's an idea with potential Daniel that's for sure,' said my mother. 'Peter, Tony, what do you think of going into the forest to learn a little more about the environment?'

Tony jumped in and he was quite excited. 'Gran' that's great. Coming from the city it's all a brand new world to me and I think it's a fab place to learn.'

'I think so too Grandma, even though I'm far more at home in the woods than Tony but I think kids would like the chance to see what we have. Don't forget the farm and the work Auntie Stephanie's doing. It would add something new to the estate.'

'Daniel you said you had two ideas son. What was the second, some sporting thing you said? Should we invest in you going on the professional golf tour?'

'No Dad, that wasn't what I had in mind, although it is an interesting thought. The other idea was less expensive, well probably and that was competitive orienteering. Now the estate is not really very big but there is a fair amount of diversity and we could talk with some of the neighbours maybe at allowing such events over a larger area if that was necessary. Again, it means more people on the estate and again the question of liability. We'd have to talk with a lawyer about either idea but they are both green, non-destructive and perhaps more importantly they are investments in children, in the future.'

'Grandfather, I like both Uncle Daniel's ideas. I'm sure as I grow older I will like them even more and would feel very happy to be associated with ideas that help the future. I think they would enhance the reputation of the Lord family name.'

I could see that my father was quite impressed with such a profound statement from the young heir to the estate. He smiled and told Peter he thought they were pretty good too.

'Anthony, can we put those two good ideas on hold for just a moment and think outside the boundaries of the estate. Last time we discussed whether there might be some financial investment we might make if this sale went through. I know Samantha mentioned Betty Ferris and her pies and I think that is a good local idea and we may pursue that next week but is there anything bigger that appeals?'

'Tony might want us to invest in Tottenham Hotspur,' I suggested. 'I hear that several of the larger football team associations have shares and investors.'

'Could we Uncle Daniel, could we? That would be a smashing idea.'

'It's a good thought Tony, and yes I can understand why you are so excited,' said my mother, 'although it is a little outside my sphere of expertise.'

'Is there any benefit in re-investing in Rosalind's company, or even what she turns Brainware into?' asked Samantha. 'You and dad know quite a lot about that kind of business and which companies or technologies have potential. Perhaps we should ask great uncle Matthew? Have you thought about that Mum?'

My mother mused on this and then she turned to dad. 'Maybe Anthony this is too fast. Everyone has only just learnt about the sale so maybe we should wait a week or two to give people a chance to think about the next steps. Even I haven't really got my head around any serious options. Let's just celebrate step one and agree to come back in a couple of weeks with some thoughts.'

'Will we have trifle Grandma?'

'For you darling we will have a special trifle. I'll ask cook to put a gingerbread cookie shaped like a horse dancing on top of the trifle and she will jiggle as you shake the bowl.'

'Smashing,' James agreed.

On this cheerful vision Christina gathered up Peter and Tony and took them back to Home Farm.

Thursday morning I had been busy around the forest. After checking on the progress of the gang thinning out the Douglas fir I had another couple of sites in the forest to see. We were having some drainage problems in one of the compartments and several of the trees were stagnating as their roots were flooded. I did a careful inspection to see where we could cut some ditches and channel the flow under the road with a series of culverts. Then on again downstream to make sure I didn't just move the problem to another location. Nature and man I thought, always a challenge to get us to work together. All the time I was out in the forest that morning I also kept a weather eye out for my two proposals from last night. There was certainly a lot of variety from an educational point of view. Our woodlands were still an eclectic mix of sites and environments so we weren't just a tree farm. If we did lean in that direction we might even change some of the tree species into shrub or even grass sites to add to the mix of habitats. I realised that I would have to discuss some of those thoughts with a wildlife biologist as birds and bees weren't really my speciality. Katya would be pleased though I thought. Katya, ah yes Katya, roll on Friday.

When I came home for lunch I found that dad had taken a telephone message for me. It was Detective Inspector Field. 'What did he say Dad?'

'He didn't Daniel. He said he wanted to talk to you, quite secretive he was. Couldn't understand why he didn't tell me whatever it was but he said specifically he wanted to talk to you first. Perhaps he thinks you don't know something I know and wants to get a first reaction or something without you knowing the details. Anyway, his number is on the pad.'

I looked at the number and wondered what it was that was so special. Thinking over yesterday evening's conversation at the cottage I couldn't imagine anything we hadn't already discussed. Well I told myself, you won't know Daniel will you until you phone so do it lad, do it. I picked up the phone and dialled the numbers.

'Detective Inspector Field please. Ah, it's you. I hadn't realised this was your direct number. Yes, my father gave me your message but he said you were very tight-lipped about any new information. It's about the bones. Yes, well I sort of guessed it might be. They're what? You're sure? Hell that does put a different complexion on things. Two young males you think. But how old, how long have they been there? Your lab thinks they have been there about the same time as the other bones, the dog bones. So you think, well you said you were suspicious but now you seriously think that the dog bones were just a cover for the human ones? But who? No Inspector, I suppose I was just thinking out loud. So where do we go from here? You're tied up with something else this afternoon but you would like to talk with Ferris again this evening. Fine, I'll come down to the cottage this evening around six. In the meantime can I tell Ferris to expect you? Yes, but don't tell him anything else. Yes, I understand Inspector, and I won't tell anyone else either. No, no, rest assured I'll not even tell my family.' I laid down the phone and scratched my head. Two young males buried there about eight years ago. Whoever were they and why were they buried in that cottage? Norton never had any other family surely. Idwal and John never had any mates so who?

'Dangerous thing son.'

'Sorry Dad, what did you say?'

'I said it was dangerous, talking to yourself Daniel.'

'Yes Dad, no Dad, I'm not sure. What did you say?'

'Never mind Daniel but what did that Detective Inspector chappie want, or perhaps what did he say that was so secret?'

'He was interested in the background of the Ferris family.'

'Daniel, I know much more about the Ferris family than you do so try again.'

'Sorry Dad, I promised my lips were sealed.'

'Okay son, no doubt we will all learn something soon enough if it is important but let's have lunch shall we? Your mother has been re-arranging numbers all morning and my head is going round in circles. I think I shall be glad when this deal is finally done and we can get some peace and quiet.'

'Granddad, granddad, mummy wants to take me out riding this afternoon and she wants to know whether you wanted to come out and see me ride? Do you? Do you?'

'Well James that is a very tempting offer but can I think about it over my lunch?'

'If you must but it is a really simple question and yes will do just fine.'

James sped off to find Samantha and I could hear him explaining how granddad had to eat before he could think. 'Isn't that funny Mummy. I don't have to eat before I think. Do you have to eat before you think?'

I listened carefully to my sister's answer as Samantha traditionally acted long before she thought let alone had to wait to eat.

I managed to keep any conversation away from my telephone call during lunch and as soon as I could I took off to find John Ferris. Behind me in the house I caught part of the conversation detailing James going riding and how he would teach Dainty new moves. Always on the move you are James I thought, so like your mother even without any competition. That brought me round to my brother Michael, who had been the main competition for Samantha. Michael, eight years ago, what had been happening brother I mused? You were very friendly, well sort of with Norton Ferris. You probably knew most about the goings on in that cottage. Who else might know? Who else was here? There was Enrico of course and Bob Edwards had been the foreman. There were a couple of the present crew working for us back then. Young Freddie Dunster was one and Norton used to give him a real hard time but he's still alive, and being a pain with John Ferris too. We have Garry Templeton working for us and he was around in 1990 but I can't remember whether he was on the work crew. Too young I thought.

It was hard trying to think back that far, especially as I had been at school much of the time. Still, I could talk quietly with Bob Edwards and with Enrico after I've found out some more from Terence Field. Very soon I arrived at the thinning operation and carefully parked away from any falling trees. I found Bob Edwards trying to show a new worker how to safely operate a chain saw and so I waited until Bob was done. He stepped away from Ronnie Gould, the new employee and I managed to catch Bob's eye.

'How's it coming along?'

'We're doing just fine Mr. Daniel. Most of the lads know the drill well enough but Ronnie here still needs a careful watching. He's a little sloppy with that chain saw but he'll learn. I've kept him apart from the rest of them so any mistakes don't affect anyone else. Otherwise we're on schedule and should be through tomorrow or Monday at the latest.'

'That's really good Bob. Everything looks pretty tidy and I see much of the cut material has already found its way to the yard.'

'Yes Mr. Daniel. I got Freddie involved in that to try and keep him from sniping at John.'

'Actually it is John I have come to see. He's a couple of rows over?'

'I've put him in the farthest row Mr. Daniel with old Tom Hawke next to him. Tom never says 'owt all day and so I thought John would work better without any interference.'

'Good thought Bob. I'll just go and have a word. Looks like a good thinning, even if you and I did the marking. Perhaps we know what we are doing after all?'

Bob laughed and patted my shoulder. 'Make a good team Mr. Daniel. We do all right.'

I walked across the thinned rows looking upwards most of the time. The crowns of the young trees were virtually all free now and there would be lots of light reaching down into the stand. With the reduced competition the remaining trees would grow that much better and we could look forward to a productive plantation. Must have my commercial hat on for a moment I thought; just seeing money in the trees. That wouldn't please Katya. Well Katya, the open trees would let other things grow and a rather sterile plantation may develop into a more diverse woodland. We may even get birds in here. Feeling cheerful I whistled.

John had just finished trimming the tree he had felled and heard me whistling through the trees. He turned and looked at me with a rather worried and uncertain expression.

'Looking for me Mr. Daniel?'

'Aye John but don't look so worried lad. I'm not bringing bad news, well I don't think so. Inspector Field wanted me to check you would be home tonight. He wanted to see you again but he couldn't come this afternoon and so he asked me to tell you he would come and visit around six this evening. I said I'd tell you and also I will be there too.'

'What about Mr. Daniel?'

'I don't rightly know John but I expect it's about his further digging in that hole. Still, he didn't sound too fierce on the phone and so it may just be some more routine questions.'

'That's as maybe Mr. Daniel but that Inspector doesn't have to be fierce. He's a canny man he is. He has those eyes, sort of look right through you. He gives me the shivers Mr. Daniel. He's quiet, soft-spoken but once he gets his teeth in I don't reckon there's any letting go.'

'John, there's something niggling in my mind, perhaps something I'm not letting go but didn't you tell me that Idwal mentioned something about gardening? I'm sure I remember you saying you were surprised. You said it sort of stuck in your mind because it was so unexpected for Idwal to mention such a thing. Can you remember what you said, or better what Idwal said?'

John put down his saw and pushed his hard hat and safety goggles higher up on his head. He took off his work gloves and scratched his head. 'Can't rightly remember Mr. Daniel. Idwal never said anything

234

special in the cottage so it must have been when we went to the pub. We were sitting there drinking, reminiscing really almost like old times but Idwal kept harping on about revenging our dad. He had this fixation Mr. Daniel. I suppose he had spent much of his time inside going over and over it until it had become an obsession.'

'Yes John, I understand that. Well I don't really understand that but I do hear what you say. But didn't he say something that caught your attention?'

'Right Mr. Daniel, now I remember, he asked about Flo Whelks? He asked whether she still lived in that old cottage of hers on the edge of the village. Now our dad used to do some deals with Larry Whelks but then you probably know all about that Mr. Daniel?'

'Yes John but Larry Whelks has gone and what was special about Florence Whelks?'

'It's funny Mr. Daniel because it wasn't the cottage Idwal was interested in but the garden, or rather the garden path. He mentioned something about some special path she had and that he might have to go and do some gardening. Yes, that was it, that's why I remembered because Idwal wouldn't know gardening if he fell over it. He's never been interested in gardening and that was what struck me as unusual. Don't know why though.'

'Did he say anything else? What was special about this garden, or this garden path?'

'He didn't say. Actually he wouldn't say and when I asked him the same question he just told me to forget it, forget he ever asked. He changed the subject right away.'

'Florence Whelks eh? Well yes your dad certainly did some deals with her son Larry but he's long gone. Actually he disappeared about the time your dad died and we fired you.'

'Maybe Mr. Daniel. I was still in shock probably what with dad getting killed and then Idwal and I out on our ears so to speak. Don't blame your father Mr. Daniel. Our old dad was a bit of a cheap villain with sticky fingers and a poor head for any scam. Idle bugger he was too if truth be told. No Mr. Daniel I don't hold any grudge against your family. Your dad came looking for me and your mum made me proud when she offered me my old job back. Helped me get back on my feet and gave me some confidence. I wouldn't have had the courage to go asking after Betty if that hadn't happened thanks to your family.' John stopped and shook his head.

'John, let's not go there,' I said. 'We're all working towards a better future and maybe this evening we can clear up some of the mystery of the hidey-hole. Seeing as you never knew anything about it there are no worries as far as you are concerned. So, this evening around six o'clock and hopefully we can get this sorted.'

I left a somewhat puzzled and woebegone John Ferris and walked back to my Landrover. Larry Whelks disappears, well gets killed up in Bristol by Idwal Ferris. Now, after all this time Idwal Ferris remembers he is still interested in Florence Whelks's garden, well garden path. Perhaps we should go and take a look. Old Florence never does anything in her garden. No one ever sees her. Larry used to live there and he did everything for her. Wonder how she survives now?

It didn't take me long to drive from the plantation out through the southern end of the estate and onto the road running towards the village. Florence Whelks lived in an old very ramshackle cottage on the outskirts. Because of the bend in the narrow road you couldn't actually see the village and the cottage property was fairly extensive. There was a large mass of vegetation in what had been a front garden and a laneway led up beside the house towards two large dilapidated wooden outbuildings. Everything was still, quiet and peaceful. Just a corner of quaint old

England I thought with the humans being overrun by nature. Perhaps the plants in the garden are triffids?

Chuckling at my vivid imagination I pushed open the front garden gate. Needless to say this didn't have any effect and the gate fell down in front of me as it came completely off its hinges. I must have blushed and felt a little foolish as I stepped over the gate into the garden. Shrubs, grasses, wildflowers and three very old fruit trees overwhelmed this garden. The windows at the front of the cottage peered at me like large eyes, somewhat accusatively as if I had broken the gate and trespassed. I walked further into this English wilderness. A rather irregular gravelled pathway led from the now dismantled gate towards the front door of the cottage. Several large flagstones occurred haphazardly in this gravel path. The edges of this indistinct path were lined with little stones that looked as if they had been painted green. I walked rather slowly and hesitantly up the path towards the door of the cottage and I wasn't quite sure what I was looking at or for. I must have been peering rather myopically at the path and concentrating because the screech of the door and the louder screech of Flo's voice made me leap out of my skin and I assume I jumped a mile in the air.

Samantha was leaning over me and peering rather worriedly into my eyes.

'Daniel, are you all right?'

'Samantha, why are you here? What happened?'

'Daniel I was just riding past with James when I saw you lying on the path and not moving. I suppose James saw your Landrover at first and I was paying attention to him so he didn't fall off with all his twisting about. When I was sure he was safe I turned and suddenly saw you lying on the path. Whatever are you doing?'

'Where's Florence?'

'I don't know Daniel. She's certainly not obvious.'

Samantha stood up and I assume she was scanning the horizon for any sight of the source of that incredible screech. She crouched back alongside me. 'Daniel, I'll just go back and check on James and then I'll come and help you up. You still seem a little groggy.'

I flopped back onto the path and felt my head very gingerly with my fingers. Jesus, that was some bump. I suppose I must have jumped when I heard that God-awful screech and banged my head on the flagstones when coming back to earth and passed out. I tried to sit up but my feet couldn't find any purchase as I kicked along the path.

'Daniel, wait up a moment. I'll help. James is fine but he can't understand why you are lying down in the middle of the afternoon.'

'Just tell James I'm waiting for the train. No, better not or he'll want to come and lie beside me. Tell him I'm listening for earthworms, or space invaders or something. Help me up Samantha.'

'Say please.'

'Samantha this isn't the time to play big sister/little brother. Help me up please. I seem to be having difficulty finding my feet.'

Samantha managed to half sit me up and I rolled around onto my knees. Shaking my head a little I slowly pushed myself upwards and managed to stand.

'What are these Daniel?'

'What are what Samantha? I'm having a little problem seeing straight. What are you babbling about?'

'This,' she said and she held up one of the small green stones that had been edging the path.

'I don't know.'

'What were you doing here anyway? I think I asked that before but you were still only semi-conscious.'

'Yes, let me stand a moment. Where's old Flo'?'

'Daniel, forget Flo'. She's not in sight and you haven't answered my question.'

'Well, if you must know I had a call from Detective Inspector Terence you know who Field.'

'Yes yes Daniel, I know you had a call and you kept very quiet about it at lunchtime. So, what did Terence say?'

'That I wasn't to tell anyone else.'

'What?'

'I just said I wasn't to tell.'

'What weren't you to tell? Heavens Daniel, you can be very obtuse at times little brother.'

'There you go again with the little brother routine. If I stand up straight. Ouch, that's painful. As I was saying if I stand up straight Samantha I am now as tall as you are, perhaps taller, so let's have less of the little brother please.'

'Yes yes Daniel but you are avoiding the question. What did Terence say?'

'My lips are sealed, but what I will tell you is that I went to see John Ferris after lunch.'

'And? Daniel, this is like getting blood out of a stone.'

'Well I've just been putting blood on the stones,' I said as I felt a sticky patch on the back of my head.

'And what did you tell John Ferris that you can't tell me?'

'I didn't tell John Ferris anything.'

'Like me!'

'But I did ask him something.'

'What?'

'If you must know John had mentioned earlier to me that Idwal had said something strange when he was here before all the trouble.'

'Which was?'

'Patience. Let me tell the story please before my head explodes. Can I go and sit in my Landrover and you'd better check on that mounted warrior with you before he and Dainty take off to pastures green?'

'Oh yes James. Mummy's coming darling.'

Samantha stopped her inquisition to go and check on James. Fortunately Dainty is a wonderfully docile little horse and she had quietly stood there with Gypsy at the now flattened garden gate. I walked very slowly down the path towards the two horses. Gypsy lifted his head and snickered at me. I gently stroked his nose and held my throbbing head against his. Dainty moved slowly over to stand beside me and she too nuzzled at me. I stroked her forehead too and just rested for a moment.

'Uncle Daniel did you hear any earthworms?'

'No James,' I whispered. 'There were too many horses going past and so all the earthworms rushed away to hide.'

'Uncle Daniel you're funny.'

'I'm glad you think so James. You look pretty good up there. You're coming along really well as a rider.'

'Mummy says we will be jumping soon.'

I winced. I wasn't sure whether it was the pain in my head or the thought of my sister teaching her son to jump at such an early age. Your son Samantha I thought. Wonder what I would do?

'Daniel, you wanted to sit down. You wanted to tell me what this was all about.'

'Yes and no Samantha.'

I sat down in the Landrover and Samantha slowly led the two horses so we were all close together and safely off the road.

'You are sitting Daniel and now it is story time. Idwal said something strange. Shall we continue?'

'John told me Idwal had asked about Florence Whelks's cottage.'

'Here?'

240

'Yes, here and John had said Idwal had asked about the garden.'

'Which is a word that probably wasn't in Idwal's normal vocabulary?'

'Mummy what's vocibelly?'

'Vocabulary darling, it's words. All the words you know fit into your vocabulary.'

'And this Idwal didn't have garden in his? Everyone knows what a garden is Mummy. He must have been a very weird man Mummy. Was he Italian like Enrico? Idwal doesn't sound very Italian. Perhaps he was....'

'James love can we hold it for a moment and let Uncle Daniel finish his story about this garden?'

'Of course Mummy. I only asked.'

'Daniel, the garden, Florence Whelks's garden and Idwal, him of the weird vocabulary?'

'John said that Idwal was interested in knowing whether Florence still lived here and then he asked about the garden. John said he mentioned there was something special about the path and that he, Idwal might have to come and do some gardening. When John questioned him further about why Idwal just clammed up and changed the subject. Told John to forget he ever asked.'

'So you did a Samantha?'

'A Samantha, I don't understand.'

'You came charging down here without any thinking and plunged straight in. Looking at the gate it appears you didn't even wait to try and open it but bull-dozed straight through it. That's a Samantha brother.'

I laughed but it hurt my head so much that I soon stopped.

'I must have been looking at the garden and the path and not really knowing what I was looking for when Florence opened the door and screeched. I'm not sure which made the most noise but I was so engrossed looking I must have jumped, fallen over and knocked myself out. The next thing I knew was you peering at me. I must have appeared surprised because you seemed quite worried.'

'Beast,' Samantha said, 'I was worried Daniel. You weren't moving, you were just lying there. I jumped off Gypsy and ran up the path to see what had happened.'

'Well now you know as much as I do. I couldn't see anything special in the garden and we still don't know where or why Idwal wanted to do any gardening.'

'What was special about the path?'

'It's rocky and it's hard,' I said feeling my head again.

'Look into my eyes Daniel.'

'I'm not Terence you know.'

'Daniel this is Dr. Samantha talking. Look into my eyes. I want to see whether you're concussed at all. This is clinical Daniel.'

'Yes Doctor,' I said. 'Actually it might be better if Katya looked.'

'Daniel for heavens sake hold still. You're worse than James.'

'I didn't do anything Mummy, honest. Can we go now? I'm getting hungry and even Dainty is trying to find something good to eat.'

'Just a moment poppet and I'll be right with you. I just need to check your Uncle Daniel is safe to drive home. He wasn't content with flattening the garden gate but he had to dig up the path too. You'll have to come back Daniel and apologise to Florence and mend her gate, such as it is. Replace it may be a more realistic word than repair. I think you're okay. How do you feel Daniel? Can you see straight? How many fingers?'

I gave myself another shake and a quick mental checkover. I flexed my fingers and stretched the toes. Slowly I turned my head but that hurt. 'I think I'll make it back home. Thanks. I'm glad you were there in the road when that all happened. I don't think old Flo' would have come to my rescue.'

'Mummy!'

'I'm right there James. Your uncle is safe to drive I think and so we can sit and watch him to start with. Then we'll walk slowly home.'

'But I want to go fast.'

'James love let's walk along the road and then we can go in past the big old oak tree and maybe move a little faster when we are in the woods.'

'Smashing Mummy.'

I slowly turned the Landrover around and drove carefully back to our gates and up my father's precious long stately drive to the house. I parked round in the yard but continued sitting in the Landrover for a while. After I felt a little better I walked into the house through the kitchen. Feeling a little groggy I got as far as one of the kitchen chairs before I felt I had to sit down.

'Master Daniel, whatever have you done? You look as white as a ghost. Is that blood I see seeping down your neck? My goodness just you rest there and I'll get some warm water and a flannel. You safe to sit there? You're not going to fall over or anything? Should I go and get your mum?'

'No cook, I've just had quite a bump and still feel a little woozy. I'll rest here a moment and then go and get cleaned up.'

'Master Daniel, you just sit still there please. I'm going to get your mother and then we'll see what's to be done.'

Cook scurried off and a moment later my mother came striding back into the kitchen.

'Daniel whatever has happened? Cook says you nearly fainted and crashed on the floor.'

'Mum it's not quite that bad although thank you cook very much. I was out at Florence Whelks's cottage and looking for something when I got such a shock I must have jumped and fallen over on their flagstone path. I can only assume I banged my head when I fell over.'

243

'And next thing you knew was me looking at you from close up,' Samantha added as she came into the kitchen with James.

'Uncle Daniel was listening for worms Grandma. But he said we frightened them off with the horses. That can't be true as Dainty is always very quiet, isn't she Mummy?'

'Hush darling, your uncle is still feeling the effects of knocking himself out.'

'Daniel let me look at that bump and bathe it a little. After that we'll get you to lie down somewhere before you frighten cook any more.'

'More, more, yes more, more gingersnaps cookie please. Do you have any more gingersnaps, please?'

The rather wistful request of James brought all the three ladies round to look at him. My mother was about to say something but then I saw her close her mouth and smile. Before Samantha could say anything cook had the tin down from the shelf and opened it for James. 'Here you are love. Take two 'cos I'm sure you'd like two.'

'Thanks, two, yes thanks.'

My mother turned back to me.

'Now you've taken care of that little hungry invalid Mum perhaps you could look at my bonce? I know it's bleeding and quite a lump but I did manage to drive back here you know.'

'I'm not a evil-lid Uncle Daniel I'm just hungry.'

'James you're a little rascal,' I managed to say with a smile on my face and the word you're trying to say is invalid.'

'What was special about Florence Whelks's garden path Daniel?'

Now I had been sitting here wondering when my mother would start her questioning and so I deliberately prevaricated.

'That's just what Samantha asked,' I said, stalling for time.

'And what did you tell Samantha?' Mum asked as she gently swabbed at my aching head.

'I told her my lips were sealed Mum. I promised Inspector Field I wouldn't say anything until later this evening. He wants to ask some questions and he doesn't want his witnesses corrupted with advance knowledge or misconceptions.'

'Piffle Daniel. What can Florence Whelks possibly have done to affect our situation? We've never had any dealings with her or with her cottage. Her husband Tom used to work on the estate but that was years ago. He died before you were born Daniel. So why were you in her garden?'

'Truce Mum. Let's say I remembered something John Ferris said to me a week or so ago and it was rather unexpected so I went to investigate.'

'And?'

'Yes Daniel, you sort of left me there at this same halt in the story back at the cottage.'

'You were at Florence Whelks's cottage too Samantha? What were you doing there?'

'Picking Uncle Daniel up off the path Grandma but Uncle Daniel couldn't stand up and mummy had to sort of lift him. His feet kept scrabbling on the path and I .....'

Samantha gently placed her fingers across the little lips of Master James and squeezed.

'Mum, James and I were riding past when James saw the Landrover and cried out. Just after that I saw Daniel lying stretched out on the garden path and not moving so I jumped off Gypsy and went to see what was the matter.'

'And he was.....- oo, sorry Mummy.'

'As Daniel said Mum he'd had a shock, fallen over and knocked himself out. We helped him up and sat him down in the Landrover until he could drive back here.'

'So we're still in the dark Daniel as to why you were there in the first place.'

'All right, I suppose I can tell you part of the story. John Ferris had mentioned to me that when he was drinking with Idwal in the pub that first night his brother mentioned something very uncharacteristic, well uncharacteristic for him that is. Idwal had asked whether Florence Whelks still lived in her cottage.'

'Nothing strange there Daniel. Larry Whelks used to live with his mother in that cottage and Norton Ferris used to do some shady deals with Larry Whelks. We all knew that.'

'Yes Mum but it was the next bit that was strange because then Idwal asked about the garden and the garden path and hinted to John that he, Idwal, might have to do some gardening there. Now the idea of Idwal doing any gardening was so unlikely that John remembered and he told me. So, after talking with John this afternoon I thought I would go and look what was special or unusual about Florence Whelks's garden path.'

'There's no gate Grandma. Mummy thinks Uncle Daniel flattened it. It was on the ground when we were there.'

'And was there anything special about the path? It seems you had a very low-level inspection. Actually a close encounter I'd say.'

'Sure, of the third kind. But I was looking Mum, trying to see anything that would interest Idwal. I suppose I was really concentrating when the front door opened with a fantastic screech accompanied by a banshee wail from Florrie herself and together these startled me out of my skin and I must have crashed over.'

'And the path?'

'Even after the close encounter there was nothing special that I could see.'

Everyone thought this was a rather tame ending and after my mother patched me up I managed to walk slowly into the drawing room where I gratefully flopped onto the couch.

The taxi from the railway station slowed down and passed the Whelks cottage and its flattened garden gate. The driver stopped the cab and after a conversation with the passengers he reversed a little and turned down the laneway that led to the outbuildings and the back of the cottage. The rear door of the taxi opened and a large stout man emerged slowly struggling with a case. On the other side the door also opened and a skinny long-haired girl dressed all in black kind of slid out. She looked about her and sniffed. The stout man moved round to the boot of the taxi and with the help of the driver he retrieved four large suitcases. Looking carefully into his wallet the stout man paid the taxi driver and the car slowly backed out of the laneway and returned to the station. Phillip Whelks, Larry Whelks's brother and Florence Whelks's son had come home. He had also brought with him Margaret Whelks, his daughter, although she liked to be called Vanda. Vanda dressed in black, wore black makeup on her white pasty face, thought in black and was a beautiful exotic product of Australia.

Phillip, or Phil Whelks was Larry's younger brother and at age fifty one he had come back to see his old mum. When he was a teenager Phil had run off to sea out of Bristol docks. Eventually the life proved too bloody boring and so Phil jumped ship in Sydney Australia and set up business as a small-time thief out of Kings Cross. Women had come and gone but about twenty years ago Phil had ended up with a daughter which for some reason he kept. Margaret Whelks had grown up in the colourful environment of Kings Cross and emerged at this time as a Goth, a dyke, a drug addict, entranced with her pierced body parts and an ardent believer in kinky sex – just what a quiet little Somerset village needed. However, she was a dab hand at darts.

When Phil pushed open the back door he was nearly bowled over by Goebbels, Flo's Jack Russell terrier who was true to his breed with non-stop energy and a barrel like body. It was only after a screech from Florence that Goebbels paused and looked at his mistress. Margaret Whelks looked at the dog and dared it to move. It was an interesting reunion.

After a discussion with her mother Samantha decided that her brother was in no fit state to drive to meet up with Terence at Ferris's cottage and so she decided to drive me. My head still hurt and I didn't feel too stable on my legs so I reluctantly accepted my sister's offer. However, I did force an agreed-upon silence from Samantha at the meeting.

Inspector Field was already at the cottage when we arrived. I quickly explained why Samantha was there, just as my driver, and why I had a bandage wrapped around my head. The Inspector looked at me and then he looked at my sister as if daring her to open her mouth. She just smiled and drew her finger across her lips inferring they were zipped. We all walked in through the back door of the cottage. John was expecting us, well he was expecting Inspector Field and myself and so there were only three chairs.

'John don't worry about it. I'll just stand here against the wall and listen. It's Inspector Field's visit rather than mine. I suppose I'm as interested in the answers and the outcome but he's the one with the questions. Samantha sat down quietly on the third chair and smiled supportively at John.

'Mr. Ferris you told us you never knew anything about your father's hidey-hole?'

'That's right Inspector. First I knew of it was when I came back to the cottage that evening with Mr. Daniel here and PC Meadows.'

'And neither you or your brother, or your father ever had any dogs?'

'No, nothing like that.'

'And nobody ever came to call?'

'As I said before not that I knew about. Dad might have had people over when Idwal and I were out working, or when we were down the pub like but not when we were here.'

'So you know nothing about the bones?'

'Honest Inspector, nothing about the bones and nothing about that bloody hole.'

'Who worked with you on the forest gang Ferris back in 1990, when your father was here?'

'Christ I can't remember that after all this time. Mr. Daniel here would probably know better than I would. Leastways his dad would have the employment records back in the Forest Office. That's right Mr. Daniel isn't it? You'd have all those records?'

I kept quiet. This was Inspector Field's show and I didn't want to disturb the scene. Terence Field let the silence hang in the air. John fidgeted about on his chair. 'There was Bob Edwards of course. He was the foreman under dad. Enrico was working then and there was Peter Buckley, Harry Thomas and perhaps Tim Middlewich, although perhaps he was too young then. Of course Freddie Dunster sometimes worked with the crew. It all depended on what the job was. There were probably two or three others that I've forgotten. Why do you ask? They're still around, well except for Harry Thomas 'cos he died three years ago now.'

'Who was Larry Whelks?'

'Inspector I told you that last time. He was a character who lived in the village and used to buy and sell things. Dad used to talk with 'im.'

'He never had any relatives this Larry Whelks?'

'Only his old mum. Larry lived with his mum. She's still there although Larry disappeared. Is it him down in the hole? Is that who's down there under those bones?'

'Larry didn't have a son or anything? Didn't have any kids?'

'Not that I know Inspector. I never really knew Larry. It was always our dad that talked to Larry. I suppose Idwal talked to him a bit, especially just before the time that dad got killed. I remember that Larry was really pissed off the night our dad got killed. I think our dad was trying to sell some fence posts on to Larry Whelks and when Idwal and I went into the pub that night Larry grabbed both of us and wanted to bash our heads together.'

'About?'

'I dunno really Inspector. Idwal hinted that dad was trying to sell these posts and Larry had a sale already done for them but of course dad hadn't delivered on time. He was late or something and that buggered up Larry's deal. Larry was really mad trying to find dad that night. When Larry started talking about the posts Idwal thought he knew where dad might be. That's when we went looking Mr. Daniel and found your brother's Landrover upside down in the stream. Gave us a real fright that did 'cos we thought Mr. Michael was in the Landrover. Charged up to the Big House we did and told your father. Your dad took over and Taffy Williams came up with his tow truck and we managed to winch the Landrover out of the stream. Your mum Mr. Daniel nearly slipped down into the stream she was so upset trying to reach the Landrover. When we finally opened the door it was our dad inside and not Mr. Michael.'

'So you don't know anything more about Larry Whelks, or his mother?'

'Only what I was telling Mr. Daniel here Inspector, earlier today.'

Inspector Field paused and turned his face to me.

'You spoke to Ferris after our telephone conversation?'

'Yes Inspector,' I said. 'I told him we would meet tonight here at the cottage, and I asked him about something he had told me before that seemed out of character.'

'Out of character for whom?'

'Idwal Ferris Inspector. John had told me before that Idwal had seemed interested in Florence Whelks's garden and suggested he do a bit of gardening.'

'And did Idwal do any gardening?'

John was becoming quite agitated. 'No Inspector, he didn't have any time did he? He was with me in the cottage at first, then the pub which was where he mentioned the garden, and after that we all know what he did.' John's face reddened with the memories of what Idwal had done.

'What about the afternoon, before the fire at the stables?'

'I had the van, didn't I Mr. Daniel? There really wasn't a lot of time in between.'

'But you and Daniel couldn't find him in that time could you Ferris? You don't know where he went.'

'Inspector, for what it's worth I had asked John about Idwal's funny comment and after that I deliberately went down to Florence Whelks's cottage and looked. Unless it was all a hoax there must have been something special about that garden. Idwal wouldn't dream of gardening. As I said it was out of character and so I went to look and that is where I got this bang on the head and why Samantha is here as my driver because I am still a little woozy. However, I didn't say anything else to Ferris this afternoon.'

There was another pregnant silence while Inspector Field digested the last little speech.

'Ferris, I'm going to have my people here again tomorrow looking in that hole. It stays off limits you understand?'

'Yes Inspector.'

'That's all for now. I'll leave you to your peace and quiet. Thank you Mrs. MacRae and Mr. Lord but I would like a word with you both outside. Night Ferris.'

John grunted and slumped back into his chair.

'Night John, we'll see you tomorrow as usual on the crew.' Samantha and I left and followed the Inspector over to his car.

'Daniel no harm done but I wish you had informed me about the trip to the Whelks cottage. Somehow that family is involved in all this but I don't know how.'

'Terence, what were the other bones? I heard in there that you deliberately didn't mention them. You obviously were waiting to see whether John knew anything about them or even if he might think of someone they could be. So what were they?'

I watched Terence Field turn this question over in his mind and I could guess he was thinking how much to tell us. Finally he looked at Samantha and me and said, 'let this go no further for the moment but we think we have the skeletons of two teenage males. We're trying to track them through our "Missing Persons" files but we're not sure exactly how old or whether they are local. Our experts think they are the bodies of two young teenagers, thirteen or fourteen but Ferris didn't offer any suggestions. Look, I'll tell you something else. It's in the public record so it's really no secret and I did mention it before but it may explain my interest in Whelks. Idwal Ferris was convicted of manslaughter in 1991 and the man he killed was Larry Whelks.'

'So that's why he disappeared.'

'Yes Samantha, Idwal killed him up in Bristol. It was rather a convoluted case although it appeared that Idwal and Larry were partners in some deal with one of the heavy mob in Bristol. If I've got the story right Larry knew the Bentley brothers. That was Ken and Ron Bentley and they were big time villains in 1991 in Bristol. They were into most things but particularly buying and selling stolen property, especially jewellery and precious metals.'

'So why did Idwal kill Larry?'

'Larry had set up this deal, this sale with the Bentleys. Sometime into the deal either Larry did double cross Idwal or Idwal thought he was being double-crossed. Perhaps the Bentley brothers thought they could do a better deal if there was just one seller so they told Idwal that Larry was trying to sell on his own and cut Idwal out. Idwal went ballistic and killed Larry, somewhere in the Bristol docks. Idwal wasn't all that smart and we tracked him down and eventually he ended up in court. It wasn't very complicated although we never did find out what Larry and Idwal were trying to sell. From the word on the street Ken and Ron Bentley never got whatever it was.'

'So when you were asking John in there about Larry's family you wondered whether the bones might be a relative of Larry's?'

'Just turning over the odd stone.'

'Terence, this might be nothing but we did find something unusual in Florence Whelks's garden.'

I turned to look at Samantha. 'We did?' I asked.

'Yes,' she said and she smiled before she added, 'it was a team effort Terence. Daniel fell over and I rushed to help him up. He had fallen on the path and banged his head on some flagstones. As I helped him up he couldn't get his feet to obey him. He was still a little groggy. So here he was scrabbling his feet about while I tried to lift up his arms. Net result was a vertical Daniel and several of these kicked about the path.' Samantha reached into her pocket and pulled out two of the green pebbles I had seen lining the edge of the path. 'For part of the path these seemed to be along the edges. I really wasn't paying much attention as I was trying to help Daniel stand up but they did seem a little odd. Almost without thinking I slipped these two in my pocket. I don't know what they are, or even if they are anything at all but all this talk about the path got me thinking. But, before we go any further the path also has several flagstones down the middle and perhaps those are just as important or relevant. What do they say though Terence, it's all in the details?'

Terence took the two stones and looked at them. He scratched one with his fingernail but all he managed to do was break his nail. 'Thanks Samantha. I'll let someone clean these up and look at them. As you say they might be nothing but we need to look at everything. That cottage is involved somehow.'

'Long time no see Ma.'

'Good riddance it was. Glad to see the back of you. Useless you were but you sure pissed off your dad when you ran away.' Florence Whelks cackled.

'Where's Larry? He said he had something for me. Actually he said he was coming out to Australia but then he never came.'

'What did he 'ave? Never had much ever did he? Small-time painter, small-time carpenter and small-time thief that's all he ever was. Skulking around in the shadows and filching this and flogging that. He never had a pot to piss in. Why'd you think he stayed here all the time? Free rent that's why. Cheap bugger he was so don't you go believing he ever had anything for you. Come out to Australia? In your dreams son.'

'No Ma, straight up. He got real excited. Christ he wrote me two letters. Full of it he was. Said he'd won the Crown Jewels. Out on the next boat.'

'Doesn't show up though does he?'

'So where is he now?'

'Six feet under you stupid git. He never had anything or if he did it died with him. Got killed didn't he? That young loser Idwal Ferris killed him. They all got mixed up with some high-flying losers up in Bristol. Big fight and everyone screaming about who stole what and bang-bang. Poor old Larry.'

'So that's why he never showed.'

'Phil, don't try and put one over me son just 'cos you think I'm old and past it. That was nearly eight years ago so don't come the innocent as if it's just yesterday. Why you here? And who's this waste of space next to you dressed like the wicked witch of the west? Got a tongue girlie? You are a girl ain't you?'

'Mum this is Margaret, my daughter.'

'I'm Vanda you foul-mouthed old bag, slagging my dad off like that. Christ we come back to see how you are and all we get is a piss and vinegar greeting.'

Florence cackled and Goebbels pricked up his ears. 'She's got spunk this one Phil. Takes after me.'

Just as quickly Florence turned and asked again, 'so why you 'ere? What have you done? You never did social visits so you're probably running. Who's after you? Not that I'd do much about it. Leave off girl, that ain't for the likes of you. Enough Phil, get Polly here to go and put the bloody kettle on and we'll all have tea.'

Lord's Legacy

Bones in the Ferris cottage: I wonder if that is what happened all those years ago? Freddie Dunster sat at his mother's kitchen table and tried to remember all those years ago. I never told anyone and probably no one ever knew, and Auntie Violet probably never cared or even noticed if what the twins said was true.

When was it now, just after New Years 1991? I'd caught them skulking around our house when mum was out and I was back here skiving off from work. Suppose they must have been about fourteen, just a couple of years younger than me. Shit, I didn't even know who they were. Mum had never said anything about her having a younger sister.

'You're Freddie? You must be Freddie, and your mum's Rosemary right?'

'Who the fuck are you, skulking around our 'ouse? How do you know my name, and me mum's?'

'Freddie you got anything to eat. We're starving cous'. We ain't eaten since day before yesterday. Got any bread and dripping? Any sugar butties?'

'Who are you?' What do you want?'

'Give us a bite and we'll tell you. We're related but we're also fucking starving. Come on cousin.'

I must have had some difficulty both taking in this incredible information and trying to understand the scouse accent. I rooted around in the kitchen and dug out some bread and jam which the two of them scoffed at an alarming rate.

'Any chance of a cuppa?'

I made some tea and we ended up finishing off the loaf before they gave any sign they would speak again.

'We're Jack and Lennie Cotton.'

'So?'

'Your mum's our mum's sister – we're cousins. Your mum Rosemary Biddle had a younger sister called Violet. She's our mum. Anyway, our mum must have run away from here when she was a kid.'

'Where?' Although I could guess the answer just listening to their voices.

'Liverpool, home of John, Paul, George and Ringo.'

'Fuck that, so what?'

'Well our mum went and got married to this bog-stupid Irishman so we're Jack and Lennie Murphy now.'

'I thought you said your name was Cotton?'

'We'll get there Freddie, 'old your 'orses. Our dad was a drunk and turned our mum into a drunk. He never did a day's work and we lived on the dole yer know although that wasn't good enough so he turns our mum out on the streets.'

'What do you mean out on the streets?'

'He put her on the game didn't he? Then the silly sod got killed and so mum had no protection. So we went through a bloody parade of uncles if you know what I mean.'

I was sixteen at the time and living in a quiet country village and so I didn't really know what the two of them were talking about. I nodded as if I knew what they meant.

'Life was the shits Freddie and we were getting the rough end. One of the blokes decides he will adopt us and change our name into Cotton. He thought it sounded better than some bog Irish name and he wanted to put us out on the streets too. Rent boys like. Thought twins would be a good puller. Well this all happened recently and Lennie here decided he wanted out. He wasn't going to be no bum boy just because our mum was on the game so we decided we'd leg it.'

Lennie took over the story from Jack although looking at them or listening to them I couldn't have told one from the other. They were talking about a world I'd never seen or even heard about.

'So, where to go like? Now our mum has her odd sober moment and we learnt that she had a sister, your mum. Where, where mum? Christ it was hard trying to find out where she came from, or where her sister was. Even when we learnt the name it took us a while to find where in the fuck you were. Jesus this is nowheres-ville. What the fuck do you people do here? No, don't bother. Got any more butties?'

I dug around in the kitchen and unearthed some old cake. This disappeared in nothing flat.

'We ain't going back. That bully Lester Cotton will have us out on the streets like our mum. We ain't peddling our arses for no one. So Freddie, where you going to 'ide us? Mum will probably never know where we've gone. Even when she's sober she's not really with us. Old Lester don't know fuck all about where mum came from but we don't want no one to see us for a while. Let all the dust settle and we can appear. So, where can we go?'

I suppose I must have sat there in the kitchen somewhat stunned. Half of me was keeping an ear out for my mum because I was supposed to be at work although there was bugger all going on in the garden this time of year. Garden, garden sheds, now that was a possibility. There were lots of possible places up in the yard.

The twins didn't have much; a few odd clothes crudely tied up with rope and two old plastic shopping bags. I rummaged around in my room and found a couple of odd gloves, an old scarf and a jacket that would fit one of them. In the closet I dug around until I found an old blanket we used to have that was a bit scorched. There wasn't much left to scrounge in the kitchen but I pinched one of mum's rather battered pots and a couple of tins of beans. In the kitchen drawer I took out two spoons, an old knife and a rather rusty can opener. 'Look, I'll try and get some better things tomorrow if I can but this will help for now.'

'Great Freddie but where we going?'

'There's several sheds up on the estate where I work. It's fairly quiet right now and I'll take you up there. I'll try and find a better place tomorrow when I've had a chance to think. This is a bit of a shock but it might be quite a lark too. Never knew I had any family like you two. Mum never said she had any sister. Jesus, cousins, think on that?'

'Sure Freddie but let's get out of 'ere before your mum returns and we blow the whole fucking charade. We ain't here remember; not for a couple of weeks anyway. Come on Jack, let's move it.'

I took them up to the Estate yard the back way rather than prancing down Sir Anthony's precious driveway. The twins muttered on about so many fucking trees and grass but I could only understand half of what they were saying. At the back of the feed barn were a couple of dilapidated old stalls that we hadn't used for years. There was still a lot of hay around and that would keep them warm. Very carefully, making sure no one was about I showed Lennie where the tap was for water. I told them the hours the crew worked but they were not likely to be up here. I also told them who was in the Big House and that any of the family might decide to go riding at any time and be in and out of the stables and this feed barn. As I usually looked after the horses there shouldn't be many other people wandering about in here. I told them to keep their heads down and I would talk with them again tomorrow. I'd try and get some more food but I had to be careful not to tip off my mum. Fortunately there wasn't much work going on at this time so I could probably pop down to the village shops.

Looking back I suppose I was quite excited. Suddenly I had more family, cousins, two cousins, and there was the high of something secret, something illegal probably and something only I knew about. I spent some time working around the sheds and the stables like any normal day but everything was fairly quiet. I tried to think how best to get some more food and whether there was a better place to hide the twins. When I had finished work I made sure nobody was around and went and did a last check with Jack and Lennie before I went home. They had bedded down and looked tired but less starved. I said I'd see them tomorrow.

Fortunately my mum was all excited about something that had happened in the village and she didn't really notice that we'd run out of bread and other things. Carefully I tried to be helpful and offered to go down to the shops and pick up anything she might want. With her mind still on events in the village I conjured up a list that included some extras for the cousins. I told mum I'd get the money for groceries out of her purse and managed to slip an extra couple of pounds into my pocket. That should help for a little while. It was when I was walking back from the shops and thinking where I could hide my extra supplies when it struck me. I had been thinking about hiding places for the food and trying to decide whether our root cellar would be safe enough when I suddenly had a brain wave – the cave.

I had heard Enrico talking about a cave with young Master Daniel over Christmas time. Daniel had been all excited about it. I had thought nothing much about it until I later heard it might contain some treasure. Now being a teenager this was a possible adventure and so I had casually asked Enrico where it was. Enrico was a very trusting old man and I had always got on well with him. I unobtrusively slipped it into a different conversation and learnt where it might be. I knew the forest pretty well and it didn't take me long to find this very old tree that used to have a fork in it. The first time I was a bit spooked and scared but the cave wasn't very big and there was nothing there anyway. But, it would be a great place to hide. I managed to slip back into our house and hide away the extra food while mum was doing something else. Tomorrow I thought it will be safer for Jack and Lennie to be in the cave. There was a little spring just along the edge of the cliff I remembered and so they'd have water. No one was going to go up there this time of year I thought. No one would see them up there.

So the next day at work I quietly found the twins and gave them the spare food and explained my plan.

'You'll be safe up there,' I told them. 'Look, I'll come and find you around lunch time when I'm off and everyone else will be eating somewhere inside. It's a great idea.'

The twins were quite happy where they were. It had been warm in the shed with the hay and they had water to hand. 'But there are too many people around the yard. It's too easy for someone to see you here. Up at the cave there'll be no one around. I can bring you food and after a couple of weeks you can appear as you planned.'

I suppose at the time I thought this was brilliant. Living in a cave would have been exciting. Pity I couldn't go and join them I had thought. Mum's little cuckoo clock suddenly went into its routine and chimed the hour. Wonder whether I would still be alive if I had gone to join them? Wonder if I would be rich? Wonder what really happened and how they disappeared?

We had all moved camp around lunch time as I said. When we reached the cave the twins were quite excited too. They thought the place was neat although a bit weird with all the swishing trees. I gave them a couple of boxes of matches I had pinched from home so they could light a fire and cook up the beans, even make themselves a brew. We had carried up a couple of bundles of straw and I had given them a torch. It didn't take long to get them organised in the cave. I couldn't be away too long over lunch time and so I left and told them I would be up tomorrow around midday.

That night as I lay in bed I wondered how I could keep them supplied with food. Maybe I should ask cook in the Big House whether she had some leftovers. I was a growing lad. No, too dangerous and too many people getting to know too much. Early next morning I raided mum's larder again. I slipped down early to the bakers and bought another loaf. Packing my lunch bag I made sure mum gave me an extra couple of apples.

'Why you going to work today Freddie? It's Saturday son?'

'Got something special to do Mum. I promised Bob Edwards I would finish it and I didn't have time yesterday and so I thought I'd go in today and get it all done.'

'You're a good lad at times Freddie. You make sure that Bob Edwards knows you went in special to get the work done.'

'Sure Mum' and I slipped out of the house. Christ, I'd forgotten it was Saturday and nearly blew it; just too much fucking excitement.

So as not to arouse any suspicion I did some bits and pieces around the yard making it look like I should be there. Lunchtime, when I hoped everyone would be eating I slipped away carefully and walked up the thirty minute trip to the cave. There was nobody about and I walked up to the entrance of the cave. Outside I called. 'Hey, you two in there? Jack, Lennie you there mates?'

Lennie crawled out. 'What you got us? Christ, this ain't no good life Freddie. We're bored to tears in 'ere, going fucking bonkers. We were better off in that shed mate. At least it looked like somewhere human. This place gives me the creeps, all these fucking trees and they never keep fucking quiet.'

I slapped my hand on the big old oak tree by the cave's entrance. 'This one don't make any noise Jack. It's like a watchman, keeping guard for you. Come outside a bit and walk about. You'll get used to the trees. If you stay in that cave you will be crazy. Where's Lennie?'

'I'm Lennie you dumb birk.'

'Shit I can't tell you apart. Where's Jack then?'

'Inside dreaming up what to do next. He's the one with the brains.'

'Well look then. Here's some more food and I got some more matches and an old candle. That'll save the batteries in the torch. I can't stay but I'll get back tomorrow. I ain't heard nothing in the village. There ain't nobody asking any questions and I know mum hasn't got any letters or anything so it looks like no one knows you're here. See you tomorrow around midday again. Cheerio.'

When I got back to the cave the next day both Jack and Lennie were outside and waiting for me.

'You got to get a rope Freddie. We need a rope. It's important. It's fucking amazing. We'll all be rich.'

I suppose I just stood there, bowled over with their rabbiting on. 'What are you talking about?'

'Look, look you ignorant cunt. See 'ere in me 'and. What's this? What's this then? Bloody treasure mate.'

'Where'd you find that?' I managed to ask.

'That's why we need a rope arsehole. Get a rope and we'll get some more.'

Gradually the story unfolded but Jack and Lennie made me go back almost straight away and get a bloody rope. I returned and by this time Jack was up in the old oak tree and tugging at something in the fork.

'What you doing up there?'

'Throw up the rope and I'll show you.'

'Lennie, what's he doing up in the tree?'

'Freddie just throw him the rope mate and you'll see. Do it.'

I threw up the rope but still didn't know what was going on. Jack caught the rope and seemed to dig around in the rotten wood in the fork. Curses came tumbling down out of the tree along with mouldy wood, leaves, twigs and bits of bark. Eventually Jack shouted out, 'bonanza!'

Balancing carefully up in the tree Jack tugged on the rope and a large chest or box thing slowly appeared out of the rotten trunk. He grunted and looked down at us.

'Be careful down there. This is bloody 'eavy.' He tipped the box off the edge of the fork and carefully braced himself as he lowered his discovery. Lennie rushed forward to catch the box before it hit the ground. It obviously was heavy as Lennie couldn't hold it in his hands and he stumbled on the loose uneven ground. The box slid out of his arms and thumped down onto the ground and tipped over on its side.

'Let me at it,' cried Lennie as he tried to stand up again.

'Oy, wait for me you two. Let me get down out of this bloody tree. Lennie, stand up beside the tree again brother so I can get down.'

Lennie was still looking at the box and trying to turn it over.

'Freddie, stand up against the tree and hold me feet. I've got to get down. Up against the tree. Other side you stupid prat. You're too low that side. Right. Hold still. Catch me foot. On your shoulder. Now the other foot. Steady, steady. Stand still for Christ's sake. Lennie come and help Freddie before I break me bloody neck.'

Eventually the three of us got sorted and looked at the box. We turned it over. It was a metal box with large bands around it. It had two hinges on one side and opposite was a thick band with a clasp and what looked like a key hole but it was hard to see as the box was filthy and covered with dirt.

'So where did the thing you had in your hand come from Lennie?' I asked.

'Up in the tree you dumb bugger, where do you think? Jack here decided to play Jack up the bean stalk 'cos he was bored stupid being in that stuffy cave. I helped him up and he was digging around when he saw this coin thing. When we saw what it was we went digging further into the tree. There's quite a hollow up there and Jack thought he had found something.'

'And I did,' said Jack. 'I found this bloody box but it was too heavy to lift out. Then you arrived and we got the rope.'

'So what do we do now?'

'Open it you stupid sod. Where do you think this coin thing came from? This box is so heavy it must be full of coins. Hundreds of 'em, thousands. I tell you we're rich.'

We turned the box over again but there was no obvious way in. 'We need to smash it open. We don't have no key and so let's smash it.'

I looked at Lennie and Jack. 'A hammer Freddie, a bloody great hammer, a sledge hammer. Go and get one.'

'I've got to get back. I'm late already. People will ask questions and then we'll all be in the shit. It's Sunday you know and I'm not supposed to be here. I told my mum I would only be out for a short time. She wanted me to do something for her and I had to make an excuse just to get out for a little while. Tomorrow. I'll bring a hammer tomorrow. The box ain't going nowhere. We'll do it tomorrow.'

That was the last I ever saw of them. Seeing as the next day was Monday I had to work in the morning and so I couldn't skive off until lunchtime. When I went back there was no one there. I didn't have a torch so going in the cave didn't make sense. I tried shuffling into the entrance but it was so dark and there were no answers to my calls. Back home I didn't know what to do. The next day, the Tuesday another event completely overwhelmed any minor mystery I might have had. Norton Ferris was killed and that occupied everyone's attention. I had gone back on the next day after missing the twins and I did take a torch and go into the cave but there was nothing there. Everything had gone.

When I heard that Michael Lord had been shot right outside that very cave a couple of days later I suppose I must have decided to keep quiet. I didn't know what else to do. There were never any questions. I asked mum whether she had heard from anyone and she asked what was I talking about. Who should I have heard from? I kept my mouth shut and never asked again. Gone with the box I thought. Scarpered.

Unbeknown to me someone had seen me going from the yard on the Saturday. Idwal Ferris had been told by his dad to check on some of the supplies that were supposed to be up by the stables. As Norton Ferris didn't want anyone to know what he was looking for he sent Idwal and told him to walk up there. If he was asked why he was up in the stables he was to say his dad was looking for some fencing staples that he thought were up in the sheds. Now Idwal knew this was just bullshit but he didn't know what his dad was really up to. He had come very quietly and cautiously into the stable yard and saw Freddie before Freddie saw him. Idwal hid and watched Freddie who was acting very suspiciously, looking about very carefully and then moving quickly away to the forest. Wondering what that useless little shit was up to Idwal decided to follow. Moving very quietly though the forest Idwal saw Freddie walk up to the northern end and down along the line of the cliff. Wondering what the fuck was going on Idwal continued to watch Freddie and saw him stop by the big tree and then talk to the cliff. Must be off his fucking nut thought Idwal – talking to the bloody rocks. But then, surprise surprise for someone suddenly appeared next to Freddie. Where the fuck did he come from? Who was he 'cos I 'aven't seen him before, and now they're both talking to the bloody rocks? Idwal waited in the plantation to see what would happen next. After some more conversation that Idwal couldn't hear Freddie left and started walking back towards the Big House. Do I stay or do I go thought Idwal? I know who Freddie is and where he is going so who are you mate, you in the cliff? Suddenly Idwal's eyes widened as another young lad miraculously appeared and the two of them started chatting. Idwal moved a little closer and hunkered down to watch. The two lads wandered about, got some water in a pot and made a fire. Idwal decided they looked like they were staying put and so he quietly crept away. Food for thought: should I beat the story out of Freddie or should I see what happens tomorrow?

Back in the stable yard Idwal carefully found what his dad really wanted and walked quietly back to their cottage. When old Norton gave him shit for taking so long Idwal just spun a story about too many people being in the yard and he had to wait to pick the right time to get the stuff.

It was Saturday night and Idwal and John were down in the pub, along with their dad. They all played darts and John won which pissed Idwal off no end. Larry Whelks came over and he and Norton went into a huddle. All Idwal could hear were promises about getting things on time and there would be no problem. When John won the next game of darts Idwal decided he would get plastered and drink his brother under the table, something he thought he could win. As a result there was no Sunday morning for Idwal, well not one that he remembered. In the afternoon he still felt so rotten he gave John a hard time for spiking his drinks. He quite forgot about the two young lads and their disappearing act until late that Sunday evening. Idwal slapped his hand down hard on the kitchen table. 'Tomorrow,' he shouted, 'I'll sort it tomorrow.'

'Idwal, what you shouting about? You've been hungover and bloody morose all bleeding day and suddenly you're shouting your head off.'

'Nothing John, it's nothing. Must have been something rotten in those pork scratchings last night. I'll go down the pub tomorrow and complain. Yes, that's it, it was those bloody scratchings.'

The following morning Idwal learnt that his dad needed John for a trip somewhere, and that Norton and John would be out that night organising something for their benefit. Idwal took the opportunity to make sure he got a special task from Bob Edwards so he could be alone for most of the day. As soon as he could Idwal quietly returned to the northern end of the estate. He could hear the two of them before he saw them.

'Smash, crash. Fuck, hold it steady Lennie. Smash, thunk. Come on you bastard open. Open fuck you.'

'Here, let me try. Move over. Tip it a little.'

The noise continued interspersed with curses and grumbling. Idwal stepped forwards.

'Can I help?' he asked quietly. 'Think I know how to open that for you.'

The twins started and looked at Idwal suspiciously.

'Who are you mister? We ain't doing any 'arm. This 'ere is our box and we've got it stuck shut. My silly brother here's gone and lost the key and we need to open it.'

'Sure lads, sure. I understand. I work here, you know along with Freddie. He thought you might need some help. Told me you had a little problem so I came to help.'

'Freddie never told no one,' said Jack suspiciously. 'Freddie never told no one we was 'ere. How come you're 'ere?'

'Like I said, Freddie told me you had a problem and I told Freddie I would help. I know it's all a big secret and so I know just how to help. Always kept things to myself and no one need know anything more. Still, let me help you with that. Staying here are you? Friends of Freddie I can see that.'

'How the fuck can you help? Freddie said he'd bring... ouch, what you'd do that for Jack. Christ you almost broke my leg kicking like that.'

'Look, why don't we move this box where we can get it open. That's what you were trying to do and I can help. I know just the place where we can open it and keep it safe. Know a better place for you two to doss down too.'

Idwal had picked up on the accent and tried to make the twins less suspicious. 'My dad's from Liverpool like you two. He'll help. He ran away when he was a lad and he'll know what to do.'

'How do you know we're from Liverpool?'

Idwal smiled and put his hand on Jack's shoulder. 'Son with your accent you can't come from anywhere else. My old dad will like you. He'll want to just listen to you speak. Misses his home does my dad. Anyway, let's fix up a way to carry this box and we'll get it open and safe. Back at our cottage I've got just the tools to help you get this open and we've a spare room so you can camp out there. It'll be warmer and better than this place. Bloody cold up here in winter and it looks like snow. Come on down to the cottage and get some real grub.'

Jack and Lennie were already fed up with the cave. It wasn't warm and they were hungry again. Also they couldn't open the box. There were two of them and Idwal wasn't a very big man. Looking at each other the twins passed a message and agreed.

'Fine Mister but just remember it's our box. We've just got it stuck shut but we could do with some help.'

The three of them scrounged around the site but the twins were not very forest savvy and it was Idwal who found a couple of springy poles and making a cross piece they lashed the box to a crude frame so that they could carry it rather like a stretcher.

'Just grab your gear and we'll move you both to the cottage.'

It didn't take the twins very long to wrap up their belongings and with the plastic bags and old duffel the three of them took turns carrying the stretcher down through the forest. After nearly thirty minutes, with Jack and Lennie going on about how far was it they came out into a clearing.

'Neat, that's neat. Through the woods to grandma's house,' said Jack.

'You two hungry?' asked Idwal.

'Bloody starving,' said the twins in unison.

'Right then, I'll fix you both a fry up and then we'll have a look at your box. First though I'll show you where you can kip and stow your clobber.'

Idwal took them out of the kitchen and around to a shed that was really a lean-to against the back wall.

'Just drop your gear here and sort of tidy the place up so it's clear for you to sleep in. I can get some bedding and we'll make it warm and better than where you were. That old cliff must have been a cold place to doss down.'

'We was in a cave. Weren't cold really but it was damp and you couldn't see fuck all inside without a light. Drove me bonkers sleeping there. Like being in a bloody grave.'

'It was just behind the tree then?' asked Idwal.

'Yea, little entrance behind our tree. Standing guard on us that tree was Freddie said. Well, it was good to us wasn't it Jack? Fuck off kicking me all the time.'

'Sort yourselves out lads and I'll go and do you a fry up. There's a pump in the yard if you want to sluice some water over your faces. You both look a little grubby after living in that cave of yours.'

Idwal was thinking furiously during all this chitter chatter. Box was heavy: kids were excited: no one knew they were here except that mongrel Freddie but I can keep him quiet. What's in the box then? Obviously ain't theirs so where did it come from? Perhaps they found it in that cave. Moving around in the kitchen Idwal set about cooking. First things first and let's be friends with the little buggers. See how it goes from there.

'Caw that smells smashing. Look Lennie four eggs and bacon, bloody fantastic greasy bacon bro'. Shit we've landed in heaven.'

'Here you go then lads. Get your choppers around that lot. Like fried bread do you? Another slice then? I've got the kettle on the boil. Strong cuppa' and then we're ready to look at your box. I'll go and find a couple of tools to help us.'

While the two lads tucked into a greasy breakfast Idwal went and found the tools he would need. He laid out a sledge hammer, a tool bar and a shovel. That should do it he reckoned.

When Jack and Lennie had got their hands around their second mug of tea Idwal led them outside and the three of them squatted down around the box. 'Let's undo it from the poles first lads and have a good look shall we?'

Separated from the poles Idwal turned the metal box over and over. It still looked sturdy and solid. The two hinges on one side were carefully recessed into the body of the box and not easy of access. The clasp over a keyhole was also guarded by two extra heavy bands.

'Well lads, when you had your key did this clasp come upwards to open the lid?'

'Yes mister. It kind of hinges upwards when we unlock it.'

'Bullshit son. It ain't yours is it?'

'Maybe, but we found it and so it's ours. Let's just open it anyway. Whatever's inside is ours. We might share to pay for our grub.'

Idwal picked up the tool bar and tried to insert the end under the clasp but there wasn't enough room because of the heavy bands. Looking carefully at the box Idwal realised how he could open it.

'I need another tool lads. Drink your tea before it gets cold and I'll be right back.'

Lennie looked at Jack. 'What do you think?'

'I don't know. Think he can open it but then what?'

'He seems all right. Knows about Freddie and says he works here. Seems to live here. Says his dad is from Liverpool.'

'Keep your eyes open,' Jack said. 'Let's see what's in this bloody box. If its coins like I found earlier then we could always share.'

'Hush up, here he comes.'

'Finished your tea lads? Right, let's see whether this will work.'

Idwal had brought out a big heavy chisel and a hammer. Carefully placing the chisel on the metal of the clasp he wanted to cut through this thinner band. Thump, thump he pounded on the chisel. Lifting it up Idwal could see he had made a sharp indent. He pounded three more times and looked again. The indent was getting deeper and the edges of the clasp had split a little. Another five smashes with the hammer and the chisel cut through the clasp and severed it. Careful not to catch his fingers on the jagged edge of the metal clasp Idwal slid the tool bar under the severed end and prised. The old metal bent upwards and the beginning of a slit appeared in the dirty side of the box under the clasp. Picking up the hammer Idwal tapped all the way round the box at the line of the slit. This must be the lid he reasoned. Bits of dirt and crud fell off the box and the two lads watched intently.

After a little more prising with the tool bar and a couple of smashes with the hammer the tight-fitted lid creaked open and revealed the contents of the box.

'Jesus Murphy, have you ever seen the likes?'

'Bonanza Lennie, just what I told you.'

Two quick swings with the tool bar and both Jack and Lennie sprawled on the ground with blood seeping from their smashed heads. Idwal looked around the yard and the clearing. Nothing stirred, nobody appeared, all was quiet and peaceful. Dead still.

Carefully moving out the brooms, brushes and other household items from the closet Idwal quickly prised up the first floorboard and set about opening up his dad's hidey-hole. When it was clear Idwal found an old piece of sacking and using that he spent an hour working with the shovel to deepen the hole. When he had gone down another three feet in the sandy soil he stopped and wiped the sweat off his forehead. Thirsty work he thought and found a beer in the kitchen.

Wrapping up their heads in plastic bags so the blood wouldn't spill everywhere Idwal carried each boy into the house and stacked them flat in the pit. Just as you said lads he muttered. Just like sleeping in your cave, just like a grave you said. How right you were. Sleep tight lads and goodnight. Idwal shovelled the dirt back over the bottom of the hole and covered the bodies. He put the sacking down on the floor of the hole. Very methodically he put back the boards, the brooms, buckets and brushes and looked at the closet. All seemed the normal messy sight.

Outside in the yard Idwal washed the tool bar, picked up the chisel and sledge hammer and put them back with the other tools. He gathered up the rope and the springy poles. He coiled the rope and hung it with the other gear. The poles he just propped up by the wood shed. Carrying the shovel Idwal went over to the lean-to and gathered up the bits of gear the two lads had carried down from the cave. He carefully made sure he had collected everything before he walked into the edge of the bush and dug a shallow pit. There he buried the useless bits and bobs. Painstakingly he re-arranged the disturbed soil to look just natural. The shovel he returned to the tool shed.

Coming back through the yard Idwal picked up the two tea mugs and brought them back into the kitchen. There he cleared away the plates and the knives and forks and set about putting everything back to normal. Satisfied there was no trace of any visitors Idwal finally went back out into the yard and looked at the box. He crouched down to lift it up. Although it wasn't very big it was heavy. Idwal grunted as he heaved the box up in his arms. He had already thought where he was going to put it, well temporarily at least. Very carefully he stashed it away and tidied up any loose dirt and sand.

Finally Idwal stood in the yard and scratched his head as he thought. Two more things he muttered to himself, well maybe three if I'm going to profit out of this. First of all Idwal went back to the northern edge of the Estate and found the tree and the entrance to the cave. Turning on his torch he went inside. All that was really left was some of the straw the lads had carried up for bedding, a candle stub and the matches, their torch and the wrapping from a cut loaf of bread. Idwal gathered these things up and carried them outside. He looked up and down the line of the cliff and then stood and listened. Again, all was quiet except for the swish swish of the conifer branches. Just to make really sure Idwal walked a little way around the tree and the cave entrance. He picked up a couple of pieces of paper and an empty tin of beans. He scattered the few sticks and stones the twins had used to make a fire. Thinking which way Freddie had come to the cave Idwal carried all these bits and pieces the opposite way along the line of the cliff. It was easy to bury and scatter the few items in a natural setting. There were lots of boulders under one part of the cliff and satisfied he had taken care of item number one Idwal carefully walked back through the forest.

Back at the cottage Idwal sat down and made himself a cup of tea. So, item two. Where do I find a dog? Idwal heard a car pull up outside the cottage. Footsteps came across the stone-flagged yard and there was a knock on the cottage door.

'Anyone at home? Norton you in there?'

'Come in Bob. I'm not sure where dad or John is. Think dad said they had some special job to do over in the pines, Compartment five I think he said. That's why I asked for that solo job today. I've cleaned up most of the saws and checked on the wire strainers.'

'So what are you doing here then?'

'Well it's lunch time now ain't it. There wasn't a lot to do and so I thought I'd come back here to make myself a cuppa' with my lunch. Pot's still warm. Do you want one?'

Bob Edwards stood in the kitchen wondering how much of this was true. Still he thought, there wasn't a lot going on at this time in the forest and so no harm done. Didn't seem any point in getting on his high horse and so he smiled at Idwal and said, 'sure, could do with a mug of hot tea.'

Idwal calmly got up, found a mug and poured the tea. 'Milk and sugar Bob isn't it? Two spoons?'

'Thanks Idwal. Makes a nice change from my old thermos. Did you finish the saws?'

'No, got three more to do I think. What about I look at the planting tools? They could probably do with a sharpening. That should keep me busy through 'til tomorrow.'

'Good idea. We won't need them for a while but it'll do no harm to get them ready. Good tea.'

'Tell me Bob, where did you get that dog of yours? Big hound isn't he?'

'He's only an old mongrel Idwal but yes he is a big dog. Daisy Mullett in the village keeps dogs and she's always got a few extra. Why, your dad thinking of keeping a dog? Have to tell Sir Anthony, well ask anyway.'

'No, nothing like that. Dad don't like dogs really and we never would have the time to look after it proper. No just wondering 'cos he seemed right friendly. Good with the kids.'

'You're right there. Soft of mouth and soft of head old Dasher is but he's good company. Still, thanks for the tea. You going back up to the office yard to finish those saws?'

'Right away.'

'Give you a lift if you like. I can go back that way before I go and check on the rest of the gang.'

When he finished that afternoon Idwal walked down into the village and knocked on the door of Daisy Mullett's house. Five minutes later, in the dark as it had gone five o'clock Idwal walked two large gangly dogs quietly down the road and within minutes they had all disappeared into the forest.

After his dinner Idwal sat in the kitchen and wondered exactly what it was his dad and John were doing. Dad had been talking with Larry Whelks earlier in the week, and the way that they were talking it usually meant some deal was going on. What could dad be doing now at this time of year? And John was so thick he wouldn't cotton on to what his dad was up to. Slow was brother John. Never was one to think on his feet and grab the opportunity; soft too, no real fight in him.

Larry Whelks, now there's a thought. Actually there's a good thought. What was he telling dad about some yahoos up in Bristol? Who were they now? Larry was bragging, which is a little unusual for him about knowing these big-time villains in Bristol. What did he say; buy and sell anything? Yes, well my dad never had much that was of any real value, always piddley stuff, but the box, now that wasn't piddley stuff. Maybe we should be a little careful and test the waters. Let Larry take one of those coin things to Bristol and see what reaction we get. I needn't let on I've got a box full.

Dad and John came in around nine looking tired but happy.

'Had a good day?' Idwal asked. 'Assume you've eaten? I've finished off those bangers.'

'No son, we're right. John and me's had our suppers and a couple of pints but yes it's been a good day.'

'Right on Dad,' added John.

Next day was Tuesday and Idwal and John drove with their dad to the Forest Estate offices for the seven thirty start. Somewhat surprisingly Michael Lord was there looking clean-shaven and sounding bloody-minded. He picked on Norton right from the start. Idwal and John got their orders and Idwal checked with Bob Edwards about continuing what he was doing yesterday. Everything seemed normal and Idwal never did hear the continued dialogue between Michael and his dad.

About five o'clock the two Ferris brothers were sitting in their kitchen wondering where Norton was. John told Idwal about the bollocking he had heard Michael giving their dad. He just hoped they'd all have a roof over their heads at the end of the week. John went on to talk about some deal he thought their dad had with Larry Whelks and Idwal sat and listened and thought. After a short time the two brothers decided to go down to the pub and see whether their dad was there.

It was a rude shock when Larry Whelks grabbed both of them by the scruff of their shirts and virtually man-handled them across the pub floor. 'Where's that no-good shit of a father of yours? I've just lost two hundred quid thanks to him and I need to sort him out.' The two brothers managed to get Larry to let go and after getting their pints the three of them settled in a corner and Larry had another go. It seemed that Norton Ferris had some "items surplus to requirements" that Larry might want. 'Bloody right I want,' exclaimed Larry, 'and I had a buyer all lined up but your dad's fucked it all up again like always.'

'We'll find him Larry,' Idwal said. 'Don't worry we'll find him. Come on John I can guess what the silly old bugger has done. Bet I'm right too.'

Idwal stood up and started to go. John followed. 'Where we going?'

'Go and start the motor. I'll be right there after I've had a piss.'

John left the pub and got in their old car and waited.

Idwal watched John leave and went over to Larry who had just come back into the pub again. 'Got a moment?'

'Now what the fuck do you want? Not sure I want any more dealings with your family. You've never got anything worthwhile and when you do you manage to fuck it up.'

Idwal brought one of the coins out of his pocket very surreptitiously and with his back to the crowd in the pub he slowly opened his hand and showed Larry.

'Where'd you get that? Fuck me, you know what this is?'

'What's it worth? Quietly now, I don't want the whole bloody pub to know.'

Larry took it and bit it.

'Can find out,' he said. 'Got any more?'

'Find out what it's worth and we'll talk again. Make sure it comes back to me or else.'

'Or else what?'

'Fuck you Larry, just find out what it's worth and then maybe we strike up a deal. Gotta' go. Gotta' find my dad for you. See you.'

Idwal walked out and over to the car.

'Jesus, you pissing in some competition or something? You've been for ever.'

'Had to see a man about a dog,' said Idwal and he laughed as he shoved John over and got into the driving seat.

John and Idwal Ferris found their dad that night but not where Idwal thought, well not exactly. Norton had been loading fence posts into Michael Lord's Landrover, ready to take to Larry Whelks for a quick sale when a pile of recently cut logs cascaded down the hillside and knocked the Landrover and Ferris into the stream at the bottom of the hill. Norton Ferris was very dead when the rescue crew Anthony Lord had organised pulled the overturned Landrover out of the stream. Most of the fence posts burst out of the back of the Landrover and tumbled down the cold water.

The next day, the Wednesday Idwal and John Ferris got told they were fired, after they were questioned by the police of course. Anthony Lord had had enough of the Ferris family and this was the last straw. Idwal and John got a week's notice. Between them they sorted out the funeral arrangements and started thinking about where they would go. Idwal started thinking about the box. Heavy box full of things that were too obvious.

The shop door jingled open and Larry Whelks walked in quietly and tapped Idwal Ferris on the shoulder. 'What you thinking of painting now you've got no home? Can't be that old car, wrong colour. Green wouldn't look good on that old car. By the way Idwal I've found someone rather interested in your treasure.'

'You have?'

'Why green? What you going to paint? Perhaps we should talk? I've got some friends and you've got some problems, well a valuable problem maybe.'

Idwal paid for his paint and a brush and walked out of the shop on a Saturday morning.

'Heard you were out on your ear by next Tuesday is it? Where you going to go? What will happen to your golden friend, or is it friends?'

'You say gold? Did I hear you right? Shit, that's real money Larry.'

Sunday afternoon saw Idwal and Larry Whelks carefully lining up a whole parade of coins on a set of planks laid out on saw-horses in the back shed of Larry's mum's cottage.

'Where we going to hide them then? In fact why are we painting them?'

'Best place to hide something Larry is right under your nose. Make it so obvious that you can't see it. Sort of it's there but you don't see it's there. Magic. My old dad used to run a rag and bone cart in Liverpool when he was a kid and he told me several tricks for hiding things.'

'Why green?'

'Just suppose your friends decide they would like to find more of these little pieces. Suppose they come looking for you and where you live. It's like in our old cottage you know. It wasn't good and I never meant to leave them there for long. Too bloody obvious but now we're out of there I had to move a little faster and so your garden will do just fine.'

'Garden, but there's no hiding place in the garden? It's all a bloody jungle out there.'

'Useful things jungles Larry. You ever read a book called the "Just so Stories"?'

'I've never read a book in my life Idwal. Ain't got time for any of that crap. Life's too short. Anyway, what was this so-called story all about?'

Idwal chuckled. 'It was about a giraffe and a zebra and how they could vanish in the jungle.'

'You've lost your marbles mate. Giraffes and zebras.'

'Camouflage Larry, make it fade into the background, maybe make it be the background. Just paint mate. We'll do one side and let them dry and then turn them over. Now what about this golden answer? What are they worth?'

The following Wednesday two things happened to Idwal Ferris. First he met Ken and Ron Bentley up in Bristol. That was both a frightening and an exciting meeting and Idwal came back to the village with Larry rather wound up. Back at the cottage he met an equally frightening apparition in Florrie Whelks, Larry's mother. Just what she wanted she said. Make the garden look neat and tidy. Those little stones in the shed would do just right. Larry, right now you and this young lad put those stones down along my path. Use them to line the edges and keep them straight you hear me you useless lummox. Flo' Whelks wielded an old walking stick and thumped Larry hard across the shoulders. Do it she screeched.

With a big smile on his face Idwal knelt in the garden and carefully lined the path with a neat array of green stones. 'Right in your face Larry and you don't see them. Just like I said mate. Obvious but so obvious you don't even see what you're looking at.'

'Christ Idwal, you're a devious sod. I'll say that for you. Mum don't even know she's got a highway paved with gold.'

'Keep your gob shut mate. Keep shtum. We need to go back to Bristol tomorrow and see whether those two friends of yours have got any likely customers. They seemed interested although they tried not to show it. I'll crash here tonight if that's okay seeing as I have no other home partner.'

Idwal shook Larry's hand and walked back up the golden green path.

I probably never knew the half of it thought Freddie. Did the twins escape with the box or did someone find them? Bones in the Ferris cottage. Wonder what bones, wonder who's bones? Keep you ears open Freddie. If John Ferris can kill his brother who knows?

FRIDAY ON THE GOLDEN PATH

THERE WERE RUMOURS FLOATING ABOUT everywhere that Friday morning. Somehow word had got out about bones in the Ferris cottage and now new bones. Terence Field was more interested in Samantha's gift, well piece of evidence really. The lab had taken his two dirty green pebbles and managed to clean up the original article. Two gold pieces lay in his hand. Florence Whelks cottage he thought again. Somehow that cottage is involved.

'Daniel how do you feel this morning? How's the head?'

'Better thanks. Did you want to talk to Samantha? I think she's just taken James to nursery school.'

'No Daniel it's you I wanted to talk to. Can you spare me some time this morning? I think you know some part of this story that I don't know. I only came here five years ago and much of this mystery seems to revolve around events back in 1990. You knew most of the people involved and the discovery yesterday made me realise you were a major player. Can you meet me later this morning?'

I pensively held the phone away from my head and thought about Inspector Field's words; a major player. Wonder what he really means by that. I spoke back into the telephone. 'Sure Terence. Are you going to come here?'

'No Daniel but could we meet at Florence Whelks's cottage? I want another look at that garden path. I'll fill you in on the details when we meet. Samantha gave me something very interesting yesterday that you found.'

Freddie had been stewing all night. He hadn't slept a wink and now he was certain. Ferris killed the twins, his cousins. Idwal or John had seen the twins up at the cave. Surely that was it. Poor little buggers wouldn't have stood a chance with either Idwal or John. Someone obviously cleared up after them. If they had run off they wouldn't have left the place so neat and tidy. Someone cleaned up at the cave. So where's the box then? Bloody heavy that was and did it contain more coins like the one Lennie showed me? Neither Idwal nor John ever flashed any money around. Christ I'll beat it out of John. He's already knocked for a loop and so it should be easy to get him to talk. He can't do anything anyway 'cos he's out on bail and needs to keep his nose clean.

Margaret Whelks looked out of the window. Bloody wilderness she told the world. Place full of no-hopers. Still, there's got to be someone in this pitiful place who can get high. Jesus dad what a dump. Still, you had to run didn't you? Could have left me behind you stupid hourn. I was doing all right. All the right contacts and life was a laugh a minute. No, too many boys in blue asking questions and none of your mates too tight in the lip department. Thought I'd squeal. Dad there's times when you're just a waste of space. Christ I've gotta' pee. Wonder where's the fucking dunny in this hell-hole?

'That you Margaret? I'll be right out.'

'Sure Dad, whatever.'

'Put the kettle on girl.'

'Do it yourself. Where can a girl piss in this dump?'

'Out the back.'

'With the bloody snakes and spiders I suppose? This is worse than some of the flea-pits in the Cross.'

Florrie cackled and Margaret jumped.

'Shit, you made me piss myself you silly old cow. Frightened the life out of me standing there like a bloody ghost in that white shroud and cackling. Perhaps I should just stand here and piss, right at you?'

Flo' cackled again. 'You're full of piss you are missee but if you have to, go and do it outside. I'll put the kettle on and you can tell me all about the Cross.'

'In your dreams. I'll go before I piss down the other leg. Out of the way then before I flood the place.'

'Good to have some young life back in the place again son,' Flo' said to Phil as he walked into the kitchen.

'Don't you believe it Ma, that girl's trouble. Should have left her behind in Oz.'

'But you didn't trust her to keep her mouth shut?'

About an hour later Margaret, Vanda please Whelks wandered up the quiet peaceful main street in the village. It was like another world. It was like being in the Cross at eight o'clock in the morning, not that Vanda had ever been walking about in the Cross at that time of a morning. No one, no cars, no noise, absolutely fuck all.

'Now you look like you could do with something to help you fantasise a little. I heard you exclaiming how unreal it all was and from the accent you're not local.'

'Well aren't you a bloody marvel? Mr. Fucking Amazing. Crawl back under your rock.'

'Actually I prefer grass. Tastes so much sweeter and the aroma heightens the pasty complexion like yours darling. Dressed in black and sporting a white face you must think you're a piece of gothic art, or perhaps late art deco? Which is it darling?'

'Did my darling say grass?'

'Or whatever. You look just the type for some of the whatever. Have you had breakfast? Got a name?'

'Vanda Whelks, Mr. Whoever who peddles whatever.'

'Don't tell me you're related to old Flo'?'

'She's my gran' Mr. Whoever.'

'Come in luv and let's see whether what I have for breakfast will interest you. Fancy old Flo' having a granddaughter. Christ, I would have liked to be a fly on the wall when you walked in to that little retreat Flo' calls home. I'll bet you brought colour back into the old crone's cheeks. Not that you've got any colour yourself of course. Grass is it to start with?'

Tom Daley closed his door and Margaret Whelks entered another world.

'Freddie get off him. Get off I say.'

Sitting square on John Ferris's chest Freddie raised his fist. 'Bloody murderer, that's what you are. Killed my cousins. I know you did.'

'Freddie off now!'

Bob Edwards hauled Freddie off John Ferris and thumped him down on the ground. 'Now smarten up lad or you'll be down the road. Mr. Daniel has had enough of you and your sniping away at John here. So back off.'

Bob turned round to help John Ferris back on his feet.

'What was that all about John? How did that start?'

John slowly shook his head. 'I don't know Bob. One minute I was working on this saw and the next thing I know Freddie here is knocking me over and then hitting me with that axe handle. Bloody nearly broke my shoulder before I fell over. Quick as a flash he was sitting on my chest and going to punch me. I never said anything or did anything. Ask the other lads here Bob. Just ask them.'

Bob Edwards turned and looked at Freddie. 'What have you got to say lad? John telling me the truth? Speak up lad, you were doing the attacking.'

'I reckon he killed them.'

'Who lad, who are you talking about?'

'Those bones in his cottage. Not the first lot but them new bones they found later, the second time they came. I heard they were human those bones.'

'What's that got to do with you Freddie?'

I had just arrived when I heard Bob ask this question.

'Bob, I think I need a word with Freddie here please. Just get everyone else back to work can you? I think I might know a little more about this.'

Bob talked to the men and slowly they sorted themselves out and went back to work.

'Right Freddie, over here and I need some straight answers. You know something, or think you know something so I want to hear you. Remember I know that you have been giving John Ferris a hard time and I spoke to all of you about that a week or so ago so right now I'm rather pissed off with your attitude. Straight answers Freddie.'

Freddie sat down on the ground and shook his head. I let him think through what he wanted to say. Finally he looked up at me and I saw there were tears in his eyes. I squatted down beside him.

'What do you think Freddie? What do you know?'

'It's all so long ago Mr. Daniel. I never did know what happened to them. I kept quiet because no one else knew they were here.'

'Who are we talking about Freddie? Who are "they"?'

Freddie sat on the ground and he spent the next fifteen minutes slowly explaining the story of Jack and Lennie Cotton.

'And you never saw them again? They just disappeared?'

'Safe they were up at the cave Mr. Daniel and gone the next day when I went up there. No sign of them anywhere.'

'Why did they leave do you think? What happened up there? Anything frighten them, make them want to run away?'

'No, they were all excited. They wanted me to get a hammer right away. They wanted to smash it open. They thought it was something special. It was heavy enough. If it was full.....'

'What Freddie? What are we talking about? What did they want to smash open?'

'The box Mr. Daniel, the box they found in the tree. They wanted to open it but it was all bound up. I didn't have time to get a hammer as I was late already. I'd already been back for some rope.'

'Freddie, can we go through this slowly and in some order?'

Rather slowly Freddie revealed the story of the box in the tree, the found coin, the box on the ground and then poof – nothing, nobody, all gone.

'And you think John Ferris killed your cousins and it is their bones in his cottage? That's why you attacked him just now. You heard a rumour about some new bones and made a great guess. Just wanted another excuse to have a go at John Ferris?'

'Well if it wasn't him then it was his dad or his bloody brother and both of them are dead so John's the only one left to hit. That family always gave me a hard time Mr. Daniel. Old Norton was always bullying me and hitting me. He just thought it was funny. Well now the boot is on the other foot.'

'No Freddie, no it's not. You can't make such sweeping assumptions and then beat people up. I won't have it. Perhaps I can understand a little more after hearing your story but that's no excuse. Come on, I want you to apologise to John right now and then you and I are going to tell the story all over again to someone else.'

I took Freddie with me in the Landrover down to meet Terence at Florence Whelks's cottage. He was already there standing by his car. I talked briefly with Terence and we all went and sat in his car. There I got Freddie to repeat what he had told me. Terence asked Freddie a lot of questions about the family, the timing, the locations and the box. He also asked about what Jack had found that started the excitement.

'Looked like this?' he asked and he showed Freddie a gold coin.

Freddie's eyes blinked. 'Where'd you get that?' he said. 'Looks just like I remember the other one, the one that Jack found.'

I kept quiet for the moment and didn't say anything about Katya's find. I'll tell Terence about that another time.

'I'll run Freddie back to the gang Terence and come straight back. I thought you would be interested in hearing what he had to say as soon as I heard it. I'll be about fifteen minutes.'

When I got back I found Terence sitting in his car and going over some notes.

'Daniel I can't officially go traipsing into that garden, not without a search warrant. I was thinking over how best to do this. Samantha says you kicked up those coins when you were on the path. Now it looks as if the path is lined with those green pebbles but it is rather hard to see from out here.'

'Terence there is something else you should know.'

He looked at me. 'Said you were a major player in this story Daniel. You seem to have many of the answers, or rather you keep finding new bits of evidence for me. What else should I know?'

'A couple of days ago Katya and I were up at "Michael's cave".'

'That's where he was shot, just outside some cave?'

'Yes. It's a long story.' I stopped and laughed and Terence looked puzzled. 'Sorry, every time I say that Katya reminds me that everything about this family is always a long story.'

'Short version then.'

'Michael was supposedly looking for some Lord family treasure. We all thought it was in the cave. He didn't find anything and was shot there. We still don't know who or why. Anyway, Katya and I were up there the other day and Katya found a coin. Well it turned out to be a gold coin when she got it back to Oxford, cleaned it up and showed it to a friend. It was in the roots of the old tree outside the cave. Just last Sunday she climbed up the big old tree outside the cave and in the fork she found another coin. All this sort of confirms Freddie's story of cousin Jack's find and the box in the tree. Let's suppose the box is the real treasure and it did contain coins. Let's also suppose one of the Ferris family discovered Freddie's cousins, the box and the content. So now we have Freddie's cousins and the box at the Ferris cottage. We have bones of two male teenagers at the Ferris cottage. We have John supposedly knowing nothing about the hidey hole, so if that is true he is not the villain. Now Norton Ferris was an "on again off again" partner in crime with Larry Whelks but it was Idwal Ferris who killed Whelks. After Norton was killed we fired both the Ferris boys and Idwal was seen around the village with Larry Whelks. Idwal is kicked out of the cottage and so he moves the box. Didn't you tell us that Larry Whelks knew some big-time villains in Bristol and his death by Idwal took place in Bristol? Suppose Idwal and his new partner Larry Whelks were trying to sell whatever was in the box to the blokes in Bristol. Would they have bought and sold gold coins?'

I watched Terence mull over all that I had said. 'Continue your suppositions. You can do that while I have to deal with evidence rather than suppositions. Could all be possible but go on.'

'Idwal and Larry Whelks decide to hide the coins somewhere safe. Out of the Ferris cottage and not tidily in some box here in Flo's cottage. The blokes in Bristol might decide to come and take the lot in one fell swoop and Idwal was a crafty bloke when he had to be. He was much smarter than his dad and John too for that matter.'

'So, Idwal paints the coins and plants them down the pathway. Clever, obvious but not obvious.'

'You said the court case in Bristol about Idwal Ferris brought out some details about a double cross gone wrong. Those two Bentley brothers was it ended up as witnesses? Told some story about Idwal thinking his partner was trying to cut him out of the deal. Could be the Bentley brothers might have just wanted one seller to deal with and deliberately used Idwal to kill his partner? Anyway, that doesn't matter. Idwal and Larry hide the coins here, well some of them by the look of it.'

'Fine Daniel, but how do we prove any of that? Perhaps more importantly how do we look further in this garden?'

'If you have Katya's coins and you have the ones Samantha gave you can't some expert tell you they are the same, the same date, same coin and so they are all part of the same package? Then, you know where we found the first one. Freddie's cousin found one with the box so we have a tie in with the cave and then the boys' bones in Ferris's cottage plus now you have the same coins down in this garden. Surely that's enough evidence to get a search warrant? You're looking for stolen property and have grounds to believe it is here in this garden, associated with a possible murder. I'm assuming that it was murder, those bones you found?'

'Yes Daniel, both skulls had been smashed at the back so it looks like murder.'

'Can you do any checks to determine whether the bones at the cottage are related to Freddie or Freddie's mum? Aren't there some genetic tests, DNA or something you can do? Now you've heard Freddie's explanation you have a place to start looking for the names to go with the bones. I realise no one is going to corroborate Freddie's story. His mother didn't know and neither did anyone else in this village. Sounds like the mother in Liverpool didn't care, couldn't remember even if she is still alive.'

'You've certainly got a vivid imagination Daniel but you could be right, well about most of it. But yes, from what I have learnt I think I can get a search warrant and take an official look at that garden.'

'Look, can I go and see John Ferris again? Without fouling up your inquiry can I ask him what he can remember about the time we laid him and Idwal off? I know it's nearly eight years ago now and so John will have difficulty remembering but I might be able to jog his memory with things I can remember. I might be able to get more out of him than you just questioning him. That legal?'

'He's your employee and living in your cottage, well it was your cottage when this all happened. You've every right to ask what happened in that place and have him explain what the family did there. Keep it low key, sort of non-accusatory.'

'Terence I might be wrong but I still think John Ferris is a rather simple bystander in all of this. Sure he killed his brother but that was a "crime of passion" if we were in France. Apart from that I think all of the other stuff would be unknown to him. I really believe he never knew about that hole.'

Terence sat and thought. Finally he turned and just said, 'yes, do it. Keep me informed.'

I got out of his car and went over to my Landrover. Coming up the road walking very slowly in a rather erratic fashion was a slender apparition in black. She looked at Terence in his car and obviously said something but I didn't hear what she said. Carrying on walking she turned in to the laneway leading to the back of Flo's cottage.

'You looking for Flo'?' I asked.

'Who wants to know?'

'I do.'

'You with that copper in his car?'

'No, I live in this village and thought I knew everyone here. Flo' never mentioned any daughters, or granddaughters,' I said as I looked closer at the apparition.

'Flo' don't mention much does she? Keeps to herself. Doesn't go asking nosey questions.'

She carried on walking slowly towards the back of the cottage down the laneway. Before she reached the corner a large stout man came charging out of the back of the cottage hotly pursued by Goebbels. Now Goebbels we all knew but I didn't know the man.

'Margaret, where the hell have you been? Your old gran' has been cackling for you all bloody morning. She thought you were a real firecracker. I just think you're trouble girl. Now come in here and don't go wandering off.'

Just then the stout man realised that I was watching. 'Christ,' I exclaimed, 'it's Larry Whelks.'

'Think again cobber. Larry's dead.'

He turned and bustled Margaret whoever back into the cottage, again hotly pursued by a charging Goebbels.

I stood by the door of the Landrover and rolled some thoughts around in my mind. If Flo' is gran' then you must be Phillip Whelks, Larry's younger brother who ran away and the black apparition must be the daughter. Terence had already driven off and so I filed this information away but thought he should know next time I saw him. Phil Whelks returns, just when we find he has a path of gold on his doorstep. Now let's go and see what John can remember?'

'So where've you been?'

'Finding the main man in the village Dad.'

'What do you mean?' asked Phil

'Who do you mean is more important?' asked Flo'. 'Who's the wheeler-dealer girlie?'

'Some bozo called Tom. Has some interesting internet addresses.'

'That would be Tom Daley,' said Flo'.

'What internet addresses Margaret? We had the boys in blue sniffing around about that back home. Now what are you up to?'

'Hey, cool it pops. I was only looking you know. Anyway, I was more interested in what he had to sell.'

'Which was?'

'Something smelling good that helps lift me out of this pisspot burg. More important he seems to be the man to know. Says he can access most of the action around here. Knows who is doing what. Always useful to know where to find things Dad. This Tom seems to be a good source.'

'What did he say about us? More important did you tell him who you were?'

'Just a friend. No names no harm done eh?'

'So who is on the take in this pisspot burg as you call it?'

'Don't work that way. You have to trade. There aren't any freebies.'

'Ma what really happened to Larry?'

Florence Whelks sat in her old rocking chair and slowly moved to and fro. Goebbels sat at her feet and looked up at her with his eyes bright and ears pricked up. 'We don't really know do we doggie? One moment he was excited and next thing I learn he's dead.'

'Who was he dealing with? He was always into buying and selling. You said Bristol. Who'd he know in Bristol, and why Bristol? He was usually small time. How come he steps out into the bigger stream?'

'Found something didn't he? Well, his friend found something and thought Larry could help him move it.'

'What friend Ma? Larry never had no friends.'

'My uncle sounds a right loser. No wonder he's kicking up the grass.'

'Shut it girl. Let me finish. We might be on to something. When Larry got killed nothing was ever discovered eh Ma? Whatever they had never showed up anywhere? Could be still here? Who Ma, who was this so-called friend? Wasn't he the one that killed Larry you said?'

Florence rocked to and fro and peered at her son. 'Put the kettle on girlie and let's see whether we can remember before your dad does my head in.'

'What you think I am, your skivvy? I'm off. I don't need this happy families shit.'

Margaret, Vanda please, stomped out of the room. Goebbels looked up at his owner but Florence just shook her head. The back door slammed.

'I'll put the kettle on Ma but we need to talk. Might be good for both of us.'

Over cups of tea Flo' Whelks slowly remembered most of what happened eight years ago and told her younger son.

Up in the village Vanda wandered slowly up the curving road. She passed Tom's house and continued. Just past the general store was the George and Dragon. Vanda stopped and looked.

'Christ, a pommie pub, straight out of the bloody history books. Still, a pint would be better than any of that old witches's brew.' She pushed open the pub door and stepped down into the gloom of the public bar. George looked up from the paper he was reading on the bar. He automatically wiped the counter and looked at the potential customer. 'What'll it be luv?'

Vanda walked over to the bar and put her face up close to George's. 'You're not my type luv and I'll have a draught.'

George didn't back off from the close encounter. He was used to all sorts of customers and had been the landlord here for a long time. 'Of what luv?'

'Beer. You sell beer?'

'Ale, lager, Guinness, or perhaps I should ask which State you come from lass?'

'New South Wales. Why?'

'So it's Tooheys you want? What is it they serve in Victoria though? What's the expression – having a Piss, that's it. Great name for a beer that is. Anyway luv we don't have any Tooheys, although I've heard that Tooheys Old is quite good, sort of malty meaty flavour.'

'You done pulling your weenie?'

'A pint of lager then is it?'

'When you quite ready. I'll be over there.' Vanda pointed across to the corner of the room by the dart board and she walked over and picked up the darts. Slowly and deliberately she stood at the line and threw three perfect twenties.

George pulled her pint and carried it over. He put it on the table by the chairs and then stood there watching. Vanda pulled out her three darts and returned to the line. Three nineteens followed then three eighteens. George stood and watched. When she was down to twelve one of the darts caught the doubles wire and bounced out onto the floor. She picked up the dart, looked at the tip and drew her fingers along the line of the feathers. She reached down and picked up the glass and proceeded to drain it. Carefully putting the empty glass back on the table she ran her finger over her wet lips. She turned to George who was still standing there watching. 'Same again mate.'

George watched as Vanda spent the next hour slowly consuming pints and going round the board. She went down from twenty to one and then back up again to twenty. Going round the doubles ring she wasn't quite so consistent but she was good, bloody good thought George. The customers in the pub came and went but a few stayed and watched this weird bird in black with the pasty face calmly throwing darts. Even the young lads kept quiet. After an hour she walked back to the bar and settled up without saying a word. Turning round at the bar she slowly scanned the people in the room. A sort of hush fell and the conversations fell away. Later George said it was kind of spooky, like a freeze-frame in some film.

'You're right you pommie bastard, Tooheys Old is good,' and she walked out.

There was an immediate hubbub of voices right after Vanda left, everyone wanting to know who in the hell she was. George said he hadn't a clue. 'She just walked in and threw darts. Australian, from Sydney. I got that much before she started throwing darts. Girl's got a good aim, that's for sure. Never seen her before.'

'When she comes back George put her on the team mate. We're playing the lads from the Red Lion next week remember. With her as a ringer we could clean up.'

'Sure throws better than you do Ken.'

'In your dreams Ray. It's your space she'd take.'

'How about a quick play-off then? Just to see who ends up the spare.'

'You been in the pub?'

'No Dad, I lost my way and had to take a piss. What the fuck do you think?'

'You don't know no one here.'

'It only takes one hand to lift the glass not a bloody team. Used the other one for throwing arrows didn't I? Made a few of the bozos in there look though. Aren't there any girls in this burg? I could do with a real muffin muncher.'

'Margaret, wash your mouth out girl. We had enough trouble with all that in the Cross, you and your fucking girl-friends.'

'But that's just what I want. Girl can get sex-starved. Aren't there some nice juicy virgins around or is this place full of dried-up old prunes like gran'?'

'What did George say when you walked in?'

'Who's George, the bozo killing the dragon?'

'The landlord. His dad used to be the landlord when I was here and George was just a kid helping out. Ran in the family for years. Never was sure whether his real name was George or he changed it. What did he say?'

'Asked which State I came from.'

Phil took Margaret back into the pub and talked with George. Now everyone in the room really kept their ears open while making out they were talking amongst themselves. Phil wanted to ask George some more about his brother. He knew that Larry frequented the village pub and thought George could fill in some of the gaps that his mum couldn't or wouldn't remember. Margaret just stood at the bar with her back to the room and listened to her dad.

'So he was always dealing with this Norton Ferris bloke, a scouse you say. But he's dead, killed up on the Estate? You think he was doing some job for Larry? And this Norton had two sons you say but they got fired around the same time as their dad got killed. Jesus what sort of a family runs this bloody Estate? Cruel bastards to chuck the kids out when their dad's just been killed. Oh, they hired one of the boys back again later. What about the other kid? Not kids, men they were, and you think it was the older brother who was involved with my brother. What was his name? Idwal Ferris. But you know that he's dead too. What, never, his own brother killed him? When was this? Bloody dangerous place to live here in this village George. Thought living in the Cross had its moments. So this Idwal was away from the time of his dad's death, away from the time of Larry's death and then comes back sniffing around. Talking about some kind of revenge you think and the two brothers were here in this bar. Then the younger one kills his own brother. Who was that then? Let me get this straight. It was Idwal with Larry and then just recently this brother John kills Idwal. So now John Ferris is in gaol for killing his brother? He's out on bail, working here on the Estate? Is he dangerous? You think it was all a mistake, the brothers fell out over something?'

Phil bought a pint while talking with George. Vanda just stood there. When Phil was done he just pulled her out on to the street. 'You hear that girlie? Your old gran' was telling me about some deal that was going on with this Idwal Ferris. Him and Larry were trying to sell something to a couple of Bristol high-flyers.'

'What's Bristol? Thought that old pommie Londoner you used to know called tits bristols? What was it he said, something about Bristol City rhymed with titty? Jesus, why can't the poms speak proper?'

'Bristol is Bristol City you dumbo. It's a place, the big smoke around here.'

'So what?'

'Think, think, this Idwal and Larry fall out and my brother gets killed. If gran' has got it right this Idwal does time for killing Larry and then comes right back here. Why? Why does he come back here? They never found what it was that Larry and this Idwal were trying to sell up in Bristol. So it's hidden somewhere and Idwal comes running back here. Fights with his brother, probably arguing over how to split it or what to do with it and so John kills him. Think on it girlie, Larry dead, Idwal dead and still no whatever found but this loser John Ferris is still walking around. Of course he'll do time for offing his brother but right now we can get him to tell us what he knows. Maybe where it is?'

'You're fucking obsessed.'

'No, I'm fucking smart and I'm looking out for number one.'

So there I was back with Bob Edwards and the gang for the third time that morning. After talking briefly with Bob I walked through the plantation to find John Ferris. It was coming on to lunch time and so I found John and the rest of the gang walking out to the forest ride between the compartments.

'John, a moment if you please.'

We sat down in the gentle but weak sunshine on the grassy side of the ride. John unpacked his lunch bag and looked ruefully at whatever he had put together that morning.

'I don't know no more Mr. Daniel. It's all a bloody great blur.'

'I want you to think back John, not over the recent events but back nearly eight years ago. Remember I was only a kid then but you may remember some things if I try and think back too. I was here for much of

300

December and even the start of January. It was that first week in January that your dad got killed wasn't it? 'I had just gone back to school on the Monday. That was the sixth. Wasn't it Tuesday that it happened?'

'Mr. Daniel, I can't remember that far back.'

'Look John, my brother Michael had come down from London after some bloody great fight with Melanie Roger's family. That had been on Saturday, the fourth. None of us knew where Michael was over the weekend but I heard that he showed up at work on Tuesday morning really pissed off. Now I can remember my father telling me that Michael was at work here in the forest that day, that morning. There was another big row up at our house and Michael had talked to Norton that morning apparently. He had warned him he was going to get my father to fire you all and that he would be away part of the morning. That's what I heard when I came back a few days later. So, your dad was doing something in Michael's Landrover that Tuesday, loading up with fence posts if I remember right.'

'And then someone let loose that pile of sawlogs Mr. Daniel. Let them loose to knock old dad down into the stream below. That's what Idwal thought. He was sure it was Enrico that let those logs loose. That's why he came back. That's why he wanted to hurt Enrico. He was so sure that Enrico had sent those logs crashing down.'

'What was your dad like that week John? Who had he been talking to? Who had been at the cottage?'

'No one Mr. Daniel, no one ever came to the cottage. I told you and that Inspector chap. We never had no one at the cottage.'

'So who did your dad talk to elsewhere, in the pub for instance?'

'Well he was talking with Larry Whelks. He must have been 'cos when Idwal and I went to the pub that night to look for dad Larry Whelks grabbed us both as soon as we walked in. He was hopping mad he was. He was going to brain our dad. When Idwal heard it was to do with fence posts that's when he thought he might know where dad was. That's how we found Mr. Michael's Landrover 'cos Idwal knew where we had recently unloaded fence posts for that new plantation, around that larch cutover.'

'Was that all your dad was doing with Larry Whelks, just the fence posts?'

'Hell I don't know Mr. Daniel. It's about the level of dad's dealings, small stuff, nothing heavy just petty pilfering. Our dad wasn't smart enough to do any different. He even buggered that deal up as he was already a day late according to Larry.'

'What was Idwal doing that week, the week before your dad got killed? Did Idwal meet anyone or talk with anyone?'

'Let me think back Mr. Daniel. It's all so long ago now. Just after New Year you say, well my dad and I had a special job and I don't know about Idwal. Yes, that's right, it must have been the Monday. Dad was all mysterious and he told Idwal he would be out all day and he took me to look at some sheep. Jesus it was way out and gone. I never knew where we were going and dad was ultra cautious when we got close. We met a couple of blokes who had some sheep, well they said they had some sheep and did my dad want to buy some and keep them in the forest. Of course dad thought this could be a free grazing deal but he wanted me there 'cos he thought I would look after them. Now it turned out that these two blokes never had the sheep, leastways not yet and so the whole bloody day was a bit of a loss except dad was excited over a possible deal when they did get the sheep. We didn't get in until late that night. At the farm where we had gone the two blokes treated us to some fry up and a couple of bottles of beer so dad thought he was one up already.'

'And what had Idwal been doing?'

'Dunno' but I remember the next day, the Tuesday I suppose that Bob Edwards asked about the saws and whether Idwal got them all done.

I would guess that Idwal was just cleaning up the tools as it was a pretty quiet time at the start of the New Year. There wasn't much going on in the forest at that time Mr. Daniel.'

'So Idwal might have been alone that day?'

'Could be. Ask Bob Edwards, he might remember.'

I mulled this over.

'What happened Tuesday?'

'As I said, Idwal and me went to work and we never knew where dad was. In the pub we couldn't find him but Larry Whelks gave us a hard time.'

'And Idwal knew where he might be, your dad that is?'

'He said he thought so.'

'So you both rushed out with Larry Whelks chasing you and drove off to find your dad?'

'Yes, that's right Mr. Daniel. No, wait a minute. Larry left the pub before that and then I bumped into him as I went out to start the car.'

'You went out, although it was Idwal who knew where to go and look. Why didn't Idwal drive?'

'He did drive.'

'But you started the car. Where was Idwal?'

'He had to take a piss didn't he? Well that's what he said and so he told me to start the car.'

'So Idwal's having a piss and Larry has gone back into the pub. Did they talk?'

'Fuck I don't know Mr. Daniel. I was in the car wasn't I? I just told you.'

'But Idwal and Larry could have talked, while Idwal was having this maybe piss?'

'Could be, who cares? Idwal's dead so what does it matter?'

'John, if your dad wasn't smart enough and you never knew about the hidey-hole then the most likely person to know about the bones would be Idwal. If no one ever came to the cottage then it was very likely Idwal who was responsible for the bones.'

'But they were dog bones weren't they? Who cares about dog bones?'

I kept quiet about the new set of bones that definitely were not dog bones.

'The day after your dad got killed my father gave you a week's notice if I remember right. Then on the Thursday, the next day my brother got shot.'

'Idwal never did that Mr. Daniel, he never did.'

'No John, you're right. Your brother was never a serious suspect for Michael's death, neither were you.'

'But we both got questioned. We both got seriously questioned.'

'What was Idwal like that week? Did he go anywhere unusual, see anyone unexpected? Just think, he knew about the hidey-hole and now all of a sudden he was having to leave your cottage. What if he had stashed something else in the hole and then had to move it? Did you see him move anything?'

'Mr. Daniel this was eight years ago and a lot has happened since. I smartened up, found Betty, had kids and everything was going wonderfully. You're asking about a past life. One I'm trying to forget. Now you're dragging all that up again.'

'Okay John, I'll back off. I was hoping you might remember something if I nagged enough. I'm trying to find out what is down in that hole and why. If I could find out who is responsible that might help. Inspector Field agrees with me that we don't think you had anything to do with the hole but just think who did know about it? The list seems to include only Idwal and your dad and I would put my money on your brother John. I don't think it is the kind of thing your dad was into but your brother was a different kind of man. Who would you pick if you were me?'

John sat on the grass and looked up into space. 'Make it all go away Mr. Daniel. It's all too much to take in. I suppose it's more like Idwal, especially knowing what he did later.'

'I'll let it go John. Sorry to bring up old hurts but those bones need to be sorted and Inspector Field thinks I know more about the cottage, the forest and the people than he does. He's only been in the area a few years and this is history, sort of before his time.'

I got up and walked over to Bob Edwards. Freddie watched me and got up as I came over.

'So did he confess Mr. Daniel? You spent enough time asking a lot of questions. Did he finally say he did it?

'What are you talking about Freddie?' Bob asked.

'Another time Bob and I'll explain,' I said. I turned to Freddie. 'Freddie, just keep your story to yourself, and no, John is not responsible so keep you assumptions to yourself.'

'You sure, after what he did to his brother? Fell out did they, dividing the spoils and John ended up killing him? Where's the box?'

'Freddie I said shut it.'

'Ain't right Mr. Daniel. That box should be mine now. Never was in the cave was it? Your brother got killed for nothing, well looking for nothing.'

Bob Edwards stood there with his mouth half open. He stuttered and eventually managed 'Freddie what are you talking about lad? I thought you were pissed off with John over killing his brother.'

'Bob,' I said, 'it's a long story and it appears to go back nearly eight years ago now. While Freddie's yapping I may as well ask you whether you can remember back eight years ago. We're trying to put together

305

what happened around New Years and early January 1991, right around the time that Norton Ferris got killed. Remember that?'

'I wasn't there that actual night Mr. Daniel, not when you hauled the Landrover out of the stream but I was here the next day when the police were asking questions. Freddie was there though, weren't you Freddie?'

'Sure was, upside down it was and bloody funny with all those fence posts bouncing out of the back and bobbing away downstream. Cold it was too, really icy on that slope. Your mum nearly slipped into the stream Mr. Daniel.'

'Hold on, hold on, it's not the accident that interests me but both before it and after it. Now, the accident happened on a Tuesday. Bob, John has been telling me that the day before, the Monday, he and his dad were off all day on some special job so you would have been in charge. Cast your mind back if you can Bob and try and remember what everyone was doing. It was early January and so we probably had a small crew and there wouldn't have been much work. What were you all doing on that Monday?'

Bob scratched his head. Freddie also went into some kind of thinking mode.

'Didn't we put all those fence posts out on the Monday Bob? Norton forgot to do it the previous Friday and your dad Mr. Daniel gave him a bollocking for forgetting so when he rushed away on the Monday with John we put them out then. It was the Tuesday that Norton tried to collect up some of the "spares" and the logs came down.'

'So all of the gang were out on the Monday laying out the fence posts?'

'No, now I remember we had Peter Buckley, Harry Thomas and Enrico was driving the truck that Monday. We didn't need any more than that for the job. Freddie here was doing something around the yard and Idwal, yes Idwal asked to look over all the tools and sharpen what

306

needed it. I had a variety of inspections to do and I remember checking in the yard and not finding Idwal. I went down to their cottage and he was there having a cup of tea.'

'Alone?'

'As far as I know Mr. Daniel. He'd gone back to his cottage to have lunch as it wasn't far and he was half way through he said.'

'So Idwal was alone that day and apart from you seeing him in the cottage around lunch time no one would have seen him?'

'I suppose so Mr. Daniel, but what's this all about? John was out that Monday with his dad and then with his brother on the Tuesday.'

'Freddie, did you see Idwal that Monday?'

'No Mr. Daniel. I told you I went up to the cave around lunch time but there was no one else there. I didn't see Idwal anywhere that day, or any of the rest of the gang.'

'Bob can you remember John or Idwal doing anything special or unusual that final week, the week they were working out their notice?'

'Other than being late most days and not really being any use to anyone no I can't. They sort of appeared and then by next Tuesday or Wednesday they were both gone.'

'Where did they go?'

'Well John pissed off and I never did see him until your father hired him back about five months later.'

'And Idwal?'

'He was still in the village for a couple of days. I saw him in the pub one night with Larry Whelks. Don't know where he was staying but he was around for nearly a week I think. This is a long time ago Mr. Daniel. Most times I can't even remember what I did last week let alone eight years ago but I do remember seeing Idwal and not John.'

Back at the Big House I scrounged around for a late lunch, primarily by raiding the kitchen. Cook was more concerned with my head but I told her I felt much better and so she was quite prepared to feed me. Coming out of the kitchen into the hall the telephone rang and when I picked it up I heard a rather jubilant Terence Field telling me he had obtained a Search Warrant. He asked whether I could come down to the Whelks cottage and help him understand the situation with the garden path and the green pebbles? So, for the third time that day I was back outside the Whelks cottage looking at the still horizontal garden gate. As Terence Field's car was not there I sat in the Landrover and waited. Sitting in the car I thought over all the things I had heard and they still didn't make sense. I looked out of the window at the garden. Was this where the so-called hidden treasure ended up?

The arrival of Terence's car brought me out of my musings. Terence got out accompanied by a constable, although I didn't know this at the time as he was in plain clothes.

'Daniel I asked you down here as an observer really. You know more about the people here than I do and certainly more than PC Goodfellow here. By the way this is PC Goodfellow and constable this is Daniel Lord.'

We shook hands.

'I've got a Search Warrant that covers the entire property. I had to explain that the area of interest may not be the cottage itself but elsewhere on the property. It took a while to make the authorities understand the importance of the entire property but your adventure with the path yesterday and Samantha's find helped. Round the back then constable and let's see whether we can unearth the mystery of the garden path?'

I followed Terence and PC Goodfellow round to the back of the cottage and Terence thumped loudly on the door. The only response was a scrabbling of feet, a solid thud on the inside of the door and a loud outburst of barking. Apparently Goebbels was home. Terence thumped on the door again. 'Police, open up please Mrs. Whelks. I have a Search Warrant here for your property.'

Goebbels responded with a series of growls, yelps and a very aggressive crescendo of barks.

'Mrs. Whelks we are coming in. This is the police.'

As Terence reached forward to hold the handle and open the back door the handle suddenly sprung away from his hand and the door flew open. Florence Whelks stood there holding Goebbels by his collar. She said, 'what do you want?' and Goebbels uttered a menacing guttural noise from the bottom of his throat. Not at all taken aback Terence stepped forwards inside the doorway and politely said, 'may we come in please?' I grinned inside when I remembered John Ferris's description of Terence Field when he had said 'quiet, soft-spoken but once he gets his teeth in I don't reckon there's any letting go'. You're right John I said to myself and he's got his teeth in.

Terence didn't stop in the doorway but continued his forward motion into the kitchen. Florence had to back up or brazen it out. Goebbels looked like he might make a positive stand but Florence did turn and walk back into her kitchen. I followed PC Goodfellow on the heels of his leader.

'What do you......'

'Mrs. Whelks I have a Search Warrant here to search your property,' and Terence flourished his valuable entry document.

I'll give Florence her due as she wasn't particularly cowed by this aggressive attitude. Once inside the middle of her kitchen she straightened up and let go of Goebbels collar but only after she had uttered 'stay'. Goebbels obediently stayed but the tail and the body motion suggested a change of attitude was to hand if needed.

'What can I do for you officer?'

Terence opened his wallet and so did PC Goodfellow and they both stated who they were while showing Florence their I.D.s. 'Mrs. Whelks we have the authority to search your property. We would like you to accompany us and answer any of our questions please.'

'Who's he?' Here Florence pointed her finger rather rapier-like at me. 'He was trespassing in my garden. Have you arrested him? Looks dangerous to me officer. He was here yesterday but I sorted him. Should have seen him jump. Could be in the Olympics,' and here Florence cackled and her whole body convulsed.

'See you banged your head sonny. Well you shouldn't go poking your nose into other people's business now should you?'

'Mrs. Whelks, our search if you don't mind.' Terence wasn't going to be diverted by Flo's rantings. 'Can we start in the garden? Constable go through and open the front door.' As PC Goodfellow started to walk towards the hallway leading to the front door Goebbels quivered and growled. The good constable halted in his tracks at the reaction.

'The front door constable,' said Terence looking pointedly at Flo'.

'Stay.'

PC Goodfellow reached the front door and succeeded in producing that frightful screech I had heard yesterday as the rarely-opened front door reluctantly opened inwards.

'Shall we Mrs. Whelks?' offered Terence and pointed with his arm that Flo' should follow the constable. Goebbels couldn't stand the strain and he torpedoed his barrel body down the hallway and shot like a cannonball out into the garden. Turning in mid-air he landed part way down the path and looked at the humans as all four of us reached the garden.

Terence slowly walked down the overgrown path to the gate at the end.

310

'He did that,' said Flo' and she turned to look at me with that puzzled look. Terence didn't look at the gate or comment but walked slowly back up the path. He turned to look at his constable. 'What do you see PC Goodfellow? What catches your eye?'

I didn't know what Terence had told the constable and so I listened carefully. I saw that Florence too was quite interested in both the question and the answer.

'Rough gravel path with irregular flagstones sir leading from the door to the gate, flattened gate that is. Garden looks a mess with no obvious pattern and there doesn't appear to be any disturbances or unusual vegetation. Strange edging to the path though sir. A bit of a mix up of pebbles that look like they line the path but some are missing and look kicked up sir.'

'My Larry did that for me. Wanted to keep them in the shed when he had painted them but I thought they would look better lining my path. Made him edge the path for me. They were neat when he first did it. Tidy it was then. He was a good boy looking after his mum.'

Terence crouched down and tapped at a couple of the irregular flagstones. He spread his fingers over the gravel and casually picked up three of the green pebbles. He turned them slowly over in his hands.

'Know what these are constable?' he asked.

'Hey, my Larry put those down officer. You've messed up the edging.'

'Constable?'

PC Goodfellow took one of the green pebbles and looked at it more closely. 'They all look about the same size sir and they are rather round for ordinary pebbles. Did they come from a stream or something? They are all very smooth like they were worn down by water.'

'Why paint them Mrs. Whelks?'

311

'Look good in green. Larry and that other bloke were painting them green and I thought they would look good in my garden. The other bloke agreed although Larry didn't at the time. Still, I made them lay them down out here in the end.'

'What colour were they before Larry painted them Mrs. Whelks?'

'I don't know do I? They had done all of them, laid out in the shed back there to dry when I first saw them. Just putting the paint away when I found them. Goebbels found them didn't you boy? Fund of information this dog is officer. Why do you think I call him Goebbels?'

'So constable, any more thoughts?'

'Beginning to think they didn't start off as pebbles somehow sir but I'm not sure what they might have been originally.'

'Like this,' and Terence flashed one of Samantha's finds out of his pocket although now the green pebble was a rather dull gold coin.

'Struth,' said PC Goodfellow.

'They're mine,' extorted Florence, 'all mine, the cottage, the garden and the garden path.'

'I think not,' said Terence very quietly, 'but I think we can discuss this further in the comfort of your kitchen Mrs. Whelks,' and Terence walked slowly back into the cottage.

PC Goodfellow scratched his head and looked at the array of pebbles lining the path. His gaze slowly travelled up one side of the path to the gate and moved back on the other side to the front door. 'Amazing, who'd have believed it? Right in front of your face, under your feet and not knowing.' He lifted his gaze and looked at me. 'You knew?'

'I had a very good idea constable and I also think I know where they came from too but let's go into the cottage and see whether your boss can persuade Florence to explain a little more about these pretty painted pebbles.'

Once again we had to contend with the furiously moving legs and barrel body of Goebbels as we re-entered the cottage and all re-assembled in the kitchen.

'Why don't you sit down Mrs. Whelks and Constable Goodfellow here will put the kettle on. I think a strong sweet cup of tea might help you get over some of the shock.'

'But they're mine,' muttered Florence.

When we had sorted out the niceties of tea, milk, sugar and settled Florence in her chair Terence lifted a wooden kitchen chair and having reversed it he sat in front of Flo' looking at her.

'So how about you explain Mrs. Whelks how these pebbles got here? Let's walk backwards can we? Larry and his mate put them in the garden for you after you asked?'

'Yes, that's right. Didn't take long but I did want them neat.'

'Where were the "pebbles" before you had Larry and his mate put them in the garden?'

'In the back shed. That's where I found them doing the painting.'

'And in this back shed Larry and his mate had laid out these pebbles and had painted all of them?'

'They were spread out on a set of planks on saw-horses. Larry always had lots of wood and stuff in that shed so it wasn't hard to set up some sort of table to paint them.'

'What else did you see in the shed? What were Larry and his mate doing?'

'Painting them of course like I told you.'

'So they had brushes, paint cans and what else?'

'I don't know. What else would you expect? They were painting them so that's all there was?'

'What had the pebbles come in? Was there any sack, any suitcase, any box? Larry and his mate must have got them from somewhere Mrs.

Whelks? Who was this mate then, this other painter and path layer? The one who thought your garden path was a good idea?'

Florence Whelks stiffened. Her hands shook and the cup rattled on the saucer. The spoon tipped off the saucer and tumbled to the floor. Goebbels turned his head and looked up at his mistress. There was a pregnant silence in the kitchen. 'The mate?' Terence asked very quietly.

'Murderer, murderer,' screeched Florence and the cup and saucer crashed to the floor to be followed by a series of piercing barks from the Jack Russell. 'He killed my Larry didn't he? Murderer murderer but he got his comeuppance.' Here Florence looked point blank back at Terence Field. 'His patsy brother killed that bloody murderer and good riddance. Heard he slashed his throat. Gaol was never the right answer for murder. Should have hung him but fate caught up and hung him for me. His mate officer was Idwal Ferris, may his soul rot in hell.'

Rather unthinkingly I had picked up the scattered pieces of the cup and saucer and stacked the shards on the table. Florence suddenly seemed to notice me. 'You hired him,' she screeched, 'your family hired all of them. That useless Norton, Simple Simon he was, but his son Idwal was different. Rotten through and through Idwal was. John's more like his dad but then he turned out good after they all left. He'll be all right officer won't he? John was a good lad and he and that Betty Travers have done well. Good kids they've got too. John will get off Inspector, crime of passion surely?'

Terence quietly sat there without changing the expression on his face. 'Where did the pebbles come from Mrs. Whelks? Did Larry find them? Why was Idwal Ferris here?'

'Came here when the Lord family fired them, kicked them out of their cottage didn't they?' Here Florence turned and glared at me. 'Hard your mother is Daniel Lord. Father dies and the same day them boys were fired.'

I was about to respond that it was my mum who hired John back again but remembered that this was Terence's investigation and I was just here as an observer. I kept my mouth shut.

'Idwal Ferris stayed here Mrs. Whelks?'

'Probably, long time ago, couple of nights maybe. I don't remember.' Flo' seemed to have shrunk back inside herself. The memory of her son being murdered dragged back again hadn't helped. The colour had seeped from her face and she looked all of her eighty eight years. Her body looked frail in the large chair.

'Long time ago,' she muttered. 'Larry never found them Inspector. I'm sure they weren't here until Idwal appeared. Where he got them from.....', and Florence passed out.

'Cup of water constable please. Here Mrs. Whelks, just sip this slowly. Breathe gently and take little sips. Just rest there a while and we'll check on that shed out back. Mr. Lord here will stay and look after you. Just let her sip slowly Daniel. Come on constable. Let's look at the "painting studio".'

'Just who the fuck are you and what are you doing to my ma? Hey, you were skulking around here before when we came yesterday. What you fucking doing in here now? Who let you in? You trying to poison my ma? Hold him Margaret while I thump him.'

'I would recommend against that Mr. Whelks. It is Mr. Whelks isn't it, Mr. Phillip Whelks, brother of the late Larry Whelks?'

'And who the fuck are you mate? Christ, it's like a bloody merry go round in 'ere.'

'He's that freaking copper I saw yesterday Dad. Outside he was but a copper through and through.'

'Right, that's it. Out, out the bloody lot of you.' Phil Whelks moved forwards and all Terence did was thump him on the chest with his Search Warrant. 'Read that sir,' he said calmly, 'and I think you'll find it all in order. We've come here to search your mother's property and very helpful she has been. How is she Daniel?'

'She's okay Terence but a little frail I think.'

I felt Florence grip my forearm in her thin arthritic claw of a hand and she hissed, 'frail sonny, just let me catch my breath and we'll wade into round two.' I turned to look at her and her sharp eyes revealed an inner core of fire. 'Old Ma Whelks doesn't back out of any fight sonny and don't you ever forget it.'

I smiled and winked. Her face broke into a hideous smile and she cackled. 'Frail' was all she said and she let go of my arm and cackled again.

'Mrs Whelks I'm going to get PC Goodfellow here to put police tape around your garden, well around your path and I expect you to respect that tape. We don't want you or anyone else inside that taped area. Do you understand me? I think you know why.'

Florence nodded. 'Later today I'll come back with a couple of officers and we will gather up your garden path pebbles and then take the tape away and the garden will be all yours again. I've spoken with Mr. Lord here and he will see that your garden gate is restored after we have finished. I don't think there is anything in the shed that interests us any more at the moment and so there is no tape there, just around the path.'

Florence slowly moved herself more upright in the chair and some colour returned. She looked at me and murmured 'frail,' and then looked straight at Terence. 'Understood Inspector. They looked good when Larry first put them down but now I think I'll let them go. Seems they've got too much blood on them.' She tried to stand and I quickly held out my arm to help. Once again she murmured 'frail' and managed to stand. Goebbels thumped his tail on the floor and looked around. He saw Margaret and growled. She promptly squatted down and growled back in his face which really surprised him and his tail suddenly collapsed between his legs.

'Seems the witch has spoken,' said Florence. 'Takes after me that one,' she told the room. Phil bristled but no one was paying any attention. Terence turned his wooden chair around and placed it back by the table. 'I think we've done all we need to do constable. Thank you for your cooperation Mrs. Whelks. We will return shortly.' He turned and made for the back door and PC Goodfellow followed.

'Oy, what about me copper? Don't I get no apology? Frightening my ma like that and him,' and here he turned to point his finger at me. 'How come he's here, breaking up the place?'

Terence turned. 'Mr. Whelks your mother will explain everything but at the moment I would advise you to wait until we have all left. I wouldn't want to hear something that later I might have to use, if you know what I mean? Daniel coming?'

With one last look at Flo' I walked out of the kitchen.

When we were standing back by the cars Terence held my arm. 'Thanks,' he said.

'For what?'

'For being quiet and helping in there. I think that mad old lady quite likes you,' he said with a grin on his face, 'even if you did flatten her gate. Oh, by the way, I assume that you replacing the gate is no great inconvenience. I thought that one good turn deserves another.'

'Did you learn what you went there for?' I asked.

Terence turned to his fellow officer. 'Well constable, what did we learn?'

'Looks can be deceiving sir, and hiding stolen property in plain view is very clever sir. Did Idwal Ferris really have the original goods sir?'

'Not proven yet constable but we're getting closer. Suppose we'll never really know whether Larry Whelks ever knew about Norton Ferris's hidey-hole. If he didn't then Idwal was very likely the source of the coins and we think we know how he got those. Don't we Daniel?'

I started. I suppose I hadn't really been listening to Terence and his constable. It was getting on for Friday evening and I had to phone Katya. 'What Terence, what did you say?'

'It'll keep Daniel. Come on then constable. We need to collect a carrying bag for our booty and fill in some precious police procedure forms.'

'Yes sir.'

Still feeling the effects of the bump on my head I drove slowly back to the Forest Office and rather carefully lowered myself into the office chair. I briefly scanned over the Day Planner to make sure I hadn't forgotten something in the day's series of roundabout trips. What was it Terence asked his constable, my question about whether we learnt anything. I suppose I could check tomorrow just to make sure. Ladder, that was it, that would make it easier. Katya, God yes Katya, I'd forgotten all about you: must be the bang on the head. I checked the clock and automatically lifted the telephone.

'You've got to go to a lecture this evening? Oh, it's really relevant and your tutor expects you. No Katya, no love that's fine. I understand. I'm disappointed of course but I do understand. Tomorrow then, fine, about nine? Not nine, then when? Now I'm doubly disappointed. I understand. See you tomorrow, can't wait. Bye love.'

Rather dejectedly I put the phone back on the cradle. Tomorrow, I'll have to wait until tomorrow. My quiet self pity was suddenly rudely interrupted when James with the wobbly helmet came thundering into the office and energetically leapt into my lap.

'Uncle Daniel, Uncle Daniel I did it, or rather we did it.'

Somewhat startled and trying not to drop James off my lap I awoke from my dreaming of Katya to respond to my nephew. 'We did what James?'

'We jumped Uncle Daniel, we jumped over the hurdles. Tall ones, huge! This high.'

With a quick series of wriggles the arms went into motion and performed all sorts of height estimates. The mouth went non-stop at the same time just proving that men can do two things at once.

'That's amazing James,' I exclaimed, 'and did your partner enjoy it too?'

'Dainty thought it was smashing, well perhaps better would be awesome, although we did sort of smash through the hurdles the first few times.'

'And did you whisper "well done" in her ear?'

'No, should I?' came an inquisitive voice accompanied by a rather wistful face.

'Well it was a team effort James and it is always good to praise your partner when you do something well together.'

'I'll go now and tell her.' James gathered up his arms and legs and hurtled off my lap just as fast as he had arrived and sped out of the door accompanied by a loud shout of 'Dainty, Dainty, you were great, good, fantastic, where are you?'

Then I heard the rather quieter voice of my sister explaining she had moved the horses to the edge of the yard to avoid the trucks coming in at the end of the day. End of the day I thought. I sat upright and rethought. Tomorrow we'll sort out the details Terence and wrap it up.

CLIMAX

THAT SATURDAY KATYA COULDN'T COME down from Oxford until midday and so it was early afternoon before I could get her alone. I spent most of the time in the Landrover driving to the cave filling Katya in on the events of this past week. She was quite delighted with the idea about an Education Centre but said she didn't know anything about orienteering.

'How was golf on Wednesday Daniel? Did your wrist feel any better?'

'Wednesday was typical Katya, up and down. When I thought of you and imagined you with me I played really well and had three birdies.'

'Smashing birdies? You know the ones that Tony likes? Never mind. But you didn't think of me all the time? I'm hurt Daniel. What happened to the score? I bet you had a double bogey and that'll teach you not think of me.' She laughed and tossed her head of hair. Then she reached across and put her hand on my arm, 'but I must confess kind sir I didn't think of you all the time either. Daniel this thesis stuff is a bit of a grind. There are days when I go round in circles.'

320

'Not smashing, no, one over, yes and it will all come right in the end.'

Katya looked at me with a puzzled look on her face. 'Is this a quiz or something Daniel?'

Now it was my turn to laugh and I said, 'no but I answered your questions and tried to help with you going round in circles. Actually it was bones that kept intruding into my thoughts during my golf. That hidey-hole is slowly doing my head in. I just hope that Terence's white-coated wizards don't find anything else puzzling down there.'

'Where are we going Daniel, and why the ladder?'

'I thought I'd try and determine whether there is anything else in that old tree by the cave. The more I think about it the more I think you were right.'

'I was?'

'Yes, remember you thought that the X-mark on the plan of the cave might be just an indicator, like we use nylon flagging in the forest. You've used flagging to mark the start of some traverse to find an actual plot in the forest which is unmarked. You don't want to mark the actual plot because someone will see it and do something special or unnatural in the plot itself. You want the plot to merge in to the rest of the forest. Well, I think the mark in the cave was similar. The treasure or the box of coins was like the plot and close by but not where the X-mark was. That was merely a flag.'

'So we're going to look at the plot so to speak?'

'Which may or may not be violated or vandalised so to speak.'

I told Katya the story of Freddie and the twins.

'So the coins I found could have been dropped when they got the box down?'

'Or when the box was put up there. We'll never know whether the tree was the first or last hiding place for the box but what I want to do now is see whether there is anything else stuck up in that tree.'

The ladder was awkward to carry over the rough ground leading to the cave and the old tree but we carefully picked our way down along the edge of the cliff.

'Here, let's brace it on the downhill side. There's more room down here and it's long enough to reach up to the old fork.'

'You want me to go up while you hold it?'

'No Katya, I'll go up this time. Can you just hold the bottom and watch it's stable for me please.'

'What about your wrist? Is your head still woozy? Let me look in your eyes Daniel?'

'Willingly,' I said, and we kissed gently.

'Daniel I thought we were going treasure hunting?'

'I've found my treasure,' I said and kissed again.

'Work first and play afterwards Daniel. That's what my father taught me.'

'And he is quite a southern gentleman with all the proper etiquette.'

'And he likes you so behave for a moment and then we can relax having solved the world's last mystery.'

We both laughed and kissed once more before I slowly and carefully stepped up the ladder.

'See anything? I couldn't find anything up there when I looked but I was trying to hold on and stand on your shoulders. It wasn't as easy as on a ladder.'

There was nothing very obvious in the rotten fork. Leaves, twigs, bark, fragments of rotten wood and the odour of decay wafted about as I rummaged in the cavity. It looked as if the box had been the only man-made item hidden up here. I had brought along a short-handled rake and I used this to dig about further into the rotten trunk. A shower of debris rained down on Katya.

'Daniel you don't have to throw it all my way you know. There are other sides to this tree.'

'Sorry, sorry but I think I've found something. Yes, I have.'

'What is it? If it's more solid than the debris you're throwing down give me a warning. I'll go and get a hard hat.'

'No, I've just got to get the edge under. Sod it it slipped again.'

'Watch your weight on the ladder Daniel. Don't lean too far to the right or you'll push the ladder from under you.'

Hush woman I whispered under my breath. I'm fine but just let me catch the edge again. Ah, there, up you come my beauty. The rake had caught the edge of a small slender box which at one time had been fine smooth leather. Years of living in the tree had disfigured the leather but it was still in one piece and I tapped the box. It sounded like the leather was a decorative covering for a wood or metal case.

'What have you got Daniel? You're very quiet and the rain of debris has stopped. You safe up there?'

'A box, yes and yes again.'

'Daniel, cryptic comments don't become you. What box?'

'Just let me check one last time in this hole. I think I have dug around enough but I would like to be sure. Watch out below Katya.'

'You're not going to throw the box down Daniel?'

'No, that's safe but I'm going to dig one last time.'

I couldn't find anything else and so I was soon down at the foot of the ladder and kissing Katya again.

'Daniel, the box, the other box, what's in it?'

'I'm not sure I agree with your priorities lady,' I said as I kissed her again.

'Daniel, we agreed, work first play later. The box!'

I put down the rake and we both sat at the foot of the old tree. The box was pretty grubby and I found a handkerchief to wipe most of the black composted debris off its surface.

'It looks like a ladies jewellery case Daniel. What's inside?'

'Mystery upon mystery,' I chanted.

'Well open it then mystery man.'

Inside lay a golden necklace with a pendant that looked a like a large pearl.

'Daniel that's beautiful, it's exquisite.' Katya delicately lifted the golden strands and examined the jewel. 'It really is a treasure,' she murmured. 'You did find your treasure.'

'I told you I found my treasure,' I answered and put my arm around her shoulders. We kissed.

Vanda paid another visit to Tom Daley and feeling rather relaxed and mellow she wandered into the George and Dragon. It was still early evening and the bar was only half full. Having secured her pint and listened to George rabbit on about Australian beer she once again wandered over to the corner with the dart board. Slowly she started to throw her way around the board only this time she started at one. On her second beer she threw the three darts unerringly into the twenty and sat down and looked around the room. Doesn't look like there's much talent in this burg she thought. Where do all the pretty young things with thongs and pert nipples hang out? Dad we need to move before I get sex-starved.

Just at that moment there was some activity at the bar and Vanda turned to watch. Two lads had come in and they were having some kind of argument with a new face behind the bar. Now there was a potential lover thought Vanda as Gloria Manson flirted with Freddie Dunster and Gary Templeton. Having spent ten minutes chatting and buying their beer the two lads moved away to another part of the room. Vanda glanced across at Gloria. The girl behind the bar was a local but she hadn't lived in the village since she was eighteen, some seven years ago now. Gloria had recently come back into the village from London and there were all sorts of rumours why. Slim, blond, and built like a girl Vanda noticed. Full lips, pretty pink tongue and a cute little clit thought Vanda. Now that's more like it. She wandered over to the bar and eyed Gloria up and down.

'You're much better to look at than George.'

'What'll it be love?' came back the London drawl still with a west country inflexion.

'How about half an hour on the sofa in the back?' suggested Vanda.

'Fifty quid for you sweetheart but are you sure I swing both ways?'

'You'll never know until you try.'

'Jesus, an Ozzie in drag. Are you going to vamp me all dressed in your black get up? Black bra and panties I suppose?'

'What's a bra or panties? Bet you taste sweet.'

'Gloria, you've met our new Australian beauty queen have you? This is old Florence Whelks's granddaughter, just come over from Sydney. Drinks like a fish and throws darts like a pro. What'll it be, Vanda isn't it?'

'George I was just telling your little nympho here that I would like her but she went all coy.'

'Got her wrong there Vanda. Our Gloria has just come back from the big city and she is quite used to dealing with funny questions.'

'George, I'm also quite capable of dealing with funny customers, so now love, as I asked earlier, another pint is it?'

Vanda wandered back to her dart board with her pint thinking how to get into Miss Blondie's knickers? Wonder whether she was on the game up in London? Certainly not taken aback by my questions and answer. Well, early days and so we'll see. She brushed off those two lads easy enough. Back at the dart board Vanda started on the double ring.

'Care for a game? I could use some competition. Throw a good dart myself. What'll it be? Like another pint for starters?'

Slowly Vanda turned her gaze from the dart board to the owner of the voice. The man was probably in his early thirties and looked clean and tidy enough. He smiled. Wonder how I could fuck him she thought?

'Mine's a lager and yes I'll give you a game. Think your cock can stand the embarrassment when I beat you, or do you like being beaten? Perhaps I'll tie you up later and beat you.'

Back at the bar Gloria pulled another pint and the man brought it over to Vanda's table.

'There you go love. Name's John and who are you?'

'She's the witch's daughter, or granddaughter,' called out Gloria.

Vanda turned and looked at Gloria. 'Wonder what you look like dressed as a fairy,' muttered Vanda, 'and I would slowly pull off your wings and pin your cute little body to a board with my darts.'

'Jesus, you're a weird one? Do you always dress like that? Where you from 'cos you speak funny.'

'You want to throw arrows or are you just all hot air Mister? How does 501 grab you with doubles to start and finish or is that too much bloody funny talk?' Vanda took a long swallow on her beer as she looked at John over the rim of the glass.

'No, as you like, 501 sounds okay. Closest to the bull starts?'

'Fine, throw.'

Before John even had a chance to throw Freddie's voice rang out across the crowded room. He and Gary had been talking in the corner and half watching a football game on the TV when suddenly Freddie noticed who was playing darts. Standing up Freddie called out, 'you watch him darling. Cuts people up does our John. Just keep out of his line of fire love or he'll pin you to the floor with those darts. Walking....'

'Freddie, I've told you before, any more of that lad and you're out of here. Now just sit down and watch the match or talk with Gary here. Gary, keep a hand on his shoulder lad and any time our Freddie wants to stand up just persuade him to stay seated. Freddie you hear me son?'

Freddie sat down and grunted into his beer. 'Tosser,' muttered Freddie, 'still, looking at that bit of crumpet he's welcome. Jesus, who does she think she is and where did George say she came from?'

'Said she was old Flo's granddaughter. Larry never had no kids did he? Thought George said she came from Sydney. That's in Canada isn't it Freddie, Nova Scotia or somewhere? Does she look Canadian to you?'

'She looks like a fucking nightmare to me mate but she can throw darts. See that? Never bloody misses? John is good, well so they say but that bird's got his number.'

Vanda let John win the first game. She started off with her doubles easy enough but then kept missing the twenties and sliding into the fives or the ones. Occasionally she'd hit eighteen next to the one to make sure John didn't notice her mistakes. She downed her pint and carried the glasses over the bar.

'Same again gorgeous. Still think you'd look good on that sofa. I've got a tongue that works wonders.' Vanda slid her tongue forwards and the little stud in her pink tongue jiggled at Gloria. 'Just think of that tickling you. Makes you go weak at the knees and wet in the drawers eh love? Thrill a minute me.'

'Six pounds please.' Vanda pouted her lips and then turned and carried the two glasses over to John.

'You're right mate, you are good. Still, perhaps I'll get luckier this time.'

'No luck involved, Vanda wasn't it? Did someone say you were from Sydney? Heard that's a big city. Place with that bridge isn't it? What do they call it? Saw it on the tele a while back – the coat-hanger that was it. Funny name for a bridge. Don't they walk over it too, right over the top? Christ that must be bloody terrifying. Done that have you?'

'In your dreams sport. You ever going to throw those bleeding arrows?'

During the second game Vanda got closer to John in the scoring but she let him get his doubles to go out in style. Gary Templeton had let go of Freddie's arm for a moment and was back at the bar chatting to Gloria and trying to buy another couple of pints. He was chatting much more seriously than he was buying and Gloria flirted away leaning across the bar and letting Gary get a good view of the goods on offer. She could almost see his tongue hanging out. Still, he was well built and smelled okay for a Saturday night.

The interaction at the bar got interrupted when Freddie decided that Gary was too bloody slow getting his round in and Freddie was thirsty.

'You going to ogle those tits all night mate while I die of thirst back there? You're supposed to be buying pints Gary, beer that is not milk pints. So come away from the milk fountain and get my pint. I've got to go and take a piss. I'll expect my pint lined up on the table when I get back.'

Freddie deliberately walked towards the dart board. 'Leading you by your nose John she is, or perhaps by your cock. Still, looking at her I don't think I'd fancy her pulling my cock.'

'Freddie, George told you to put a sock in it so sod off mate. At least I've found someone who can play darts and give me a little competition.

Helps make the evening worthwhile. So bugger off and leave us in peace.'

Freddie grinned and leered at Vanda. 'Pulling his cock you are you wicked witch. I watched you before going round the board. Never missed did you and now you can't throw worth a shit. Bewitching, glad it ain't my cock. I prefer my birds to look like birds. Now our Gloria there, she'd make me turn tricks and she looks like a goer.'

George came up from the cellar and saw Freddie. 'Freddie!'

'I'm just off George, need to see a man about a dog landlord, honest I do.'

Freddie took off for the gents.

'Sorry about loudmouth there. I think you look.... well different, quite interesting in fact. Never seen anyone look as startling as you. Want to try and get your honour back?'

Vanda smiled inwardly. Get her honour back? Fuck you chump, my honour don't have anything to do with it. I'll startle you though you stupid prick. Could be a different trip and perhaps a new life in this dead hole. We'll see, the evening is young. If Miss Blondie pants won't play then maybe this fine young man will be my giggle for the night. Feel like a new sensation and I'll startle this bloody virgin out of his fucking mind.

'So shall we play for real now? I'll buy you another pint to drown your sorrows.'

'Darling, I'm just getting warmed up.'

'I'll warm you up,' muttered Vanda as she walked slowly over to the bar and stuck her tongue out at Gloria so the stud jiggled. 'Two more of your finest gorgeous and your finest are quite gorgeous aren't they?' Vanda hooked her finger between Gloria's breasts.'

'Leave off you little tart or I'll have George throw you out.'

'You don't know what you're missing. Heard you've come down from the big smoke. Must have learnt a thing or two up there surely? I think I could make you pant Gloria. Should give it a try.'

Vanda picked up the two full glasses and walked back to John.

'You'd better watch that one Vanda. Heard she was in trouble up in London, getting too hot for her in the club scene or something. Rumour is she was working in a club and saw something or heard something she shouldn't. Came down here back home pretty sharpish with the unfriendly blokes from London sniffing around. Just warning you 'cos you're new in the village. Wouldn't like you to get hurt. She's a hard case is Gloria. Might come across all smiles and giggles but she can show some claws I hear.'

'I don't know about that John, I just think she's gorgeous. Look how that friend of Freddie was all over her. He practically had his tongue down her blouse.'

John blushed and Vanda caught the reaction. 'Still, I like a man with a bit more maturity who likes to try new things. Anyway, drink up and let's see whether I can get the hang of this game. I'm getting better every time so watch out or I'll beat the pants off you.'

'I might like that.'

'Well, we'll have to see about that later, but right now it's you to throw.'

Katya and I were standing in the hall. We had planned to spread a map of the Estate out over the large table in the library so that we could discuss the various options that we would envisage in an Education Centre. After a rather leisurely return from the cave and old tree we were explaining to my mother why we were so dirty.

'We were exploring some of the possible sites for orienteering Mum. There still are a few tough places on this Estate and compass work could be a real challenge in a couple of areas.'

'I understand that Daniel but did you have to bring some of the remnants of those tough places all through the hall? You've left a trail that any orienteer could follow.'

'Well we couldn't really strip off outside in the yard could we Mum?'

My mother looked at me and then she looked at Katya. 'I could ask why not Daniel but I will spare Katya blushing. What's the expression people say now? Yes, I remember, "get a room".' Chuckling my mother left us looking at each other.

'Nothing much gets past your mother Daniel does it?'

'Let's go and shower and change before my mother makes any more double entendre remarks.'

'Willingly Daniel. I'll scrub your back if you'll scrub mine.'

I put my arm around Katya's waist and we slowly walked up the staircase. We were quite engrossed in each other and James's sudden descent almost caught us off guard.

'I've missed you Katya. I've missed my friend but now I've found you. Come and see. Mummy took some photos of me jumping with Dainty. They're really good. No they're more than good, they're stupendous. You must see.'

James proceeded to pull Katya up the stairs only to be met by the unyielding legs of his mother.

'James darling, my impetuous treasure, can we let your friend get cleaned and changed before the grand display of you jumping with Dainty?'

Absolutely impervious to any adult sarcasm or motherly admonition James continued to pull on Katya's hand. 'Come on Katya come on.'

I decided that action might be better than words and so I reached up and lifted James off the staircase. His legs continued a climbing motion but the mouth activity suddenly stopped, for a moment. 'Mummy I'm flying. It's just like jumping but without Dainty. Do it again Uncle Daniel.'

I gently offered the mass of arms and legs to my sister and reached for Katya's hand. 'I think a rapid advance would be in order Katya before the jumping monster overwhelms his mother's maternal clasp.'

We ran down the corridor and turned into the bathroom. I locked the door and turned to find Katya in my arms. 'Well, we've found a room Katya as my mother suggested.'

Half an hour later I cautiously and quietly unlocked the bathroom door and peered down the corridor. 'All clear love.' Katya scooted quickly down the corridor to her room clad in a bathroom towel. Once she was there I walked to my room and sat on my bed. I almost hugged myself I was so happy.

Over dinner dad decided he needed to be brought up to date on the various activities and discoveries of Terence Field. He told us he thought he had all the informed people sitting at the table, perhaps with the exception of Terence himself but he reckoned we should tell him the story to date. Mum kept quiet but I could tell she was all ears. Bearing in mind that we had James at the table with us I went over the story of the bones and discreetly turned it into a treasure hunt like a game for James. I did include the story Freddie told us and the possible involvement of the twins. Looking at my mother I told her that Katya and I had been to the cave and what we had found there. Katya slipped the gold coin out of her pocket and laid it rather reverently on the table. James gasped. 'Is it real Uncle Daniel, real treasure?'

While James was deeply involved in his dessert, and with him that could be literally involved as he shortened the distance from bowl to mouth, I described the activities at the Whelks cottage and what Samantha and I had found there. Samantha couldn't produce any coins like Katya had as Terence Field had kept them as evidence items but we explained they were all very similar.

'So Terence collected all of the green pebbles from the garden path?'

'Yes Mum. We think they all came from the same place, the tree by the cave.'

'So Michael was looking in the wrong place all those years ago?'

'Mum, don't go there,' I said. 'We didn't say anything about where we had gone or what we had done until the discoveries of the bones and then Freddie's story. Terence has still got a lot of questions to ask people including Freddie's mother. He's spent quite some time with Florence Whelks. By the way did you know that Larry's younger brother Phil has just come back from Australia?'

'The one who ran away to sea, years ago now? You say he's come back? I can't imagine that will please old Flo'. She always said he was a waste of space and she was glad to see the back of him.'

'That isn't all Mum. Phil brought back a daughter and what a daughter. Old Flo' thinks she is dynamite although I can't see it myself.'

Samantha decided to intervene and provide a feminine description of Margaret Whelks. 'Mum I got this from Daniel but imagine a thin wraith with long black hair wearing a flowing full length black dress, black shoes and a sort of black shawl. In a complimentary fashion the little bit of very white pasty skin that is showing is artfully adorned with black lipstick, black eye shadow and sporting gold rings through her nose and eyebrows. Imagine Miss Goth World 1998 with other pierced body parts I'm quite sure although I wouldn't like to try and find out.'

'What did Florence Whelks say to this product of the southern hemisphere?'

'She thought Miss Margaret, who likes to be called Vanda by the way was just fine and "full of spunk" if I remember Flo's words correctly.'

'Daniel will Terence be coming here again? Sounds like he has some of our property?'

'Dad I don't know but I would think so. He will probably want to check who was working here back at that time and likely ask you and mum whether you can remember anything relevant. Look, I know that was not a good time for any of us in this family but Terence will only be interested in events and people concerning the Ferris family and the Whelks family. Samantha, does Terence know about our concerns of January 1991? Have you explained some of our sorrows?'

'Yes Daniel, yes Mum and Dad, Terence knows what happened then and I'm sure he will show the same empathy and consideration I have seen him show before. He really can be a very sensitive man. I agree with Daniel Mum, he'll only be looking for some facts about who was here. He might, in fact he almost surely will ask whether either of you saw or heard anything unusual to do with the Ferris family at that time. The story about Idwal killing Whelks in Bristol and being found guilty of manslaughter does sort of answer some of our earlier questions. I think Terence will be very discreet and considerate.'

'Mum, on a brighter note Katya and I found something for you. You could think of it as green revenues or you could think of it as something good coming out of something sad. Here, we found this today and Katya and I want to give it to you.'

Katya reached down under the table and brought up the slender box we had found in the hollow tree. I had managed to clean up the leather covering so it looked a lot more presentable than when I first found it. Katya offered it to Sylvia and said, 'I hope you find this a joyful gift as Daniel and I give it to you with all our love.' Katya reached out and held my hand as she extended her other hand holding the box to my mother. Dad sat quietly very attentive at the head of the table and he realised he needn't ask what it was as he would find out soon enough and any question from him would disturb the beauty of the moment. Even Samantha was taken in by the atmosphere.

My mother took the box and she smiled at Katya. 'Thank you my dear. I think I understand your words and I am doubly grateful. I suppose I should open it Daniel before your father's eyes pop out of their sockets. Katya, Daniel, it's beautiful. It's truly a work of art and the delicacy of the chain with that magnificent pearl is enchanting. Thank you both. Here Samantha, let your philistine eyes feast on this ladylike bauble and tell me you can't see the beauty and charm of this lovely creation?'

For once my sister was short of words. She reverently lifted the necklace from the box and held it in her fingers. Somewhat uncharacteristically Samantha lifted it up to set it against her neck.

'Mummy that's lovely. I think that's really pretty. Can I have one Uncle Daniel, please?'

'James we will have a special treasure hunt for you next week. This week Katya and I went hunting for something for your grandmother. Next week we'll look for something for you.'

'What about Grandpa? Doesn't he get something?'

'Bravo James, it's good to hear someone stick up for me now and again. What do you think Daniel should find for me?'

'Perhaps Uncle Daniel has already found it Grandpa.'

I watched my dad looked puzzled and all the adults around the table looked at each other and wondered what revelation would come next. I decided to be the one who had to ask. 'What James have I already found that Grandpa would like?'

There was a hush around the table and James smiled. I caught my sister trying to decide whether to silence her little darling or brazen out his answer.

'Another daughter of course Grandpa and Uncle Daniel's found Katya.'

Samantha drew in a deep breath and I watched her mentally wipe her hand across her forehead with relief.

'James, you are one smart young man,' dad said. 'You have chosen exactly what I am looking for and I am delighted that Daniel has found Katya for me.'

'Of course I found her too Grandpa, and King Delaney and Queen Deidre.'

The table quietened down again and mum passed the box up the table to my dad. James returned to the small amount of dessert left in his bowl and I gently put my hand over the top of Katya's. 'Seems you are a treasured find for all of us Katya.'

'I must say Daniel it was a relief to hear James's choice. Personally I agree wholeheartedly with my son Katya but for a moment there I wasn't sure exactly what to expect. Remind me Daniel to guard against any more train trips for James for a while.'

Of course Samantha had mentioned the magic word and within five minutes I carefully watched engine driver James pilot "King Henry VIII" around the track with a trio of passenger coaches. Katya stood beside me and together we listened to James describe the life of everyone in the little village and where they might be going on the train. The monologue came to a grinding halt with one of James's typical out of the blue questions. 'What's a Goth Uncle Daniel?'

'So I have one hundred and twenty seven to finish John? Well, watch and weep mate. Triple nine, triple twenty and double top. How do you like that for talent? Your shout I think.'

336

John just made it to the bar and ordered up his pints before George shouted for last orders. Gloria plonked the glasses down hard on the counter. 'She'll sew you up in a web just like a black widow spider that one.'

'Naw, just letting her think she's winning. This time I'll show her who can play.'

Walking very carefully because he felt rather light-headed, and absolutely blind drunk, John carried the two glasses back to the dart board corner.

'Winner takes all mate. Start with a double and you lead off.' Vanda drained half her glass and looked at John. He swayed but managed to pick up the darts. With a dedicated amount of concentration John threw his three darts but only one managed to find the board.

'You drink up mate before George closes up. I'll take that as a win after your last effort. Come on John, time we took you home.'

The pub cleared as George shut up for the night and Vanda carefully steered John down the street. Once she was a little way along and in the shadows she propped John up against the wall and told him to hang on for a moment. Carefully Vanda took some of Tom Daley's grass and rolled a joint. Once alight she took a deep toke and handed it over to John.

'Here lover boy, take a deep breath and you'll feel over the moon. Big breath now.'

John gasped, spluttered and let out a long sigh.

'Dreamy isn't it? Well, don't go to sleep on me 'cos we've got the whole night ahead of us and I'm feeling deprived. After all the times I beat you in the end I think you owe me something. We'll just walk a little further and then we can play some other games.'

John was half out of it but he had one arm around Vanda and she was rubbing her hand up and down his chest. By the time she had walked him down the laneway and into the shed at the back of the cottage her hand had slid lower and she was gently rubbing against his stiffening cock. Once inside the shed Vanda struck a match and found the old lantern. Soon there was enough light for her to turn John round and press her body full length up against him. She felt him respond.

'But I've got to piss.'

'Course you have to lover. Here, let me help. I always love holding a man when he's taking a piss. Cor, that feels good. Looks like a big hose pipe. Let me pull the skin back and you spray away.'

When John had done and Vanda had shaken off the drips she spun John around and told him to help her slip her dress off. 'Just lift it up over my head.' As John dropped it Vanda leant back against him and took his hands to rub over her nipples. She was wearing a black leather halter that lay both above and below her small breasts and so the hard pointed nipples were free for attention. Holding his hands she pressed them over her nipples that stood up like little volcanoes and then drew them down the sides of her body and round onto her buttocks. Vanda was wearing a kind of black leather garter belt with a waist strap and two sides panels that were sewn to leather thigh loops. Each thigh loop had a series of brass studs set in it. She pressed the hands onto her buttocks and then moved them quickly round to her bush of pubic hair. Having thrust one hand deep between her legs she felt John's cock with her other hand. Rubbing against him she could feel his excitement. Provocatively she lifted his creamy fingers from inside her to her mouth and licked his fingers. She heard him gasp.

'I said I'd beat the pants off you,' she muttered, 'so let's see what you look like without your pants.' Vanda slowly peeled the rest of John's clothes off and she stepped back and looked up and down. 'Time for a little beating. I know just what you would like. Turn round and lean over that saw horse while I get some things to help you enjoy yourself.

Men love a little bondage but I'll bet you've never tried, have you John? Tonight gorgeous I will give you a thrill like never before. Just let Vanda introduce you to the wonderful world of S&M.'

He was so far out of it and yet awake enough to realise he was living in a world he had only fantasised about. Naked, draped over a saw-horse which Vanda padded with his clothes, she tied his ankles and wrists to the legs of the wooden frame. All John heard was a swishing noise as he couldn't turn his head far enough to see what Vanda was doing. He heard her strike a match. 'Another couple of deep drags and you'll love every moment.' He inhaled deeply on the joint and his head swum further into orbit.

Slowly at first he felt the whip on his buttocks. Vanda slid the smooth steel rod over his back, down along his backbone and slid it gently between his cheeks. The end slid further down his leg and then slap, slap it beat sharp, stinging and exciting on his taut buttocks. The rod slid between his legs and nudged against his penis. He swelled, he couldn't help it. The rod rubbed against him and then again slap, slap and his whole body tensed with the excitement.

'Here, two more drags and then I'll give you something so you can really let go.'

Again John sucked in deeply on the joint and after he had exhaled Vanda slid a gag in his mouth and tied the ends behind his head. She whispered in his ear, 'now you can shout and scream and really let go John as I help you into the next world.'

The rod was a little faster now, a little harder and more demanding. The strikes were sharper and his penis responded. Vanda leant underneath him and slid a tight greased ring down the length of his rampant penis. He gasped. Again he could hear Vanda doing something but could not see. Now the anticipation was mind-blowing and the stroking and the whipping became more intensive. It hurt but it was exhilarating. 'Shout,' cried Vanda. Suddenly John felt a hard massive dildo thrust deep inside his body and Vanda's hand squeezed the ring on his penis. He was being squeezed tight and split in half all at the same time. It was an orgasm like never before and once again his penis streamed. Vanda ripped off the ring and ripped out the dildo. She grinned as she looked at the collapsed man's body in front of her. Women make far better sex slaves she thought. John had passed out.

As she went through his wallet Vanda noticed it didn't contain much money. Paid for most of the beer I suppose she murmured. His driving licence fell out onto the shed floor. As Vanda picked it up she gasped and then growled. The latter noise would have terrified Goebbels. John Ferris, John fucking Ferris who killed his brother, who killed my uncle. The fucking Ferris family who buggered around with my gran's head, here in our shed. Suddenly all of the aggro at having to come here, to come to this pisspot of a place, and to find someone who killed her family all boiled inside Vanda's drunken and stoned head. First she sat on a bale of hay and fumed but she couldn't sit still. Without thinking, without a second thought she ripped open her bag and pulled out her flick knife. 'Bastard, bastard, bastard,' she shrieked as she stabbed, stabbed, stabbed and slashed at John's balls. John screamed and screamed. His body arched and fought against the lashings. With a last ghoulish cry Vanda plunged the knife deep into John's rectum. 'Bugger you mate, you killed my family,' and she collapsed on the floor utterly out of this world as blood flowed out of John's ruined body.

Phil stared at the scene in disbelief. Goebbels ran round and round sniffing all the time.

'Jesus girl, what have you done?'

Walking across the shed floor Phil looked around him. He thought he had seen most things in his life but this was another world, his daughter's world. In Sydney he had never inquired too much as Margaret just dismissed him as a small-time loser. He had never known the weird world she had lived in. In his time Phil had tried being a thief, a fraud, a con artist and even a sort-of violent heavy but not this drug-driven perverted world of un-natural sex, pierced bodies and sadomasochism. He didn't know where to look. Goebbels licked Vanda's face and she rolled over on the floor and opened her eyes. Seeing the dog she screamed again and Goebbels barked as he jumped all over her body on the floor.

Another light suddenly appeared in the shed doorway and Phil wheeled round to see who was there.

'Seems she's full of madness as well as full of spunk,' cackled Flo'. 'Goebbels here.'

'Why Goebbels Mum?'

'What?'

'Why'd you call the dog Goebbels?'

'You're too young to know. You was born after the war.'

Phil was trying not to look and think about the scene in the shed and was rambling to keep from going slightly mad himself. Flo' looked around and cackled again. Seems the fella' over there's almost the same as the dog.'

'What, what are you talking about?'

Flo' stood looking around and quietly sung to herself,

'Hitler, he only had one ball,

Goring had two but very small,

Himmler, was very similar

And poor old Goebbels had no balls at all.'

Phil looked for somewhere to sit down before he collapsed. It was all too much. His mother was a raving loonie and his daughter, Christ his daughter was a bloody mess. Vanda stirred herself on the floor and gazed around with a glassy far-away look on her face. 'Far out, Jesus that was some fuck, but I still think women are better. Look at this useless tosser Dad? Know who he is this naked piece of shit? Thought he could beat me at darts the silly bugger but I showed him. I gave him a thrill he'll never forget. I beat the pants off him,' and she collapsed on the floor in a fit of giggling and convulsions.

Flo' put down her light and walked over to Vanda. She bent down slowly and lifted Vanda's head up by her hair. Slap, slap, slap her hand cracked across Vanda's face and the giggling stopped. She let go of the hair and Vanda's head flopped back onto the ground.

'Fetch a shovel son, we've work to do.'

AND JOHN MAKES THREE

OVERNIGHT A COLD FRONT HAD come through and the wind was still blowing hard when I woke up early that Sunday morning. That in itself wasn't too bad but the horizontal rain looked positively threatening. As was usual on a Sunday morning I planned to play golf and Katya was up early as well to come out and caddie. We were both walking around the dining room munching on bowls of cereal when the telephone interrupted our breakfasts.

'Larry, this is a bit early. Our tee-time isn't until around nine this morning. They've what? Oh, yes I understand, and they decided to try and repair it straight away. Well I suppose that makes sense although it will piss off a few members. You've already called Alan and Peter. It can't be helped and so we'll see you next Wednesday then? True, it's not the end of the world but I was looking forward to beating you again today. Yes, I do have my secret weapon with me and Katya and I are starting to like the success of our partnership. Sure, I'll tell her. See you Wednesday, bye.'

'That sounds like golf is off Daniel?'

'Yes, apparently the wind did some damage to several trees around the course, especially on three of the holes. The rain has backed up to flood a couple of spots that were dammed up with the debris. Course closed for the day.'

'What will we do?'

'We could always go back to bed?'

Katya put her cereal bowl down on the table and walked round to hug me. Pushing my spoon to one side she kissed me and I could taste weetabix, milk and Katya's tongue.

'You two could come and help me instead of playing golf, or whatever it is you two are playing now.'

'Samantha I didn't hear you come in.'

'Apparently not Daniel. Good morning Katya. I see you like passion fruit for breakfast.'

Katya giggled and waved her hand at Samantha. 'I'm trying to console your brother Samantha. He really wanted to go out and play golf in this delightful weather and now he's deeply disappointed the course is closed.'

'Obviously a bunch of wimps at your course Daniel. Going out in weather like this is what made us Englishmen men.'

'Weak-chested, rheumatic, plagued with coughs and having fungus between our toes.'

'Daniel that's gross, especially when I'm eating my breakfast.'

'So, seeing as you are so disappointed about not being let out to play in the storm I can count on you to come out in the rain with me and help me on my errand of mercy?'

'Can I finish my breakfast Samantha or is this another "rush out and bowl over" errand of mercy like with Betty?'

Katya sat down with her bowl and spoon watching and listening to the verbal sparring. 'I never had brothers or sister,' she said, 'and so this is quite an education.'

Samantha allowed us to finish breakfast and the three of us made sure we were suitably dressed for the great outdoors before I opened the back door. 'What about James?' I said as I suddenly realised it was quieter than usual.

'I sent him into mum's room when he woke up. Last I heard there was an animated conversation going on about Dainty, jumping, polo and Uncle Daniel listening for earthworms.'

'Listening for earthworms Daniel? Whatever were you doing for James to think that, or did he imagine the story all on his own?'

'Just don't tap his head Katya, it's still rather sensitive. Daniel decided to fall over and when I looked into his eyes to see whether he was concussed all he could say was he preferred your eyes looking at him from that distance.'

'What's that to do with listening for earthworms? No, don't tell me, it's a long story!'

We all laughed and I opened the door of the Landrover for the two girls. I climbed into the driver's side and drove slowly out of the yard.

'So you're running messages between Betty and John now Samantha? I thought they weren't supposed to meet. Does Terence approve of this undercover operation? Will Katya and I get charged as accomplices? You know Terence still thinks I am more involved in this than I'm letting on Samantha?'

'Daniel, I bumped into Betty in the village and spent some time talking with her. I was trying to keep her aware of what was really happening out in the forest and the cottage rather than her hearing the silly rumours running around in the village. I'm still very keen on the idea of helping her with her pies and the capital for that would easily come from the sale of the cottage.'

'So we're going to tell John he has to move out?'

'No, don't be obtuse Daniel. We're going, well I'm going to tell John how Betty feels about the cottage and let him think about selling it with Betty. He can still stay there and rent it from us and continue working. Nothing else need change.'

The clearing was empty when I drove the Landrover around to the back of the cottage. John's old car wasn't there and everything was quiet. The rain continued to lash down and the occasional violent gusts really made the trees sway. The three of us sat in the Landrover and looked at the cottage.

'I'll go and knock Samantha. Either John's not here, which maybe another problem or he was so drunk last night in the village he walked home rather than try and drive. If he's hungover we may not get much sense out of him. I was talking with him at work on Friday and he really was a bit of a mess. His mind was all over the place although I suppose I didn't help as I wanted him to remember about the time his dad was killed.'

'Whatever were you asking Daniel?'

'Terence thinks there is a connection between this cottage and Flo' Whelks's cottage and we both think the connection is Idwal rather than Norton Ferris. I was asking John whether he could remember what Idwal was doing around that time. We were trying to establish a definite link, a real piece of evidence Terence said. He thought my imagination was too vivid.'

'Yes,' said Samantha, 'at times Terence is very methodical and thorough.'

'Which is why the pair of you get on so well,' I joshed. 'They say opposites attract.'

346

'Daniel, get out before your sister tries to bump the other side of your head and I will have to look into your eyes.'

'Now there's an offer I can't refuse.'

'Out Daniel, out, into the rain with you and go and do something useful.'

Samantha laughed and congratulated Katya on her treatment of men.

I opened and quickly closed the door of the Landrover and jogged over to the cottage.

'John you there?' I knocked loudly on the door but there was no answer. After calling out a second time I opened the door and walked into the kitchen. Everything was quiet.

'John are you about?'

Silence greeted me. The cottage was empty and there was no sign of anything unexpected so I assumed John never made it home last night. Closing the door behind me I ran back to the Landrover in the pouring rain.

'No sign of him girls. I can only assume he never made it home last night. Any suggestions?'

'Where would he have gone Daniel, yesterday evening I mean?'

'Well Saturday night and Saturday was the village day so I would assume he went down to the pub. He really had nowhere else to go. He never had many friends before this last event and now I would imagine there are only a few people willing to even drink with him.'

'He was with some drinking companions a couple of weekends ago Daniel, when Terence and I were in the George. Freddie Dunster was giving him a hard time. I told you about it Daniel.'

'So the pub is certainly an option but what about Betty? Could he have gone there?'

'I doubt it Daniel. I don't think he would have got a very warm reception from Mary and Toby.'

'But Betty might know whether there were any other friends?' suggested Katya.

'That's a good idea Katya,' I said. 'Let's start there Samantha and likely progress to the George. Betty and the family are more likely to be up at this time whereas George is probably recovering from a Saturday night.'

'If you talked to Betty yesterday Samantha she is also likely to understand why we are anxious to find John.'

'True Katya but I'm wondering whether telling Betty we can't find him will start her worrying all over again, perhaps unnecessarily.'

'Well ladies, we have to pass the George to reach Toby's place so why don't we look before we knock so to speak? I know that's not your style Samantha but it may obviate upsetting Betty.'

'Right Daniel, I'll accede to your diplomatic approach. Let's go.'

Katya looked at the pair of us and giggled. 'Being out with you two English Lords is such an education. I don't know why I bothered to go to Oxford.' Before Samantha could think of a suitable retort I put the Landrover into gear and loudly splashed our way into the forest.

It didn't take me long to drive from John's cottage into the village. Sunday morning in the pouring rain things were quiet and as we came to the George and Dragon we saw John's car parked beside the pub.

'So answer number one is he went to the pub last night but then what?'

'Or then where? Daniel, wake up George rather than Betty. I think we'll only worry Betty rather than learn anything useful.'

'That's fine. We might even find John sleeping in his car so why don't we look there first?'

Unfortunately John's car was empty and the engine was cold so away I went up to the public bar door and hammered.

'Hey up George. You awake in there? We need a word?'

I did my best imitation of Terence with his official rap on the door and turned and grinned at Samantha.

'I've been out with Terence so much lately I'm beginning to feel and sound like a policeman.'

'Knock again Daniel, louder. I'll come and do it.'

'Katya put a lock on my sister will you for a moment before we have the whole street awake.'

Bolts sounded coming undone and the door swung open to reveal George in a tattered string vest, orange pyjama bottoms and yesterday's stubble. Wiping a hand across his chin and face he growled, 'Daniel Lord, don't you know this is the Sabbath and all god-fearing people like you should be in church?'

'Yes George and we love you too but my sister is on an errand of mercy and that is only appropriate on Sundays, and as you so rightly said today is the Sabbath.'

'Daniel you spent too much time in school lad. Still, I suppose I should be lucky it is you knocking and not your sister. I've been told by some very respectable police constables that your sister tends to flatten people in her path when she is on errands of mercy. Morning Samantha, morning Miss,' and George pulled his forelock in a sign of acknowledgement.

'George, now that we've got all of the niceties out of the way we were looking for John Ferris. We see his car is in the parking lot and so we assume he was here last night?'

Hitching up his orange pyjamas and moving the weight from one leg to another George wrinkled his face. 'Aye.'

349

'Can you add to that cryptic reply or are you going to answer word by word?'

'Sure Daniel, he was here. He ended up having a skinful. When he bought his last pints just before I rang for last orders he could hardly carry them back to the table. He certainly couldn't throw the darts any more.'

I suddenly realised that Samantha had decided this was going too slowly when she brushed me aside and moved up close to George. 'Pints George, carrying them to the table and playing darts. So, obvious question, with who?'

'With whom?' I added.

'Daniel,' said an exasperated Samantha. 'George, with whom was he playing darts?'

'That weird granddaughter of Flo' Whelks, the black spectre from the lost lagoon of Sydney or wherever. She can certainly drink. Going pint for pint with John she was and there's no body on her to absorb all that drink. She can sure play darts though. John thought he had found some competition because he is quite good but that little Miss from the dark side wiped the floor with him.'

'And?'

'I don't know Miss Samantha. I called for last orders and started clearing up. Gloria served them and I had some things to do out the back. Gloria bolted the doors and closed the bar.'

'His car's still here.'

'The state he was in he sure wasn't going to drive anywhere. He could hardly walk let alone drive.'

'So this Margaret Whelks possibly wheeled him out of here. Could she walk?'

'She was doing fine when I last saw her. She wanted to play one more game but John could hardly stand. She stood there and threw three into the treble twenty and finished off her beer. That was the last I saw of her but she seemed pretty sober, well upright at the time.'

I decided George had told us as much as he knew and that Samantha should back off.

'Thanks George, we'll take it from there. Sorry to have disturbed you. Glad Samantha didn't have to flatten you.' I purposely propelled Samantha back to the Landrover and we all sat there thinking on the next step.

'Daniel I don't flatten people do I?'

'Samantha, my dearly beloved sister, you exhibit a charming array of approaches to questions and problems. I think Janet and her clients are going to be pleased out of their minds by your innovative methods. Actually, talking of Janet, how is that idea coming along? Did you decide to join forces? Now there Katya would be a team to handle anything. Maybe we should consider hiring Heritage Adventures to research some historic background and characters to add variety to our Education Centre. It needn't just be Natural History.'

'You think with Samantha's help it could include unnatural history?' asked Katya.

'Cut it out you two, we need to find John. Well I want to find John.'

'Actually Samantha so do I. Dad put up the bail and we stood surety for his behaviour and that included keeping away from Betty.'

'Betty or Florence Daniel?'

'I suppose I could go and look at the flattened gate. Terence promised I would replace it and so I could pretend I was looking to measure it up.'

'Sure, and we're there to give you protection against Flo' and the teeth of Goebbels?'

'We can give it a try Samantha. Katya could hold an umbrella over me while I pretend to measure up the gate. You could run interference Samantha.'

'How's this going to find John? Why don't we just go and knock on the door and ask? According to George they were together most of the night and it sounded as if John couldn't walk straight. Unless this black witch just dropped him somewhere she might have taken him home, her home I mean.'

'That sounds more like it Samantha. That's my sister Katya. In your face.'

'Daniel, drive and I'll do the talking.'

I reversed and drove back out of the village. We skidded to a stop on the slippery edge of the road by the Whelks's laneway. 'Want to drive down to the back door?'

'Look, why don't we try a two-front approach? I'll knock on the back door and you scout around the front path. Did Terence remove all of those green pebbles? Could be Idwal hid some of those coins in another "in your face" place. We never did look and I'm not sure Terence checked.'

'I'll bet he did knowing him, but yes we could divide and conquer, and I could take a look at that gate if I'm supposed to replace it. Come on Katya. Yell Samantha if you have any trouble.'

Samantha took off at her usual speed and was soon down the laneway. Katya and I stepped over the gate and I looked about me. Sure enough all of the green pebbles had been collected and I casually walked up the path towards the door. I could hear some talking going on in the cottage and then some shouting. Turning to walk back down the path to go round into the laneway the shouting increased and the door behind me screeched open and Phil Whelks came roaring out of the cottage. I slipped on the wet flagstones, tripping over the edges and heard Phil cry 'you again.' As I looked up I saw the weight of Phil about to drop on my stooped body.

'Daniel look out, look out,' shouted Katya.

My feet went from under me as Goebbels bounded out of the door and knocked against my legs and then I was crushed under Phil's mass. My head was still quite bruised from two days ago and Phil had his arms and fists going non-stop. I tried hard to protect my head as Phil decided to use feet as well as fists. At the same time Katya had found an umbrella in the Landrover and was wielding it as best she could on Phil's head and shoulders but to little effect. I rolled over on the path to try and escape Phil's feet and scrabbling with my hands I grabbed a rock off the path. Almost on my knees now I managed to parry one of the feet with my rock and quickly raised it and smashed it down onto Phil's bare foot. I grabbed another bigger rock and tried to smash at the other foot but Phil's fist thumped down hard on my shoulder and I dropped it.

Katya must have distracted Phil for a moment because there was a pause in the fists and I levered hard to lift a larger flagstone and roll this over onto the bare feet. All of the rain pouring down was making the ground really slippery and I managed to flip this rock just as Phil slipped. It caught his ankle rather than his foot but he fell heavily onto the ground. As quick as I could I stood up and looked around me. Katya was safe and still wielding the umbrella like a golf club. She would have been really effective with a golf club I thought. Phil was up on his knees and his face wasn't pretty. He had cut himself on the stones and had a substantial gash down his cheek that bled quite profusely but his eyes were a mix of rage and desperation. I braced myself for a further onslaught.

Right in front of me Goebbels was digging furiously and as Phil lurched forwards he slipped over the dog on the wet ground and banged his jaw on the stones. He must have had his tongue somewhere between his teeth when his jaw crashed as his mouth suddenly spewed forth another gush of blood. Phil groaned but this time he didn't get up but half rolled over in the rain. Goebbels refused to stop and as the ground became looser and wetter he enlarged his hole in the middle of the path.

Flo's screech stopped Goebbels in his tracks, and frightened the living daylights out of me for the second time. Phil stayed groaning lying on the ground and blood still streamed out of his mouth. I carefully found my feet and stood up. For a moment we were a still life tableau. Samantha's cry shattered the silence. 'I've phoned Terence. He's on his way.'

All I could think of was 'how?'

'On my cell phone brother, on my Canadian but works in England cell phone. Should be useful working with Janet.'

My sister never fails to amaze me.

'Daniel, are you all right? You were getting a frightful beating and I couldn't pound hard enough with this stupid umbrella.'

'Katya love I'm fine. Thanks for helping. You managed to distract Phil just enough for me to change tactics. Fighting in bare feet can have some disadvantages. Still, I'd better look at Phil because he hasn't moved and he is still bleeding profusely.'

'You've killed him,' screeched Flo'.

'No Flo',' I managed to say, 'he's still breathing and groaning. I think he just knocked himself out falling over Goebbels. Get this dog out of it Flo' for heavens sake and let me look at that bleeding.'

'Don't you touch him, don't you dare touch him. He's mine, my son. Lost one I did and I'm not going to lose the other one.'

'Come on then Flo', come and look and see whether we can stop this bleeding. Just let me hold him upright a little, get his head higher and that should help slow the blood down. You look while I hold him.'

Clad in a white cotton gown of some kind, which I could only assume was a nightgown and wearing a white woollen nightcap Flo' slowly advanced down the path in a ragged pair of mules. She shuffled along and bull-dozed the wet earth and gravel aside as she approached her son. Thin thin arms stretched out and with her arthritic hands she gently touched Phil's face. I lifted Phil into a half-sitting position and braced him up against my knee. He was a heavy mass and I was still feeling the effects of being beaten. I grunted trying to keep him stable. The rain continued to fall heavily on this odd assortment of people on the garden path.

Flo' opened his mouth and looked. 'Bitten his tongue silly sod. Hold him still Daniel. Got a handkerchief girlie?' she asked Katya.

'A tissue do?'

'Nobody uses proper handkerchiefs these days. What good are bits of paper?'

I managed to dig in my pocket with my spare hand and pull out a handkerchief. 'Here Flo' use this.'

She looked at me and once again a spark passed between us and just as quickly she was trying to stem the flow of blood and make sure Phil didn't choke.

Samantha hadn't been idle all this time. She saw that the scene in the garden looked stable for a while and so she had gone to look for John, our original quest. I didn't know this at the time as Flo', Katya and I were attending to Phil who was still only semi-conscious. Going in through the back door Samantha entered the kitchen and looked around. Obviously our visit had interrupted breakfast with half-eaten toast and unfinished cups of tea on the table. Walking slowly and cautiously Samantha looked around her in the kitchen. All was quiet and John's body was not obvious. Had he ended up in bed with this black witch from Sydney? I suppose he and Betty had been apart for several weeks now and people don't lose the urge thought Samantha. Perhaps this Margaret girl had urges too. John would have been an easy target. Daniel said he was all mixed up emotionally and after being cooped up in the forest all week a night on the town could lead to all sorts of urges. Do I go in with all guns blazing or do I knock and ask? Shit, it's not really my problem. Why don't I wait until Terence comes and then I'll surprise him by acting out of character? Can't let him get complacent about who I really am. Don't want to be too predictable Samantha. Tiptoe out again and wait for the cavalry.

I began to get very tired propping Phil up. 'Flo', I said, 'I've got to change arms or do something. My knee's going to sleep and Phil here is heavy. Have you stopped the bleeding?'

'Yes Daniel but I'll leave the handkerchief there and not tear any clotting. He's breathing easier and doesn't seem to be choking or anything. Just lower him gently can you Daniel?'

'Katya can you find anything so we can put it behind Phil's back and let him sit upright a little? As he's stayed unconscious I think it would be better if his head stayed elevated. Can you look in the Landrover. I may have some pillows or cushions there?'

We ended up with Phil lying on the wet ground but semi elevated.

'Flo' we need to call for an ambulance. Phil's still groaning and as his eyes are shut I don't know whether he's concussed or not. Katya, where's Samantha? She can call for an ambulance on that magic machine of hers, that cellphone thing.'

'All under control Daniel. Done that. Supposed to be fifteen minutes or thereabouts.'

'Found John?'

Flo' stiffened and suddenly looked frightened. She shivered and I realised that she must be soaking. The cotton nightdress clung in an angular form about her skeletal frame.

'Flo' I'm sorry, I should have noticed. Katya can you take Flo' indoors and find her some warm clothing. She's soaking and freezing. I was so concerned about Phil here I hadn't noticed.'

'Good idea Daniel,' said Terence as he walked over the garden gate. 'Can you manage Katya while I look at Daniel and Phil here? Samantha can you keep a weather eye out for the ambulance as Phil needs attention I think? Katya, Constable Goodfellow here will help you with Mrs. Whelks and look after her.'

Having deployed his resources Terence turned to me. 'Daniel, you seem to be involved a lot with this family? Samantha said you had been attacked. Care to explain? No, before you do that are you all right? You look pale and you've got blood on you. Don't faint on me Daniel.'

'Terence I'm probably okay although I do feel a little battered. Here's the ambulance now. We should get Phil looked at first and then we can go inside. Sitting on wet ground is not good for my piles.'

The ambulance attendants took care of Phil and Samantha had a quick word with Terence before it left. I slowly and painfully walked along the torn up path towards the cottage door. As I turned to look at Terence and Samantha I caught my foot on one of the tilted flagstones and pitched forward full length again. Opening my eyes I saw that I was looking into Katya's eyes. Once she and PC Goodfellow had dried and wrapped up Flo' Katya had come back out of the cottage to find me.

'That's better,' I said, 'much better.'

'Daniel, what are you saying?'

'Last time I knocked myself out on this path I woke up looking into my sister's eyes and told her I would sooner be looking into yours. Now I am and it is much better.'

'Let's get him up Katya before he swoons again. Here you take the other arm and we'll carry this lovesick puppy into the dry.'

The three of us managed to get into the cottage and through into the warmth and relative comforts of the kitchen. Flo' was wrapped up with blankets around her and a towel wound around her head like a turban. She was clutching a steaming cup and so I assumed that PC

Goodfellow had made a brew. Sensible chap I thought. Train them to handle priorities in the force.

Terence took charge. 'Samantha I understand that you instigated this expedition?'

'I wanted to ask John Ferris about the cottage Terence. Betty wants to sell and I was to ask John whether he would agree and then continue to stay in the cottage.'

'Paying you rent?'

'That's up to mum and dad but knowing dad I doubt whether that would be a question.'

'You went looking for John?'

'And decided that my brother and Katya here would benefit from a walk in the rain. Daniel was going to play golf but he wimped out and that's not a Lord characteristic. I decided Katya should see the family as it really is.'

'Daniel what really happened?'

'We drove to John's cottage Terence and there was no one there. No John. Yesterday was Saturday and so we went looking in the village and found his car outside the pub.'

'Normal procedure for Ferris isn't it, Saturday night in the George?'

'It's his only day out Terence and at least he can drink with some friends or acquaintances. He can have some company and a possible game of darts.'

'Just as we saw him a couple of weeks back Terence, when we were there.'

'But he wasn't at the pub although his car was?'

'We woke up George and he told us that John had been playing darts most of the evening. Playing and drinking with Margaret Whelks.'

The cup in Flo's hands crashed to the floor. She lurched forwards half out of the chair. Katya reacted first and she knelt in front of Flo' and held her arms so she couldn't fall further forwards out of the chair. She looked rather wildly about her in desperation and then slumped back into the body of the chair. Katya slowly released her hold on Flo's arms when she realised Flo' was safe in the chair.

'I drove here Terence and while Samantha went to ask about John Katya and I walked up the garden path again. Katya was interested in seeing where the coins had been hidden. Remember she had found a couple of them earlier and was fascinated by the story of their travels. She hadn't been here before.'

Terence held up his hand. 'Fine Daniel.' He turned to Samantha. 'You knocked? Who came to the door?'

'Yes Terence, for once I knocked rather than bowled anyone over. Flo' opened the door.'

'And?'

'I asked whether John Ferris was here?'

'And?'

'First of all Phil Whelks pushed his mother out of the way and shouted at me to get lost. There was a whole stream of abuse Terence and I probably shouted back.'

'Terence, I heard the shouting and was going back down the path to come around the laneway and find out what Samantha was up to when the front door opened again and Goebbels knocked me over on the slippery flagstones. Next thing I knew Phil had landed on top of me and was kicking and thumping the shit out of me. As I was still feeling bruised from a couple of days ago I was primarily warding off blows rather than fighting back.'

'Daniel couldn't move Terence,' added Katya. 'It was wet and he kept slipping and the dog was jumping all over the place and digging the path up. I'd grabbed the umbrella to hit Phil and try and distract him so Daniel could at least get up.'

'In the end Terence I used the stones in the path to smash Phil's bare feet. May not have been very sporting or gentlemanly but bloody effective. Somehow in all the chaos of mud, dog, rain, smashed feet and exchanging blows Phil ended up crashing down.'

'He tripped over the dog Terence and suddenly there was blood gushing out of his mouth. Next thing Daniel was trying to make sure he didn't choke on his blood or his tongue.'

'I wasn't sure what had happened Katya and then Phil was beside me and gushing blood. I suppose I switched from fighter to firstaider in one fell swoop. Then Flo' is right beside me screeching I had killed him and between us we tried to stop the bleeding. Samantha told us the cavalry was on the way. You arrived and end of story.'

'Not quite Daniel but I understand.'

PC Goodfellow walked quietly back into the room and spoke into Terence's ear. He just nodded.

'Mrs. Whelks do you feel strong enough to answer some questions for me please?'

Flo' drew the blanket tighter around her but she straightened up in the chair and looked straight at Terence.

'Aye laddie, I can answer your questions.'

'Was your son here last night Mrs. Whelks?'

'Yes, he was here.'

'And his daughter?'

'No, she was out until late. I was asleep whenever she returned as I had gone to bed soon after ten.'

'So she did return. She is here?'

'Suppose, but I ain't seen her. Suppose she returned. Strange girl and Phil reckons she's trouble but she found out who was who in the village pretty quick. Smarter than my Phil. Sharp tongue but the girl's got fire in her belly. Takes after me.' Here Flo' looked around at all of us and cackled.

'Did your son see her come home?'

'Dunno do I? Was asleep like I told you.'

'But this morning you were up and talking to your son when Samantha knocked on the kitchen door. You were having breakfast together. You must have talked? You must have asked about this sharp-tongued girl who takes after you?'

'Maybe.'

'My constable tells me your granddaughter is in the next room.'

'Well then, she came back here. She did return like I said.'

Suddenly Terence turned and looked at me. 'Phil came flying out of the front door?'

'Yes,' I said cautiously not knowing where this was going.

He turned and looked at Flo' quickly, 'why?'

'Why what?'

'How did your son know Daniel was in the front and why did he rush out of the front door so wildly?'

'Dunno. Ask him?'

'We will Mrs. Whelks.'

'Goebbels come here.'

'What do you want with my dog?'

'Come on Goebbels, this is an inquiry and we need to ask you some questions.'

'He don't know nothing. He's just a dumb dog. Stay!'

'No Mrs. Whelks, I need Goebbels to further my inquiries and remember I still have a Search Warrant.'

Terence was about to lead Goebbels by the collar down the hallway and out into the garden when the bedroom door opened and the black apparition made a dramatic entry. 'Gran' I fucked up. It was a fabulous fuck but I fucked up. He killed Larry, or his brother killed Larry. Who gives a shit? He was a useless tosser but I fucked him proper Gran'. Nobody should have killed my dad's brother.'

'Hush child, you don't know what you are saying.'

'I should have had that blond bitch. Great tits she had and I bet she is a goer. Slagged me off she did so I decided to beat the pants off that dart's artist. Well, he thought he was good but I beat him Gran', and then I fucked the life out of him.'

We all sat there listening to this thin stoned voice speaking in a flat monotone. It droned across the room. Vanda let go of the door-frame and collapsed on the floor still mumbling on.

'Constable, call for another ambulance. I think we have another casualty. Go with the ambulance and stay at the hospital with both of them 'til I get there. I won't be long here.'

'Terence, shouldn't we do something for her?' Samantha asked. Without waiting for an answer Samantha strode across the room and knelt down beside Vanda's sprawled body. She checked her pulse and spoke gently to her. Carefully Samantha lifted back one of Vanda's eyelids and looked at her eye. 'I think she's stoned out of her mind Terence. I don't know what but she's got a weak fluttery pulse so that ambulance had better hurry up.'

'Samantha keep an eye on her for me can you? Daniel, look after Mrs. Whelks, no perhaps Katya can do that better as you're still looking rather battle-weary. Constable, a quick look outside I think. Bring the bloodhound.'

We sat in that kitchen and looked after each other. No one said anything and I could see that Flo' had shrunk back into her chair again. Her face was almost the same colour as her nightgown and Katya had taken hold of one of her hands to re-assure her. Re-assure her I thought, when her world had suddenly brightened with the arrival of her son and granddaughter only to be turned upside down in another calamity.

The ambulance took Vanda and PC Goodfellow away and Terence returned to the kitchen, along with his new accomplice. 'Mrs. Whelks I'm going to ask Katya here to go with you into your bedroom and let you get dressed. She'll help. After that I think we need to go down to the station for a longer more official conversation. I've radioed for some uniforms to come here and tape around the property and stand guard. I believe we are going to do another search. Do you understand all I have said?'

'Yes Inspector, I hear you. Come on then missy, let's go and get dressed. Wouldn't do for old Flo' Whelks to be in her nightie at this time in the morning. What would the neighbours say? Got to look strong and not frail. That right young Daniel Lord? Not frail am I?'

'No Flo', you're tougher than all of them. Good English stock, salt of the earth.'

She turned and looked at me. 'Don't you ever forget it son, salt of the earth.'

Leaning on Katya's arm Flo' slowly shuffled into her bedroom. I turned and looked at Terence.

'Yes Daniel, I'm sure we will find John Ferris in the golden path.'

'Norton, Idwal and John makes three.' I turned to face my sister. 'Seems we have an answer to your question Samantha.'

'Daniel?'

'We started this morning, after the wimpy cancellation of golf looking for an answer to the fate of the Ferris cottage. I understood that Betty wants to sell and it looks like I should tell mum and dad to start preparing some papers.'

The rest of the day went by as a grey continuum. Once Terence had everything organised I drove Katya and Samantha back to the Big

House. We were all very subdued and we sat with my parents describing the morning.

'I shall tell Betty,' said my mother. 'In fact I will do that this afternoon. Samantha do you think that Terence has already done that? Won't he need Betty to identify the body or some such ghoulish thing? No, I'll do it now.'

'Sylvia, isn't that rather impetuous? Isn't that what Samantha would do?'

'Dad!'

'No Anthony, well yes and no. Samantha what should we do?'

'Mum I'll phone Terence and ask. I think you're right but dad has already stated the obvious.'

The telephone rang in the hall and I was closest. I listened carefully and slowly replaced the receiver. 'Terence anticipated your reaction. He had WPC Nicols summoned from wherever she was this Sunday and instructed her to go and see Betty. Remember Mum she was the WPC Terence had with him when he first went to Betty's cottage.'

'Betty thought she was good Mum,' added Samantha. 'She told me, in fact she told us when we went to Mary's house to see her that she thought Terence and Evelyn Nicols were really sensitive people. Terence has done the right thing Mum.'

I spent much of the afternoon with Katya upstairs in the Railway Room. Carefully training our new young engine driver James was a welcome distraction from the events of the morning. Sure enough there was some trauma and the occasional burst of excitement when James wanted to drive two engines at the same time but this was low-key compared to the morning. James insisted on coming with us when I ran Katya back to the station for her return to Oxford. He also insisted on a goodbye kiss as Katya was his friend too.

'Remember next weekend is special Katya,' James said. 'Don't tell about the secret.'

'No James, my lips are sealed. Actually my lips taste a little bit of your lunch but I won't forget. Bye Daniel love. I'll look forward to next weekend. I'll promise you a secret too. Bye James.'

As most English people expected the weather that had turned bloody-minded on Sunday changed its tune on Monday. Now that the weekend was over the sun shone and the breeze was light. I managed to have Bob Edwards get the gang organised and away to work on time without too many questions. Freddie tried to find out what was going on but I just told him to zip it.

I returned to the Big House and found mum and dad in the dining room having a leisurely breakfast.

'Samantha taken James to nursery school?'

'Yes Daniel. I think she has to phone Janet when she returns. Janet called yesterday morning when you were all out and asked Samantha to call her this morning. I believe there is a client that Janet wants your sister to handle. Canadians I think Janet said.'

'Everything okay Daniel?'

'Depends what we're talking about Mum. It's good to see both of you here at this time in the morning instead of already out at the office. So that's okay.'

'The work gang?'

'Bob Edwards has them all gainfully employed and the Douglas fir plantation where they are working looks really good. We should get some first class sawlogs out of that stand.'

'No questions?'

'Told Freddie to smarten up and keep quiet for the moment. I'll talk with Terence today and we'll decide what should be said and when.'

'And Katya?'

'Katya's fine Mum.'

'Yes Daniel, she is. I like her and I think you do too son. Think you can persuade her to stay in England when she's finished next June?'

'I hope so Mum, I really hope so.'

Cast of Characters

The Lord Family

George Lord   Born 1880. Dies 1946.
The eldest son and heir. Went to Public School of Bristol House. Into the army and fight in Boer War. Stayed in S. Africa for 4 years and made some money in diamond business. Home to UK in 1904 with lots of money to return to family farming estate in Somerset plus be a partner at Lloyds. Married Virginia Milne in 1908 at age of 28. Goes to Europe in 1911, 1912 and 1913 to mountaineer and learns to ski, as does his wife. Builds Fotheringham Manor = House of Lord in 1908 to 1910 on family estate. In 1914 he is 34 and re-enters military as artillery officer. Spends first part of the war in training but later Regiment is posted to fight with the Italians in the dolomites against Austrians. Ski capability plus artillery knowledge leads to working with Italian alpine troops. Gets to know Dolomites area and works well with Italians. Impressed with their mountaineering skill and courage of alpine troops. Albert Templeton is in the same regiment. Dies at age 65.

Virginia Milne   Born 1883. Dies 1966.
Daughter of Lord and Lady Exmoor, minor gentry from the West Country. Well travelled young lady and had done the Grand Tour in Europe. Swept off her feet by dashing George and marries George Lord in 1908 at age of 25. Has a strong influence on children and grandchildren. Dies at age 83.

George and **Virginia** have four children**, Desmond, Harriet, Veronica** and **Matthew**

Desmond Lord   Born 1910. Dies 1968.
The eldest son and heir. Went to same Bristol House boarding School. At age 18 = 1928 goes to Oxford University to study mathematics and forestry but becomes enamoured with flying. 1932 graduates from Oxford and helps father George manage the estate but spends all of his spare time with a flying school. Learns to fly 1935 to 1939. During that time his father George and mother Virginia (ages 55 to 50) take Desmond to Europe, especially the Dolomites where he learns to climb along with Italian guides. Married Rosamund DeWinter in 1938 at age of 28. In 1939 WWII Desmond enlists as RAF pilot. Is a fighter pilot in Battle of Britain and shot down severely breaking a leg in the

process plus losing the use of one arm. Gets redeployed in WWII to communications, encoding, ciphers and misinformation. After WWII Desmond continues to oversee his father's estate and continues until retirement. Arranges for Anthony, Charles and Stephanie to go to Europe and learn to ski and climb whilst teenagers = 1950s. Grandmother Virginia goes too as chaperone. Dies at age 58.

Rosamund DeWinter   Born 1912. Dies 1987.

French parents but born and brought up primarily in England. Is fluently bilingual and highly educated in mathematics, statistics, puzzles and codes. She is very studious but a hopeless romantic about men in flying machines. Falls in love with Desmond and marries in 1938. In WWII Rosamund is enrolled at Bletchley to work with codes, deciphering, misinformation. Being bilingual helps. After the war the intensity gets to Rosamund and she becomes eccentric, especially after birth and upbringing of Charles. Rosamund very upset over death of Charles but in no state to look after his children in 1966 – see Stephanie Lord. Dies at age 75 slightly gaga.

Harriet Lord   Born 1912. Dies 1933.

Second child. Gets caught up in the whirl of the twenties, burns out and dies at age 21 of an overdose.

Veronica Lord   Born 1913. Alive 1998.

Born 1913. Is Mummy's pet. In 1936, 1937, 1938 goes to the Dolomites with Desmond and parents and learns to climb and to ski. Works in WWII as a WRNS – competing with elder brother and works well in London with Admiralty brass. Marries 1946 to a monied ex-Admiral older man. Lives at Dartmouth.

Matthew Lord   Born 1914. Alive 1998.

Is a strong child. Goes to Bristol House from 1921 to 1932 (age 18) and then goes to Cambridge University to study science from 1932 to 1936. Learns a lot about sound waves, radio, and ultimately radar. Works as a boffin in WWII. At end of war (1946) is age 32 and starts a company involved in early electronics and basics of computer hardware. Travels to the US and learns about ENIAC etc. Very involved in the whole evolution of computer hardware. Ends up influencing Anthony in developing software.

Desmond and Rosamund married in 1938 have three children: **Anthony, Charles** and **Stephanie**

Anthony Lord   Born 1940. Alive 1998.

Eldest son and heir. As parents busy all three children brought up by their grandparents George and Virginia. Rosamund's parents were both dead. Anthony learns a lot from his grandfather up to age 6 when George dies. Virginia continues to influence his life. Goes to Bristol House from 1947 to 1958. Climbs in the Italian and French Alps in 1955, 1956 and 1957. From School goes to Imperial College London to study mathematics and computer science 1958-1962. Continues climbing while at Imperial College, including North Wales and the continent. Graduates and does a crash PhD at Berkley, California from 1963-1964 in computer science. Whirlwind meeting, romance and marriage with Sylvia Trelawney in late 1964. Anthony starts his own company called Brainware in software development. Expands into several different specialties, including security, communications and encryption following in the steps of his father and mother, and abetted by Matthew Lord, his uncle. Continues to manage company through 1998. Very successful.

Sylvia Trelawney   Born 1942. Alive 1998.

Daughter of parents owning China Clay workings in Cornwall. Conventional schooling going to L.S.E. from 1960 to 1964. Climbs in North Wales while at L.S.E. and does meet Anthony but no real connection. Marries Anthony in 1964. Provides economic backing and knowledge to Anthony for the company. Strong woman active in outdoor sports. Gets on well with grandmother Virginia but finds Rosamund a little strange. Gets on well with Desmond while he is still alive, and with sister-in-law Stephanie and Aunt Veronica.

Charles Lord   Born 1941. Dies 1966.

Second son born after the trials of the Battle of Britain. Problem child and inherits latin temperament from mother Rosamund. Brought up by grandparents but a tearaway and rebellious. Goes to Bristol House from 1948 to 1959. Had gone with brother Anthony and sister Stephanie to Alps in 1955, 1956, and 1957. Becomes an avid and brilliant climber. In 1958, in last year of school at age 17, goes to French Alps for some big climbs. Meets Helene Forcier (age 18). She is also a brilliant climber. Charles finishes school in 1959 and goes straight to France, partly to avoid the draft in England. He and Helene do some big climbs and celebrate by getting Helene pregnant. Son Marcel born in 1960. Charles stays in France climbing. Son Henri born 1961 and daughter Giselle in 1962. Charles stays in Europe doing big climbs until he and Helene are killed in 1966 at age 25.

Stephanie Lord   Born 1942. Alive 1998.

Brought up by Virginia particularly as both father and mother very busy in the war. Likes her brother Charles despite his tantrums. Goes to good schools and finishes High School in 1960. Goes to Bristol University and studies Veterinary Science intending to be a country vet from 1961-1963. Goes into practice locally but doesn't marry. In 1966 when Charles and Helene killed Stephanie takes on the adoption of Marcel (6), Henri (5) and Giselle (4). Anthony and Sylvia very supportive, as is Grandmother Virginia. Practices research in genetics, especially of sheep working at Home Farm at Fotheringham Manor.

Anthony and Sylvia Lord marry 1964 and have 4 children: **Geoffrey, Michael, Samantha, and Daniel.**

Geoffrey Lord   Born 1965. Dies 1990.

Eldest son and heir. Pupil at Bristol House School 1972 to 1983. Goes to Oxford University 1983-1987 and obtains a MBA. Works for father from 1987. Is prime inheritor named when 21 in 1986. Anthony and Sylvia introduce children to rock climbing in late 1970s and 1980s, and to sailing. Marries Christina DeLucci in 1988 and have son Peter born 1989. Lives in Home Farm at Fotheringham. Killed climbing with brothers Michael and Daniel in North Wales in June 1990 leaving Peter heir to the Estate. (*Full details in the novel Michael*).

Christina DeLucci   Born 1965. Alive 1998

Born in Italy and only daughter of Giuseppe and Sophia who are vineyard owners and in the import/export business in Italy. Marries Geoffrey in 1988. Son Peter born 1989. Somewhat emotional and very family oriented. Lives on Home Farm at Fotheringham with son Peter.

Michael Lord   Born 1969. Dies 1991.

Second child. Boarder at Bristol House School from 1976 until 1988. Goes to London University (Imperial College like his father) in 1988 to study mathematics and electronics – is intelligent student and gifted. Reckless and self-centred. Sails at Burnham on Crouch. Limited rock climber but good endurance. Is engaged to Veronica Matheson, then to Melanie Rogers and takes Danielle Made as a mistress. Is father of son Tony with Danielle Made. Shot to death in January 1991. (*Full details in the novel Michael*).

Danielle Made   Born 1970. Dies 1998.

Born in Mozambique. Came to England in 1989 at age 18 and became mistress of Michael Lord. Has son Anthony (Tony) born August 1989. Lives in London 1989-1998 when she flees down to Fotheringham. Killed 1998 at Fotheringham. (*Full details in the novel Samantha*).

Samantha Lord   Born 1972. Alive 1998.

Born in March. Grows up a tomboy with two older brothers. Learns to sail at age 6 with Great Aunt Veronica and to climb at age 7 with father in Cornwall. Goes to a private school at age 5 and then a Lycee in Switzerland at age 11 in 1983. Home for Geoffrey's 21st. in 1986 and his wedding in 1988 when age 16. In 1990 (September) goes to Cambridge University studying Marketing and Sociology. Skis for University Team. At Fotheringham for Michael's 21st. in December 1990 and then his funeral in January 1991. Meets with Danielle Made and Rosalind Cohen in summer of 1991. Rocks climbs very aggressively. Talks with older relatives and studies mathematical modelling in 1992. While skiing in Switzerland (1992/3) meets Andrew MacRae (forestry student at Oxford University) and marries him later in 1993. Both Andrew and Samantha do post-graduate at Oxford from 1993-1996. Son James born August 1994. Moves to Canada in 1996 where Andrew does fire research. Andrew dies in forest fire in August 1998. Returns from Canada in September 1998 with 4-year old son James to family home at Fotheringham. At Fotheringham meets up with Danielle Made and son Tony, Donald MacLeod, and an old Lycee friend Janet Donaldson. (***Full details in the novel Samantha***).

Andrew MacRae   Born 1972. Dies 1998.

Born in the Isle of Skye, Scotland. Studies Forestry at Oxford as undergraduate 1990-1993 and postgraduate specializing in forest fire modeling research from 1993-1996. Marries Samantha Lord in July 1993. Son James born 1994. Works at Forest Research Centre in Canada from 1996 until death in August 1998 in Ontario.

Daniel Lord   Born 1974. Alive 1998.

Born October. Starts climbing when age 5 (1979) but not keen. Goes to Bristol House from 1981-1992. Takes an early interest in model railways and golf from 1982 onwards. Climbing with Geoffrey and Michael in June 1990 when Geoffrey killed. Goes to Oxford University studying Forestry from 1992-1996. Works for his parents as Estate Manager for Fotheringham Manor from 1996 onwards. Helps his sister Samantha during the attacks, arson and murder at Fotheringham on her return home in September 1998. That same week while taking nephew James to see steam engines he meets the Howard family and brings them back to Fotheringham. (***Full details in the novel Samantha***).

Charles and Helene Lord had three children: **Marcel, Henri and Giselle**
Charles and Helene killed in 1966.

Marcel Lord   Born 1960. Alive 1998.

Born in France. After parents killed in 1966 adopted by Aunt Stephanie. Brought to

England. Becomes an avid sailor. Meets and marries Marie in 1980 and have sons Jean in 1981 and Philippe in 1982. Marcel becomes a professional yachtsman. Marie lives at Dartmouth.

Henri Lord   Born 1961. Alive 1998.
Born in France. Adopted by Aunt Stephanie in 1966. Grows up to be a climber like his father. Lives in Bristol and works in financial planning and investments. Has a "partner" Leslie Asher who is a spiteful journalist who resents Charles being second son, Henri being second son and therefore dislikes Anthony/Daniel Lord family and its traditions. Henri is a rambler/hiker as well as a climber.

Giselle Lord   Born 1962. Alive 1998.
Born in France. Never really remembers her parents and is brought up by Aunt Stephanie. Doesn't really like rock climbing or sailing but does develop a talent for languages. Goes to University from 1982 to 1985 with a First in Modern languages. Giselle speaks Italian, French and Spanish and works as an interpreter for a Government office in Bristol.

Other Lord offspring include

Peter Lord   Born 1989. Alive 1998.
Born August. Son of Geoffrey Lord and lives with mother Christina DeLucci at Home Farm, Fotheringham Manor. Heir to the Lord family estate after death of his father in 1990.

Tony Lord (Made)   Born 1989. Alive 1998.
Born in London. Mother was Danielle Made and father was Michael Lord. Lived in London with his mother most of his life. Adopted by Christina Lord after his mother killed in September 1998 and lives with Christina and Peter at Home Farm. Keen on football and swimming.

James MacRae   Born 1994. Alive 1998.
Born August. Son of Andrew MacRae and Samantha Lord. Raised by Anthony and Sylvia Lord for most of his first year. Went to Canada with parents in 1996 and returned with Samantha in 1998 to Fotheringham.

Jean Lord   Born 1981. Dies 1990.
Born in Devon. Elder son of Marcel and Marie Lord. Keen to sail like his father but afraid. Dies from drowning while out sailing with Michael Lord in 1990. (**Full details in the novel Michael**).

Philippe Lord Born 1982. Alive 1998.

Born in Devon. Younger son of Marcel and Marie Lord. Bullied by Uncle Henri. Goes to Bristol House School with fees paid by Stephanie Lord.

The Howard Family

Delaney Howard IIIrd.

Manager of Forest Operations for International Paper Company in Jacksonville Florida. Married to Deidre. They have one daughter, Katya.

Katya Howard

Born 1976. Only daughter of Delaney IIIrd. and Deidre Howard from Jackonsonville, Florida. In 1998/9 is studying Forestry at Oxford University and in her final year. Special friend of James MacRae.

The Ferris Family

Norton Ferris Born 1925. Dies 1991.

Born in Liverpool. Joined the army in 1942. Got his face slashed by a knife from a scam gone wrong in Naples, Italy. Developed a hatred of the Irish, Italians and any authority. Survived to the end of the war working for Colonel Quimby Travis, an eccentric forester. References from Col. Travis helped him get into Forestry College. Works in Forest of Dean for the Forestry Commission 1948 to 1983 when retired by FC for embezzlement and drunkenness. Married to Blodwyn Williams in 1958. Two children, Idwal and John born 1960 and 1963. Blodwyn dies 1980 in drunken accident. Hired by Anthony Lord as a Forester in 1984 working under Ronald O'Rourke and lives with two sons in cottage on the Estate. Becomes in charge when O'Rourke dies in 1987 and bullies forest work crew especially Antonio and Enrico Branciaghlia and young Freddie Dunster. Dies in January 1991 in an accident on Fotheringham Estate. (*Full details in the novel Michael*).

Idwal Ferris Born 1960. Dies 1998.

Elder son of Norton Ferris. Forest labourer works at Forest of Dean and then Fotheringham Manor. Single. Lives with his Dad and his brother up to 1991 in cottage on Fotheringham Estate. Fired January 1991. Leaves local area but returns in 1998 after supposedly serving time for manslaughter.

John Ferris Born 1963. Dies 1998.

Younger son of Norton Ferris. Forest labourer works at Forest of Dean and then

Fotheringham Manor. Fired in January 1991. Rehired in May 1991. Married in 1991 to Betty Travers.

Betty Travers   Born 1968. Alive 1998

Eldest child of Toby and Mary Travers who run the off-licence and the greengrocers shops respectively in the village. Betty is famous for her pie-making. Married John Ferris in 1991. They live in the Ferris cottage on the Estate. Have two children, Katey and Paul.

The Branciaghlia brothers

Antonio Branciaghlia   Born 1920. Dies 1990.

Born near Cortina Italy. Grew up in father's trade as a stone mason. Enlists in Italian army in 1939 and captured in North Africa in 1943. Transferred from P.O.W. Camp to Fotheringham Manor Estate in 1944, where George Lord and Albert Templeton remember the skills and work ethic of Italians, and need employees. Parents killed in Italy during the war and decides to stay at Fotheringham in 1945. Well respected on the Estate and in the village. Makes toys for the Lord children and other children in the village. Killed in a tree-felling accident in August 1990.

Enrico Branciaghlia   Born 1922. Alive 1998.

Born near Cortina Italy. Became a woodworker making furniture, house repairs, roofing, plus carving animals for children. Enlists in the Italian army in 1939 and captured in North Africa in 1943. Transferred from P.O.W. Camp to Fotheringham Manor Estate. With brother trained as a forest worker and stays at Fotheringham after the war. Well respected on the Estate and in the village. Also makes toys for children. Stays on in Estate cottage living alone after brother killed in 1990. Retires in 1997.

The Templeton Family

Albert Templeton   Born 1880. Dies 1950.

Grew up on the Fotheringham Manor Estate as a gamekeeper's assistant. Good with guns, traps, pheasant coops, and general estate work. In WWI was 34 and fought in the same artillery regiment as George Lord. Fought in Italian Alps. Married to Annie and had son Edward, born 1914. Works all his life on the estate. Is 59 in 1939 for WWII. Teaches Enrico and Antonio when they come to the estate in 1944. Dies at age 70.

Edward Templeton   Born 1914. Dies 1978.

Brought up on Fotheringham Manor estate as son of gameskeeper. Follows in father's footsteps. Develops a love of machinery and cars. Becomes a good mechanic for the estate. Leaves school at age 15 in 1929 and is ready to take over from father when WWII breaks out. Age 25 in 1939 and joins up. Becomes a fitter for the RAF including working on the squadron where Desmond is a pilot. Married in 1938, same year as Desmond Lord, to Sally Sanders. Has son Brian in 1944. Takes over from his father in 1945 (Albert now 65) as head gamekeeper but also forest agent. Woodlands in need of attention after devastation of war. Lots of clearing, replanting, pruning, fencing, control of rabbits. Less attention to shooting and more to forestry. Works well with Enrico and Antonio. Stays very traditional in forest actions. Dies at age 64.

Gary Templeton   Born 1973. Alive 1998.
Grandson of Edward Templeton and son of Brian Templeton. Works as a labourer on the Fotheringham Manor Estate. Longtime friend of Freddie Dunster and Gloria Manson.

The Edwards Family

Ernest Edwards   Born 1914. Dies 1988.
Starts work on Fotheringham Estate in 1930. Marries Gwen Biddle in 1950. Son Bob born in 1957. Foreman on the Estate from 1978 until 1988 when he dies at age 74.

Bob Edwards   Born 1957. Alive 1998.
Son of Ernest Edwards and Gwen Biddle (who is the Aunt of Rosemary and Violet Biddle – see Freddie Dunster and the Cotton twins). Marries Frances Tetley in 1984 and have a son Dennis born in 1985 who is mad about soccer. Worked on the Fotheringham Estate and became foreman in 1988 on the death of his father Ernest.

Tilley Edwards   Born 1953. Alive 1998.
Daughter of Ernest Edwards and Gwen Biddle. Elder sister of Bob Edwards. Marries Walter Manson a trucker at age 19 in 1973 and Gloria born in 1973. Son Wendell born in 1983. Walter Manson a bully who was born in 1951 and dies in September 1998 in fiery lorry crash.

Gloria Manson   Born 1973. Alive 1998.
Daughter of Tilley Edwards and Walter Manson. School friend of Freddie Dunster and Garry Templeton. Runs away to London at age 18. Returns in October 1998 to work at the George and Dragon Public house.

The Biddle family

Freddie Dunster   Born 1973. Alive 1998.
Son of Rosemary Biddle and William Dunster. Worked at Fotheringham Manor Estate from 1990 onwards. Friend of Gary Templeton and Gloria Manson.

Jack and Leonard=Lennie Cotton   ·   Born 1975. Die 1991.
Twins born in Liverpool. Sons of Violet Murphy (nee Biddle) who was younger sister of Rosemary Biddle. Violet ran away to Liverpool when a teenager. Twins came back to Fotheringham in 1990.

The Whelks family

Florence (Flo') Whelks   Born 1909. Alive 1998.
Lived in the village all her life. Married to Thomas who had worked on the Fotheringham Estate until he died at age sixty in 1970. Had two sons, Larry and Phillip. Is a little mad and a recluse by 1990. Has a Jack Russell spaniel called Goebells.

Larry Whelks   Born 1943. Dies 1991.
Elder son of Florence. Lived with his mother in village cottage. Small-time fence, house builder, tradesman, painter. Partner in crime with Norton Ferris for several years. Killed in Bristol in 1991.

Phillip (Phil) Whelks   Born 1946. Alive 1998.
Younger son of Florence. Lived in village until a teenager when ran away to sea and ended up in Australia. Lived in Sydney. Has daughter Margaret born 1978. Returns to England in October 1998 with daughter.

Margaret (Vanda) Whelks   Born 1978. Alive 1998.
Born in Sydney Australia. Age 19 in October 1998 when she comes to England with father Phil. Is a dyke, drug addict, with pierced body parts and into S&M. Plays darts well.

Other Characters

Ronald O'Rourke   Born 1939. Dies 1987.
Born in Killarney Eire. Forestry graduate from Oxford in 1962. Works in Devon from 1962 to 1966. Becomes the professional forester for Fotheringham Manor Estates in

1966 the year after Geoffrey born when work, family, and estate prove too much for Desmond and Sylvia. Works well with Edward Templeton and with the two Italians. Is killed accidentally in the big storm of 1987 at age 48.

Janet Donaldson
Closest school friend of Samantha Lord from Lycee in Switzerland. Starts a private company called Heritage Adventures. Becomes one of James MacRae's "hot women". (*Full details in the novel Samantha*).

Donald MacLeod
University friend of Andrew MacRae and Samantha. Research mathematical modeler. Keen on Samantha romantically but no real response from Samantha. Proud to be from Isle of Skye and to be Scottish.

Terence Field
Born 1966. Detective Inspector in 1998 at time of Samantha/Daniel. Regional Crime Squad investigates September incidents at Fotheringham. Becomes friend of Samantha. City born and bred, unfamiliar with country.

WPC Beverley Nicols
Works for Detective Inspector Terence. Climbs with Samantha MacRae (nee Lord). Special friend of James MacRae.

Rosalind Cohen (nee Townsend)
Owns and manages Cohen and Townsend in London, a Security Company. (*Full details in the novel Michael*). Buys Brainware (the software development company) of the Lord family.

George Doone
Is George the landlord of the George and the Dragon public house in the village

PC Timmy Meadows
Is the village police constable

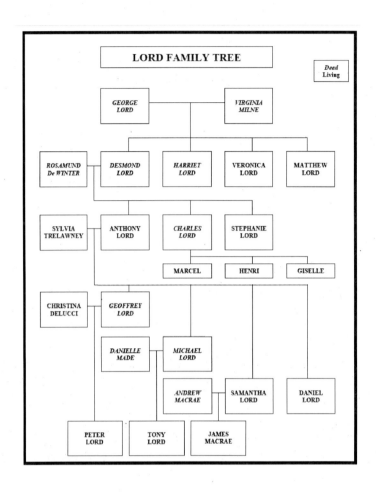

LORD FAMILY TREE

Dead
Living

ABOUT THE AUTHOR

John Osborn was born in 1939 in Ipswich England but grew up in the East End of London where he learnt to sail. In North Wales he graduated as a professional forester and rock climbed three days a week. After working as a field forester for three years in Australia John went to Vancouver, British Columbia for postgraduate studies and the Flower Power movement of the sixties. While working for thirty years for the Ontario Ministry of Natural Resources, both as a forester and a systems analyst John sailed competitively, climbed mountains and taught survival and winter camping. He finished his professional career with three years consulting in Zimbabwe, walking with the lions. Now retired, although working part-time at the local Golf Club, John lives with his wife in Kelowna, BC where he hikes and x-c skis from his doorstep.